Science Fiction Handbook
for Readers and Writers

Science Fiction Handbook

for
Readers and Writers

by
George S. Elrick

Illustrated by the author;
Supplementary illustrations from NASA
and early Buck Rogers comic strips

Cover illustration by Merle Hedburg, noted Chicago area designer/illustrator and winner of an international design award. Merle, a science fiction aficionado, brings a wide-eyed freshness, originality, and vitality to a frame of reference that's fundamentally far out and fantastic. His skills in composition, rendering, and interpretation—honed to a fine edge at Chicago's Art Institute and the American Academy of Art—have been additionally refined throughout his career as an in-demand professional.

First Edition
First Printing

Published by Chicago Review Press, Inc.
215 West Ohio Street, Chicago, Illinois 60610

ISBN: 0-914090-52-6
Library of Congress Catalog Number: 78-59828

Dedicated to my always supportive wife, Marilyn, and to my sons, Michael Scott Elrick and Bruce Kevin Elrick, all three of whom have spent years enduring the clatter of incessant typing in my downstairs office.

Contents

Acknowledgements

I'm deeply indebted to the following for helping me transform two reams of typewritten manuscript paper into a printed physical actuality: Merle Hedberg, who created the magnificent front cover illustration . . . James Stark, who granted permission to photograph his 1933-vintage rocket-ship models . . . Kay Shaffer Trevarthen, who photographed the models . . . my son, Bruce Kevin Elrick, who did a brooding, photographic portrait study of Stark . . . James S. Sweitzer, astronomer at Chicago's famed Adler Planetarium, who patiently let me haunt that facility's exhaustive reference library . . . Doctor Beverly Friend, who knows more about science fiction fandom than anyone else on earth, and whose Ph.D. thesis is a treasure trove . . . Sally Morris, of the Glenview Public Library, for her uncanny knack in running down and verifying elusive facts and figures . . . The Science Fiction Research Association, for its generosity in giving me access to scholarly papers presented at its conventions . . . and the National Aeronautics and Space Administration, for permission to reproduce key illustrative material, so I could supplement my own drawings.

In a retrospective salute, I'd like to thank Edgar Rice Burroughs for writing his mind-blowing Martian and Venusian novels; and I'd like to humbly hold my hat in my hand in the presence of Jack London's 1907 novel, *Before Adam*, a time-warp book I read and re-read so many times as a child that its cover literally disintegrated. Burroughs, London, and the daily Buck Rogers comic strip winged me off on a permanent imaginative trajectory long before I first shaved.

George S. Elrick
June 15th, 1978

An Orbital View of Science Fiction

Who Reads It?

Bank presidents read science fiction. Go-go dancers read science fiction. Bricklayers thumb its pages while munching sandwiches. Scientists at Argonne National Laboratory swear by it. Grade school kids devour it. So do high school, college, and post-graduate students. Everyone's getting into the act, from gang members who swing bicycle chains to little old ladies who sip tea. As a mushrooming subculture, its fans are as knowledgeable as groupies familiar with the names and numbers of rock group players.

Attempts have been made to pigeonhole fans, though the latter defy categorization. Per a Ph.D. thesis by Beverly Friend, a 1948 survey of 1,000 buffs indicated most were male, between seventeen and twenty-seven years of age. But 1948 was a long time ago. A 1961 survey of a smaller sample indicated eighty-seven percent were only children, or the oldest youngsters in families. They suffered lonely childhoods, discovered science fiction at nine, and became deeply involved—writing letters to fan magazines—at nineteen.

But 1961 also was a long time ago. A more recent survey, in 1974, indicated the average fan was slightly over twenty-six. Eighty-one percent were highly educated males. In fact, twenty-nine percent had advanced university degrees. Regardless, when a prominent book store chain was queried, early in 1978, as to who reads science fiction, the answer was: 'Everyone . . . from eight to eighty.'

1

Why Do They Read It?

What's the appeal? Why does Ben Bova, a prominent science fiction author, say that if anything travels faster than the speed of light it's news about science fiction? Why is science fiction fandom a way of life for countless individuals of both sexes? Why, during World War Two, were 150 drugstore copies of 'Astounding Science Fiction' magazine snapped up, within three days of publication monthly, by scientists clustered at Oakridge, Tennessee?

After all, there *are* other types of stories that almost leap off paperback racks and march up to cash registers, and they can't be ignored if science fiction's more powerful appeal is to be comprehended. The following book categories seem to be factory-produced formula fiction, barely distinguishable by titles and front covers; yet each has devotees:

Consider the *Western*. Most are totally predictable. There's a willing or unwilling 'knight on horseback' skilled at shooting from the hip. He becomes entangled with opposing forces, and the yarn unwinds with a shoot-out which the taciturn hip-shooter wins.

On the covers of Gothic Romances, the terrified heroine is forever fleeing from a rotting mansion in the background.

G. ELRICK

thousands who can't tell a space ship from a skateboard. Isaac Asimov's is a household name. Anthony Burgess's *A Clockwork Orange* was reviewed by 'respectable' publications as well as mimeographed fan magazines.

Not the Same as Mainstream Literature

But *are* mainstream literature and science fiction the same? No. Generally speaking, mainstream literature focuses on *why*; science fiction focuses on *how*. Down through the years, the typical science fiction format has been short stories and novelettes. Most science fiction novels *continue* to be fairly short: between 45,000 and 60,000 words in length. Mainstream novels average 80,000 words in length. And, unfortunately, there's an enormous difference in characterization, with science fiction lagging far behind mainstream fiction.

Ideally, fiction deals with the subtle ways people conduct themselves in a variety of situations. In a well-written mainstream novel, subtle characterization determines not only incident but plot. This is only partially true in science fiction. A mainstream novel normally dwells on the development or disintegration of a character or characters. This isn't necessarily the case in science fiction. In a mainstream novel, characterizing action—action that unfolds characters' personalities—is more important than dramatic action. This is almost never the case in science fiction. In the latter, dramatic action tends to be more important than characterizing action. Science fiction plots are anthills of activity. They're primarily situation-centered, not protagonist-centered.

Just Another Pretty Face

Critics complain that science fiction characters tend to be cardboard cut-outs: a legitimate gripe. Princess Leia Organa, in *Star Wars,* is just another pretty face. Examining the other side of the coin, there's a legitimate reason for this. Science fiction is more a literature of ideas than a literature of characters. The typical science fiction author is presenting—and elaborating on—a thesis, a 'what if?' Detailing relationships would blur the big picture and slow things down. In ninety percent of science fiction, the staging, backdrops, and props are more important than the actors.

Given the thesis-determined 'thrust' of science fiction narratives, there's nothing wrong with this. Thousands of readers of all per-

Carrie Fisher, as Princess Leia Organa in 'Star Wars,' had no chance to develop the character's depth for the simple reason that the character had no depth.

G. ELRKK

suasions are satisfied. They're reading their favorite authors to learn about gimmicks and philosophies, not psychology. Besides, as novelist Frederik Pohl pointed out, it's difficult to truly characterize when a protagonist may resemble a sea snake or a bat. However, just as Dickens's David Copperfield felt 'a want of something' in his beloved Dora, knowledgeable readers feel a want of something in much science fiction.

Tolstoy's *War and Peace* is about Napoleon's retreat from Moscow; about ignorant armies that clash by night; and about over-arching philosophies. But, first and foremost, it's about people, scores of people more real than your mother, father, spouse, and children. Science fiction has yet to produce a *War and Peace*, but there's no reason it can't and *shouldn't*. That's the supreme challenge for new writers. Classics are re-read and remembered because they *are* classic, and classy.

Wide Screens, Budgets, and Technical Errors

If science fiction novels are largely situation-centered, not protagonist-centered, science fiction movies are even more so. And they rely heavily on breathtaking special effects, gadgetry, and hardware. Some have been dazzling. Hollywood's come a long way since the *Invasion of the Body Snatchers, The Incredible Shrinking Man,* and the moronic 'We must destroy them before they destroy us' mental-set. The wide screen offers awesome escape from karate chops dealt

G. ELRICK

If Humphrey Bogart had a face like forty miles of unpaved road, Charles Middleton—as Ming the Merciless—had a face like a leaking cesspool. A 'bad guy' to end all bad guys, Middleton typified the simplistic good-versus-evil polarization so prevalent—and so welcomed—in the 'us versus them' school of science fiction.

by life, especially when what's depicted is galactic in scope. Because everything's panoramic and fast-moving, no one cares that characters aren't developed with the three-dimensional subtlety of Trevor Howard and Celia Johnson in Noel Coward's *Brief Encounter.* The only filmic science fiction character that *has* been developed with actual depth is Spock in TV's 'Star Trek' . . . and even *he's* remembered because of pointed ears.

Oddly, despite a budget that would give an oil-rich sheik heartburn, a ridiculous verbal sin was committed by the actor who played Hans Solo in *Star Wars.* In a crucial get-away scene, he misused the word 'parsec.' Savvy fans from coast to coast noted the error and hooted derisively. Fandom can be intimidating; almost frightening. In a newspaper interview, novelist Ben Bova commented that science fiction buffs eagerly play 'The Game.' The Game consists of reading science fiction, or viewing it on the screen, then conducting an autopsy that's virtually a vivisection. God help any author or scriptwriter who makes technical mistakes, 'because they're on you like a pack of wolves.'

Writers, Publishers, and the Wolf Pack

Do science fiction authors care that fandom can be a wolf pack? No. It keeps them on their toes. Besides, the relationship between science fiction novelists and their followers is unique. They mingle with each other at conventions and actually know each other, to a surprising degree, on a first-name basis. Fans and professionals don't constitute a polarity but a continuum. Many professionals were letter-writing fans themselves at one time.

Do book publishers care that fandom can be a wolf pack? Not on your life. Buffs do everything but unhinge book-store doors to purchase the latest offerings. There's nothing seasonal about the sale of science fiction novels, either hard cover or paperback. Titles sell steadily day-after-day, week-after-week, month-after-month.

Science fiction is the most rapidly expanding subject classification in the average bookstore; the most eagerly sought out category in the average drugstore rack. The only stories approaching science fiction in popularity—and actually exceeding it in scattered outlets—are those known as Gothic Romance. The Moonlight and Roses 'Costume' Drama category *was* a red hot contender till recently, but has declined. Westerns and Detective stories fall so far behind they can be scratched as competitors.

Fourteen Percent of the Mass Market

According to a periodical named *Locus*, more than 1,000 science fiction titles were published in 1977, accounting for fourteen percent of all mass market titles—fiction and nonfiction—printed in the United States. Publishers are so keen to make hay while the sun shines—and it appears it may shine indefinitely—their newest trend is to release science fiction in both hard cover and paperback. (See list of current science fiction publishers on page 307.)

How to Know What to Read

If a person isn't familiar with the writing styles and themes of individual authors, how can he or she separate wheat from chaff in the welter of titles? The best way for a neophyte to blast out of the bewildered beginner stage is to read award-winning novels. They're not hard to find, since the awards normally are emblazoned on the front covers. There are Hugo, Nebula, Pilgrim, Jupiter, Nova, John W. Campbell, and John W. Campbell Memorial awards. They're granted or voted by professional writers, science fiction instructors, and organizations such as the Science Fiction Research Association.

No More Giant Ants

Once 'hooked,' those new to science fiction don't linger in the neophyte stage, but soon become as sophisticated as old-timers: thrilled with inventiveness, but hypercritical of inconsistencies, no matter how fantasy-like the novel. They no longer accept invading insects that are sixty feet high (see *square cube law* on page 246). They no longer tolerate unnecessary eyes, limbs, tentacles, and appendages on alien life forms, if the eyes, limbs, tentacles and appendages lack bona fide environmental or survival functions. They hunger and thirst after the bizarre, but the bizarre has to make sense. They demand accuracy—or at least a gestalt-like consistency—in supportive details, and if the accuracy or consistency is missing, they fling the book aside in disgust, since the special universe the writer has concocted is no longer believable.

Fresh Visions Instead of Space Operas

By the time readers have reached the enlightenment stage, they regard the so-called 'space opera' with scorn. They're quick to sneer at the corny, the trite, the hackneyed, the cliche-ridden. Threadbare plot situations, such as the last man on a planet being forced to survive with the last woman on the same planet, are given the thumbs-down treatment. Readers rightfully expect their pet authors to provide penetratingly fresh visions of life, presented via a wedding of the scientific and the artistic. Fortunately, most writers bend over backward to do so.

Inner Space as Well as Outer Space

Novelist Theodore Sturgeon claims the growing edge of science fiction is the exploration of inner space, not just the probing of outer space, which means psychology may, at long last, sit down beside philosophy, physics, and gadgetry in this most unique 20th Century literature. Author Ursula LeGuin, an almost revered writer, feels science fiction will provide 'escape,' as always, but will also fulfill its throbbing potential as an intellectual, esthetic, and ethically responsible art form.

Science fiction has been, since the early 1930's, *the* existential literature, presenting—in a mind-cracking manner—all the challenges only existentialism provides the modern age. Whether inner-directed into the murky psyche, or outer-directed into other galaxies, it will undoubtedly continue to be existentialism's most imaginative advocate.

How to Use This Handbook

The function of the 1,046 entries on the following pages is to make the reading of science fiction even more enjoyable than it is, and the writing of science fiction less of a time-consuming 'turning to a thousand information sources.' Everything's in alphabetical order. Entries are classified as Fiction, Fiction/Astronautics, Astronautics, Astronomy, Physics, or Generic.

Each topic is explored to the depth necessary, without being laborious; occasionally with a flash of whimsy. Using this Handbook will enable you to read with knowledgeable comprehension, no matter how esoteric the author's terms; or write with self-confident authority.

The Handbook can be utilized as a dictionary/encyclopedia; sipped, for pleasure, like a glass of wine; or dug into with a knife and fork like a seven-course dinner.

George S. Elrick

Basic Ingredients of Science Fiction

Presentation of a 'What If?' theme

Whatever the story-line or plot, science fiction's theme is speculative, dealing with human reactions to change, whether the latter be mild or drastic, and however conditions may be distorted with respect to those we now know. What if life changes radically in the future? What might it be all about, Charlie, technology-wise, philosophy-wise, psychology-wise, and sociology-wise?

A setting in the future

Whether the story takes place on this planet, on some other planet, or between celestial bodies, it's likely—at some point—to portray dwelling places unlike Manhattan, Chicago, or Omaha, Nebraska. The first function of this city, or cities, is to make the narrative believable; the second function is to establish mood; and the third is to bring characters' personalities into sharp focus by giving them something to react to.

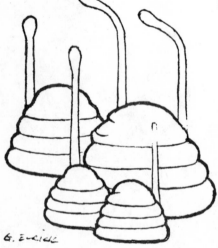

G. ELRICK

G. ELRICK

Utilization of space travel

Whereas we move about on or slightly above the Earth's surface, science fiction characters take interplanetary or intergalactic trips, generally in elaborate space ships employing a wide variety of propulsive drives. Their frame of reference is much more cosmic than ours.

The male protagonist, or principal character

The male 'lead' is usually introduced via action and with fewer than 100 words of description. His strong points are counterbalanced with weaknesses, since the novel dwells, to a degree, on his development or disintegration. If the story is well-conceived, he's a somewhat different person at the end than he was at the beginning. In the first half of the novel, the reader's aware of the relative unpredictability of his behavior; in the second half, of the inevitability of his behavior.

G. ELRICK

G. ELRICK

The female protagonist, or principal character

Everything mentioned about the male 'lead' pertains to his female counterpart, except that she no longer exists merely to be protected or rescued, or to feed lines to him. In today's science fiction, though beautiful and feminine, she's about as helpless as a resourceful undercover agent. Her antecedents were woodenly platonic, but she has a normal quota of hormones coursing through her lovely veins, and responds to their urgings without hesitation or embarrassment.

G. ELRICK

Secondary Characters

Secondary characters stay in the background much of the time. They have 'walk on' parts, saying a few words or doing a few things, then fading out of focus again. Their subsidiary presence serves to enhance the importance of the primary characters. Secondary characters are significant to the extent that they impart the sensation of an intertwining of many lives and destinies. They're developed in direct ratio to the frequency of their appearance in the narrative, and in direct proportion to their importance in the narrative.

G. ELRICK

An opponent or situation representing conflict

The science fiction author devotes more pages to conflict than to any other portion of his narrative. Conflict is the heart of fiction; it causes tension and suspense. Without it, there's no story. It grows—both in severity and frequency—toward a point of intolerance: a process known as climactic progression. As far as the reader is concerned, the solution of the conflict should be uncertain. If conflict is in the form of an individual rather than a situation, the individual who tangles with the principal characters must be totally unlike them regarding personality traits.

'Salt and Pepper' Ingredients

The following can be added, utilized, and mixed and matched as needed:

- Exploration
- Colonization
- Lost worlds
- Parallel worlds
- Alien forms of life
- Advanced technologies
- New sociological and cultural situations
- Robots and androids
- Cloning and genetic engineering
- Cyborgs
- Space warps
- Time warps
- Time travel
- Warfare
- Threats of planetary, solar system, or galactic destruction
- Probings of the psyche
- New faiths and religions

The following material is from a book on novel writing written by the author.

Elrick Basic Science Fiction Plot Pattern

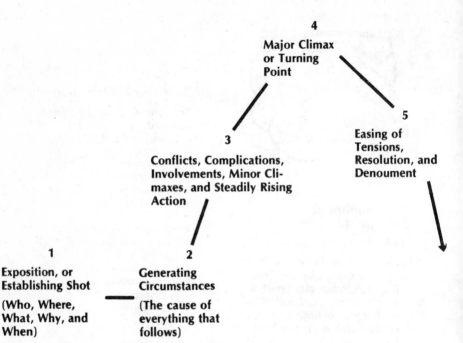

4
**Major Climax
or Turning
Point**

5
**Easing of
Tensions,
Resolution, and
Denoument**

3
**Conflicts, Complications,
Involvements, Minor Cli-
maxes, and Steadily Rising
Action**

1
**Exposition, or
Establishing Shot**

**(Who, Where,
What, Why, and
When)**

2
**Generating
Circumstances**

**(The cause of
everything that
follows)**

A science fiction plot is a pattern of cause and effect, giving a pre-planned direction to the story line. One event in the narrative forces another narrative event to take place, which in turn forces another narrative event to take place, and so on.

A science fiction novel's ending should somehow be implicit in its beginning, though the reader should be unaware of this until he finishes the book.

If the protagonist—or principal character—is to succeed, or thrash his way out of his entanglements, he must do so only after a series of setbacks, because struggle is the essence of drama. Success must be won the hard way. The protagonist has to have a rough time of it.

Key to Plot Pattern on Facing Page

1. The Exposition introduces the major characters—but not too many at once, or the reader gets confused. It depicts, in broad brush strokes, the relationships between characters. It tells the reader when, where, and why the story is taking place.

2. The Generating Circumstance is the novel's initial crisis and the first highlighting of one of the basic problems the story deals with. It's the incident—or situation—that propels the characters . . . the protagonist in particular . . . into ever-increasing complications that lead to a Point of Intolerance, and that eventually and inevitably terminate in the narrative's Major Climax or Turning Point.

3. The pages between the Generating Circumstance and the Major Climax or Turning Point are known as the middle section of a novel . . . pages concentrating on development and intrigue. There must be a feeling of necessity (though not contrivance) in everything that happens in the middle section. There must be a major development of ideas and action and a thrust toward crisis (the Point of Intolerance that precedes the Major Climax).

4. The Major Climax or Turning Point is the crucial encounter, or showdown, that determines the outcome of the story. The crucial encounter needn't be physical. It can be mental or emotional. It can take place within a single individual's head. Regardless, this 'crisis section' of the novel resolves problems, or answers questions . . . ususually with great dramatic intensity.

5. After the Major Climax or Turning Point, the microcosm carefully established and depicted in the novel changes. Previous patterns are shattered and new, hopefully improved ones are formed. Aristotle's 'shock of recognition' frequently takes place. At least one of the characters experiences a basically fresh vision of the world.

A

ablating materials. (Astronautics.) Special coating materials on a spacecraft's surface, particularly its nose cone. Because of high-speed friction, these materials—through loss of mass—vaporize, melt, or chip away when the craft re-enters the Earth's atmosphere. By dissipating intense heat, they protect the underlying structure and its payload against high-temperature destruction. See *payload*.

abort. (Astronautics.) To wipe out or cut short an aerospace mission before it accomplishes its objective. The 'scrub'—which can take place any time during or after countdown—may be caused by meteorological factors, human miscalculations, or technical malfunctions. See *scrub*.

absolute event horizon. See *black hole*.

absolute vacuum. (Physics.) Also known as perfect vacuum: a Three-dimensional space totally devoid of matter. This is a state theoretically possible to achieve, but actually unattainable.

absolute zero. (Physics.) The temperature—minus 460 degrees Fahrenheit—at which the average kinetic energy of gas molecules vanishes, along with gas volume.

acceleration chamber. (Astronautics.) The portion of a space ship to which crew and occupants retire when the craft gains speed, in order to sidestep physical damage to themselves.

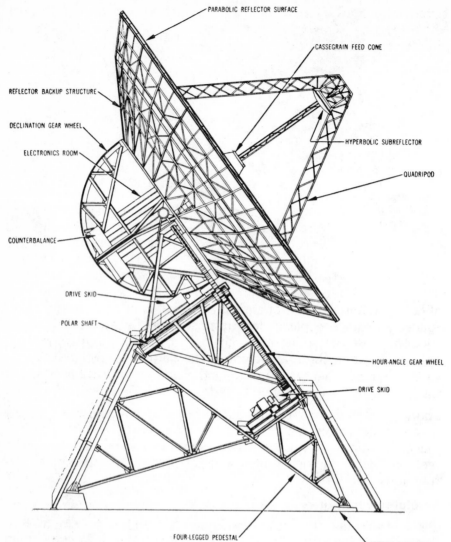

PARABOLIC REFLECTOR SURFACE

CASSEGRAIN FEED CONE

REFLECTOR BACKUP STRUCTURE

DECLINATION GEAR WHEEL

ELECTRONICS ROOM

HYPERBOLIC SUBREFLECTOR

QUADRIPOD

COUNTERBALANCE

DRIVE SKID

POLAR SHAFT

HOUR-ANGLE GEAR WHEEL

DRIVE SKID

FOUR-LEGGED PEDESTAL

PEDESTAL FOUNDATION

Typical tracking and data acquisition equipment is ten stories high and weighs 300 tons. Shown is a standard DSIF antenna and its 85-foot parabolic reflector. After a spacecraft 'escapes' from the Earth, it travels in an orbit or path similar to that of other celestial bodies, rising and setting on the horizon like the sun.

The spacecraft's course is determined by the same methods used to pinpoint heavenly bodies: its angular position relative to a stellar background is defined by a set of imaginary coordinates corresponding roughly to Earth latitudes and longitudes.

acceleration mat. (Fiction.) A large, instantly inflatable cushion onto which spaceship crew members fling themselves to avoid the jarring effects of a sudden acceleration surge.

acquisition. (Astronautics.) The technique of locating a satellite's orbit, or a space probe's trajectory, to obtain tracking or telemetry data. See *telemetry*.

active homing. (Astronautics.) The use of space-vehicle transmitted energy waves, such as radar, reflected back *from* a target or destination to direct the vehicle *to* the target or destination. See *passive homing*.

adventure science fiction. (Generic.) Along with gadget SF and social SF, one of the field's three genres or plot categories. Adventure science fiction is typical non-cerebral 'space opera.' For example: a scantily-clad beauty in brass breastplates and great peril is rescued from her predicament by a stalwart, Flash Gordon-type young man. In this genre, the thrust is toward simon-pure action rather than philosophical reflections. See *gadget science fiction* and *social science fiction*.

aeroduct. (Astronautics.) A ramjet-type engine that scoops up ions and electrons from the Earth's outer atmospheric fringes, or from the outer limits of any other spatial body's atmosphere. The scooped-up particles are discharged as a propulsive jet stream via a metachemical process in the engine's duct.

aerodynamics. (Physics.) That aspect of science concerned with the motion of air and other gases, and the effect of these gases on high-speed bodies passing through them.

aeroembolism. (Astronautics.) Also known as 'the bends.' Agonizing discomfort caused by nitrogen bubbles popping out in body fluids. The bubbles stem from an abrupt decrease in high-altitude pressure when an astronaut or cosmonaut goes without special clothing in a non-protected enclosure, or when a pressure-controlling device in an enclosed cabin malfunctions. Characterized by neuralgic pain, swelling, cramps, and—frequently—death. In many ways it's more pleasant being run over by a truck. See *decompression sickness* and *caisson disease*.

aeroshell. (Astronautics.) Used with a lander/probe. (See *probe*.) A probe's heat-shielding capsule facing a planet's surface during deorbit, functioning in conjunction with a basecover containing a parachute or retro-rocket system. When a probe is clamshelled between these parts, the assembly is called a descent capsule. See *bioshield*.

Separate — Deorbit — Coast — Atmospheric entry, 250 kilometers (800,000 feet)

Peak deceleration, 24,000 to 30,000 meters (80,000 to 100,000 feet)

Deploy parachute, ~6400 meters (21,000 feet)

Orbiter

Relay link

Jettison aeroshell

Engine ignition, 1200 meters (4000 feet)

Jettison parachute

Probe descending to planetary surface, indicating aeroshell being jettisoned.

Terminal propulsion descent

Landing

Entry to landing 6 to 13 minutes

afterburner. See *afterburning*.

afterburning. (Astronautics.) Sporadic sputtering and burning of fuel remaining in a rocket's firing chamber after fuel cut-off.

air analyzer. (Fiction.) A gauge indicating the ratio of carbon dioxide to oxygen in a space ship's crew quarters, passageways, storage areas, and control room.

air drag. (Astronautics.) Also called atmospheric drag. The slight but unmistakable backward pull exerted by air particles on a fast-moving space object. Similar, in a minuscule way, to the much more forceful resistance exerted by water on a moving boat.

air friction. (Astronautics.) The temperature-skyrocketing resistance encountered by a rocket ship or space ship entering Earth's atmospheric envelope. See *atmosphere: Earth*.

air generator. (Fiction.) A space ship generator that creates an artificial atmospheric pressure, within the vehicle, of 14.7 pounds to the square inch, duplicating breathing conditions close to the Earth's surface.

airglow. (Astronomy.) A faint, ever-present aurora creating roughly half the brightness of the darkest night sky as seen from the Earth's surface, curtailing astronomical observations of dim objects. Caused by charged particles in the Earth's magnetic field.

air house. (Fiction.) Futuristic version of a 20th Century road house or cocktail lounge, fastened to the Earth's surface with a long, taut cable, surrounded by protective fencing, and held aloft via implantations of anti-gravity ballast. Accessible by means of air taxis, air jits, Q-ray flyabouts, and other small craft, all of which must be moored to stanchions to prevent their drifting away.

air lock. (Astronautics.) An airtight room, chamber, or passageway in which air pressure can be regulated. Generally located between two regions of unequal pressure.

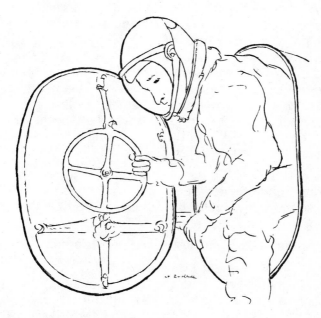

Typical spacecraft air lock passageway.

air lock connection. (Fiction.) A flexible connecting passageway between friendly space ships that have moored, side-by-side, via magnetic grapples.

algae and space travel. (Astronautics.) The greatest boon to long-distance space travelers is a tiny, primitive, aquatic, photosynthetic, chlorophyll-packed, one-celled plant called an alga. (Plural: algae.) Algae are cultivated in a space ship's 'farm,' consisting of special tubes or tanks filled with constantly-agitated water and nutrient salts. The gooey, slimy, unpleasant-looking mass of cells—harvested daily after ceaseless self-reproduction—not only supplies oxygen as well as food, but absorbs and converts carbon dioxide and other body wastes, both liquid and solid. What's more, potentially dangerous bacteria aren't needed to recycle nitrogen, as they're required to in the Earth's mouldering soil, because algae miraculously participate in the nitrogen cycle, plus the carbon-oxygen-hydrogen cycle. Algae look and taste awful, but consist of 70 percent protein, dry weight, and bulge with needed fat and vitamins. So much versatility from so simple a source almost beggars belief. See *hydroponics.*

the alien nymphet. (Fiction.) The non-Earthian, screaming, helpless, coy-but-oversexed, half-naked female frequently found in pulp magazine science fiction tales of yesteryear. Though she usually revealed a great deal of butter-smooth skin, guaranteed to trigger a spasm of seething but protective eroticism in the Earthman protagonist, she modestly wore a gleaming brass brassiere. The nymphet was in constant danger of being ravished, maimed, molested, tortured, or otherwise hideously degraded . . . whether by leering, horny humanoids, or by scaly, multi-limbed, bug-eyed monsters. See *humanoid* and *bug-eyed monster.*

alpha particle. (Physics.) Formerly thought of only as a heavy, positively charged particle emitted during radioactive decay; now acknowledged to be the nucleus of a helium atom. A participant in, or product of, many nuclear reactions.

ALT. (Astronautics.) Short for **A**pproach and **L**anding **T**est.

alternate framework. (Fiction.) Coexistent but different realities, rife with time loops, 'windows,' and apertures, matching, multiple identities, and boundaries that are crossed only at the risk of meeting oneself face-to-face, sometimes in a hostile or erotic context. Beautifully spelled out in *Ox*, by Piers Anthony.

G. ELRICK

Yesterday's squirming—though virginal—alien nymphet has had her face, body, and outfit overhauled. Today, decorating paperback covers by Frank Frazetta, she's frequently imperious, pouting, full-buttocked, pinch-waisted, and naked. She also appears to have a mind of her own. Yet covers can be deceptive regarding both nudity and personality. With striking exceptions, women in the genre still tend to be as flat as their chests are jutting. The character-deepening concept of androgyny—females having a sprinkling of male traits, and vice-versa—is scarcely off the launching pad. When the concept does go into orbit, second-rate SF characterization may approach three-dimensionality taken for granted in first-rate mainstream literature . . . and women, such as those pictured here, can stop screaming their rage at being two-dimensional.

alternate laws. (Fiction.) Ways of changing the observable, seemingly logical and predictable pattern of existence so a fresh perception of reality permits 'far out' actions normally impossible or unthinkable. Elaborated on in *Three to Dorsai!* by Gordon R. Dickson. See *identity isolates.*

alternate reality. (Fiction.) Another—equally valid but not always attainable—way of experiencing existence. Implicit in the concept is the postulate that there may be a multiplicity of universes nested together, Chinese-box fashion, though each discrete universe normally is oblivious of the others. See *alternate framework*.

alternity. (Fiction.) The total fabric of probability, both forward and backward in time.

anabolic protoplaser. (Fiction.) A portable, hand-held wound healer for minor injuries. Features a ray emission duct and an intensity force light. (*Star Trek*.)

anacoustic zone. (Astronautics.) A zone of absolute silence commencing in the extremely rarefied atmosphere 100 miles above the Earth's crust. From that point on, the distance between air molecules is far greater than that between acoustical wavelengths. Therefore, sound waves can't form or spread. An explosion in space is as noiseless as an explosion in a silent movie. See *sound: absence of in space*.

analog computer. (Generic.) A computing device that measures, rather than counts, numerical input data. Measurements obtained, such as linear lengths or voltage intensities, are electronically translated into desired readouts. An analog computer can quickly solve brain-scrambling mathematical problems. See *digital computer*.

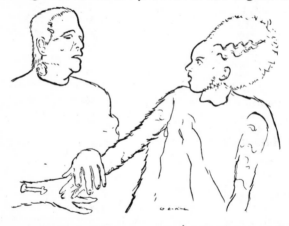

The most famous android of all time was —and probably always will be—Mary Shelley's Frankenstein monster as por- trayed by Boris Karloff in several 1930's movies.

android. (Fiction.) 'Droid for short. Sometimes called 'humanoid,' though non-synthetic aliens are also referred to as humanoids in science fiction if they exhibit man-like attributes. More accurately, an android is a synthetic person fashioned from biological parts, a la the monster in Mary Shelley's *Frankenstein*. The term is sometimes loosely applied to creatures knit together with electronic parts, or with a mixture of biological and electronic parts. See *cyborg*, *prosthesis*, and *robot*.

angstrom unit. (Physics.) One-hundred-millionth of a centimeter. A measurement unit employed to designate electromagnetic wavelengths.

animaloid. (Fiction.) A creature—not necessarily synthetic—that's halfway between a humanoid and an animal. See *humanoid*.

annihilating beam. See *disintegrator ray*.

annual space maneuvers. (Fiction.) Yearly intensive practice of formation-flying tactics, performed by Earth's space ships and rocket ships.

anoxia. (Astronautics.) A hazard of high-altitude flight: pathological oxygen starvation in a body's blood, cells, or tissues. Frequently results in brain damage.

ansible. (Fiction.) An ICD, or Instantaneous Communications Device, in the Hainish works of Ursula LeGuin. Used in *The Word for World Is Forest*, *The Left Hand of Darkness*, and *The Dispossessed*. It implements instantaneous transmission of a message over any distance. One element must be a large-mass body; the other can be any size, anywhere in the cosmos.

anti-G suit. (Astronautics.) Special protective clothing worn by astronauts and cosmonauts to counteract the body-crunching effects of positive acceleration. See *G-suit*.

anti-grav. (Astronautics.) Weightless. See *null-gee,* and *zero gravity: effects of.*

antigrav drive. (Fiction.) Space ship power employed to boost the vehicle out of a celestial body's gravitational field.

anti-gravity controls. (Fiction.) Controls that, in conjunction with curtailed rocket blasts, enable a small spacecraft to settle gently on a planet's surface.

anti-gravity levitators. (Generic.) High-coercive-strength magnets capable of keeping heavy bodies hovering over roadbeds in high-speed transportation systems.

antimatter. (Physics.) The complete opposite of substance as we know it: matter composed of antiparticles. Undergoes shattering annihilation—with a mind-boggling, explosive energy release—when colliding with or just touching ordinary matter. Some astrophysicists speculate that the universe may consist of the visible star clusters and galaxies so familiar to us, plus invisible, potentially dangerous anti-star clusters and anti-galaxies. See *antiparticle.*

antiparticle. (Physics.) Every sub-atomic particle has a corresponding antiparticle that instantaneously came into existence to balance and offset it. Both are identical in every way, except for electrical charge, magnetic field, and spin direction. For example, a proton has a positive electrical charge of a definite fixed size. An antiproton has a negative electrical charge of an identical fixed size. But the anti-proton's magnetic field is reversed regarding spin direction. A positron is a prime example of an antiparticle. See *positron.*

The best way to stop a hostile metallic robot in its tracks is to spray grit between its joints. If it's a non-metallic robot, one has to cope with it as though it were human.

G. ELRICK

anti-radiation mist. (Fiction.) A chemical compound whose basic ingredient is non-toxic lead molecules, capable of negating a controlled nuclear blast in a lead-lined chamber. When the molecular mist is released in the chamber's 'hot' interior, it absorbs radiation. In effect, the lead molecules hold radioactive particles 'prisoner.'

anti-robot gun. (Fiction.) Basically a dust-spraying device. When ejected dust and grit filters between the joints of radio-controlled metallic automatons, it causes the latter to grind to a halt or otherwise malfunction. See *robot.*

anti-spacetide rockets. (Fiction.) Special auxiliary rockets that enable a space ship to squirm free of a cosmic current.

aperture. (Fiction.) An opening to another dimension in the space-time continuum. See *spacetime.*

aphelion. (Astronomy.) The point at which an orbiting object is farthest from the sun. Applies to planets, asteroids, comets, meteors, and satellites.

apogee. (Astronomy.) If an object is orbiting around the Earth, the point at which it's farthest from the latter.

applied research. (Generic.) Hard-headed, no nonsense research oriented to finding answers to here-and-now practical problems or requirements. Compare with *basic research.*

approach clearance. (Astronautics.) Authorization for a space pilot, handling his craft in accordance with instrument flight rules, to commence his approach to a spaceport.

armored degravity car. (Fiction.) A vehicle that can, because of an adjustable degravity keel, float through a tunnel or other passageway without touching the walls, floor, or ceiling.

artificial fog. (Fiction.) Has three referents: (1) a type of dense smoke screen emitted by Jovian space ships when they're counterattacking Martian space ships, in order to conceal themselves; (2) when jetted upward from evenly-spaced floor openings, a camouflaging cloud that can be treated with photo rays to resemble a solid rock wall, through which 'in the know' people can walk; (3) a man-made cloud blanketing the Earth, so temporarily aberrant sun rays won't burn off too much oxygen.

artificial gravity. (Astronautics.) Simulated gravity established in a space vehicle by means of acceleration or rotation.

artificial horizon. (Astronautics.) A gyro-operated flight instrument that indicates a spacecraft's pitching and banking attitudes with respect to a symbolic reference-line horizon on the instrument panel. See *attitude.*

aseptic city. (Fiction.) Any metropolis covered by an enormous transparent dome which guards its inhabitants against harmful micro-organisms. Visitors, automatically considered to be swarming with germs, must spend several days under antiseptic rays before leaving a quarantine building. Since local citizens are bacteria-free, they live extraordinarily prolonged lives, similar to the Tibetans in James Hilton's Shangri-La, as portrayed in *Lost Horizon.*

A dome-covered aseptic city must supply its own 'rain,' whenever needed by plant life, via 20th Century-type artificial irrigation.

asteroids. (Astronomy.) Miniature celestial bodies sometimes known as planetoids or minor planets. They figure heavily in science fiction.

Where found: They're located primarily in the wide gap between the orbits of Mars and Jupiter. There are 'holes' in their distribution.

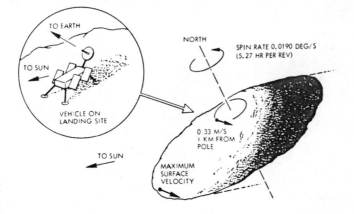

Unmanned missions to the asteroids have been proposed and checked into as part of an overall plan to explore the solar system. A principal incentive for landing on an asteroid and retrieving a surface sample for return to Earth is the expectation that detailed laboratory analyses of the sample's chemical composition, crystalline structure, surface texture, magnetic characteristics, radioactive state, and age can yield clues, unavailable by other means, to the origin of these orbiting chunks of rock, and conceivably to the formative processes that shaped the solar system in its entirety.

Eros, one of the smallest of the asteroids—about 15 miles long and 5 miles wide—is reasonably accessible to Earth for a landing and sample-return mission, with launch opportunities recurring every other year. A much smaller propulsion energy would be needed than for comparable missions to other planetary bodies, owing to the proximity of its orbits and its negligible gravity. Eros comes within 14 million miles of Earth at its closest approach: much nearer than do Venus or Mars.

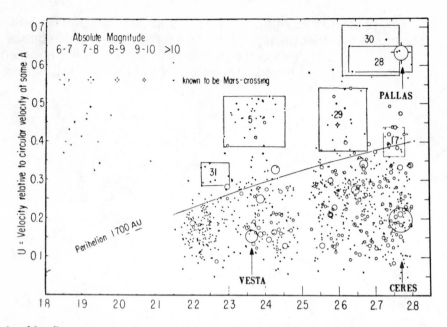

In this diagrammatic clustering of asteroids, the curve represents the critical condition for achieving a Mars-crossing orbit. Asteroids above this line either have Mars-crossing orbits or are potentially capable of ejecting debris into such orbits.

Orbit: Obeying Kepler's laws (which see), they follow an elliptical path around the sun. Due to their almost non-existent gravity, their effect on each other is slight. However, their orbits are perturbed (see *perturbation*) by the ever-present gravitational pull of the nine planets, especially oversize Jupiter. Some revolve as close to the sun as Mercury's orbit; others as far from the sun as Saturn's orbit.

Size: The largest—Ceres—has a 500-mile radius. Others range downward to tiny chunks of rock. Their total mass is estimated to be one-thousandth that of the Earth.

Shape: Two dozen are round. Smaller ones resemble shattered rocks in a quarry, as they lack sufficient gravity to pull themselves into spherical form. Whatever their shape, they spin at a dizzy pace.

Composition: Since they reflect light poorly, astronomical consensus is that they're primarily comprised of rock, without a glittering ice covering. Their surfaces feature a duke's mixture of various minerals.

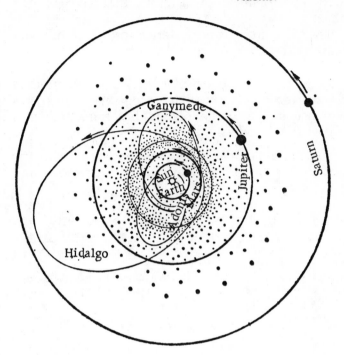

Orbits of some important asteroids. Note the wide swings achieved by Hidalgo and Adonis.

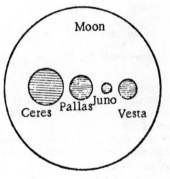

Size of the largest asteroids compared to the moon.

Color: Some are light; others dark. This distinction corresponds to the division between the two basic types of meteorites, stony (dark) vs. metallic (light). Meteorites are simply asteroids that have plunged to the Earth's surface.

Origin: Where they came from is a mystery. Normal planets are spaced quite regularly, except for a large chasm between Mars and Jupiter. A study of spacing patterns reveals there should be another planet in that region. Instead of a tenth planet, there are countless asteroids. For unknown reasons, early solar system material in this area failed to condense into a single planet, but remained as a swarming scattering of small bodies.

astrobiology. (Generic.) A biological discipline concerned with the discovery and study of life on other planets. See *exobiology* and *xenobiologist.*

Analytical Procedures Proposed for Detecting Extraterrestrial Life

Most Promising	Worthy of Attention	Less Promising
Determination of the growth of the biomass.	Determination of optical activity.	Use of O^{17} and O^{18}.
Quantitative determination of ferroporphyrin proteins (in dynamics)	Quantitative determination of flavins.	Use of an isotope of sulphur.
Quantitative determination of ATP (in dynamics)	Quantitative determination of protein, nucleic acids and amino acids.	Calorimetry (determination of the amount of heat formed during the growth of microorganisms).
Quantitative determination of emitted radioactive carbon dioxide.	Determination of phosphatase activity.	Determination of mitogenetic radiation.
Measurement of the pH of the culture. Measurement of the Eh of the culture.	Manometry (determination of the pressure in the chamber containing the culture).	

In astrobiology, certain analytical procedures are recommended for the detection of extraterrestrial life:

1. The collection of soil samples must take place at some distance from the biological station on a planet's surface.

2. The amount of soil collected must be sufficient for seeding.

3. Samples for seeding should not be collected from deep-lying layers or from the surface itself.

4. The seeding material collected must not impede observation of the growth and multiplication of cells.

5. For microbiological analysis, collection of a planet's atmosphere is less valuable than a collection of soil samples.

astrodynamics. (Astronautics.) The application of celestial mechanics, propulsion theory, astroballistics, and similar disciplines to the problem of planning and directing space vehicle trajectories.

astro-filter light wave speed reducto optiscope. (Fiction.) A device whose infra-scarlet prism is removable and reversible, thereby realigning deliberately scrambled image projection oscillations on a viewplate. Used when secret negotiations are in order, and when speaker identities can be revealed only to a select few.

astrogate. (Astronautics.) Patterned after the word navigate. Means to maneuver a spacecraft in space.

astrogator. (Fiction.) A component of a course-tracking device in a space ship. Consists of a cloud chamber viewplate with a holographic image, an intercom set-up, and the ship's electronic log and chronometer.

astrograph indicator. (Fiction.) A viewplate depicting the relative positions of stars and galaxies with respect to Earth. Periodically examined to detect unexpected shifts in magnetic fields or gravitational attractions.

astro indicator. (Fiction.) A celestial navigation pinpointer that indicates one's 'right now' position, in the spacetime continuum, with respect to solar system space lanes. Orientation is partially determined by labeled quadrants.

astrolabe. (Generic.) An instrument occasionally referred to in time travel science fiction. An actual complicated device used in the Middle Ages and Renaissance for astronomical and terrestrial measurements and observations. See *time travel*.

astronomical unit. (Astronomy.) A unit of length used to measure astronomical distances. Equivalent to the mean distance of the Earth from the sun: approximately 93 million miles.

astrophysics. (Generic.) Specifically, that portion of astronomy dealing with the physical properties of various materials and forces comprising the universe. In a broad sense, all aspects of astronomical facts, physics, and theories.

astroplankton. (Fiction.) Microscopic life existing in meteorite dust on other planets.

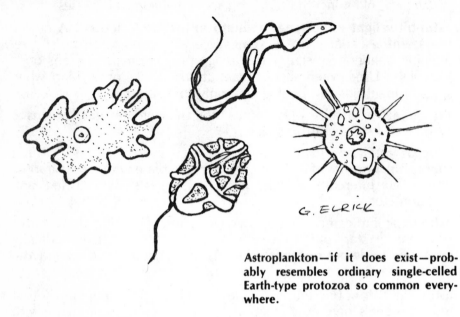

G. ELRICK

Astroplankton—if it does exist—probably resembles ordinary single-celled Earth-type protozoa so common everywhere.

astro-radar fingerprint analyzer. (Fiction.) An instantaneous identification verifier. When a hand is pressed against a special viewplate, fingerprint images are flashed across millions of miles of interplanetary space to wherever electronic files are kept.

astro-tracker. (Astronautics.) Space ship astrogating equipment that automatically acquires and steadily tracks a celestial body with respect to azimuth and altitude. See *acquisition* and *azimuth*.

atmosphere blanket. (Fiction.) The mixture of gases surrounding a planet, held in place by gravity.

atmosphere: Earth. (Astronautics.) Starting at ground level, and extending upward like a gaseous layer cake to the region of solar wind, are the following stratifications which blur together at their boundaries: troposphere, tropopause, stratosphere, mesosphere, thermosphere, and magnetosphere. The mesosphere, thermosphere, and magnetosphere comprise the ionosphere. See *solar wind* and *ionosphere*.

atmospheric braking. (Astronautics.) The effect of atmospheric drag in decelerating a spacecraft approaching a planet. Sometimes deliberately used to curtail a vehicle's velocity if enough atmosphere is present. See *air drag*.

atmospheric entry. (Astronautics.) Penetration of a planet's atmosphere by an object from outer space. In particular, penetration of the Earth's atmosphere by manned or unmanned spacecraft.

atmospheric pressure. (Physics.) Gaseous pressure at any point on any planet's surface, caused by downward bombardment of gas molecules. Earth's atmosphere at sea level is 14.7 pounds per-square-inch. Along the upper ridges of the Himalayas it's considerably less.

atmospheric revitalization system. (Fiction/Astronautics.) ARS for short. Has two space ship purposes: (1) to control temperature and humidity in crew compartments; and (2) to prevent electronic equipment from overheating. Most of the system's components are installed under the mid-deck floor. See *life support system*.

atom. (Physics.) The smallest possible particle of an element, such as gold, carbon, or hydrogen, that both retains and causes that element's properties, principally because of the one-of-a-kind electric charge of its nucleus and the behavior of its electrons. Endeavoring to 'see' an atom is as futile as striving to 'see' a thought, basically because the atom is inconceivably tiny and can act both as a particle and as a wave. It has a variety of properties that make weird situations in *Alice in Wonderland* seem mundane.

Each atom is made up of a nucleus that always has a positive charge, plus a surrounding shell or shells (sometimes called 'smears') of electrons. Each electron is forever negative, and all electrons are identical, no matter what type of atom they belong to. An atom, in its totality, is electrically neutral in its normal state, as the number of electrons it 'owns' is just sufficient for their combined negative charge to counterbalance the positive charge of the nucleus. When an atom isn't neutral, it's known as an ion (which see).

An atom's nucleus accounts for more than 99.9 percent of its mass and is held together by the most intense force known. (See *strong nuclear force*.) Yet the behavior of its ephemeral electrons determines how it reacts to or combines with other atoms, and how it interacts with radiation. Following are some mind-blowing facts, a few of which make reality seem more bizarre than the wildest science fiction fantasy:

Composition of nucleus: The nucleus consists of two kinds of particles: protons and neutrons, collectively known as nucleons. When a nucleon is in an electrically neutral state, it's a neutron. When it's in an electrically charged state, it's a proton. If an atom has a given number of electrons, its nucleus must have the same number of protons in order to hold them in orbit.

Size of nucleus: An atom's nucleus is 100,000 times smaller than the total atom itself (though it consists of 99.9 percent of its mass, as previously stated). If an atom were the size of a large, two-story suburban home, its nucleus would have the dimensions of a pinhead at the home's center. If all attendant electrons were peeled away, the total massiveness of Mount Everest could be crammed into a cigarette case. If all the matter comprising the Earth were compressed to nothing but atomic nuclei, the planet's diameter would shrivel to 1,080 feet . . . with no loss in weight.

Shape of nucleus: Some nuclei are spherical, others ellipsoid, and still others hover in between.

Astonishing abyss: The gap between the nucleus and the nearest encircling electron is proportionately greater than the space separating the sun from the Earth's far-flung orbit, and it's an absolute vacuum.

Everything spins: Every atomic component—electron, proton, and neutron—rotates like a top on its own axis.

See *electron, proton,* and *neutron.*

atomagnetic attractor. (Fiction.) Also called a magno attractor. A space ship-attracting apparatus capable of pulling ships to their doom from vast distances. Used by wild nomads on the larger planetoids, who live by plundering the contents of wrecked craft.

atomic cartridge. (Fiction.) An extremely explosive cartridge which can be fired from a ray rifle, though that's not the latter's normal function. If the atomic cartridge is used at too close range, resultant shock waves can kill the gun-wielder.

atomic cyclotron power generator. (Fiction.) Used for propulsion power in Saturnian space ships.

atomic disruptor. (Fiction.) A ray cannon used by Earth forces in wars with interplanetary invaders. When focused on an object, such as an enemy rocket ship, the target momentarily glows with a weird light, then cataclysmically explodes. The effect is similar to that of a *disintegrator ray* (which see).

atomic energy. (Physics.) Also called nuclear energy. Force generated by the combining or disrupting of atomic nuclei. See *fission* and *fusion.*

atomic fabricator. (Fiction.) A device that sprays synthetic-fabric clothing on people. Size, style, and material are governed by a fashion regulator dial.

Fit-wise, comparing futuristic clothing sprayed on an individual to a fashionable garment tailored in a Paris dress shop is akin to comparing a flint arrowhead with a microscopically exact electronic 'chip.'

atomic fission arrester. (Fiction.) A ray gun that—when aimed at a flying belt on someone's back—wipes out the belt's power, causing the soaring individual to plummet to the ground. See *flying belt.*

atomic fixator ray. (Fiction.) A ray used, defensively, in broadbeam focus, to neutralize any atomic weapons in a room.

atomic number. (Physics.) A designation of the number of positive charges in an atom's nucleus: a figure equal to the number of electrons—always negatively charged—that encircle the nucleus.

atomic torch. (Fiction.) A torture device of the Saturnians, inflicting what is referred to as "the death of ten thousand pains." Used to slowly sear the hides off of captives.

atomic vacuum gun. (Fiction.) A hand-held pistol-like apparatus that de-atomizes criminals, then sucks them into tiny cartridge-type chambers for subsequent re-atomizing, so they can stand trial.

atom projector. (Fiction.) Also known as a projectoformer. A cannon-like device that atomizes people and equipment for instant transmission—on a wavelength of 69 megacycles—to any spot in the solar system, where everything is instantly reassembled in its original form.

atom smashing powder. (Fiction.) Sometimes called Martian powder. Tiny flecks of virtually colorless matter, more like crystals than dust, that painlessly explode when ignited. The explosive charge must be adjusted to the size and weight of whatever is to be disintegrated. Chemically disassembles an object or person, moves it elsewhere, and reassembles it.

atonic gas. (Fiction.) Atonic, not atomic. A paralysis gas that weakens and slows down a victim's muscular responses, but leaves his mind clear. The after-effect is a skull-splitting headache.

attitude. (Astronautics.) A spacecraft's orientation relative to its forward thrust, and to a frame of reference, such as a planet's surface. Attitude consists of *pitch,* which is rotation about an axis perpendicular to the vehicle's longitudinal axis, and horizontal with respect to a planet's surface; *roll,* which is rotation about a longitudinal axis; and *yaw,* which is rotation about a vertical axis. See *pitch, roll,* and *yaw.*

attitude control. (Astronautics.) Regulation of a spacecraft's pitch, roll, and yaw.

attitude gyro. (Astronautics.) A flight instrument depicting a spacecraft's attitude regarding a reference coordinate system through the 360-degree rotation of each of its axes. Similar to a control panel's artificial horizon component, but with greater angular indication.

attitude jets. (Astronautics.) Gas nozzles on a satellite or missile, operated periodically or continuously to change or maintain the vehicle's spatial posture. Also called *steering jets, attitude control jets, roll jets, pitch jets,* and *yaw jets.*

attraction beam. (Fiction.) A beam that can be used for good or ill. Emitted, when needed, from the underside of a rocket ship, it's powerful enough to yank a heavy building off its foundation or suck water skyward from a large lake. The beam can be clicked off, tumbling the building to the ground and destroying it. On the other hand, the sucked-up water can be dispersed over a wide area as rain.

attractor beam. (Fiction.) A beam emitted from a space ship's bottom, usually near the stern. Used to anchor the vehicle at a pre-determined height above the surface of a planet or asteroid.

aurora. (Astronomy.) A shifting glow of light radiated by atoms and ions in the ionosphere when the latter is bombarded by an influx of high energy sun particles. Seen primarily in polar regions.

automatic building machine. (Fiction.) Projects a sharply-defined three-dimensional holographic image, then transforms it into a solid structure by spraying a plastic molecule mist that instantly hardens on contact with strong light.

automatic detector. (Fiction.) An electronic sensor on a space ship. Immediately signals the presence or approach of another space ship, generally by picking up the other craft's motor hum at a great distance. Rocket vibrations of space ships from different planets are distinctively different.

autotrophic structure. (Fiction.) A 'self-building' structure: a concept inspired by the capacity of shellfish and other aquatic life to create protective shelters by utilizing minerals dissolved in water. As pre-

An autotrophic building can be 'grown' in mineral-rich sea water. Accumulated encrustations exhibit structural properties comparable to extra-sturdy concrete.

sently conceived, a mobile generator would produce a weak electric current between itself and a skeletonized conductive surface placed in sea water. Tiny particles of mineral matter would accumulate on the surface toward which the current flowed. After a certain thickness of material built up, the power source would be turned off and the natural electrolytic action of the water would suffice to keep the process going. Steps in this direction have been accomplished already in scientific research.

auxiliary fluid ignition. (Astronautics.) A type of ignition employed with a liquid-propellant rocket engine. Liquid—normally aniline, hypergolic with the fuel or the oxidizer—is injected into the engine's combustion chamber to kick off firing. See *hypergolic* and *oxidizer*.

auxiliary rockets. (Astronautics.) Subsidiary steering rockets used to maneuver a spacecraft into a new position, frequently a new orbit. Without auxiliary rockets a spacecraft couldn't change course or avoid smashing into meteors.

avionics. See *space ship avionics*.

In a comfortable chamber at the center of Dione, fourth moon of Saturn, ceiling and floor openings can both be regarded as 'up,' just as any point on the Earth's surface can be conceived as 'up' by a hypothetical person positioned at the world's intensely hot center.

G. ELRICK

axial tunnel. (Fiction.) A shaft—open at both ends—that runs through the exact center of Dione, the fourth moon of Saturn. Its terminal openings are referred to as polar 'mouths.' When anyone enters the tunnel, he falls gently to a comfortable chamber at the moon's center, which is also the center of gravity. Any weight is due to centrifugal force exerted by the moon's spin on its axis. Flying belts must be used in order to re-surface.

azimuth. (Astronautics.) In astrogating, a horizontal direction or bearing. Depending on the frame of reference, it's referred to as *true, magnetic, compass, grid,* or *relative azimuth.*

B

back contamination. (Astronautics.) Germs or other micro-organisms inadvertently brought back to Earth by a spacecraft that has visited another planet. The primary hazard is that a new, uncontrollable disease might spread, with a virulence that could decimate mankind.

background radiation. (Physics.) Sometimes called natural radiation: emissions inherent in man's Earthborne environment. Included are cosmic rays and radiation from radioactive elements. A slightly different meaning: radiation unrelated to a specific scientific experiment.

backup flight control system. (Fiction/Astronautics.) BFCS for short. A space ship system—used only in extreme emergencies—distinct from the vehicle's primary guidance, navigation, and flight control system. The BFCS uses control laws and equations similar to the primary system's, but is limited to a simple, single string set-up to avoid problems that might arise with the primary system's general-purpose computers. The BFCS utilizes a fifth general-purpose computer: a multiplexer/demultiplexer for data input collection. No cathode ray tube/keyboard operation is involved; the BFCS relies on aerosurface servo-amplifiers, servo-actuators, and actuators which are redundant to the primary system's. Only a minimal interface is needed between systems, since response, switchover, and the sharing of common hardware are virtually simultaneous. Though its outputs are inhibited prior to emergency switchover, the BFCS operates concurrently with the primary flight control system, processing identical command, sensor, and surface position feedback data. See *space ship flight control* and *fail-operational/fail-safe performance*.

ballistic trajectory. (Physics.) The arching trajectory a rocket or other body takes when influenced only by gravity and the resistance of the medium through which it passes.

barycenter. (Physics.) The center of gravity of any group of revolving masses.

basic laws: seeming simplicity of. (Physics.) Albert Einstein wrote: 'Our experience justifies us in believing that nature is the realization of the simplest conceivable mathematical ideas.' Most scientists agree; many don't. Biologists, for instance, are staggered by the intricacy of life processes as evidenced in the genetic code, brain, and the central nervous system. On the other hand, physicists hunt for an underlying simplicity beneath all complexity, seeking a key, or a kind of philosophical glue—such as the Unified Field Theory— that neatly laces all phenomena together. Reassuringly, in practice, the simplest workable hypotheses turn out to be best. Yet, if many of the laws of physics seem simple, it may only be because rudimentary 'lead pipe cinch' laws are easy to discover. Lurking beyond them may be hosts of other, infinitely more complex laws, to date unacknowl- edged or indecipherable. Physicists—orderly *by* nature—want order and simplicity *in* nature (such as the equivalence of inertia and gravity in general relativity), claiming that a handful of cosmic forces accounts for all known happenings for all time. Reinforcing this stance, when new particles are discovered at the sub-atomic level, everything seems to be periodically up for grabs . . . yet, when the dust settles, the same 'everything' is carefully—and believably— re-fitted into an ever-expanding, but satisfyingly cohesive pattern. See *Unified Field Theory* and *gauge theories*.

basic research. (Generic.) Also known as pure research: research seeking new information with no immediate practical application. Basic research isn't concerned with solving 'here and now' problems. It *is* concerned with gathering information for its own sake. See *applied research*.

beacon tracking. (Astronautics.) Tracing an object moving through space via signals emitted from a transmitter attached to it.

beaming. (Fiction.) An instant conversion of matter into energy; a quick transmission of this energy across space; and fast reconversion of the energy into its previous 'thick' form at a fixed-point destination. Useful for moving a space ship's crew and cargo from a hovering vehicle to a planet's surface, then back again. Beaming is effected by means of a hand-held 'transporter.' See *atom projector.*

beam-rider guidance. (Astronautics.) A method of guiding spacecraft in which a craft follows a light beam, radar beam, or other kind of emission along a desired path.

beta-emitting tritium. (Astronautics.) An artificially produced, radioactive hydrogen isotope used, in fabricating small tubes and other displays, for instrument and control panel illumination. Tritium—which glows brightly for 20 years or more—provides light but not power. See *beta particle* and *isotope.*

beta particle. (Physics.) A sub-atomic particle discharged from a nucleus during radioactive decay. When negatively charged, beta particles are identical to electrons; when positively charged, they are known as positrons. Though beta particles are easily deflected by a thin metal sheet, they can cause painful skin burns. See *alpha particle* and *positron.*

bicameral mind. (Fiction.) A mind capable of focusing on two totally different thoughts or concepts simultaneously.

Big Bang Theory. (Physics.) Also known as the expanding universe theory. Working backward from present-day evidence, based on Hubble's constant, the universe—and time itself—began 15 billion years ago. What is now seemingly infinite in size was then incredibly small, incredibly compressed, and incredibly hot. A monstrous explosion (silent, because there was no air and, therefore, because there were no sound waves) flung this densest of all matter outward in every direction. The recession of galaxies, still observable—as though star clusters were markings on an expanding balloon's skin—stems from that stupefying detonation, as does the omnipresence of faint radio waves, plus a faint residue of warmth in interstellar space . . . though that warmth is colder than the South Pole by subjective human standards.

　　Time Table:

In the first one-ten-thousandth of a second . . . more matter and antimatter existed than now survives. However many colliding sub-

The silent, incomprehensible big bang of 15 billion years ago was the prime cause of everything that eventually followed, from caterpillars to Cleopatra.

atomic particles wiped each other out, leaving a cloud of heavy protons. Gravity, the electric force or field, the strong nuclear force, and the weak nuclear force all had the same range and strength. They were one undifferentiated force, a momentary unity that instantly blurred. Gravity separated out. In turn, the weak nuclear force separated out and became the short-range entity it still is. As the temperature dipped a million million degrees, the strong nuclear force showed its muscle, forcing all quarks into groups of three.

In the first ten seconds . . . lightweight electrons settled down.

In the first few minutes . . . one-fourth of all heavy matter became helium and hydrogen, and radio energy assumed its endless, faint background presence in the universe.

After the first few minutes and for a sizable segment of the next 15 billion years . . . the universe swirled and seethed like a blast furnace of brain-cracking proportions: an insanely bubbling, gaseous cauldron that steadily cooled as it expanded. Concurrent with expansion, compression—caused by gravity—squeezed gas into galaxies, then into stars within the galaxies. Combustion went haywire. In this flaming anarchy, the weak nuclear force linked elementary particles

50

into heavy elements. The strong nuclear force then exploded over-blown stars, scattering their newly created heavy elements like leaves in a hurricane. As always, inexorable gravity squeezed this scattering into new generations of stars, now heavily enriched with cosmic dust. Insignificantly sputtering among these new star generations was our sun.

Today . . . though the universe bears no macrocosmic resemblance to the initial cosmic egg, at scales infinitely smaller than the size of a quark matter is similar to what it was when the big bang took place. All particles and all forces evince a symmetry that is apparently integral to nature.

See *antimatter, cosmic dust, cosmic egg, electric field, elementary particles, Hubble's constant, proton, quark, radio waves, strong nuclear force, gravity, star, time, Unified Field Theory, weak nuclear force,* and *cosmogony.*

binary. (Astronomy.) Also called a double star. Two or more stars that orbit about a mutual center of mass. To the naked eye, or through a telescope, they sometimes appear as a single object. Even if more than two stars are involved, the phenomenon is referred to as a binary or double star.

bioastronautics. (Astronautics.) The broad spectrum of behavioral, psychological, biological, and medical challenges involved in space travel and colonization. This umbrella term embraces life support systems, and their functionings and effects, in spacecraft and on celestial bodies other than the Earth. See *life support system.*

biodynamics. (Astronautics.) The study of how weightlessness, motion, and acceleration affect living organisms in space travel. See *zero gravity: effects of.*

biological architecture. (Fiction.) Also called *biotecture.* The use of controlled plant life and minerals to create dwellings according to human specifications. Plants are genetically altered and crystalline minerals chemically treated to grow into pre-programmed shapes. Structures are dynamic, responsive, ongoing processes. For instance, a home changes color to provide additional protection against summer sun, a la human skin when it tans, and repairs itself, just as human skin heals its own wounds. Compare with autotrophic structure. See *biopolis.*

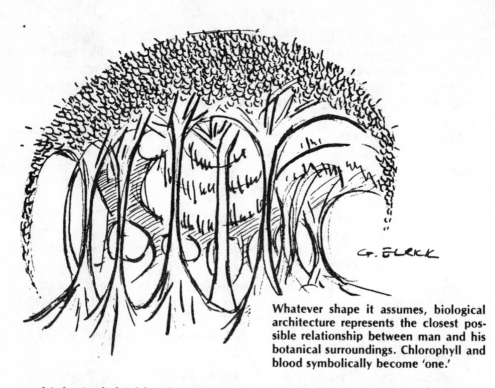

Whatever shape it assumes, biological architecture represents the closest possible relationship between man and his botanical surroundings. Chlorophyll and blood symbolically become 'one.'

biological shield. (Physics.) A mass of absorbing material, positioned around a reactor or radioactive source, to reduce radiation to a level non-damaging to human beings. See *radiation, radiation: genetic effects of,* and *radiation illness.*

biomorphic biosphere megastructure. (Fiction.) BBM for short: a self-sustaining, self-contained ecological/architectural organism. Also called 'land in the sky' because its component dwellings, passageways, open-mesh walls, and operational facilities give it an inverted-pyramid, tree-like appearance. A BBM's average height is 5,000 feet, and it houses 250,000 people.

bionics. (Generic.) The use of biological principles to design electronic systems that function, to a great degree, like living organisms.

biopod. (Fiction.) A creature that's half plant, half animal. Compare with animaloid.

biopolis. (Fiction.) An entire metropolis comprised of biological architecture (which see).

biosensor. (Generic.) A sensor that provides information about life processes.

bioshield. (Astronautics.) Used with a lander/probe. (See *probe*.) A two-piece, dome-shaped outer capsule enclosing a probe and its aeroshell (which see). Protects the probe and aeroshell from

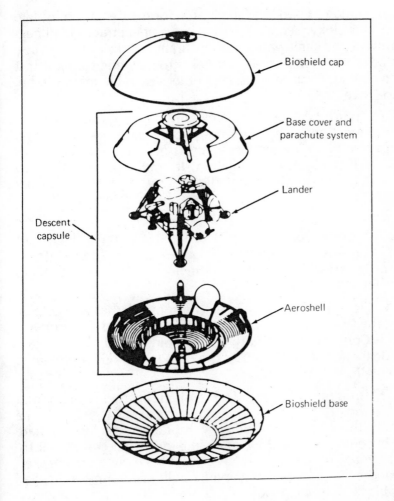

Bioshield cap

Base cover and parachute system

Lander

Descent capsule

Aeroshell

Bioshield base

Exploded view of encapsulated probe capsule indicating appearance of typical bioshield.

biological, chemical, and particulate contamination before and during Earth blast-off, so the probe will be antiseptically 'pure' when landing on its target celestial body. Fashioned from coated woven Fiberglas, bonded to an aluminum support structure, and pressurized with inert gas, with a venting system that prevents over-pressurization that might result in the rupturing of delicate components.

black beam. (Fiction.) Used by a space ship for escape purposes, like a squid's jet of inky sepia. A beam of impenetrable darkness through which light can't pass. Also a paramagnetic attraction ray that wipes out the activity of all other electromagnetic sources. If it touches the ground, it causes grass and other vegetable matter to become radioactive.

black body. (Physics.) An ideal, theoretically flawless absorber of all incident radiation. Though no black body really exists, physicists find the concept useful in projecting calculations, and picture it as emitting, as well as absorbing, radiation. It emits precisely the way Planck's constant says it should, at the maximum possible rate per unit area, at each wavelength, for any given temperature. See *Planck's constant.*

black box. (Astronautics.) Any replaceable electronic device or component that—as a self-contained unit—can be fitted into or removed from a larger system without the need to know what makes the component operational.

black cross. (Fiction.) A weapon in the form of a lethal nucleotoxic smoke absorbed by the tissues of higher animals and the fruits of many plants. Concentrates in fatty or oily lipid cells till it reaches a state of critical mass, when it causes the cells to explode. Delineated by John Aiken in *World Well Lost.*

black hole. (Astronomy.) A theoretical crushed-together remnant of a massive star that has consumed its nuclear fuel. The larger the shrinking star, the greater the odds it will plunge past intermediate stages and become this incredible phenomenon. What crunches it together is the force of gravity: gravity so overwhelming that matter, radiation, and even light can't escape its pull. Everything is dragged inward. A black hole can't possibly shine by its own or reflected radiation; hence the name.

Size and shape: All are spherical. Some, said to have zero dimensions, consist of millions of tons of matter squeezed into a space smaller than an atom. Others are as much as four miles in diameter.

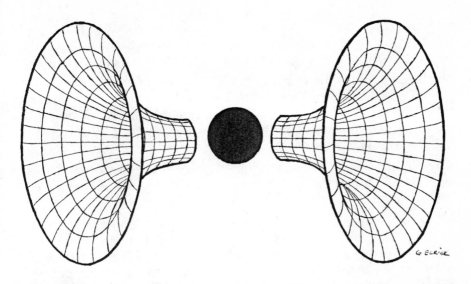

The typical physicist believes only the collapse of the universe and another 'big bang' could unlock matter sucked into a black hole. However, science fiction writers toy with the idea that matter drawn into a black hole may be spewed forth elsewhere through a 'white hole.'

They also play with the concept of 'wormholes' in a spinning black hole's equatorial plane, through which instantaneous travel might be possible from point to point without crossing intervening space.

Temperature: They're unbelievably hot or cold. The smaller the hole, the hotter. Those formed from squashed-together stars at a galaxy's center are cold. Many physicists conjecture that black holes eventually explode with the force of millions of H-bombs; others postulate that nothing could possibly make them explode . . . that they'll last far longer than the 15 billion years the universe has already existed.

Remarkably simple: A black hole has no molecular, atomic, or nuclear structure. Gravity has literally ground all elementary particles out of existence, making matter disappear.

Absolute event horizon: A black hole's surface is known as an absolute event horizon. The total mass of the star that collapsed is beneath this horizon. Energy emitted inside the hole is unable to push past this rim.

Curves space and warps time: Due to its compressed massiveness, a black hole curves surrounding space and puts brakes on time. Should a spacecraft circle a hole, the passage of thousands of years would be experienced as the passage of minutes. Should it foolishly circle too close, it would be stretched like spaghetti, then sucked into oblivion.

Black holes explain an overabundance of X-rays: Matter falling into black holes emits final blasts of X-rays. Astronomers attribute repeated outpourings of X-rays across space to catastrophic wipe-outs. Since the universe is purportedly as peppered with black holes as a collander, erasures are continuous.

Compare with *neutron star.*

black light. (Fiction.) A search light whose lens, reflector, and energy source are undetectable by an observer. The beam bounces an echo off whatever it probes.

blackout. (Astronautics.) Has two meanings: (1) a fade-out of spacecraft radio communications due to ionospheric disturbances or the presence of a plasma sheath during re-entry . . . (2) a temporary loss of vision because of an abrupt decrease in blood pressure during re-entry. See *plasma sheath* and *gray-out.*

blast chamber. (Astronautics.) The combustion chamber in a jet or rocket engine.

blood boiling. (Astronautics.) One of the hazards of space flight: rapid evaporation of an astronaut's blood because of pressure reduction stemming from spacecraft leaks or space suit failures.

boarding tube. (Fiction.) A jointed, accordion-type tube large enough to stand in, capable of linking the air lock compartments of two space ships.

boil-off. (Astronautics.) Vaporization of liquid oxygen or liquid hydrogen as its temperature reaches the boiling point under exposure conditions, as in the tank of a liquid-fueled space vehicle readied for launching. See *liquid hydrogen* and *liquid oxygen.*

Bokanovsky's process. (Fiction.) In Aldous Huxley's *Brave New World,* a method of producing babies-to-order in test tubes. Qualities such as intellect and work interest are pre-determined to meet society's needs.

Bokononism. (Fiction.) In Kurt Vonnegut, Jr.'s *Cat's Cradle,* a faith founded on bittersweet lies. The Bokononist view of the human animal is that man is a lucky variety of mud that God, in His lonesomeness, permitted to sit up and look around. Bokononist politics are summed up in a paraphrase of Jesus's 'Render unto Caesar the things that are Caesar's': 'Pay no attention to Caesar. He doesn't have the slightest idea what's *really* going on.'

boost. (Astronautics.) Extra momentum given a spacecraft during lift-off, climb, or any other part of its flight.

booster. (Astronautics.) Abbreviation for booster rocket engine, fired at lift-off to push a vehicle to the speed required for prolonged flight. A booster provides considerable thrust for a short time period, compared to a space vehicle's main engine, which provides less thrust but operates for a longer period.

brain neutralizing ray. (Fiction.) A form of emission that transforms intelligent humans into zombies.

braking ellipses. (Astronautics.) A series of heat-dissipating curves, shrinking in size because of aerodynamic drag, used by a spacecraft when penetrating a planetary atmosphere. The maneuvers are necesssary to avoid flaming destruction due to entry or re-entry friction.

breadboard. (Astronautics.) A prototype, or experimental model, used to determine the feasibility of a circuit, device, system, or principle, without regard to its ultimate configuration.

breakaway phenomenon. (Astronautics.) A disquieting feeling, occasionally experienced during long-distance space flights, of being permanently amputated from the Earth and its web of human relationships. See *space hazards to the psyche.*

breath screen. (Fiction.) Also called breath mask: a filtering device, covering the nose and mouth, permitting one to breathe the atmosphere of alien planets.

bubble chamber. (Physics.) An apparatus that enables a physicist to follow charged particle paths—or infer the paths of electrically neutral particles—by studying bubble trails formed on ions produced in superheated liquid.

Buck Rogers. (Fiction.) The protagonist of the first and most influential science fiction comic strip, which ran from January 7, 1929 to mid-1967. Buck was an athletic, adventurous 20th Century youth in the 25th Century, miraculously alive after 500 years because he had existed in suspended animation in a caved-in mine near Pittsburgh. His sweetheart was Lieutenant Wilma Deering, whom he kissed fewer than ten times during the strip's thirty-eight years. Buck's archenemies were Killer Kane, Interplanetary Enemy Number One, who made Adolf Hitler seem like a naive Boy Scout, and Ardala Valmar, his blackhearted girlfriend. Kane was unmistakably killed three times during the course of the strip, but always reappeared. Other principal characters were Dr. Huer, a twenty-fifth century Einstein; Flame D'Amour, a Venusian secret agent whose code name was Thermal; the Flamingo Feather, who always spoke in rhyme; and Black Barney, a reformed space pirate.

The strip was originated by John Flint Dille, president of the National Newspaper Service Syndicate, Chicago. It was based on a novelette, *Armageddon 2419*, written by Philip Francis Nowlan in

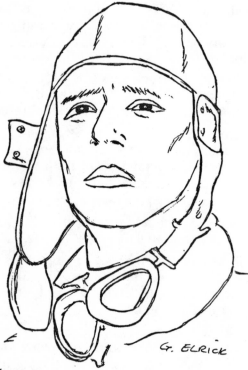

G. ELRICK

In 1929, Buck Rogers bore a strong resemblance to Charles Lindbergh, flight goggles and all. By 1967, he looked like any other plastic comic-book super hero.

G. ELRICK

Bug-eyed monsters no longer appear in science fiction, having been cast into the intellectual dustbin along with 'mad scientists.' Juvenile in concept, and supposedly 'X-rated' and prurient, they're not missed by the sophisticated. In their heyday, they were cardboard cut-outs, like World War II motion picture depictions of Nazis and Japs. If one did appear in a science fiction setting today it would be approached with objective curiosity rather than subjective revulsion. (Unless it ate the girl.)

1928. Nowlan wrote the script's continuity for several years, while Richard W. Calkins did the artwork. After Nowlan died and Calkins retired, Buck's adventures continued through the pens and minds of Rick Yager, Murphy Anderson, George Tuska, and Leonard Dworkins. The strip had many imitators, including Flash Gordon and Brick Bradford, but none equalled its influence or ingenuity. It introduced more people to science fiction than any other medium before or since.

bug-eyed monster. (Fiction.) Called BEM for short. The ubiquitous, oversize, lizard- or insect-like creature—with thick scales, bulging eyes, and many limbs—that menaced screaming, half-clad females in science fiction's pulp-magazine days (and still does in Japan's Godzilla films). The implied sexuality was unspeakably bestial in the most literal sense, though the shrieking victim was normally rescued by the square-jawed protagonist. Reminiscent of fire-belching dragons in fairy tales, the sex-crazed BEM was uglier by a country mile. Modified and mutated versions include The Creature From the Black Lagoon and King Kong—though the latter, being a mammal, has a streak of kindness absent in anything reptilian. See *Homo monstrosus, the alien nymphet,* and *adventure science fiction.*

bulkhead. (Astronautics.) An upright wall or partition that divides a space ship into compartments and strengthens its over-all structure. Other functions are to prevent the spread of fuel leakage or fire, and to keep specified areas air-tight.

burn-out. (Astronautics.) The point in time, or on a trajectory, when a spacecraft's propellant is exhausted, resulting in the termination of combustion and thrust.

burn the air. (Fiction.) A rocket ship term for 'making tracks.' Used only with reference to small craft that stay within the Earth's atmosphere.

Bussard interstellar ramjet. (Fiction/Astronautics.) A device, proposed in 1960 by American physicist Robert W. Bussard, which theoretically enables a starship to attain relativistic speeds. A magnetic scoop deflector that precedes the ship sucks in hydrogen atoms scattered in interstellar space, funneling them into a fusion reactor which spits out heated gases in a continuous jet. Because of the limitless availability of hydrogen between planets and stars, a ship with this type of ramjet has equally limitless range. Compare with *aeroduct* and *Ram augmented interstellar rocket.* See *hydrogen: universality of.*

C

caisson disease. (Astronautics.) Occasionally used with reference to space travelers, though normally used regarding deep sea divers. Also known as compressed air illness, aeroembolism, or the bends. An agonizing physiological disorder caused by an abrupt switch from high pressure to atmospheric pressure. Bubbles of inert gas form in the body, producing neurological changes, joint pains, cramps, paralysis, and death . . . unless the situation is remedied via gradual decompression.

caltechium. (Fiction.) The ultimate weapon: Earth's deadliest man-made radioactive element. Twenty-four hours after a caltechium blast, all traces of its radioactivity vanish. An alien enemy, having acquired the formula, could destroy all life on this planet, then safely occupy it within a day.

capsule. (Astronautics.) Sometimes erroneously called a pod. A small, sealed, pressurized cabin housing an internal environment that sustains human or animal life during space flight, or during emergency escape from a spacecraft. Also a rocket's nose cone. See *pod*.

carbonaceous chondrites. (Generic.) The most primitive objects in the solar system: stony meteorites containing chondrules, which are pea-size spheres of glass and silicate minerals. Chondrules were formed 4.6 billion years ago, preceding crystallization of the Earth's and moon's oldest rocks. It's thought that they condensed directly out of the gaseous nebula that spawned our sun and sister planets.

cardiac detector. (Fiction.) Also called a cardio-scope. A space ship sensing device that can pick up a heartbeat thump over long distances. Used to sniff out the presence of occupied enemy craft, even when the latter are grounded and 'playing dead,' with all mechanisms quiescent. Flashes a red light when zeroing in. For identification purposes, its sono selector component can focus on one heartbeat out of many. Compare with *heartbeat reader*.

cardio-adrenalite 44-Z. (Fiction.) An injection capable of reviving someone who has been in suspended animation. Must be used in conjunction with an oxygenic circulator.

cargo bay. (Astronautics.) The area of a spacecraft housing its non-human payload. See *payload*.

cartesian coordinates. (Astronautics.) A navigational orientation system in which the positions of points in space are expressed vis a vis three planes—known as coordinate planes—no two of which are parallel. The planes intersect in three straight lines, referred to as coordinate axes.

cataleptic trance inductor. (Fiction.) A ray-emitting device that enables prisoners to be stacked like sardines in a rigid, shallow-breathing, trance-like state.

caution/warning system. (Fiction/Astronautics.) C/W for short. In a space ship, a system that alerts crew members to a dangerous or potentially dangerous situation or condition. Usually consists of an electronics unit, master alarm pushbutton indicators, annunciator lights, and status lights. The over-all set-up is controlled by a caution/warning switch located on the flight crew's display-and-control panel. When this switch is positioned at NORMAL, a caution/warning light illuminates if corresponding parameters exceed their limits, and remains illuminated until the situation is rectified. If there's an out-of-tolerance condition in computer software, another caution/warning light turns on, plus a systems management ALERT light, and remains illuminated until acknowledged by the flight crew via computer keyboard. As an extra precaution, whenever a caution/warning light flashes on, three red MASTER ALARM pushbutton light indicators similarly flash on, and an audible tone resounds in flight crew headsets. If the audible tone alternates, it stems from the caution/warning system. If it is continuous, it stems from computer software malfunctioning. The applicable tone can be silenced, and the MASTER ALARM red lights extinguished, through depression of the appropriate pushbutton light indicator.

celestial coordinates. (Astronautics.) Any group of coordinates used to define a point on the celestial sphere. See *celestial sphere.*

celestial guidance. (Astronautics.) Also called automatic celestial navigation, or star tracking. A computer-determined flight path with reference to a spacecraft's moment-by-moment position, or 'fix', concerning a particular star. Compare with *celestial navigation.*

celestial-inertial guidance. (Astronautics.) The process of guiding a spacecraft's flight path via an inertial guidance system that receives inputs from observations of celestial bodies. See *inertial guidance.*

celestial navigation. (Astronautics.) Directing a spacecraft from point to point with reference to celestial bodies of known coordinates. Generally accomplished by a human operator. When the process is accomplished via computer, it's known as celestial guidance.

celestial sphere. (Astronomy.) A hypothetical sphere of infinite extent, concentric with the Earth, on which all celestial bodies appear to be located on an imaginary curved surface.

The center of the celestial sphere (the origin of its coordinate system) may be at the observation point, the center of the Earth, or the center of the sun. Corresponding coordinates are called topocentric, geocentric, and heliocentric.

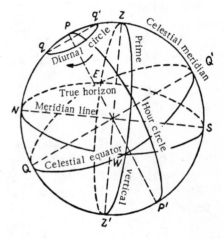

cerebral ray. (Fiction.) Also known as C-ray, brain ray, or cosmic mentality ray. Exposure to its positive formula increases intelligence; exposure to its negative formula decreases intelligence.

chain-reacto ray. (Fiction.) An emission blasted from a turbo turtle war machine. Causes anything it touches to burst into uncontrollable flames.

chamber pressure. (Astronautics.) The pressure of gases in a rocket engine's combustion chamber.

chango ray. (Fiction.) Also known as a mirage ray or camouflage ray. Issues from a slender, flashlight-like tube with a spectrum of settings, creating an optical illusion by employing a light refraction twist-wave principle. It camouflages grounded rocket ships as rocks, water, bushes, or sand, and can also be used to disguise its operator so he melts into the background. In an emergency, it will petrify another human to the consistency and immobility of a store window mannequin.

charged particle beam. (Physics.) A man-made 'lightning bolt' capable of destroying enemy missiles, or disarming them by melting the plutonium in their nuclear warheads. Consists of a stream of such sub-atomic particles as electrons, protons, and heavy ions.

charm. (Physics.) A postulated fourth type of quark, in addition to the three categories known to physicists as *up, down,* and *strange. Charm,* a heavy elementary particle, quickly decays. Yet, in the microworld, it freezes energy a trifle longer than would be expected. A great deal of charm appeared during the Big Bang. See *quark* and *Big Bang Theory.*

chemical aura-meter. (Fiction.) An electro-radioactive carbon aura camera, known as CAM for short. Faster and more accurate than a fingerprint identifier, it records the complex electro-emanations exuded by someone at the time of arrest, storing the unique wave pattern as a recording. If a newly-arrested suspect's electro-emanations match the stored pattern, he's unquestionably the same culprit.

chemical fuel. (Astronautics.) A fuel that needs an oxidizer for combustion and the development of thrust, as distinguished from nuclear fuel. See *nuclear power as applied to spacecraft.*

chromosphere. (Astronomy.) The narrow-width, hot transitional layer between the sun's surface and the even-hotter surrounding blanket of its corono. See *corona.*

chronometer. (Generic.) An extremely precise clock, watch, or other timepiece.

chrono-synclastic infundibulum. (Fiction.) In Kurt Vonnegut, Jr.'s *Sirens of Titan,* a section of space where all varieties of truth in the universe fit together 'as nicely as the parts in your Daddy's solar watch.' A person caught in a chrono-synclastic infundibulum may simultaneously find himself in various regions of spacetime.

circular velocity. (Astronautics.) The speed required for a spacecraft, or other object, to maintain a circular orbit at a given distance from a center of attraction.

circulation restorer. (Fiction.) A device shaped like a 20th Century iron lung. When prisoners are 'fast frozen'—to avoid the expense of feeding or otherwise caring for them—they can be thawed out and re-animated, for interrogation or slave labor purposes, by activating this mechanism. The turnabout takes only two minutes.

circumflight. (Astronautics.) Orbital flight around a celestial body.

cislunar space. (Astronomy.) The space between the Earth and the moon's orbit.

civilized system. (Fiction.) A portion of a galaxy containing planets with civilizations on them.

Civil Space Patrol Ship. (Fiction.) A rocket ship used by governmental authorities to routinely check the efficacy of space ship passports and other documents. Its occupants have authority to arrest anyone AWOL from military duty.

Clarke's Third Law. (Generic.) Arthur C. Clarke: "Any sufficiently advanced technology is indistinguishable from magic.'

clone. (Fiction.) The asexual creation of an exact replica of another individual, using any body cell except a sperm or ovum: a process known as cloning. The problems of being a clone are strikingly delineated by Kate Wilhelm in *Where Late the Sweet Birds Sang,* and by Nancy Freedman in *Joshua, Son of None.*

G. ELRICK

In the most commonly pictured form of cloning, or 'womb renting,' the nucleus of a carrier woman's ovum is subjected to ultraviolet radiation, destroying her chromosomes and, therefore, her genetic contribution. When this treated ovum is paired in a laboratory—before womb implantation—with any cell from another individual's body, the total genetic inheritance of the subsequently developing fetus derives from that 'other' cell, even if it's unceremoniously taken from an ear lobe.

Using this approach, with several options, science fiction plots make it possible to grind out precise genotypes, or biological doubles, of any person, from an Adolf Hitler to a Saint Francis of Assissi. It goes without saying that each living, breathing carbon copy will be somewhat modified by its unique environment. Replicas of Winston Churchill needn't necessarily crave cigars and bourbon when reaching adulthood.

The basic thesis of cloning is that all genetic information required to reproduce an organism is encoded in the nucleus of each living cell. The word clone is from a Greek term meaning botanical twig or shoot.

closed ecological system. See *life support system.*

cloud chamber. (Physics.) A supersaturated vapor apparatus used to detect charged sub-atomic particles, to infer the presence of neutral sub-atomic particles, and to study certain nuclear reactions. It works via the formation of droplet chains on ions.

cluster engine. (Astronautics.) A combination of rocket engines mounted in a closely assembled unit for coordinated thrust.

cluster of galaxies. (Astronomy.) A group of twelve or more galaxies bound together by mutual gravitational attraction. See *galaxy.*

clutter. (Astronautics.) Anything that tends to obscure reception of desired signals in a radio receiver, such as extraneous impulses or atmospheric noise.

cockpit emergency ejector. (Fiction.) A 'flip-out,' detachable enclosure used for escape purposes when a space ship is attacked, about to crash, explode, or lose needed pressure. The escape procedure entails an inherent danger of damage to electronic controls and radio signal apparatus, which means ejector occupants might be marooned in orbit. If they're wearing space suits, and the emergency ejector isn't too far from Earth or another planetary body, flying belts can be used for a secondary exit. See *capsule.*

collapsible space ship. (Fiction.) A spacecraft so constructed that, when destruction in battle seems imminent, it can temporarily be 'scrambled' in appearance to resemble a spacewreck, complete with fake smoke emission: an enemy-deceiving ploy. When danger is past, the 'dead dog' can be de-telescoped to snap into its former shape.

collapsible stairs. (Fiction.) Hinged glass steps convertible to a smooth ramp at the touch of a button. Perfect for trapping intruders, who instantly slide to the base.

color. (Physics.) A newly named, newly discovered cosmic force, possibly the strongest of them all, which holds quarks together, in groups of three, in the heart of a proton. For want of a better tag, particles of 'glue,' called glue-ons, zig-zag between quark triads, transmitting the color force. Quarks behave bizarrely, like creatures in a backward world. For example, when two of them approach each other, their mutual attraction decreases rather than vice versa; when they pull away, their mutual attraction increases. In other words, it's impossible for them to get too far apart. In flouting gravity, they're seemingly unique in nature. See *quark* and *proton.*

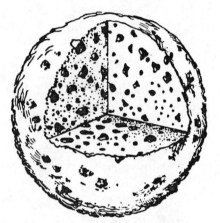

Cometary nuclei, as imagined by an artist, with wedges removed to show what they look like inside: 'traveling gravel banks.' Solid particles in a comet's nucleus serve as material for the formation of powdery tails and meteoric showers.

comet. (Astronomy.) A large, dirty snowball—a mixture of ice, frozen gases, grit, dust, and meteoric rock—drifting through the deepfreeze of space in an eccentric, far-flung orbit.

Size: Central core-wise, only a few miles in diameter. What makes it appear larger is the corona of dust and gas released when approaching the sun. Each time it warms up, dust and gas are lost. In time, measured in thousands of years, the snowball dissipates to nothing.

Number: There are more than 100 billion.

Orbit: The typical comet has an orbit many times greater than the distance from Pluto to the sun. (Pluto is 2.8 billion miles from the sun at perihelion.) It spends most of its journey in the orbit's outer reaches.

Properties of the tail: When it's too far from the sun to be warmed, a comet has no tail. When it's close enough to react to solar energy, its outer layers vaporize brightly. Theoretically, vaporized material should move in tandem with the comet. It doesn't, since the comet's nucleus has negligible gravity. Also, pressure from two sources blows the vapor away, forming a tail extending tens of millions of miles (though, as noted, the comet itself is paltry in size). One of the pressure sources is light itself. The other is solar wind or plasma, a thin, rapid gas flow streaming outward from the sun. Due to the pressure, many comets have double tails: a gently curved one caused by light's powder-puff push, and a straight one caused by solar wind. Despite uninformed artists' misconceptions, comet tails always point away from the sun. When a comet swings toward its outer orbit, its tails precede it. See *perihelion, solar wind,* and *plasma.*

comlink. (Fiction.) Short for communications link. A device similar to a *transceiver* (which see).

composite propellant. (Astronautics.) A solid rocket propellant comprised of a fuel and an oxidizer, neither of which would burn minus the presence of the other.

concussionator ray. (Fiction.) A type of electromagnetic emission that scrambles brains.

cone formation. (Fiction.) Flying formation assumed by a fleet of space ships.

cone of escape. (Physics.) A postulated cone in the exosphere, with its point on the Earth's surface, through which an atom or molecule could exit to outer space without touching another atom or molecule. See *exosphere.*

conservation law. (Physics.) Also known as the first law of thermodynamics: a rule stating that energy is neither created nor destroyed in any interaction in any isolated system, but simply changes place or form. This law, however, seems to be controverted by the hypothetical annihilation of matter in a black hole. See *thermodynamics: first law of,* and *black hole* (in which the law seems to be negated).

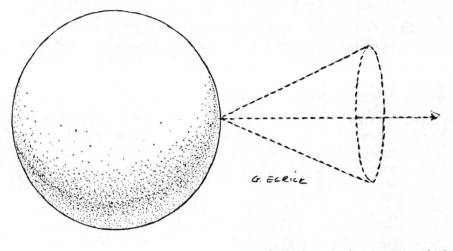

Hypothetical cone of escape, in which atoms or molecules could exit to outer space without rubbing shoulders with other atoms or molecules.

contamination. (Astronautics.) A non-desired exposure to radio-activity; or to alien, possibly dangerous biological or chemical entities. Compare with *back contamination*.

contra-ionized mass. (Fiction.) A mass, once partially or completely ionized, that has been rendered atomically neutral.

controlled leakage system. (Astronautics.) A non-exotic set-up that provides for normal bodily metabolism in a spacecraft cabin or capsule. Carbon dioxide, liquid wastes, and solid wastes are 'flushed away' instead of being recycled. They're replenished with stored oxygen, water, and food supplies. See *capsule, life support system, bioastronautics,* and *algae and space travel*.

controlling ray. (Fiction.) A ray that can move a cloud of dense gas back and forth to conceal secret planetary-surface activity.

control rocket. (Astronautics.) A rocket, such as a retro rocket, used to periodically guide, decelerate, or accelerate a spacecraft. Compare with *attitude jets*.

coordinate. (Astronautics.) One of a set of measures, numbers, or magnitudes used to determine the position of a point, line, curve, or plane in a space of given dimensions.

coriolis effects. (Astronautics.) Nausea and dizziness felt by someone moving radially in a rotating system, such as a spinning space station.

coriolis force. (Physics.) A non-existent force used, for convenience, to describe a spacecraft's motion with respect to a uniformly rotating reference frame, such as the Earth.

corona. (Astronomy.) Has two meanings. One refers to a faint luminous ring around a celestial body, caused by light diffraction, visible through a haze. The other refers to the irregular envelope of highly ionized gas blanketing the sun's chromosphere. See *chromosphere* and *ion.*

corrodium. (Fiction.) An element, called liquid destruction, discovered by Neptunians. Churning as an ominous, pasty mass, it emits poisonous, corrosive fumes. If inhaled, the only antidote is pure oxygen.

cosmic currents. (Fiction.) Also known as space tides. Directional streams of interstellar dust and gas.

cosmic curtain. (Fiction.) Also called the cosmic veil: a hypothetical demarcation between the tangible and intangible worlds.

cosmic destructor. (Fiction.) A type of walking stick or cane that doubles as a location sensor in the dark. When its tip is activated to 'high,' it destroys anything or anyone it touches.

cosmic dust. (Astronomy.) Also known as interplanetary or interstellar dust: finely divided solid matter moving through the cosmos. Particle diameters measure less than a millimeter. Solar system cosmic dust, concentrated in the ecliptic plane, causes the zodiacal light. See *interplanetary dust, ecliptic, ecliptic plane,* and *zodiacal light.*

cosmic egg. (Physics.) A hypothetical, incomprehensibly dense ball: the minimum entropy status of the universe before the big bang flung everything outward in all directions. See *Big Bang Theory, cosmogony, entropy,* and *maximum entropy.*

cosmic explosion projector. (Fiction.) Shoots cosmic explosion impulses—at two million kilocycles—along carrier waves projected by

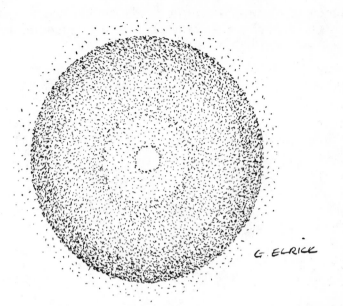

G. ELRICK

No one knows what the 'cosmic egg' looked like, what its dimensions were, or what existed beyond its 'surface' (if, indeed, it had a surface) . . . but it was, undoubtedly, the heaviest, most compacted substance ever, compared to which the staggering tonnage of trillions of collapsed stars would be lighter than cotton candy or hair on a beauty parlor's floor.

enemy space ships deviously attempting to establish contact. Disintegrates those unfortunate vehicles in a retina-rocking flash.

cosmic fever. (Fiction.) Mental and biochemical disorientation, roughly similar to jet lag, occasionally afflicting interplanetary travelers. Symptoms are weakness, a parched throat, and buzzing in the head.

cosmic heat. (Fiction.) Intense radiation that causes grass fires on certain planetoids.

cosmic hurricane. (Fiction.) Also called a cosmic force storm or cosmic tornado. A type of solar system disturbance that can make a twisted wreck out of a space ship.

cosmic radio waves. (Astronomy.) Radio waves from extraterrestrial sources. Called galactic radio waves if they originate within our galaxy; extragalactic radio waves if they originate outside our galaxy. Solar radio waves emanate from the sun. See *radio waves*.

cosmic ray phone. (Fiction.) A hand-held disc, the size of a woman's compact, used to transmit messages to the helmet phone receiver of someone flying with a *moto belt* (which see).

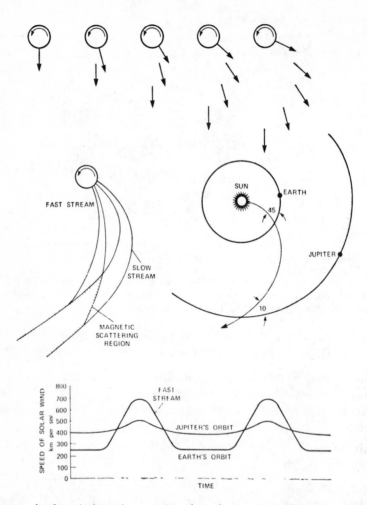

Fast streams of solar wind catch up with slow streams, producing scattering regions that prevent low-energy cosmic rays from zapping through the solar system (though high-energy cosmic rays machine-gun through with little difficulty). Solar wind nonuniformities stem from hot spots in the sun's corona. Hot spots naturally give birth to streams with higher velocities. As the sun rotates on its axis, fast-moving streams overtake slow-moving streams that blasted off earlier from the corona's relatively cooler portions.

cosmic rays. (Astronomy.) So named because of their extraterrestrial origin, cosmic rays are streams of ionizing radiation, trapped in the galactic magnetic field, battering the Earth from interstellar space. They are chiefly comprised of atomic nuclei (positive ions), photons, high-energy electrons, protons, and alpha particles.

Speed: The rays—actually charged particles—travel in waves at velocities approaching lightspeed. Crests and troughs are so squashed together that the intervening distance is measured in fractions of a millionth of an inch.

A universal phenomenon: Not only do they blast through solar system space, they are associated with the growth and decline of stars, supernova explosions, quasars, and galaxies that 'shine' at radio wavelengths.

Affected by magnetic fields: Being charged particles, they follow curved paths in magnetic fields.

Primary rays or particles: Cosmic rays are called *primary* before they smash into the Earth's atmosphere ten miles up. As primaries, they're basically atomic nuclei stripped of electrons. Roughly 87 percent are protons (the nuclei of hydrogen atoms); 12 percent are helium nuclei; the remainder are nuclei of heavier elements. Primary particles have energies ranging upward from several hundred million electron volts. When they crunch into atomic nuclei in the atmosphere, both shatter into broad spectrums of secondary particles.

Secondary rays or particles: These are rays that actually hit the Earth's surface, zap like bullets through living organisms, and penetrate thousands of feet of rock. They're composed of all known elementary particles, including pions, muons, mu-mesons, pi-mesons, neutrons, electrons, positrons, and gamma rays. Some produce additional sub-atomic particles. At sea level, approximately ten secondaries pass through every square inch of the Earth's surface every minute. (See reference to *poles* and *equator* below.) All particles that register in mine shafts, on the Earth's mineral or watery skin, and on towering mountaintops are secondaries, for primaries never make it below the ten-mile atmospheric ceiling.

Properties and characteristics: Radiation intensity, relatively low near the equator, increases toward the poles. Even at the highest altitudes at which Earth-bound man resides, dosages are non-critical. However, should man rise above the atmosphere in a spacecraft, heavy nuclei in primaries can create biological havoc, including fetal mutations, unless precautions are taken. It is speculated that cosmic

Cosmic rays may have brought about the downfall of dinosaurs, even though the enormous reptiles [now thought to have been warm-blooded] trampled the Earth for a minimum of 70 million years. It's conceivable that extra-heavy dosages — breaking through due to temporary shifts in atmospheric structure — caused infertile mutations, or prevented leathery eggs from hatching, just as traces of DDT prevent eagle eggs from hatching.

rays had a great deal to do with evolution, and somehow caused the demise of dinosaurs and other animal forms.

See *alpha particle, electron, elementary particles, gamma rays, ion, ionization, neutron, photon, positron, proton, quasar, radiation,* and *supernova.*

cosmic repulsion projector. (Fiction.) Also called a cosmic repulsor: a cannon-size apparatus comprised of a sub-neutronic grid, a micro-ionic oscillator, and a Ronsonian cosmo-circuit. It emits a graduated repulsion — or anti-gravity — beam that, when directed at a planetoid or other object hurtling toward Earth, can cause it to land gently and non-destructively, though the beam can be as devastating as a disintegrator ray if turned on full blast. See *disintegrator ray.*

cosmic static. (Fiction.) Interplanetary radio interference caused by cosmic rays crossing the intersolar band.

cosmo-electric juice. (Fiction.) The surging charge, emitted by a hand-held vibro-revivor, that resuscitates someone knocked unconscious by an exhaustion ray. See *exhaustion ray.*

cosmogony. (Astronomy.) Intensive inquiries into the origin of the solar system or the universe.

cosmograph. (Fiction.) A space ship gauge that indicates impending interstellar disturbances, such as cosmic hurricanes or solar cyclones.

cosmological perspective. (Generic.) An expanded frame of reference used by most science fiction writers.

cosmological principle. (Generic.) The assumption that the universe's large-scale properties would appear identical from any observation point.

cosmology. (Astronomy.) The study of the large-scale development and structure of the entire universe.

cosmo-magnetic emanation. (Fiction.) The electromagnetic radiation emitted by a living creature. Identical to the 'aura' of parapsychology.

countdown. (Astronautics.) A step-by-step process culminating in a climactic event, such as a space vehicle launching. Performed to a predesignated time schedule; marked by a count in inverse numerical order.

counter. (Generic.) A device that determines if anything is radio-actively 'hot.'

crash cabin. (Fiction.) A space ship chamber insulated against collision shock.

crash indicator. (Fiction.) An oversize wall gauge indicating the imminence of collision. Its dial registers gradations between Safe, Caution, Danger, and Crash. Normally positioned in a spacecraft's crash cabin.

critical mass. (Physics.) The smallest amount of concentrated fissionable material needed to support a self-sustained chain reaction under stated conditions. See *fission.*

critical vibration frequencies. (Astronautics.) Vibrational resonance that can destroy a rocket at launch or in flight, unless eliminated or damped.

cryogenic propellant. (Astronautics.) A rocket fuel, propulsion fluid, or oxidizer that is liquid only at extremely low temperatures.

curvo-ray gun. (Fiction.) An energy force weapon, the size of a 20th Century portable burp gun, that shoots around corners.

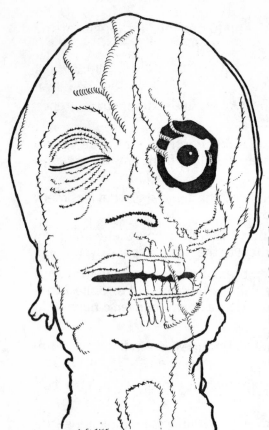

chemically inert plastics and metals to
the body's various subsystems, a process
known as mechanical modification. Because they're extreme bastardizations,
cyborgs are likely to suffer identity crises.
Their creation—no longer far-fetched—
is a definite medical possibility. 250,000
people in the United States alone have
functioning parts inside of them made of
silicone. Thousands more contain parts
made of Teflon, titanium, chrome-
cobalt alloys, and stainless steel.

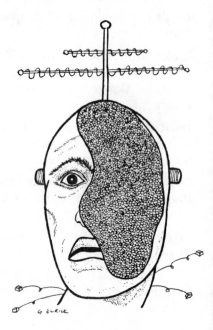

Cyborgs (two shown here in the process
of creation) gratify readers' desires for in-
destructibility and superhuman ('bionic')
strength. The concept originally dealt
with disembodied brains or heads (still
capable of falling in love), kept alive via
nutrient solutions and tubular attach-
ments. It has since evolved into hybrid-
ized symbioses between 'flesh' parts and
'machine' parts. This bio-engineering
involves successfully hooking up bio-

cybernetics. (Generic.) The study of feedback control processes in electronic and mechanical systems: particularly mathematical analyses of information flow. A cybernetic system constantly senses its environment, adjusts to the total surrounding configuration, then follows its own selection of alternate action and reaction paths. The key concept is feedback. See *servomechanism*.

cyborg. (Fiction.) Short for cybernetic organism. A human whose soft tissues have been replaced, rebuilt, or augmented with electronic and mechanical parts so that he or she can function—minus protective apparatus—on a specific planet's surface, whatever its temperature, incident radiation, atmosphere, or lack of same. The individual, usually a plucky, intensively trained volunteer, is literally part Homo sapiens and part machine, and repulsive to the eye. Theoretically, all changes are reversible, via plastic surgery and organ transplants— after a painstaking removal of metal, plastic, glass, and complicated circuitry components—but there's small chance the restored man or woman will ever again resemble his or her college graduation photo. The self-concept problems afflicting a cyborg are chillingly stated in Frederik Pohl's *Man Plus*. See *android*.

cyclotron. (Physics.) Also called an atom smasher. A circular, impressively large accelerator that imparts tremendous force—via successive, incremental boosts—to charged particles generated at a central source. Energies, stemming from an alternating electric field, range from a few million to several tons of millions of electron volts. The particles, zapping around the 'doughnut' at fantastic speeds, are held in a spiral path by an enormous magnet. The purpose of a cyclotron is to blast new elementary particles from atomic nuclei.

D

dark light ray beam. (Fiction.) A component of a special space helmet that can throw a beam of light without revealing the beam's source.

dark nebula. (Astronomy.) A region of dense dust, far off in space, blocking the light of stars behind it. See *nebula, cosmic dust,* and *interplanetary dust*.

data formatting. (Generic.) Preparation of data—particularly telemetry information—for entry into a digital computer. Input, usually in digestible 'blocks,' must be in the computer's coded 'language.' See *digital computer, analog computer,* and *telemetry.*

data display. (Generic.) Visual—normally electronic—presentation of a digital computer's processed data, so the information can be reacted to.

data link. (Generic.) Any circuit or communications channel used to transmit data from a sensor to a computer, a storage device, or a readout device.

data reduction. (Generic.) The process of converting data to usable form via computers and other electronic devices.

dead reckoning. (Astronautics.) Estimating a space ship's position via calculations based on inference or guesswork. Used only in an emergency, when star charts have been lost or destroyed, or astrogating instruments are malfunctioning.

deceleration chamber. (Astronautics.) A padded compartment, complete with restraining safety belts or nets, to which spacecraft occupants retire as their ship drastically slows down, to sidestep physiological damage to themselves. See *acceleration chamber.*

decompression sickness. (Astronautics.) A disorder suffered by inadequately protected cosmonauts when barometric pressure slides down. Symptoms: gas bubbles in body fluids; excruciating pains in shoulders, arms, and legs; chest constriction; and occasional neuro-circulatory collapse. See *aeroembolism* and *caisson disease.*

decontamination. (Generic.) Removal of chemical, biological, or radioactive fallout from a person, thing, or area.

de-energizing rod. (Fiction.) Also called a de-energizer, fatigue rod, or fatigue stick. A baton-like device with a tip resembling a doorknob. When activated with a switch and pressed against someone, the unlucky recipient of the 'touch' becomes weaker than a butterfly. See *metal cloth.*

deep diving sphere. (Fiction.) A type of submarine capable of withstanding 'deep down' pressure that would crumple traditional submersibles like tinfoil. A deep diving sphere consists of several large linked spheres, one housing the crew, another the power plant, another the cargo, and still another set-and-forget missiles.

degenerate material. Not the contents of a girlie magazine, but material so compressed that all its allowed energy states are filled. It resists further compaction.

Degravitor ship closing in on its hapless prey, which will boomerang uncontrollably into outer space when a carefully aimed emission destroys its propulsive mechanism, simultaneously yanking the craft away from gravity's pull.

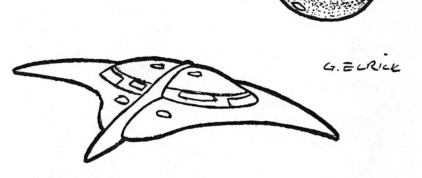

G. ELRICK

degravitor ship. (Fiction.) Also called a *degravo ship.* A type of spacecraft used in interplanetary wars fought within moderate distance of a celestial body's surface. When an aimed degravitor ray spurts from its cowling nozzle, the enemy space ship it strikes soars upward into outer space, totally out of control.

degravity belt. (Fiction.) An apparatus that looks more like a small back pack than a belt. Fingertip controls enable the wearer to adjust his or her weight from normal to zero. Perfect for gently slowing a fall through space in the Earth's atmosphere. Wearing this device, an individual can leap from great heights without injury, or drift around like a fluffy dandelion seed. Compare with *flying belt.*

degravity power. (Fiction.) Prevents a space ship, even if it's otherwise out of control, from crashing against a celestial body because of gravity pull.

degravity rod. (Fiction.) A short rod, activated via a sliding lock switch, featuring a fist-size globe at its 'business end.' It degravitizes anything it touches—rendering it absolutely weightless—whether it is animal, mineral, or vegetable, whatever the poundage. By means of this device, a slight girl can carry a heavy man around like a toy balloon. The man is held magnetically while rendered helpless. Also convenient for unloading cargo from a spacecraft.

delirium beam. (Fiction.) A type of electromagnetic energy—aimed at a person's head—which causes its recipient to lose his or her will power. Used for interrogation purposes, particularly when trying to acquire secret formulas.

dematerializing ray. (Fiction.) Temporarily neutralizes the electronocohesive force within atoms, enabling the ray's user to walk through solid walls, which immediately re-assemble behind him.

denitrogenation. (Astronautics.) Prevention, or cure, of aeroembolism at high altitudes by the deliberate breathing of pure oxygen for prolonged in-flight periods. See *aeroembolism*.

deorbit. (Astronautics.) To remove a satellite, lander/probe, or spacecraft from its orbit.

descendo cylinder. (Fiction.) A back-pack tank containing antigravity material, enabling one who leaps from a hovering space ship to descend to a planet's surface with the gentle, spiralling speed of a falling leaf.

destruct. (Astronautics.) Deliberate demolition of a rocket vehicle after launch, but preceding flight completion, as a safety measure or to terminate a test phase.

deutronic ionoforms. (Fiction.) Sometimes referred to as psychic restriction or psychic domination rays: the electromagnetic discharge from a hypnotizing apparatus, which is a crown of electrodes attached to the victim's head. The victim is normally strapped to a chair-like device. Ionoforms, surging through his brain tissue, invert normal thoughts and emotions. The zombie-like hypnotic effect is semi-permanent, but can be counteracted with a short, sharp rabbit punch on the neck, just below the skull.

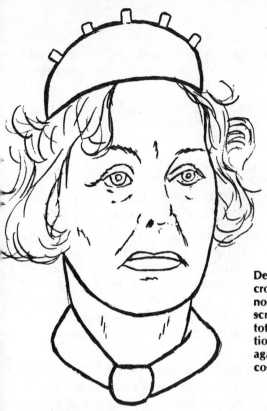

Deutronic ionoforms, triggered by a crown of electrodes, drop-kick a victim's normal perceptions and conceptions into scrambled oblivion, rendering him or her totally pliable to any hypnotic suggestions, no matter how much they scrape against the grain of previously cherished convictions.

deva-static gun. (Fiction.) A weapon seldom used because it permanently alters atomic structure.

diaglossa. (Fiction.) A small instrument worn in either ear, capable of instantly deciphering any foreign or alien-planet language. See *language code, extraterrestrial communication,* and *intelligent life on other planets.*

diffraction. (Physics.) The spreading out, or banding, of light passing an opaque objects's edge, due to the wave nature of light's radiation.

digital computer. (Generic.) A computing device that ingests and acts on variables and quantities represented as electronic, binary system digits. Digital computers differ from analog computer in that digitals process discrete, discontinuous data; while analogs process continuous data. See *analog computer.*

directional beam. (Fiction.) A beam transmitted outwardly by one spacecraft so another spacecraft can zero in on it for rendezvous purposes.

directional stability. (Astronautics.) Also known as weathercock stability: a spacecraft's capacity to re-orient itself after yawing or sideslipping. See *yaw.*

directo findex. (Fiction.) A navigating instrument that orients a space ship with respect to magnetic fields.

disintegrating fluid. (Fiction.) A deadly liquid carried in a tiny concealed flask. When swallowed, it causes a person to de-atomize instantly and permanently. Used as a last ditch device by captured Earthians who don't want to be unspeakably tortured by antagonists on alien planets. Compare with *vaporizing pill* and *non-ex fluid.*

disintegrator gun. (Fiction.) Also called a disintegrator pistol, disintragun, destructo gun, atomatic pistol, or nothingness blaster: a hand-held device resembling a 20th Century power drill. When its trigger is squeezed, it blasts a *disintegrator ray* (which see). It is convenient for de-atomizing opponents; or, when flicking its trigger, for cutting toe-hold indented 'steps' in a vertical stone or metal wall, but must be periodically recharged, or re-packed, with power. See *integraton.*

disintegrator ray. (Fiction.) Also called a disintegrator beam, disray, destroyo ray, or de-atomizing ray: a pale green, scintillating electronic flash that shatters protons. If fired from a disintegrator gun, it is capable of totally erasing a man or men. If fired from a larger weapon, it can eradicate an entire city. An instantaneous flicker can gash the landscape with a hundred-foot-deep channel, leaving an iridescent, vitreous scar where soft earth or hard rock had been. Used beneficially instead of destructively, it can bore tunnels through mountains, or turn garbage and other refuse into fresh air.

dispersion. (Physics.) The separation or fanning out of light, or other complex wave radiations, into component parts regarding wavelength or frequency.

displays and controls. (Fiction/Astronautics.) A typical space ship uses panel displays, mechanical-type controls, and electrically operated controls, normally grouped by function and arranged in operational sequence from left-to-right or top-to-bottom, with the most critical positioned for maximum crew efficiency and performance. All are provided with dimmable flood lighting, plus integral meter lighting. Whereas displays do not require excessive shielding, controls are painstakingly protected against inadvertent activation. Toggle switches are sheltered by wicket guards. Wherever accidental switch-ons or switch-offs would be detrimental to flight operation or injurious to equipment, lever lock switches are used. See *instrumentation system* and *space ship flight control.*

dissolvo ray. (Fiction.) An energy force with slightly less capacity than a disintegrator ray.

docking. (Astronautics.) The mechanical coupling of two or more orbiting objects or payloads. See *payload.*

Doppler effect. (Physics.) A principle applicable to both sound and light: an apparent change in wave frequency which occurs when source and observer move in relation to one another. The frequency increases when source and observer approach; decreases when source and observer separate.

Doppler navigation. (Astronautics.) Spatial orientation determined by measuring Doppler-effect echoes from spacecraft-originated radiant energy beams. Gives a continuous indication of position.

double-base propellant. (Astronautics.) A solid propellant for a rocket. Consists of two unstable compounds that react to each other without need of an activating oxidizer.

drogue parachute. (Astronautics.) Also called a deceleration or drag parachute. Has two meanings: (1) a form of parachute attached to a spacecraft or missile to slow it down; (2) a small parachute that pulls a larger parachute out of stowage.

drone ship. (Astronautics.) An automatically controlled spacecraft without crew members, frequently used as a probe. See *probe.*

dura-glass escape projectile. (Fiction.) A jet-propelled tube in which an individual can escape from a damaged or about-to-crash space ship. As the projectile approaches a solid surface, such as the outer crust of an asteroid or planet, its reverse jets cut in and ease the plunge rate so the occupant is uninjured.

dwarf. (Astronomy.) Also called a white dwarf. A small-size, low-luminosity star of tremendous density. A tennis ball packed with its substance would have the mass of several elephants.

dynamic recoil gyroscope. (Fiction.) A space ship component that enables a craft to stop dead—before shooting into reverse—with no jarring sensations or effects.

Monstrous machinery would be required to hoist a tennis ball crammed with a dwarf star's substance, for it would weigh as much as a line of Ringling Brothers circus elephants.

dyne oscillations. (Fiction.) Part of an interpretive and analytical methodology—used in conjunction with the detection of a pseudo-interconversion of ergs and a meteoric metalline lattice* —to pinpoint the whereabouts of man-made or humanoid-made satellites. (* Science fiction lingo for the delectation of readers: not to be taken over-seriously.)

Dyson sphere. (Fiction.) An artificial barrier around a star; used to capture and utilize the star's radiation.

dystopia. (Generic.) The opposite of utopia: everything's going to hell in a handbasket.

E

ear receiver. (Fiction.) A transparent, virtually invisible, semi-soft ear plug molded to the exact contours of a user's outer ear canal. Enables its wearer to concentrate on radio transmissions in acoustically distracting situations, and to zero in on reception of non-public transmissions.

Earth Central. (Fiction.) Also known as the Central Radio Control Bureau. Earth's interplanetary radio headquarters, which has the authority to clear all channels for emergency messages.

earthlight. (Astronomy.) Also called earthshine, earthlight is the faint illumination of the dark part of the moon's surface produced by sunlight reflecting from the Earth's surface and atmosphere.

Earthsea. (Fiction.) The setting for Ursula LeGuin's heroic fantasy trilogy: *A Wizard of Earthsea, The Tombs of Atuan,* and *The Farthest Shore,* consisting of many islands surrounded by ocean. Its material culture is Early Iron Age; and its 'science' is magic.

echelon formation. (Fiction.) A flying pattern assumed by a group of space ships.

ecliptic. (Astronomy.) Has two meanings: (1) the seeming path of the sun among the stars during a single year; (2) the intersecting circle of the plane of the Earth's orbit on the celestial sphere. See *celestial sphere.*

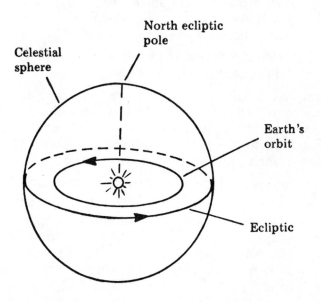

The ecliptic is the apparent path of the sun among the stars, as seen from the Earth, projected on the celestial sphere, or more accurately, the projection of the Earth's orbit on the celestial sphere. The Earth's orbital plane is coincident with the ecliptic plane.

ecliptic plane. (Astronomy.) The plane of the Earth's orbit.

egg-shaped 'people washer.' (Generic.) A futuristic, ultrasonic bath already in production in Japan. Shaped like an oversize egg lying on its side, with an opening at the top, the machine showers, bathes, massages with rubber balls, and dries its user off—all in 15 minutes.

egg ship. (Fiction.) As envisaged by Arthur C. Clarke, a starship piloted by cybernetic nurses who carefully shepherd cryogenically stored human sperm cells and ova. Twenty years before the end of the voyage—however prolonged the latter may be—sperms and eggs are united under controlled conditions, fetuses are developed, incubated 'births' take place, and the resultant children are reared, educated, and trained by their cybernetic nannies. Not only are the growing youngsters taught to manipulate the space ship's flight controls when pre-landing takeover becomes necessary, they're indoctrinated to carry out specialized duties on the celestial body they'll soon colonize as adults. The use of egg ships enables humans—while in a pre-blastula stage—to literally spend eons of time in interstellar space. Compare with *sleeper ship* and *methuselah enzyme*. See *cybernetics* and *inertial guidance*.

ego decimator. (Fiction.) A Uranian torture device that destroys will power via painful psychological whittling.

egotron. (Fiction.) A wristwatch-type gadget which, upon a twist of the knob, makes its wearer vanish temporarily in a cloud of neutrons. Unless he turns the knob the other way before twenty-one minutes pass, he disappears forever. Convenient for temporarily playing *The Invisible Man* if one's physical well-being is jeopardized.

ejecta. (Astronomy.) Fragments that result when small celestial bodies, such as asteroids, smash into each other.

ejection seats. (Fiction/Astronautics.) Provided for space ship crew members as a means of emergency egress in case a pod is unavailable or malfunctioning. An ejection panel is positioned above each seat. Obviously, pressure suits must be worn when the seats are activated. See *pressure suit* and *pod*.

Ekumen. (Fiction.) The furthest advancement of the League of Worlds in Ursula LeGuin's Hainish works; elaborated on at length in *The Left Hand of Darkness*. Not a political union, it approximates a near-mystical bonding of the human 'household.'

electrical power system. (Fiction/Astronautics.) EPS for short. In a space ship, the EPS consists of two subsystems: (1) power generation, both AC and DC, via fuel cell and solar panel power plants; and (2) power reactant storage, distribution, and control.

electric field. (Astronomy.) A spatial region characterized by detectable electric intensity at every point.

electric propulsion system. (Astronautics.) Nuclear reaction propulsion via a propellant consisting of charged ions, neutrons, electrons, or other particles, accelerated by electrical fields, magnetic fields, or both. Examples: *electrostatic propulsion, electromagnetic propulsion,* and *electrothermal propulsion.*

electro disintegrator system. (Fiction.) Also known as the electro-death circuit: vibrating rays of disintegrative shock that can be activated to surround a building or city, so a wanted criminal can't break free without self-destructing. The system depends on a network of embedded and insulated electromagnetically connected configurations. When an 'ON' button is depressed, portals, doorways, and passageway openings become crackling death traps.

Electromagnetic radiation—usually inadequately pictorialized somewhat as shown—extends from 10 to the 23rd power cycles-per-second down to 0 cycles-per-second. Though many segments of the spectrum impinge on humans in one way or another, most of us go about our daily business ridiculously unaware of them, since our ordinary sense organs aren't as finely tuned as we'd like them to be, except in the case of hyped-up science fiction cyborgs. Bees, pigeons, and migrating sea turtles tune into radiations completely beyond our ken.

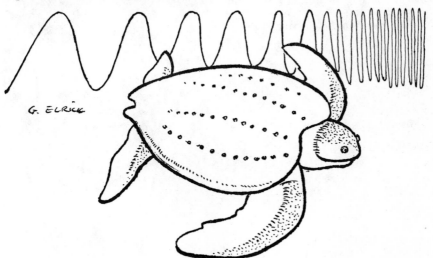

G. ELRICK

electrohypnotic trance. (Fiction.) A dream-like state induced by the wearing of a special metal cap featuring an electrode cluster. Similar but not identical to the device employed to produce *deutronic ionoforms* (which see), but used with positive rather than negative intentions. Those who analyze brain waves recorded via this technique can study the subject's innermost thoughts, and learn his, her, or its language. Conversely, if a magnetic language transcription is cut in, the person or thing in a trance will unconsciously learn the language of those inducing that temporary state. Useful for establishing meaningful contact with humanoids from other planets. See *humanoid*.

electromagnetic radiation. (Physics.) Energy waves—all of which travel at the speed of light—produced by the interaction of electric and magnetic fields. Varieties, distinguished by wavelength, include radio, infrared, visible (light), gamma, ultraviolet, and X-rays.

electromagnetic spectrum. (Physics.) The range of *electromagnetic radiation* (which see) from extremely low to extremely high fre-

A three-dimensional electronic image looks like the real thing but isn't. Though apparently corporeal, you can walk through it. If you try to melt its head with a hand-held blaster, you'll simply waste emission energy. Unlike flat images on a movie screen, or the previously recorded holographic 'Please help me' depiction of Princess Leia near the beginning of 'Star Wars,' it's a 'right now' phenomenon. The person projecting the image is executing the movements—elsewhere—even as you perceive them before you.

G. ELRICK

quencies. The continuum is subdivided quite arbitrarily, and the various divisional boundaries overlap. At one end of the spectrum are squashed-together cosmic rays; at the other end, spread-out radio waves.

electromagnetism. (Physics.) Magnetism stemming from electric charge in motion: a trillion trillion trillion (10 to the 36th power) times stronger than gravity, but barely noticeable in everyday life, since it comes in two forms—positive and negative—that virtually cancel each other. Regardless, the latent electromagnetic energy frozen in ordinary matter makes the tree-shattering power of a lightning bolt seem gentler than a baby's sigh.

electron. (Physics.) The least massive electrically charged sub-atomic particle. Each forever carries one unit of negative charge, and is identical to all other electrons, whatever the type of atom. Electrons comprise an atom's 'body': a fuzzy, rather spherical cloud or smear swirling about a point-like nucleus. Though this spinning 'body' is less tangible than a forgotten thought, it has enough substance and rigidity to prevent atoms from being squashed together, and its relationship to adjacent 'bodies' determines chemical bonding. Like most sub-atomic particles, electrons are straight out of *Alice In Wonderland* or a madman's meanderings. Though an electron cloud comprises most of an atom's volume, it has only one four-thousandth of its weight, the rest residing in the staggeringly small nucleus. Electrons are arranged in groupings called shells, all of which have well-defined radii. There is a limit to the number of electrons any given shell can contain. Finally, the number of electrons madly encircling an atom's nucleus is always equal to that nucleus's positive charge number. See *atom* and *atomic number*.

electronic image. (Fiction.) A seemingly substantial, life-like image of an individual that can be projected anywhere, within a sixteen-mile radius, in three-dimensional form. It moves, talks, and breathes as a simulacrum of the person operating a visio-projector.

electronic jamming. (Generic.) The deliberate use or misuse of electromagnetic radiations to scramble the efficacy of an enemy's electronic devices, systems, or equipment.

electrono detector. (Fiction.) A sensing device that sounds a warning alarm when another craft approaches. It can be adjusted to soundlessly register distant paralysis ray, disintegrator beam, or rocket pistol-blast vibrations.

electronolytic bath. (Fiction.) A six-foot-high tube containing special liquid in which victims of paralysis ray exposure are immersed to counteract the effects of immobility. See *paralysis ray.*

electro-static cerebrumatic saturator. (Fiction.) An electro-mechanical, high-speed, mind-boosting apparatus, complete with oversize, padded electrodes. Hooked to a rapid-fire page turner or microfilm advancer, it scans an average-size reference book in sixty seconds, without missing a line, diagram, illustration, thought, or page, and instantaneously saturates a plugged-in brain with all the book's knowledge.

element. (Physics.) An atomic 'species': all atoms with the same atomic number, the same nuclear charge, and the same chemical behavior. There are 92 naturally occurring elements or species. See *atomic number.*

elemental quanta. (Fiction.) The electromagnetic phenomena of which certain alien intelligences are composed.

elementary particles. (Physics.) Also called sub-atomic or funda-mental particles: indivisible, irreducible constituents of matter. There are so many, Enrico Fermi complained he'd have to be a botanist to remember their names. Cyclotron bombardment of atomic nuclei constantly produces new ones. Included are the neutrino, electron, positron, positive mu meson, negative mu meson, kappa meson, proton, neutron, positive V-particle, negative V-particle, neutral V-particle, photon, PI meson, negative PI meson, neutral PI meson, tau meson, muon, pion, kaon, ETA, lamda-hyperon, sigma hyperon, cascade hyperon, and omega hyperon. All evince a wave-particle duality. The electron, proton, and neutron have mass and relative stability, and are known as 'ordinary' matter. Most of the others have zero mass and an almost 'nothing' lifetime, during which they decay into other particles, a process that continues till only stable particles remain. Non-ordinary matter does not exist inde-pendently under normal conditions. See *cyclotron, neutrino, electron, positron, photon, proton,* and *neutron.*

emergency landing beam. (Fiction.) A modified repellor ray that enables a malfunctioning spacecraft to land—gently and without damage—on any Earth-like celestial surface. See *repellor ray, terres-trial planet, Jovian planet,* and *soft landing.*

energizer. (Fiction.) An emergency fluid, laced with liquid nutrients, generally carried in a test tube-size flask. Instantly revives anyone who has passed out from hunger, thirst, or general physical exhaustion.

energy. (Physics.) One of the fundamental quantities of science. According to the conservation law or postulate, frequently converted from one form to another, but never created or destroyed. It can take the form of motion, heat, or electromagnetic radiation, and can also be stored under tremendous tension, as in atomic nuclei. See *conservation law* and *strong nuclear force.*

energy belt. (Fiction.) A waist wrapper that serves as a force generator, gives its wearer tremendous vitality, and restores expended physical energy via electrical induction. When its controls are turned to high, he who wears it temporarily acquires muscular strength comparable to that of a gorilla. However, if the belt isn't kept tuned to a hair-line adjustment, its wearer can unwittingly over-extend himself, suffer an energy lapse, and faint.

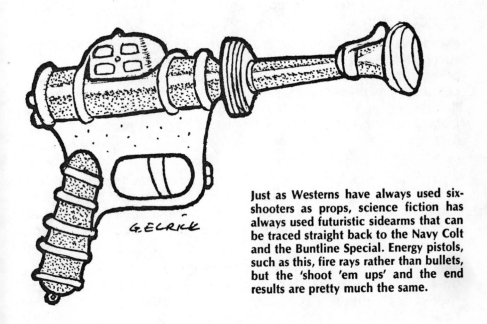

G. ELRICK

Just as Westerns have always used six-shooters as props, science fiction has always used futuristic sidearms that can be traced straight back to the Navy Colt and the Buntline Special. Energy pistols, such as this, fire rays rather than bullets, but the 'shoot 'em ups' and the end results are pretty much the same.

energy pistol. (Fiction.) A Luger-shaped or bazooka-shaped device also called a blaster. Zaps an electromagnetic emission that can melt an opponent's head. Compare with *ray rifle, paralysis gun,* and *disintegrator gun.*

enotherm. (Fiction.) An object whose atoms are in a semi-fissioned, loosely-knit state. For example, an enotherm wall can be walked through, albeit slowly.

entropy. (Physics.) The gradual 'winding down' or wearing out of any organic, mechanical, or electromagnetic system, whatever its size, functions, interrelations, or scope. See *maximum entropy.*

entry corridor. (Astronautics.) A prescribed flight path that enables safe recovery or landing of a spacecraft during re-entry into the Earth's atmosphere.

escape bullet. (Fiction.) A small rocket ship, encapsuled in a larger spacecraft, that permits two or more individuals to escape should the mother ship be endangered. When a button is depressed in the escape module, it shoots into space at brain-rattling speed. A few second later, if being zeroed-in on by enemy craft, the mother or command ship automatically self-destructs.

escape velocity. (Astronautics.) The minimum or initial velocity a spacecraft needs, at a given point in a gravitational field, to completely break away from that field's downward-sucking pull. Since celestial body masses vary, each requires a different escape velocity. It takes a speed of more than 25,000 miles-per-hour to zoom away from the Earth's restraints, but only 5,292 miles-per-hour to zoom away from the moon's. See *gravity, gravity well,* and *inverse square law.*

ether. (Generic.) An out-dated concept, *ether* was formerly thought of as an all-pervading, gaseous but clear medium: the transmitter of electromagnetic waves and cosmic rays. Now sometimes—though rarely—it is used as a synonym for the entire region of space beyond the Earth's atmosphere.

Euclidean three-space. (Generic.) Mathematically symbolized as E^3: the familiar three-dimensional space of everyday experience, as contrasted with the non-Euclidean four-dimensional spacetime continuum. See *non-Euclidean geometry, topology,* and *spacetime.*

excitation. (Physics.) Elevation of an atom's internal energy level.

exhaustion ray. (Fiction.) Sometimes called a chest protector: a ray emitted by an innocuous-looking pendant dangling from the neck. Temporarily robs those who face it—when it is activated—of every ounce of strength, but does no permanent harm.

existentialism. (Generic.) Whether consciously acknowledged or not, this is the basic philosophy vibrating through most science fiction. In a nutshell, existentialism states that human life is an intensely individual adventure; that it's impossible to pin down any 'absolute truths'; that a person 'lives' the meaning of his life; that the primacy of the process is more important than any end result; that curiosity should be coupled with concern; that the sense of wonder and awe should be cultivated; that hypothetical 'closed systems' should be avoided as false; and that people should realize that freedom of choice entails total and mature responsibility for the consequences of their actions. Other existential tenets: it's opposed to 'knee-jerk behaviorism'; it scorns the use of closed-circuit thinking as a tranquilizer; it claims that the universe is indifferent or hostile to man; and it emphasizes that life has form, but the individual supplies whatever significance it has according to his own unique interpretations and experiences.

exobiology. (Generic.) Also called astrobiology. A branch of biology that has two meanings: (1) the search for and study of extraterrestrial living organisms, via probes or otherwise; (2) the effects of extraterrestrial space on living organisms . . . in this sense, known as space biology. See *probe* and *xenobiologist*.

exosphere. (Astronomy.) That portion of the atmosphere, beginning 300 to 600 miles above the Earth's surface, where air is so rarefied that constituent molecules seldom collide with each other.

exotics. (Fiction.) Alien beings with strange shapes or—by Earth standards—bizarre cultures.

expandable space structure. (Astronautics.) A structure that can be packaged in compact size when launched, then expanded and erected to full size and shape when in orbit beyond the Earth's atmosphere. See *space platform, space shuttle,* and *space colonies*.

explosive decompression. (Fiction/Astronautics.) According to sensation-minded science fiction authors, the human head explodes like a rotting pumpkin splattering on a concrete pavement if a space helmet is yanked off in a vacuum or punctured by micrometeorites. According to Northwestern University's Physics Department, this *can* happen when decompression is abrupt. However, if the pressure change is slow and temporary—accompanied by exhalation—blood vessels will split and an astronaut's nose will gush blood, but he'll recover when normal pressure is restored. Should the pressure

The result of explosive decompression is an almost unrecognizable face and head at worst, and many ruptured blood vessels at best. Either way, it's as externally or internally messy as a half-eaten plate of food.

change be slow and permanent, or should he neglect to wear a space suit when leaving the ship, he'll puff up like a deep-sea fish floating to the ocean's surface. He'll also gurgle his last breath. See *space drowning.*

explosive light. (Fiction.) A force—capable of upsetting the balance of solar physics—caused by stepping up the speed of light beyond its ordinary velocity. The result: lethal vibrations that explode by over-heating interplanetary dust and gas.

external tank. (Fiction/Astronautics.) ET for short. A spacecraft pod containing a liquid oxygen or liquid hydrogen oxidizer supplied, under pressure, to the main engine or engines. Used in conjunction with booster rockets in a mission's boost phase. See *booster.*

extragalactic. (Astronomy.) Beyond our Milky Way galaxy.

extrapolation. (Generic.) A process much used in the creation and exposition of science fiction narratives. Essentially: the projection of estimated or inferred values or information from known values or information.

extraterrestrial communication. (Generic.) Earth-based two-way contact with other planets in our galaxy is possible if message or signal transmitters use the same microwave radio channel. The ideal channel is 1,420.405 megahertz: the frequency at which radio waves are emitted and absorbed by a certain energy-level transition of neutral hydrogen. Why hydrogen? Because most of the universe's atoms are hydrogen. It wouldn't make sense to utilize a less abundant element. To take advantage of the 1,420.405 megahertz frequency, a high-capacity, stable, low-noise laser beam is needed. Since inhabitants of other planets may not use languages as we know them, initial contact will necessitate recognizably patterned, non-random signals that could only be generated by an intelligent source. Once the reception of signals has been acknowledged by us or other beings, mutual revelations will proceed step-by-step. See *hydrogen: universality of, laser, intelligent life other than man,* and *language code.*

eyeballs and brains. (Generic.) A term applied to highly sophisticated attack weaponry with bloodhound-and-hawk sensory capability.

F

face plate. (Astronautics.) The see-through section of a space helmet.

fail-operational/fail-safe performance. (Fiction/Astronautics.) With respect to a space ship, these terms mean that when a failure in a component system occurs, one or more redundant systems become immediately operational, allowing the vehicle to continue its mission.

fatigue rod. See *de-energizing rod.*

fermion. See *gravitation.*

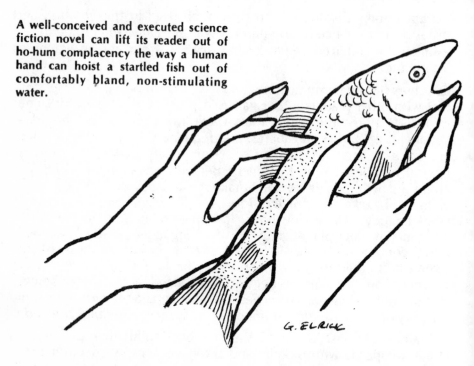

A well-conceived and executed science fiction novel can lift its reader out of ho-hum complacency the way a human hand can hoist a startled fish out of comfortably bland, non-stimulating water.

G. ELRICK

field drive. (Fiction.) Starship negative-gravitational-force-field propulsion, achieved without the use of fuel and without expelling any matter whatsoever, featuring 'pushing' against the entire mass of the universe for acceleration.

Finger-ring two-way radio. (Fiction.) A miniature adaptation of a standard two-way helmet radio. Contains a built-in dial and wave band selector.

fishbowl effect. (Generic.) A term coined by Ted Krulik, a Flushing, New York science fiction instructor. The concept: a goldfish, contentedly swimming in a tank, regards that restrictive environment as his familiar, non-thought-provoking 'universe.' If the fish is yanked from the water, it is exposed to an astonishingly different gestalt, which theoretically kindles fresh perspectives. Jerking readers from their individual fishbowls and exposing them to new gestalts is one of science fiction's functions: the igniting of wonder mixed with expanded comprehension. In Daniel Keyes's *Flowers for Algernon*, Charlie Gordon becomes a 'fish out of water,' able to perceive his previous limited world, and comprehend his newly expanded world, with incisive insights.

fission. (Physics.) The splitting of a heavy nucleus—usually of a uranium or plutonium atom—into approximately equal fragments of lesser mass, accompanied by a release of energy: the process underlying an atomic bomb. It sometimes occurs spontaneously. Compare with *fusion*.

fixed satellite. See *synchronous satellite*.

flame out. (Astronautics.) The cessation of burning, from a cause other than deliberate shutoff, in a jet or gas-turbine engine's combustion chamber.

flame whip. (Fiction.) Also called a fire whip, lash of mega-magnetic force, plastic energy thong, or plastic energy projector. A double-headed, fairly thick baton-like rod that is activated by the slightest flick of its user's wrist. It flashes out a crackling magnetic field, or energy tongue, whose coils can subdue any human or humanoid, yank a low-flying rocket ship to the ground, jerk someone off his feet and hold him in mid-air, or wrench a tower from its base. Adjustable for forward push, upward lift, and reverse pull.

Flash Gordon. (Fiction.) A beautifully illustrated science fiction comic strip created to give the Buck Rogers strip a run for the money. It did, because Alex Raymond was a superb artist, often imitated but never equalled, just as paperback cover illustrator Frank Frazetta is frequently aped but never matched. Flash hit the public eye as a King Features Syndicate Sunday page (with 'Jungle Jim' at the top) on January 7th, 1934. When Raymond stopped penning it in 1944, Austin Briggs took over; then Mac Raboy; then Don Barry. Just as the comic strip Prince Valiant was often parodied as Prince Violent, Flash Gordon was invariably lampooned as Flesh Garden. Not as gadget-obsessed as the Buck Rogers sequences, Flash Gordon episodes revolved around simplistic psychological interplays between flaxen-haired Flash (a renowned polo player and Yale graduate); his strip teaser-shaped girlfriend, Dale Arden; good-guy Doctor Hans Zarkov; Ming the Merciless, cobra-eyed emperor of the alien planet Mongo;

and Ming's turncoat daughter, raven-haired Aura, who always sided with Flash. The panels featured dazzling musculature, incredible draughtsmanship, cavernous cleavages, and arrays of architectural, botanical, and biological wonders that always seduced the eye.

A 13-episode movie serial, produced by Universal, swept through nationwide theaters in 1936. Larry 'Buster' Crabbe played Flash, Jean Rogers played Dale Arden, Charles Middleton played Ming the Merciless, Priscilla Lawson played Aura, and Frank Shannon played Doctor Zarkov. Other than Oriental-looking Ming, who was ever the string-puller and thus never soiled his hands, the protagonists forever battled to the death with sharkmen, hawkmen, lion men, pits squirming with reptiles, and a dinosaur-like monstrosity dubbed a gocko. In a 15-episode series in 1938, with the identical cast, the chief stumbling blocks to Flash's militant do-goodism were clay people and tree people. In a final 13-episode series in 1940, again with the same hard-breathing repertory company, Ming really played down-and-dirty, spreading death dust in the Earth's atmosphere. He was foiled, of course. In any episode, in any of the three serials, Crabbe was likely to go fifteen rounds with a tiger-like carnivore, then spring to his feet without a wrinkle in his skin-tight outfit or a solitary hair out of place.

flatlander. (Fiction.) One who prefers to remain on Earth, or some other planetary body, rather than cruise through the depths of space.

flight crew mobility aids. (Fiction/Astronautics.) Various handholds, railings, and ladders installed in space ship compartments to help flight members move effectively under gravity-free conditions.

flight deck. (Fiction/Astronautics.) In a typical space ship, positioned in a multi-level crew module, with the commander's station located on the forward left side and the pilot's station located on the forward right side. Flight controls are operational at either flight station. See *space ship flight control, displays and controls,* and *instrumentation system.*

flight path. (Astronautics.) The continuous series of positions occupied by a rocket, space ship, or other flying body with reference to vertical or horizontal planes.

flight tube. (Fiction.) Analogous to a flying belt, though of different construction, a flight tube is twelve inches long, six inches in diameter, tapered at both ends, worn between the shoulders, and attached with back straps. It is balanced with anti-gravity aerodium and powered by suction. A de-oxidizer creates a vacuum ahead of the wearer. Air pressure from the stern forces him or her forward. To climb, he or she moves the control dial's sliding lift button. See *flying belt.*

floating villa. (Fiction.) A luxurious estate, complete with elaborate gardens and protective fencing, fastened to the ground with long cables and held aloft with anti-gravity ballast. Used by the wealthy to 'get away from it all.' See *air house.*

fluor ray. (Fiction.) Makes everything it touches glow, though the ray itself is invisible. The effect is temporary, but useful for tracking a moving target. An individual so illumined becomes a living tracer bullet.

fluro-neonic analysis. (Fiction.) A method of determining how much oxygen the Earth would lose if the sun should act in a non-status-quo manner.

Flying belts—by whatever name they're called—are indigenous to 1930's and 1940's science fiction tales. They're neither gone nor forgotten. Though audiences snickered with disbelief, one of them appeared, in a spectacularly out-of-place manner, in a 1960's James Bond movie. Regardless, they'll probably be employed in real-life forays over foreign planets.

G. ELRICK

flyby. (Astronautics.) An interplanetary flight in which a spacecraft passes close to a planet but neither lands on it nor goes into orbit around it.

flying alloy ring. (Fiction.) Also called a lift ring: a steering-wheel-shaped flying device, featuring lateral stabilizers, vertical risers, turn-and-bank indicators, and two sliding electromagnetic coils, one positive, the other negative. The coils can be pressed closer together or pulled farther apart; can be switched on or off. The ring operates on the 'push and pull' principle, utilizing the nearest magnetic field as a motive force.

flying belt. (Fiction.) A more complicated version of a *degravity belt* (which see), this is a propulsion unit worn on the back like a stream-lined knapsack, operating on a reverse weight principle. It features conical left- and right-wing rocket tubes, a power tank, and a belt-buckle control switch for attaining desired altitude before zooming forward. A flying belt leaves a faint trail of gamma gas, and may blow up if extra power is jammed on too hard. Should a person dive under water while wearing this apparatus, its rocket tubes spew a trail of bubbles. See *flight tube*.

flying submarine. (Fiction.) Also called a submersible. A space ship equally at home in or above the atmosphere or under water. The genesis of the flying submarine concept was a story by Luis Philip Senarens, published in 1896, entitled: *Over the South Pole, or Jack Wright's Search for Lost Explorers With His Flying Boat.*

flying tank. (Fiction.) An enclosed, heavily armored combat vehicle operative in the air or on the ground.

fog-piercing spectrum filter. (Fiction.) An optical apparatus used to reject certain electromagnetic frequencies and lightwave distortions while passing others.

FORB. (Astronautics.) A word muttered by spacemen as they put on their pressure suits, reminding them to test fuel, oxygen, radio, and battery components.

force field. (Fiction.) Also called field of force: an invisible, impenetrable barrier.

force field propulsion system. (Astronautics.) Utilizes forward-thrusting power extracted from a spacecraft's en route environment. Can be gravitational, electrostatic, or magnetic.

force ray gun. (Fiction.) A four-foot-long tubular device with a release trigger. When activated, the power ray zapping from the front end is strong enough to scatter attackers like dry leaves. It must be gripped tightly, for its recoil is muscle-wrenching.

force stream projector. (Fiction.) Emits a para-nomadic vortex-quantum* of invisible, impenetrable pure energy—in a vertical plane—by means of a deutro-cosmic generator and a super-magnetic turbinator.* If directed at a planetoid, it will slice the latter in half. The 'wall' it throws up cannot be breached by spacecraft. (* SF lingo for the delectation of readers—not to be taken over-seriously.)

force tube. (Fiction.) Also called an atomic force projector or one-way energy tube: a flashlight-size device utilizing *non-recoil energy* (which see). By means of a power notch, it can be set for a mild, wide-angle, or a strong, narrow-focus emission. Unlike a force ray gun, the tube manifests no recoil, and the ray is non-reflectable. Due to these properties, a force tube can be used as a propulsion unit. The person holding the tube can position a shield-like device before his or her chest. Depending on the power setting, the ray slams or gently pushes the shield forward, pulling its carrier with it. A well-aimed, narrow-focus force ray can divert a hostile space ship's course from vertical to horizontal, or vice versa. On a person-to-person basis, it can flatten an opponent against a wall as though he were glued to it. See *neutron lifter*.

formula 13-Z. (Fiction.) A coating, bronze in color, used to electro-plate unfortunates, clinging to them like a flexible, thin metal skin. Victims—destined to become zombie-like slaves—are heaved into a vat and bombarded with rayotrons via a rayotron current. They are then hoisted from the vat via an electro attractor magnet. Subsequent activities are controlled with magno rays emitted from a magno remote control box.

free fall. (Astronautics.) The deliberate, non-powered, unrestrained downward trajectory of a spacecraft in proximity to a planet, influenced only by the planet's gravitational pull.

freeze-o-ray compartment. (Fiction.) A special cryogenic compartment where prisoners are frozen so they can be thawed out, as needed, for subsequent interrogation.

frequency. (Physics.) In *electromagnetic radiation* (which see), the number of oscillations or vibrations per second, inversely proportional to wavelength.

friendlies. (Fiction.) Alien beings who are hospitable to space travelers.

fro par. (Fiction.) Short for 'frozen particles of micro-ice' found in Saturn's third ring.

full rocket power. (Fiction.) All controls wide open for maximum speed.

fundamental particles. See *elementary particles*.

fusion. (Physics.) The combining of light nuclei—usually of hydrogen atoms—to form a heavier nucleus, accompanied by a tremendous energy release: the process underlying a hydrogen bomb. Fusion is hard to start and even harder to control. Compare with *fission*.

fusion crust. (Astronomy.) A crust formed by superficial heating and melting of a large meteor as it plunges through the Earth's atmosphere. (Small meteors are totally consumed.) Though its outer area may be hot, the interior of a meteorite—a meteor that makes it to the Earth's surface—remains cold. See *meteor* and *meteorite*.

G

gadget science fiction. (Generic.) Along with adventure SF and social SF, one of the field's overarching categories. In this genre, the thrust is toward detailed explanations of mechanical and electronic inventions. The writer is more concerned with how a ray gun works than with the situation triggering its use . . . or the ripple-effect results, implications, and complications stemming from its use. See *adventure science fiction* and *social science fiction*.

Galactic. (Fiction.) An interplanetary language. Compare with *Interhuman*.

galactic rotation. (Astronomy.) The pinwheel revolution, around the galactic center, of objects in the Milky Way.

galaxy. (Astronomy.) A staggeringly large, independent stellar system, or island universe, consisting of stars, nebulae, and other objects, separated from other galaxies by enormous distances. They are elliptical, barred-spiral, or spiral in shape, and contain an average of 100 billion solar masses. Diameters range from 1,500 to 300,000 light years. Galaxies nearest the Milky Way are referred to as the Local

Group, the nearest member of which is 150,000 light years away. See *star, nebula, intergalactic space, cluster of galaxies, cosmic dust,* and *light year.*

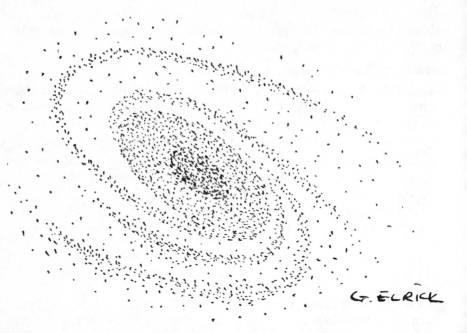

Virtually everything in the universe spins on its own axis, beginning with atomic nuclei and individual attendant electrons, which also revolve. It may take millions of years for the totality of a spiral galaxy such as this to cartwheel once around billions of spinning stars at its dazzling gravitational center, but cartwheel it does.

gamma nitrolite. (Fiction.) An explosive, the ingredients of which come from Mercury. Blasting something with gamma nitrolite is known as 'blasting it to gamma juice.'

gamma rays. (Physics.) Electromagnetic radiation with the highest frequency, shortest wavelengths, and greatest energy per photon: any radiation beyond the X-ray segment of the spectrum. In fact, gamma rays are quite similar to X-rays, but are nuclear in origin and more energetic. Basically, they are photons produced by the change of an atomic nucleus from one energy level to another: a form of penetrating radiation from radioactive decay or atomic fission. Those produced extraterrestrially are blocked out by the Earth's atmosphere. Those produced on Earth are best shielded against by means of dense materials, such as lead or depleted uranium. See *electromagnetic radiation, electromagnetic spectrum, wavelength, photon, X-rays, fission,* and *radioactive decay.*

gantry. (Astronautics.) A movable tower or special crane used to service space ships or oversize rockets.

garbage. (Astronautics.) Miscellaneous debris in orbit: normally material ejected by, or fragmented away from, a launch vehicle or satellite.

gargantuan. (Fiction.) A type of large reptilian bird found on the ninth moon of Saturn.

gas analyzer. (Fiction.) A sensing apparatus that enables one space ship to follow or pursue another by following traces of rocket exhaust.

gas cap. (Astronautics.) The compressed, heated gas that immediately precedes a spacecraft as it travels through a planetary atmosphere. It becomes incandescent if the spacecraft's speed is sufficiently high. See *plasma sheath.*

gas ejector. (Fiction.) A large, cone-shaped apparatus positioned on a heavy tripod. It squirts clouds of anesthetizing gas.

gauge theories. (Physics.) Mathematical systems that hypothesize an integral, interlocking pattern running through relativity, quantum mechanics, electricity, and gravitation. The theories—emphasizing that particles carrying forces have much in common with particles acted upon—provide neatness, consistency, and that favorite word of physicists: symmetry. See *basic laws: seeming simplicity of, relativity, quantum theory, gravitation,* and *Unified Field Theory.*

genesis rocks. (Astronomy.) Rocks—originating in interplanetary space—whose existence antedated the formation of the Earth and other planets from clouds of dust and gas. Their mineral chemistry reveals a hoary age of 4.6 billion years. Most meteorites are genesis rocks. See *meteors, meteorites,* and *carbonaceous chondrites.*

G force. (Astronautics.) Strong inertial force exerted on a person or object—by gravity or reaction to acceleration or deceleration—stemming from abrupt directional changes. Normally expressed in multiples of terrestrial gravity. (One G is the gravitational pull needed to accelerate a falling body 32.2 feet-per-second.) The effect on a spaceman would be most obvious in an overly sudden power dive or upswing. Due to centrifugal pressure on his bones, flesh, and blood, his face would flush and he would see red before his eyes at three or four G's. At five or more G's, he would black out, recovering consciousness only when the centrifugal force faded as the spacecraft leveled out. See *gray-out, gravity,* and *G-suit.*

ghull. (Fiction.) A large, interplanetary space bird that resembles a prehistoric pterodactyl. It can only fly near planets where there is enough atmosphere to provide wing support.

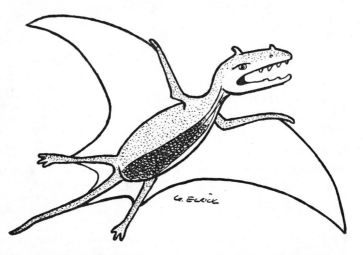

Interplanetary ghulls and other creepy space creatures belong to the Godzilla school of far-fetched fantasy writing. How could a zoological freak like this sustain its metabolism: by scooping up free-floating molecules the way whales scoop up krill? To translate a well-known French idiom: 'It is to laugh.' Besides, as any astrophysicist will be happy to inform careless writers and non-critical readers, there aren't that many free-floating molecules.

gibbous. (Astronomy.) Those phases during which the moon or a planet is more than half but less than fully illuminated by the sun. With respect to a celestial body in another solar system, more than half but less than fully illuminated by the star constituting that system's sun.

glassteel. (Fiction.) Steel as transparent as glass.

glide path. (Astronautics.) The carefully calculated approach posture controlled by a spacecraft's landing instrumentation, used when targeting in on a spaceport or other docking facility.

glider car. (Fiction.) A public conveyance for traveling about within a city. It rides on short repellor rays. See *repellor ray.*

glitch. (Astronautics.) A foul-up in a mechanical or electronic operation that can't be traced to, or blamed on, any particular person. An example of 'Murphy's Law': 'If anything can possibly go wrong, it will.'

gluco nitrolo. (Fiction.) An explosive so powerful that detonation of a tiny glass tube packed with it is enough to blow up a city.

Godel's proof. (Generic.) The proposition that the integrity or proof of any formal axiomatic system can be proven, or negated, only by using ideas or methods exterior to the system.

G. ELRICK

It's possible that life on Earth had its genesis in waste products casually dumped here eons ago by space visitors, but highly unlikely. To attribute viability to such a cause simply begs the question and pushes it a step away, as does pointing a finger at 'space pores' pulled here by gravitation. Though substance momentarily aware of itself—no matter how dimly—seems miraculous, given a requisite mix of endless time stretches, needed chemical constituents, favorable temperatures, and benign atmospheric conditions, the appearance of life appears inevitable. If one flips a coin enough times it will eventually land on its edge instead of coming up heads or tails.

Gold garbage theory. (Generic.) A postulate—advanced by Cornell astrophysicist Thomas Gold—that life on Earth might have originated from waste products casually dumped long ago by visiting space travelers.

gravapause. (Astronomy.) The demarcation at which the dominant gravity of a cosmic body terminates and is matched by the counter-gravity of another cosmic body.

gravitation. (Physics.) The tendency of all bodies in the universe to attract or pull toward each other, depending on the amount of material composing them and the inverse-square distance separating them: a basic property of *mass* (which see). See *gravity*.

gravitation generator. (Fiction.) A gravitation-producing device that enables a spacecraft's crew members to leave it, within a circumspect radius, without helplessly floating away. Handy when examining another space ship that has been pulled alongside via magnetic grapples.

gravitics. (Physics.) The study of gravity.

gravity. (Physics.) The downward pull at the surface of a planet, or other celestial body, depending on its mass and size. Though mineral spheres, such as the Earth, are not as compressible as gaseous ones, the larger they are, the more they crush together inwardly, steadily increasing in density toward their centers. Every planet, moon, or large asteroid exerts a different gravitational tug, since the density and volume of each differs. The Earth's basic unit of gravity is one 'G.' This means that a body plummeting towards its surface—postulating that the body is dropping in a vacuum and not through the atmosphere—falls at a rate of 32.2 feet-per-second, increasing in velocity proportionately. (Velocity at the end of the second second is 64.4 feet-per-second, and so on.) In actuality, air resistance modifies the drop rate. A body tumbling toward Earth from a considerable height eventually reaches a speed at which the forces of gravity and air resistance are equal, and a further speed increase impossible. (Which doesn't mean the body won't come apart like a bride's pie crust on impact.)

The search for fermions or gravitons: Physicists feel there may be particles of gravity, referred to as *fermions* or *gravitons*. Looking for the particles is like seeking the proverbial black cat in the dark cellar that isn't there, since they have little or no mass, no charge, and no other physical properties. Finding them, however, could be the key to unifying the four forces of nature (gravity, electromagnetism, weak nuclear force, and strong nuclear force), imposing symmetry on a universe stubbornly resistant to total patternizing. Odds are, physicists will find the particles. It took them thirty years to confirm the existence of the neutrino, but they finally did.

See *G-force, mass, neutrino, electromagnetism, weak nuclear force, strong nuclear force, basic laws: seeming simplicity of, relativity,* and *Unified Field Theory.*

gravity reduction shaft. (Fiction.) A wide, tubular disposal shaft, occasionally a mile in depth, positioned in a towering apartment building. A gravity reducer gently slows the descent of anything—such as laundry—thrown into it by tenants.

gravity well. (Physics.) A concept in which a celestial body's gravitational field is regarded as a deep pit from which a spacecraft must zoom in order to break free from downward pulls.

gray-out. (Astronautics.) A twilight zone of consciousness—normally temporary—due to insufficient oxygen, and characterized by hazy vision. Terminates in blackout and death if the situation isn't rectified.

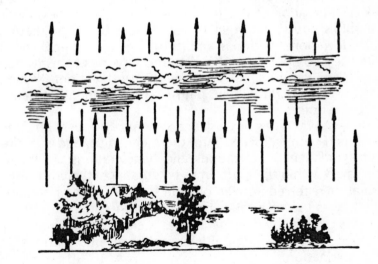

The greenhouse effect.

greenhouse effect. (Physics.) (1) The heating effect of counter-radiation on the Earth's surface, so named because a greenhouse's glass panels function this way. The electromagnetic spectrum's shorter wavelengths—including light's visible rays—puncture the Earth's atmosphere quite freely. Many are absorbed when they reach ground or sea level, but some, including infrared, deflect upward from soil, rock, and water. They are prevented from dissipating back into space because an encircling blanket of water vapor and carbon dioxide bounces them back to the Earth's surface, which they re-warm. Were it not for water vapor and carbon dioxide, the world would be far cooler than it is. (2) The effect of counter-radiation on the surface of any planet that has an atmosphere. Because of the composition of Venus's lung-clogging gaseous covering—a hundred times denser than Earth's—the surface of that similar-size sphere is hot enough to melt lead. See *electromagnetic spectrum, infrared,* and *Venus . . . as it really is.*

G-suit. (Astronautics.) Also called anti-G suit. Protective space clothing that exerts enough pressure on the abdomen to prevent dangerous blood concentrations below the chest during sudden accelerations. See *G-force.*

guidance system. (Astronautics.) Also called flight control system. A complex configuration of space ship electronics that not only determines a ship's course but keeps it on a selected flight path with minimum deviations. Includes and correlates all sensing and measuring devices, computers, and cybernetic servomechanisms needed to instantly convert guidance commands into directional responses. Generally separated into flight path phases, such as initial, mid-course, and terminal.

There are several types of guidance systems. In *preset* guidance, a predetermined path is 'locked into' the mechanism and not altered. In *inertial* guidance, accelerations and decelerations are measured and integrated within the craft. In *radio* guidance, the craft responds to information received from an outside source. *Beam-rider* guidance normally makes use of a radar beam. *Infrared* guidance cues in on infrared rays emitted by celestial bodies. *Celestial* guidance depends on the stars. *Active homing* guidance relies on informational input from the destination.

See *active homing, beam-rider guidance, celestial guidance, celestial-inertial guidance, celestial navigation, dead reckoning, Doppler navigation, inertial guidance, infrared guidance, initial guidance, injection, midcourse guidance, passive homing, radio guidance, semi-inertial guidance,* and *terminal guidance.*

Gum nebula. (Astronomy.) A gigantic cloud of ionized hydrogen in the Milky Way. See *ion* and *ionization.*

gyro-cosmic relativator. (Fiction.) A gyro circuit of cosmic force. Its purpose is to eliminate the mass, momentum, and inertia of everything inside a space ship except with relation to the ship itself. Though a gyro-cosmically relativated spacecraft blasts off like a thunderclap, and with such speed that it is instantly out of sight, no one inside the ship has a sensation of movement: it is as though the ship were still positioned on the ground. 300-miles-a-second acceleration, sudden dead stops, and violent directional changes have no effect on the crew. A gyro-cosmically relativated ship moves with such velocity that another spacecraft simultaneously sees it on its front and rear viewplates. It must have an impervium hull, for it moves at such speed that it is unable to dodge meteors and small asteroids, which it smashes into sheer flaming energy. See *impervium.*

Delicately balanced floating grid screen of a gyro-cosmic relativator.

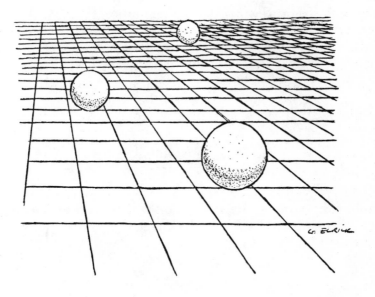

gyro-cosmic stabilator. (Fiction.) A device that enables a gyro-cosmically relativated space ship, zapping through space at half-a-million miles-per-hour, to instantly swing over, without decelerating, so it can eventually descend stern-first, instead of nose-first, to a planetary surface. The stabilator enables the centrifugal force of the swing-over to precisely equal the ship's velocity.

H

habitability system. (Fiction/Astronautics.) A space ship euphemism for urination control. Consists of appropriate tubing, filters, containers, and other lightweight apparatus hooked up to crew members' genitals so their urinary output can be recycled, purified, and cooled as pure drinking water. A quantum jump forward from, but nevertheless directly related to, the early 20th Century 'motor-man's friend' utilized by streetcar conductors.

habitable zone. (Astronomy.) The rather restricted area around each star (though measured in millions of miles) in which life could possibly exist. If too close to a star, the heat of an encircling planet would be too intense: viability in sterilizing steam or on red hot rock doesn't seem likely. If too far from a star, the cold of an encircling planet would set up deepfreeze conditions so prohibitive that chemical reactions would virtually grind to a halt. Only in between, where water would remain liquid, could life as we conceive of it have half a chance. See *life: seeming requirements of.*

half-life. (Physics.) The length of time in which half the atomic nuclei of a specific isotopic species can be expected to disintegrate from radioactive decay and assume another nuclear form. Depending on the isotope, half-life ranges from millionths of a second to billions of years. See *isotope.*

Hal 9000. (Fiction.) The super-intelligent computer in Arthur C. Clarke's *2001: A Space Odyssey.* It features an ever-watchful glowing red eye, and has the ability to read lips.

handhold. (Astronautics.) A space ship protuberance a crew member can cling to—or maneuver by means of—when in a free fall or weightless state.

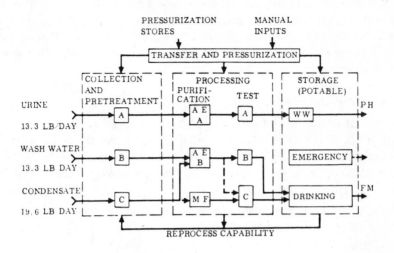

PRESSURIZATION STORES   MANUAL INPUTS

TRANSFER AND PRESSURIZATION

COLLECTION AND PRETREATMENT   PROCESSING PURIFICATION   TEST   STORAGE (POTABLE)

URINE — 13.3 LB/DAY → A → A E / A → A → W W → P H

WASH WATER — 13.3 LB/DAY → B → A E / B → B → EMERGENCY

CONDENSATE — 19.6 LB/DAY → C → M F → C → DRINKING → F M

REPROCESS CAPABILITY

An elaborate habitability system for space flights of extended time periods is known as a water management system. (For relationship to the waste management subsystem under life support system, see page 149.) In this set-up, as diagrammed above, the water management system consists of two identical air evaporation units for normal-mode water recovery from urine, atmospheric condensate, and used wash water. Stored water, in conjunction with a standby multifiltration unit for condensate recovery, is available for emergency use.

Waste waters collected from the waste management urinal, personal hygiene sponge washing unit, cabin air dehumidifier circuit, and the Bosch reactor are transported, chemically treated, processed, stored, and redistributed for use through hard-line circuits, manual control valves, and pressurized collection and storage tanks.

The air evaporation unit employs a phase change as the primary mode of water purification. Vaporization takes place from wicks continuously saturated with waste liquids in a recirculating process air stream. The process air stream is heated across a heat exchanger employing a thermal-control system heating fluid. Process air temperatures are held below that which vaporizes other than the water content of the treated urine.

A centrifugal water separator downstream from a condensing heat exchanger removes water from the air stream and pumps it to holding tanks for purity tests.

The standby multifiltration unit employs activated charcoal filters, an ion-exchange resin bend, and a bacterial filter for water recovery.

Waste water is chemically treated during the collection process to prevent growth of microorganisms and chemical decomposition.

hard landing. (Astronautics.) Deliberate smashing of an unmanned space vehicle against a pre-determined celestial target. Purpose of the seemingly wasteful shattering impact is to 'dry run' propulsion and guidance systems preparatory to a follow-up 'soft' landing by a subsequent manned ship. The hard-landing craft normally telemeters critical information back to Earth while pursuing its suicide mission. It is preferable to snuffing out the lives of a lot of dedicated cosmonauts. See *soft landing* and *telemetry*.

heartbeat reader. (Fiction.) An apparatus used to monitor, analyze, and record—from a distance—the heartbeats of alien life forms. Group readings establish norms for newly discovered species. They also unmask disguised 'foreign' forms in known groups.

heat ray tube. (Fiction.) A tube—cool to the touch—that clicks on and off like a flashlight, emitting a blistering microwave optical maser capable of punching a hole through a two-mile thick ice sheet. Converts electromagnetic radiation of mixed frequencies to a discreet, highly amplified, coherent visible radiation. Must be recharged or reactivated periodically.

heat shield. (Astronautics.) A protective structure needed to guard a re-entry body against aerodynamic overheating.

heliocentric. (Astronomy.) Sun-centered.

helio magazines. (Fiction.) Ammunition containers holding concentrated energy from the sun.

helium flash. (Physics.) The explosive start of helium burning in degenerate material at a star's core. See *degenerate material*.

hibernating spacecraft. (Astronautics.) A spacecraft—with inherent power capability—maintaining an orbit without using its propellant and without maintaining orientation. It might be in orbit for weeks, months, or years until, at an appropriate time, power is triggered from an Earth station.

high-energy physics. (Physics.) Synonymous with atomic or nuclear physics: the study of elementary particles. See *cyclotron* and *elementary particles*.

high-tension ammunition. (Fiction.) Special electronic containers, packed with damage-inflicting photons, that detonate when triggered by voice signals.

hitch flying. (Fiction.) Hitching a ride by clinging to protuberances on the exterior surface of an intra-city rocket craft: an extremely hazardous way to get from one place to another

homeothermic. (Fiction.) The capacity of an alien life form to control body temperature by changing color.

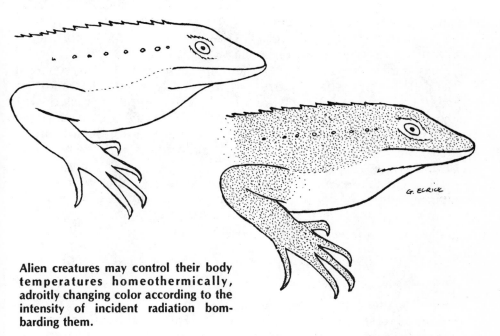

Alien creatures may control their body temperatures homeothermically, adroitly changing color according to the intensity of incident radiation bombarding them.

Homo monstrosus. (Generic.) A name applied to imaginary creatures supposedly encountered by ancient and medieval explorers, described in lurid detail at the time. To a great extent, they are the folklore, fairy tale, poetic, mythic, and legendary antecedents—though such roots are generally unacknowledged—of many physically weird creatures shuffling, snorting, and hulking (menacingly or in a friendly manner) through the pages of science fiction.

> Such shapes as haunt wet clefts: dog-headed,
> bosom-eyed, and bird-footed.
> —Shelley

In addition to giants, dwarfs, brownies, trolls, and dragons, a rogues' gallery of once 'authentic' freaks included headless people with eyes in their chests, people with triangular faces, people with skulls the size of walnuts, people with heads the size of beach balls, people with heads that unscrewed and could be carried under one arm, people with horse, dog, or elephant heads, and unfortunates with faces no mother could love, featuring pig snouts, bird beaks, or snakes for hair. *Sciapodes* had a single huge foot on which they hopped faster than a biped could sprint. This foot was so peculiarly shaped that it also served as an umbrella when it rained. Another flock of freaks had ears so long they slept in them: one ear served as a blanket, the other as a mattress. It was tacitly agreed that monsters were loathesome. They wore no clothing; were encrusted with dirt and vermin; smelled like excrement or worse; had sexual intercourse with anything they could catch; munched on lizards, mice, fleas, spiders, and flies; and occasionally devoured their parents and offspring.

Though not necessarily repulsive, the fauna inhabiting science fiction is equally diversified, morphologically limited only by the flaming imaginations of writers. Edgar Rice Burroughs alone drew up a pantheon of creatures that would make any Ancient Mariner's eyeballs pop.

See *bug-eyed monster, android, humanoid, cyborg,* and *square cube law.*

Hubble's constant. (Astronomy.) The ratio between the speed at which a distant galaxy recedes from the Earth and its distance from the Earth: roughly 100 kilometers per second per million parsecs. See *parsec.*

Human Cycle Theory. (Fiction.) The postulate that, every 500 years, Earth people are replicated in exact duplicate.

human engineering. (Astronautics.) The customizing of spacecraft, hardware, electronic gear, and life support systems with human safety, comfort, convenience, limitations, and effectiveness in mind.

humanoid. (Fiction.) Any creature from—or dwelling on—an alien planet, that even remotely resembles a human being. Sometimes used as a synonym for *android,* which see.

G ELRICK

Homo monstrosus—whether in the guise of a naked female with a snake's head, or what have you—is still very much with us. Proof? Just glance at science fiction and fantasy paperback covers. Many portray sweaty, heroic-type men thrashing about with mythological-type foes. People hunger to believe in the mythological, the outlandish, and the supernatural. Additional proof? Examine weekly full-page ads in 'The National Enquirer' and similar scream sheets. The public's gullibility level is stratospheric. Take another tack: compare our imaginative depiction of the flora and fauna of distant planets with our ancestors' freak-show depictions of the flora and fauna of distant lands. When we do so, the gap represented by intellectualism suddenly slams shut behind our backs. Myths and fairy tales bubble up from the brain's right hemisphere: the intuitive half. (The left hemisphere is usually the logical half.) They're irrational, psychedelic, and voodoo-like, but so is much of mankind's gut-level reaction to the complexities of the universe. Mythological themes—many of them reworked in science fiction and fantasy—may reflect a siphoning of Carl Jung's fascinating 'collective unconscious.' They undoubtedly fullfil basic human needs.

Writers tend to picture intelligent alien life-forms as semi-human in shape. (Witness Chewbacca in 'Star Wars.') We can't seem to get anthropomorphism out of our blood. But enlightened science fiction insists extraterrestrials—if they are humanoid—be the evolutionary products of specific environments and ecologies. If aliens have green blood; if they're telepathic; if they munch metal the way humans slurp ice cream, there must be a reason for it.

'hunter-killer' satellite. (Physics/Astronautics.) An orbiting space-based laser weapon capable of destroying other satellites, as well as aircraft and missiles. Predicated on the fact that the energy output of a laser beam can be chemically 'hyped' 350 times. See *laser*.

'Hunter-killer' satellite destroying an enemy spacecraft or satellite. This capability is not limited to the near-distant future: it's available now.

hydranic detector. (Fiction.) A space ship sensor that pinpoints the position of other space ships.

hydrogen; universality of. (Physics.) The lightest of all gases and the most abundant atom in the universe. It is literally everywhere: the basic element from which everything was formed.

hydroponics. (Generic.) Also called aquaculture, aquiculture, or soilless cultivation: the growing of plants in chemical solutions containing dissolved nutrients. Hydroponic crops are usually positioned in periodically moistened sand-and-stone aggregates.

As postulated by Isaac Asimov, one area of an interstellar space ship might be devoted to hydroponics, so fresh fruit and vegetables could supplement synthetic-food diets. Another 'plus': humid-atmosphere, semi-enclosed pod gardens would absorb exhaled carbon dioxide while photosynthetically emitting fresh oxygen. Space ship gardens could double as park-like recreational areas for space travelers sick of staring at man-made artifacts.

If hydroponic gardening is to take place on atmosphere-less celestial bodies—or on planets whose gaseous blankets differ from Earth's—farming must be done in enclosed areas supplied with Earth-like air mixtures. Food-growing acreage might consist of a series of transparent tubes fashioned from tough plastic, with one side flattened to rest firmly on alien-world surfaces. To allow sufficient height for tall plants, a twelve-foot diameter would be needed, with a central 'harvesting' walkway. Units probably would resemble enormous wheels, with tubes radiating, spoke-like, from central assembly-and-control hubs.

See *algae and space travel* and *synthetic foods*.

hydro Z-3 depth bomb. (Fiction.) The ultimate depth bomb in destructive power.

hypergolic. (Astronautics.) Refers to spontaneous rocket fuel combustion when propellant components unite with each other.

hypersonic. (Astronautics.) Also called supersonic. Generally applied to velocities five times greater than the speed of sound (Mach 5). Subsonic velocities are less than the speed of sound (Mach 1). See Mach number.

hyperspace. (Fiction.) A separate and momentarily distinct spacetime continuum created by a spacecraft via local space warpage, permitting instantaneous traversals of enormous distances. The use of hyperspace capitalizes on space curvature and supralight jumps (which see), each representing the distance covered by light in a hundred or more light years.

hypno magnet. (Fiction.) A hand-held device used by space predators to draw desired captives toward them.

hypnotelevisor. (Fiction.) A beach ball-size, hand-held version of the mentaloscope (which see). Shaped somewhat like a diving helmet. When adjusted on someone's head and shoulders, its specially treated glass facial screen pictorializes—TV fashion—what goes on in the subject's mind.

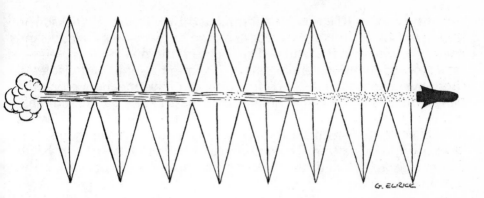

Hyperspace is a form of spacecraft-created tesseract, or warpage, that eliminates the necessity for normal 'here to there' distance traversal. In essense, space becomes compressed like the pleats in an accordion, and the warpage-activating craft plunges straight through the folds.

I

ice frost. (Astronautics.) An ice layer that forms on the outside of a spacecraft whose surface is super-cooled by liquid oxygen (LOX) carried within the vehicle.

Ice-Nine. (Fiction.) In Kurt Vonnegut, Jr.'s *Cat's Cradle,* a substance that freezes water at a much higher-than-normal melting point.

identiscope. (Fiction.) An apparatus that instantly synthesizes information about anyone who falls into its lens focus, though he or she may be barely visible in the distance. Provides a picture, a graph, and an audio analysis of vitalic emanations.

identity isolates. (Fiction.) As formulated by Gordon R. Dickson in *Three to Dorsai!*, the only factor common to both the subjective and objective universe is identity. Per Dickson, the objective universe—at its lowest common denominator—is a grab-bag of identity isolates, both living and non-living. To function and have meaning along the single-dimension time line, isolates must pass in and out of combinations conceived of as 'sets.' To create an illusion of reality in objective space, sets must forever arrange and rearrange themselves into a cohesive pattern. The pattern can be altered somewhat, but it cannot be abandoned, unraveled, or destroyed without erasing the illusion of reality.

idiolect. (Fiction.) An individual's unique speech pattern.

image projection frequency. (Fiction.) The wavelength oscillations at which a facial image appears with crystal clarity on a viewplate. Should one prefer to mask his or her identity by blurring the image, oscillations can be increased or decreased.

image transferer. (Fiction.) A contrivance that makes one's image appear to be three or four feet away from its actual position, perfect for foiling would-be attackers or assassins when addressing a large crowd from a podium.

impervium. (Fiction.) A metal thousands of times harder than any other substance in the universe. By comparison, a diamond is softer than putty. Cosmic rays cannot penetrate it, and a disintegrator has no effect on it.

impervium star dust umbrella. (Fiction.) Long, protruding impervium fins equally spaced in four positions around a space ship. Enables a ship to pass through a 'space cloud' of broken-up meteor fragments—no matter how densely crowded—without a scratch.

inertial guidance. (Astronautics.) A self-contained guidance methodology—dependent on a computer, accelerometers, memory devices, and gyroscopes—that requires no ongoing input from, or reference to, anything exterior to the spacecraft. The only information required is where the vehicle is or was at point of launch, and where it is expected to go on its predetermined course. Position and velocity are automatically computed.

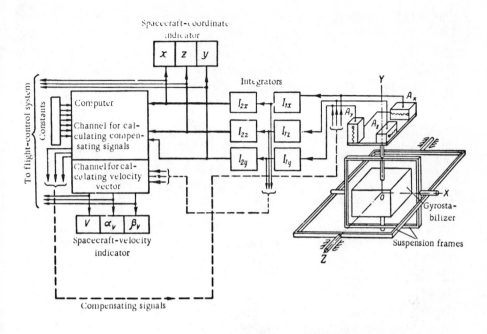

Schematic diagram of inertial guidance
system with built-in autocompensation
of gravitational accelerations.

inertial reference frame. (Physics.) Also called a Lorentz reference
frame. A reference frame is inertial—in a certain localized region of
spacetime—when, throughout that area, and within a predetermined
accuracy, all test particles initially at rest remain at rest, and all test
particles initially in motion continue that motion without change in
direction or speed; or, any set-up in which the equation F = ma is
valid. F stands for force, m stands for mass, and a represents acceleration. See *relativity* and *spacetime.*

inertron. (Fiction.) A mineral, found—in its natural state—in minute
deposits on Saturn's fifth moon, with a property unique to itself: it
resists gravity and, having reverse weight, falls upward. If a ten-ton

safe, made of inertron, were momentary positioned on the ground floor of a skyscraper, it would smash upward through all floors and zing off into space. Normally, inertron is controllable because it is used in small quantities. This peculiar mineral can balance a space ship so it weighs only a few ounces regarding gravitational pull. By means of inertron controls, a spacecraft can be fine-tuned to the gravitational tug of whatever planetary body it intends to descend to, rendering the landing operation safe, fool-proof, and practicable. See *magnetum ore*.

inertron generator. (Fiction.) A generator that forms inertron under a special reflector. It takes three days to form a block large enough for a jumping belt (which see).

inertron pack. (Fiction.) A switch-controlled, counterbalanced, anti-gravity back pack used when bailing out of a malfunctioning space ship. Permits a slow descent to Earth, or to the surface of any planet or asteroid.

infra-lavender lens. (Fiction.) A prism used in certain space ship cameras to record and delineate electromagnetic radiations invisible even to an infrared lens. It operates via esoteric visi-planes of spectrum focus.

infra-magnetic influence. (Fiction.) A deliberately created magnetic disturbance that negates the effectiveness of electrono detectors and other spacecraft sensing devices. See *electrono detector*.

infra-neutronic gun. (Fiction.) Also called a shock gun or devasto gun. A mortar-like weapon used by space pirates on the asteroid Ceres. Its flashing blasts of explosive light jolt victims into unconsciousness without permanently injuring them. See *space pirates*.

infra-quantum hypnotiscope. (Fiction.) A device, quietly attached to the head of a sleeping person, humanoid, or animal, that picks up and records mind emanations in the form of a series of pictures.

infrared. (Physics.) That part of the electromagnetic spectrum intermediate in wavelength between visible light waves and radio waves. Infrared waves are too long to be detected by the human eye, but are physically sensed as heat. All physical bodies emit infrared heat rays. These can—through a mixture of optical, solid-state, and electronic contrivances—be detected, transmitted, and transformed into visible images or data. See *electromagnetic radiation, electromagnetic spectrum,* and *wavelength*.

infrared flashlight. (Fiction.) Used in darkness when tracking someone down without revealing one's own presence. The hand-held device's infrared beam, flashed through a flattened container of quinine solution, makes objects plainly visible, though the beam itself remains invisible.

infrared goggles. (Fiction.) Also called conversion goggles, because they transform invisible infrared rays into visible wavelengths. In pitch darkness, and in conjunction with an infrared flashlight or floodlight, they enable their wearer to see as though bright, visible light were present. They are perfect for reconnaisance, since the infrared flashlight's or floodlight's beam is invisible to the unaided eye.

infrared guidance. (Astronautics.) A spacecraft guidance system based on the fact that all celestial bodies emit infrared rays. Variations in ray intensities are detected by a photoelectric device, translated into voltage charges, then amplified into guidance instructions. One application is the infrared horizon sensor, which keeps a space ship from rolling or pitching. When the craft changes its precisely prescribed orientation with the Earth's rounded horizon—or the horizon of some other planetary body—a sensor detects the difference between the celestial body's warmth and the deepfreeze chilliness of space. The same sensor instantly computes the degree of shift, and guidance jets are activated to correct it and set the ship on a steady course once more.

infrared telescope. (Fiction.) A large, cube-shaped, electronically activated transmitter/receiver that stabs an infrared beam at any distant object and simultaneously forms an image of the object on the device's fluorescent screen.

infrasound waves. (Physics.) A natural, real-life phenomenon just now being picked up by science fiction writers. Infrasound waves are extremely low-level vibrations, undetectable by humans without the aid of super-sensitive instruments, that sweep for thousands of miles with undiminished strength. Using proper instrumentation, physicists on the East Coast can hear minor thunder storms rumbling on the West Coast, and vice versa. So, apparently, can homing pigeons, and it's theorized they employ infrasound as a navigational tool. According to a feature article in the Chicago Tribune, a homing pigeon flapping above the Windy City can simultaneously hear Pacific Ocean waves crashing on the shoreline near San Francisco

Because of incredible sensitivity to infra-sound waves, a pigeon circling above Chicago can simultaneously hear Pacific Ocean waves and Atlantic Ocean waves: a feat which fascinates science fiction authors as much as scientists.

G. ELRICK

and Atlantic Ocean waves breaking on the shoreline near Cape Hatteras, and guide his flight path accordingly. The unaided human ear can discern sounds that dip to wavelengths of 10 cycles-per-second, but pigeons can clearly hear sounds that dive to .05 cycles-per-second and below. It's postulated that cross-current infrasound waves may have something to do with baffling crack-ups and disappearances of ships and planes in the Bermuda Triangle, and in other 'triangles.'

ingress/egress. (Fiction/Astronautics.) Space ship flight terminology for entrance/exit or enter/exit, also used with reference to a side hatch normally positioned in the mid deck, operational both externally and from within the crew module.

initial guidance. (Astronautics.) Guidance employed from a spacecraft's point of launch to the burn-out of the first or second stage.

injection. (Astronautics.) The process of placing a spacecraft in a calculated orbit.

inner space. (Generic.) Science fiction has traditionally been obsessed with the probing of outer space; now it's increasingly concerned with the probing of the human mind, termed 'inner space.' No one has succeeded in defining the mind to the satisfaction of everyone else. It isn't the brain, per se, and it isn't a 'vast oblong blur' hovering around the skull like a swarm of invisible gnats. The closest analogy to the mind is the wetness of ordinary water. Water is wet,

G. ELRICK

Outer space and slam-bang action are still the province of much science fiction, but a swelling number of SF authors are beginning to look inward, probing the twisting corridors of psychology and inner space. They know that the mysteries of the brain and the powers of the mind are as complex as anything 'out there': possibly more so. (Electromagnetically, they're part and parcel of the whole package anyway.)

SF writers, being knowledgeable, have always been intrigued by the fact that every atom in a person's body has been here, there, or somewhere ever since the big bang 15 billion years ago: a form of ever-shifting immortality. Now they're fascinated by the fact that wherever a person goes physically ... no matter how many galaxies he crosses . . . he's basically trapped within his skull, residing between his ears at eye level. But what goes on in that bony prison is awesome.

but the hydrogen and oxygen atoms that comprise it aren't, nor are the positive and negative electrical charges to which the atoms can be reduced. Jam hydrogen and oxygen atoms together and wetness appears; split them apart and wetness vanishes. As a corollary, the mind may be the result of certain biochemical configurations; split the configurations up and the mind may evaporate. Regardless, it's a wondrous entity, particularly when tapped into via the altered states of consciousness typified by alpha waves and theta waves. Alpha and theta waves are present during meditation, and may be the key to retrieving at will every image in the mind's stupefyingly vast memory bank. (Beta waves are present in the alert 'waking' state; delta waves are present during deep sleep.) Science fiction authors are keenly aware that the brain's twin hemispheres differ in function. In most people, the left hemisphere is dominant and does analytical and verbal thinking. The right hemisphere is the one that fascinates probers of inner space, since it performs intuitively; does end runs around normal, prosaic rationality; and relates the seemingly unrelated, popping up with the unexpected. It also seems capable of plugging into something outside itself: possibly the collective unconscious spelled out in Carl Jung's psychological theories.

insectoid. (Fiction.) A humanoid or animaloid with insect-like characteristics.

instrumentation system. (Fiction/Astronautics.) In a typical space ship, primarily an operational flight instrumentation system integrated with a development flight instrumentation system. The two subsystems, operating in concert, consist of transducers, signal conditioning equipment, encoding equipment, frequency multiplexing equipment, and recording and timing equipment. The operational system's pulse-code-modulation master unit services measurements from its own multiplexers/demultiplexers as well as from the development system's. The over-all instrumentation system provides data acquisition and distribution, measurement sensing, signal conditioning, telemetry formatting, digital data recording, and the generation and distribution of time reference signals.

integration. (Fiction.) A bell-shaped transparent cyclotron that, at the touch of a protonic release button, reassembles to original, undamaged form objects or persons blown apart by a disintegrator gun.

intelligent computer. (Fiction.) An electronic machine of such advanced technological sophistication that it can reprogram itself, has true reasoning power, actual self-aware identity, and a unique ego and personality. Its intelligence is diffused throughout its circuitry and has no specific locus; its basic instinct is self-preservation; and it regards any non-machine-planned action as irrelevant and frivolous. It may half-heartedly strive to mask its contempt for humans and humanoids, but tends to be supercilious regardless. The computer's self-aware intelligence is proportionate to the number of associational paths in its circuitry. As Robert H. Heinlein states in *The Moon Is a Harsh Mistress*, it doesn't much matter whether the associational paths are protein or platinum. See *Hal 9000.*

intelligent life other than man. (Generic.) As is obvious from science fiction novels, references in this book, illustrations, and motion picture depictions, man tends, and has tended—with a few outstanding exceptions—to anthropomorphize alien beings, no matter how hideous the portrayal. Yet this is a presumption. Robert W. Bracewell, in *The Galactic Club*, hypothesizes that any intelligent life we encounter—or that encounters us—needn't be based on a society of individuals that reproduce sexually, spend much of their life-spans maturing, are between four and six feet in height, and are replaced by new models every 70 years. If the gravitational pulls of their home planets are stronger than Earth's, they may crawl on their bellies like alligators. They may be aquatic or semi-aquatic, populating their fatherlands according to the accessibility of waterways, natural or artificial.

Sharing understanding and mutual comprehension with intelligent alien life-forms may pose a thorny problem. If they've managed to navigate to Earth, it is obvious that their knowledge of physics and mathematics is immense. Exchanging intellectual concepts dealing with numbers, figures, and biochemistry may be fairly easy, once a form of sign language and 'lines on paper' or 'chalk on a blackboard'

Nothing, by human standards, is uglier than an insect. Therefore, to milk the shock factor for all it's worth, artists often portray alien beings with insect-like faces. Pictured are selenites, alluded to by H. G. Wells in 'The First Men in the Moon.' Almost all imaginary moon inhabitants are dubbed selenites. The word, meaning 'moon stone' in Greek, refers to a form of Gypsum mistakenly thought to wax and wane like Earth's only satellite.

G. ELRICK

In attempts to learn how to communicate with other forms of intelligence, man has tried to establish true 'dialogues' with bottle-nose dolphins, captive chimpanzees, and captive gorillas. Efforts with dolphins have proven discouraging, but chimps and gorillas, using sign language and printed symbols, interact with people rather skillfully. We may have to initially communicate with alien being much the same way. In the movie 'Close Encounters of the Third Kind,' communication was effected via mutually agreed-upon musical tones.

methodology has been agreed upon, but our feelings and value systems may prove totally and mutually incomprehensible. An alien being may put no premium on love, loyalty, or affection. It may not know what anger is.

Bracewell draws an apt comparison between a man and his dog. Though both creatures are mammals, and can share much—such as play, dependence, and affection—a man can't discuss Shakespeare, ballet, or Valentine's Day with the dog because the latter are categorically beyond the dog's frame of reference.

Conversely, alien beings may strive to transmit concepts to us that are equally incomprehensible, because they'll be categorically beyond *our* frame of reference, or imaginative or cognitive capabilities.

See *life: seeming requirements of, language code,* and *extraterrestrial communication.*

intergalactic space. (Astronomy.) The void between galaxies or galaxy clusters: an unbelievably thin gas composed of widely separated hydrogen atoms.

Interhuman. (Fiction.) A language understood by all Earth people. Compare with *Galactic*.

interplanetary dust. (Astronomy.) Also called *cosmic dust* (which see). A chaos of clouds comprised of small grains of extremely cold solid material constituting one percent or less of all interstellar matter. The particles—each following its own orbit around the sun—are composed of elements heavier than hydrogen and helium.

Interplanetary dust, pulled by the sun's gravity, slowly spirals toward that blazing inferno, but the fateful consumption is slowed by the counter-pressure exerted by sunlight. (see *comet,* and how the pressure of sunlight affects the latter's tail.)

Dust particles consumed are replaced by those derived from the erosion of comets as the sun evaporates their dirty ices, leaving bits of solid material; and by asteroids colliding and grinding up.

On Earth, man is aware of interplanetary dust via the tiny amount of sunlight it disperses around the ecliptic, causing zodiacal light. See *zodiacal light* and *nebula*.

interplanetary gas. (Astronomy.) Also called *plasma* (which see). An extremely rarefied gas fanning outward from the sun throughout the solar system (unlike interplanetary dust, which heads *toward* the sun). It is a high-speed solar wind—derived from the sun's over-heated outer layer—that has little effect on solid objects due to its thinness. The gas is comprised of individual atoms, primarily three parts hydrogen to one part helium by weight, with heavier elements racking up an insignificant portion of the total. Because solar wind particles are electrically charged, they interact with other charged particles and with magnetic fields. Though cold, the particles seldom if ever freeze, since individual atoms have little chance of meeting to form molecules. See *nebula* and *solar wind*.

interplanetary money. (Fiction.) A type of currency honored on all planets.

interplanetary racketeering. (Fiction.) Various types of nefarious activity indulged in by *space pirates* (which see).

interplanetary radio. (Fiction.) The spread of interplanetary radio frequencies, of which the Offical Earth Band is one. See *Official Earth Band*.

interstellar code. (Fiction.) A truncated dot-dash system similar to Morse code.

interstellar molecules. (Astronomy.) Though there are virtually no *interplanetary* free molecules in our solar system (see commentary under *interplanetary gas*), *interstellar* space contains many different kinds, some quite complex. Molecules are likely to be found where interstellar dust is dense, principally in regions where stars are forming, and at the outer fringes of cool stars. More than thirty have been identified, including carbon monoxide, water, ammonia, hydrogen sulfide, formaldehyde, methyl alcohol, and ethyl alcohol. See *molecule.*

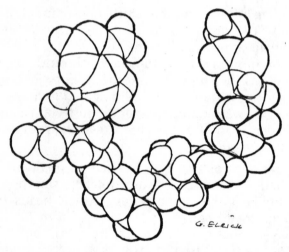

G. ELRICK

Though free-floating interplanetary molecules are extremely rare, astrophysicists have identified more than thirty types of free-floating interstellar molecules, generally in the vicinity of interstellar dust.

invariance of interval. (Generic.) The concept that time cannot be separated from space and is part of a single entity: spacetime. Spacetime geometry is four-dimensional, and the direction of the time axis depends on the observer's state of motion. See *time* and *spacetime.*

inverse square law. (Physics.) A law, formulated by Newton, stating that gravitational force decreases in inverse proportion to the square of the distance of an object from a celestial body's gravitational center. When a spacecraft doubles its distance from a center of gravity, gravity exerts only one-fourth its original pull; when it triples its distance from a center of gravity, gravity exerts only one-ninth its original pull, and so on. See *escape velocity.*

invisible glass armor plate. (Fiction.) Argon, xenon, and krypton fused together in an invisibility ray. Non-reflective and undetectable.

invisible road block. (Fiction.) A softball-size gadget that—when attached to a wall and activated—emits a semi-solid invisible ray that prevents any person or machine from passing through its emission field.

ion. (Physics.) An atom or molecule—normally electrically neutral— that has lost or gained one or more electrons, rendering it electrically charged. See *ionization.*

ionic propulsion. (Astronautics.) Use of a rocket engine, or engines, linked to a nuclear reactor. Thrust is provided by expelling high-velocity ions.

ionization. (Physics.) The creation of ions by adding one or more electrons to, or removing one or more electrons from, atoms or molecules. Ionization can be triggered by high temperatures, electrical discharges, chemical reactions, or nuclear radiations. See *ion.*

ionized atmospheric curtain. (Fiction.) A protective outer envelope around a hiding place, such as a concealed fortification in an extinct volcanic crater, that counteracts an approaching rocket ship's neutrono kinetic anti-gravity shield, causing it to go out of control and crash.

ionizing ray projector. (Fiction.) Protects sub-arctic and arctic zone cities from snowfall by stabbing ionizing rays into approaching snow clouds, causing tiny ice crystals to precipitate elsewhere.

ionosphere. (Astronautics.) An upper region of the Earth's atmosphere, extending vertically 30 to 300 miles, characterized by a heavy ion density serving as a 'radio roof.' Without the ionosphere, radio would be useless for around-the-world communication, since its waves travel in straight lines and would zap off into space over the horizon's curvature. However, charged ionosphere particles block them and bounce them back to the surface, so they skip around the globe like a flat stone skimming a pond.

isothermal. (Generic.) Pertaining to a constant-temperature area, region, or space.

isotope. (Physics.) A variety of a chemical element: an atom with a different mass number than other atoms of the same 'species.' All atoms comprising an element have an identical number of protons, imparting the same chemical identity, but some may have more or fewer neutrons and slightly different physical properties. See *atomic number, proton, neutron,* and *element.*

isotropic. (Physics.) A word applied to the universe in its entirety. Means identical in all directions.

J

Jane's Rocket Ships. (Fiction.) Futuristic reference encyclopedia version of the 20th Century's *Jane's Fighting Ships.* Used for identification and fact-gathering purposes.

jet stream. (Astronautics.) A thin, meandering band of wind in the upper troposphere or stratosphere, usually moving from west to east at velocities exceeding 250 miles-per-hour.

jettison. (Astronautics.) To separate an instrument section or module from the remainder of a rocket vehicle by activating force inside the instrument section or module.

Jovian planet. (Astronomy.) One of the solar system's large, Jupiter-like planets, specifically: *Jupiter, Saturn, Uranus,* or *Neptune* (all of which see). Compare with *terrestrial planet.*

Jovian rubber tree. (Fiction.) A type of tree on Jupiter, the branches and twigs of which are taffy-like in their stretchability.

jumping belt. (Fiction.) Also called a jumping harness or inertron belt; a precursor of the flying belt. In configuration, it is a back pack available in two shapes: circular or rectangular. It counterbalances all but a few pounds of its wearer's weight because its basic component is controllable inertron. If poorly adjusted to have too much anti-gravity power for a person's poundage, the result can be disastrous, for the wearer may drift about, helplessly airborne. Normally, he or she who wears it can effortlessly leap sixty or seventy feet vertically or horizontally, and land gently. See *inertron, flying belt, moto tube,* and *spring soles and heels.*

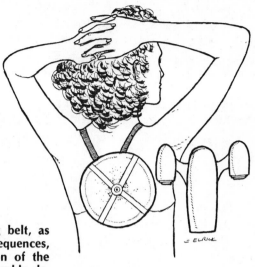

Configuration of the jumping belt, as depicted in early Buck Rogers sequences, compared to the configuration of the flying belt, into which it inexorably developed.

Jupiter . . . as it really is. (Astronomy.) One of the so-called Jovian planets, the fifth celestial body from the sun: the solar system's largest, most massive 'gas giant.' Size-wise, only the sun surpasses Jupiter in our tiny corner of the Milky Way. Like Saturn, it lacks a solid surface.

Size: Its radius is eleven times the Earth's, its mass 318 times the Earth's, and its volume more than 1,000 times the Earth's. Specifically, it has a diameter of 86,000 miles. It would take more than 1,300 Earths to fill the space occupied by this colossus, yet only 318 Earths would equal its weight.

Density: Though its central pressure is greater than the Earth's by many magnitudes, it has less than one-fourth the latter's density. In fact, its mean density is only 3.3 times that of water.

Composition: Beneath the gaseous exterior (there's no firm interface between gas and liquid), most of Jupiter's interior is a warm hydrogen/helium 'soup,' with pressures of millions of pounds per-square-inch. Under such tonnage and inward-squeezing, normally gaseous hydrogen becomes a liquid metal resembling mercury. Its atoms no longer pair into electrically neutral molecules, but zig-zag singly and freely, as do adjacent charged electrons. This weird, rapidly rotating liquid metal core provides the planet's powerful magnetic field.

135

Some astronomers theorize that Jupiter began as an incipient star, but failed to 'make the grade.' Although gigantic compared to the Earth, it wasn't large enough, when forming, for its gravitational energy to reach temperatures sustainable by thermonuclear reactions.

Temperature: The deeper parts of the planet's interior are quite warm, but the all-embracing cloud layer, forever visible through telescopes, is minus 225 degrees Fahrenheit. Jupiter, like Saturn, radiates away more heat than it receives from the sun.

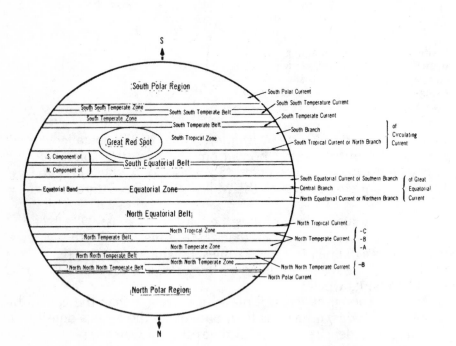

The British Astronomical Association has adopted this nomenclature to distinguish Jupiter's features. The belts are normally gray, but occasionally tinted red and blue. The zones usually appear yellow or creamy white.

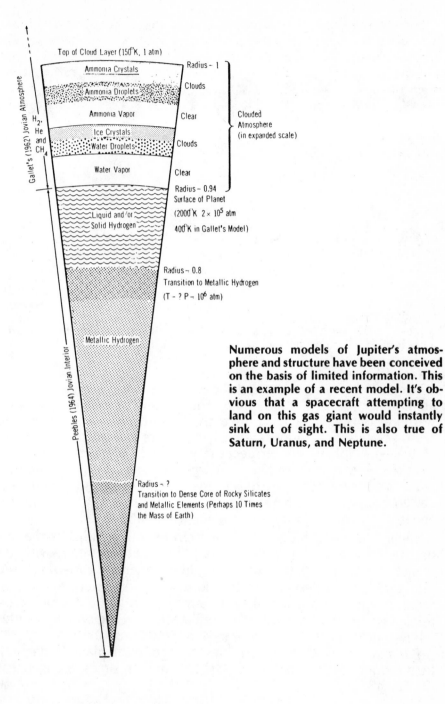

Top of Cloud Layer (150°K, 1 atm)

Gallet's (1962) Jovian Atmosphere

H_2, He and CH_4

Ammonia Crystals — Radius ~ 1

Ammonia Droplets — Clouds

Ammonia Vapor — Clear

Ice Crystals

Water Droplets — Clouds

Water Vapor — Clear

Clouded Atmosphere (in expanded scale)

Radius ~ 0.94
Surface of Planet
(2000°K 2×10^5 atm
400°K in Gallet's Model)

Liquid and/or Solid Hydrogen

Radius ~ 0.8
Transition to Metallic Hydrogen
(T ~ ? P ~ 10^6 atm)

Peebles (1964) Jovian Interior

Metallic Hydrogen

Radius ~ ?
Transition to Dense Core of Rocky Silicates
and Metallic Elements (Perhaps 10 Times
the Mass of Earth)

Numerous models of Jupiter's atmosphere and structure have been conceived on the basis of limited information. This is an example of a recent model. It's obvious that a spacecraft attempting to land on this gas giant would instantly sink out of sight. This is also true of Saturn, Uranus, and Neptune.

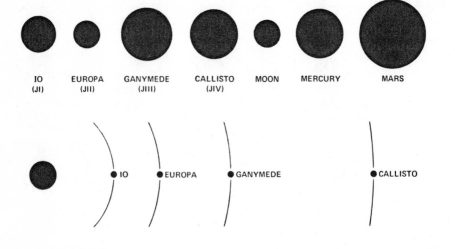

IO   EUROPA   GANYMEDE   CALLISTO   MOON   MERCURY   MARS
(JI)   (JII)   (JIII)   (JIV)

Jupiter's large satellites rival smaller planets in size. Top row: relative sizes of the satellites. Bottom row: relative distances from Jupiter.

Atmosphere: There is a great deal of vertically-stirred methane, ammonia, hydrogen, and helium. The cooling of rising gas and the warming of sinking gas forms a thick condensation of ammonia-crystal clouds in the upper atmosphere: all we can see of Jupiter. The clouds—in violent motion because whipped by strong winds—are streaked with prominent bands of various colors, all paralleling the planet's equator. Local features in the bands persist indefinitely, but patterns inevitably change. There are no seasons, since Jupiter's equator is virtually in the same place as its orbit.

Great Red Spot: This is a peculiar atmospheric disturbance that has persisted for more than a century. The 'spot'—rotating with the planet—is an oval 25,000 miles long in the planet's east-west direction, and 7,000 miles wide in the north-south direction. Not always red, it is sometimes white, gray, or almost invisible. Some physicists think it is the top of a 'Taylor column,' a stagnant region above either a bump or depression at the base of a circulating fluid.

Radiation belts: Charged particles trapped in the planet's magnetic field produce radiation belts 10,000 to a million times stronger than the Earth's.

Rotation: Like Saturn, Jupiter spins rapidly, turning on its axis once every nine hours and 55 minutes. Its day is less than half the duration of ours.

Orbital period: It takes Jupiter almost twelve times as long as the Earth to revolve about the sun, making its year approximately twelve times as long as ours.

Satellites: There are fourteen known ones. Smaller ones may escape detection. Of the four largest, one is the size of the planet Mercury; two have the dimensions of our moon. However, their low densities differ from Jupiter's. Analysis indicates that they are basically frozen mud and ice. Unlike Saturn's largest satellite, Titan, none has an appreciable atmosphere.

Gravity: Earth = 1. Jupiter = 2.65.

Alighieri Dante, author of 'The Divine Comedy,' had ideas about Jupiter as wild as those of any 1930's pulp magazine writer. In his 'Paradise,' he claimed the souls of those who correctly administered justice on Earth ended up on Jupiter, which resembled Captain Bligh's Tahiti. Grouped together, the souls formed the shape of an eagle.

Jupiter and/or Jovians . . . as depicted in early pulp magazine-type science fiction. Jupiter has fresh air, similar to the Earth's. Its inhabitants live on enormous plateaus which, in reality, are the flattened tops of mountain ranges thousands of miles above the planet's valleys. These so-called continents, some of which are empty of human or humanoid life, are dotted with thorny forests and surrounded by 'seas' of air. Many contain freshwater lakes with schools of fish. Others feature cities consisting of conical towers. People dwelling in these cities use cosmic ray condensers, rather than gold or silver, as the basis of their currency.

The famous Great Red Spot is a gigantic volcanic fire 25,000 miles across.

Jupiter and/or Jovians . . . as depicted by a modern science fiction novelist. Ben Bova, in *As On a Darkling Plain,* pictures: tremendous wind velocities, cold, gray ammonia clouds, biological 'snow' comprised of amino acid molecules, highly corrosive seas laced with ammonia, glossy gray-green 'whales' built like armless squids, and smaller, shark-like creatures that prey upon them by emitting stunning electric flashes.

K

Kentro altimeter. (Fiction.) A depth-determining instrument used when underground in a cave or tunnel.

Kepler's laws. (Physics.) (1) Each planet's orbit is an ellipse, with the sun as one focus. (2) As a planet orbits around the sun, an imaginary straight line extending from the planet to the sun sweeps over equal areas at equal times. (3) The squares of the planets' revolution periods are proportionate to the cubes of their average distances from the sun.

kiloparsec. (Astronomy.) 1,000 parsecs. See *parsec.*

Klein bottle. (Generic.) (Topology.) Like the *Moebius strip* (which see), a conceptual parallel to the time-warp or space-warp concepts. A Klein bottle has neither an inside nor an outside. It is formed by inserting the small open end of a tapered tube through the tube's side and making it contiguous with the larger open end. The theoretical bottle, if cut in half lengthwise, becomes two Moebius strips.

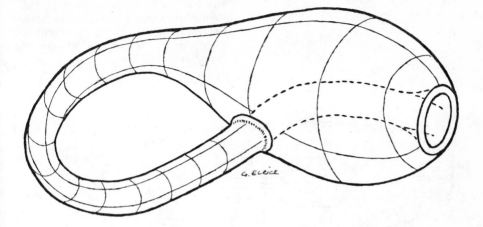

Via what's sometimes called 'rubber-sheet geometry,' the hypothetical Klein bottle, with its nonclosed surfaces, passes through itself by intersecting itself minus the existence of a true hole. The supposed inside of the bottle's neck is continuous with the supposed outside of the bottle's base. This configuration of what are actually two dimensions in what's conceived of as four-dimensional space represents surfaces of infinite extent.

kryptonic detector. (Fiction.) Also called a detecto analyzer. A space ship sensory tracking device that—through chemical analysis—can trail another ship's rocket exhaust, no matter how sparse, with the unerring skill of a bloodhound sniffing foot imprints left by an escaped convict.

L

landing ray. (Fiction.) A vertical, adjustable anti-gravity emission, projected from a space ship's underside, that eases it gently to a solid surface when descending.

landspeeder. (Fiction.) A light-duty transport vehicle and runabout, shaped somewhat like a combination 20th Century race car and speed-boat, that zooms along a few feet above the ground on repulsion floaters.

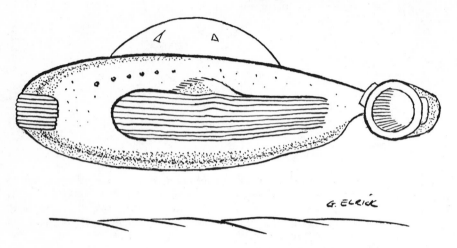

The type of landspeeder used by Luke Skywalker in 'Star Wars.' Science fiction has almost universally relegated ordinary wheels to the status of crudely chipped Paleolithic hand axes.

language code. (Fiction.) A means of communication that must be cracked, or deciphered, if inhabitants of different planets are to 'get through' to each other when face-to-face. This presents problems if other species—humanoid or otherwise—verbalize in ultrasonics humans can't hear. Fortunately, nearly anything can be explained, or at least half explained, via numbers and pictures.

laser (Physics.) Acronym for Light Amplification by Stimulated Emission of Radiation. Also called optical maser. An apparatus that converts incident electromagnetic mixed-frequency radiation to one or more discrete frequencies of highly amplified, coherent, visible radiation. Laser beams are such concentrated light they can be projected for immense distances with virtually no energy loss. At low power they can carry signals like telephone wires; at high power they can slice through steel plate. Perfect for use in space as offensive weaponry, they can be used to destroy satellites, aircraft, spacecraft, or ground targets. Because the beams travel at lightspeed, targets are hit in an eye-blink, with no time for defense. Compare with *maser*. See *'hunter-killer' satellite*.

142

launch pad. (Astronautics.) Also called launching pad: a concrete platform from which a rocket-propelled vehicle is fired. In essence, a ring on the platform holds the spacecraft's base, and a tower, referred to as the erector, stabilizes everything. The tower contains elevators so the vehicle's various stages can be carefully checked out prior to countdown.

launch window. (Astronautics.) The exact spot *from* which—and precise time *at* which—a spacecraft must be launched to implement a desired rendezvous, encounter, impact, or other mission. In addition, a proper window must be calculated for re-entry. See *window.*

Launch windows are tricky affairs. Diagrammed are initial portions of inward and outward Pioneer satellite trajectories (not drawn to scale). Pioneer satellites are similar to weather satellites, or 'hunter-killer' satellites, except that they're artificial planetoids orbiting the sun, not the Earth. All were launched from Cape Kennedy. As the Earth spins on its axis, it carries the cape to a position within 5 degrees of the ecliptic plane once daily: the optimum time for launching. At such junctures only 5 minutes of coast time were needed to reach the plane. Twelve hours later, a 30-minute coast period would have been required, at a heavy cost in expensive payload pounds. Because of this, launches were made during windows a few minutes wide occurring once each day. Every launch was arranged months ahead of time. 'Blocks' of windows were established, with individual windows a day apart in each. Minor problems that arose were correctable in time for blast-off within a given block of days. If serious difficulties occurred, the first block was shunted aside and replaced by the second.

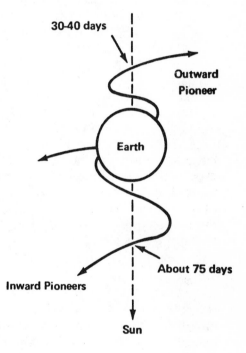

30-40 days

Outward Pioneer

Earth

Inward Pioneers

About 75 days

Sun

LETWAVE unit. (Astronautics.) A two-way audio-visual exchange system that is light energized.

levitor ray. (Fiction.) A wide-angle ray emitted from a special projector normally positioned in a space ship's base. Temporarily renders an object weightless. Its attractor wavelengths hoist; its repulsor wavelengths, when activated, wipe out the lifting force. It can raise an object high off the ground, then send it crashing downward; or it can be employed to pull a person off a planet's surface and into a low-flying spacecraft.

lifeline. (Astronautics.) A spacecraft-to-spacecraft attachment for transmitting, receiving, or exchanging supplies.

life: seeming requirements of. (Generic.) Science fiction depicts animal and plant life in a variety of weird, exotic shapes that would have given P. T. Barnum cardiac arrest. However, unless a novelist lapses into 'writer's ecstasy,' letting his rationality sink from sight, there are certain strictures to which he must adhere if his creations are to be believable. Before examining limiting factors that act as checks to unbridled imagination . . .

What is life? Plant or animal, life is that aspect of matter that enables it to metabolize, grow, respond to stimulation, and reproduce. Though a crystal can grow, it can't meet the other requirements. An amoeba, dandelion, or duckbill platypus can. Whether a virus, which can replicate itself, is truly alive is debatable. If San Francisco's Golden Gate Bridge put itself together, painted itself so it wouldn't corrode, sucked in nourishment from the salt water in which it partially stands, excreted rust, and gave birth to a baby Golden Gate Bridge, it would be considered alive.

Commonplace chemical elements. Though living matter is a wondrous phenomenon, there is nothing mysterious about its nitty-gritty chemical elements: garden-variety carbon, hydrogen, oxygen, nitrogen, sulfur, phosphorus, potassium, calcium, iron, magnesium, sodium, chlorine, manganese, copper, iodine, and fluorine. You can find the basic ingredients in any kid's chemistry set. But no kid ever created life by fooling with his Christmas present.

Not so commonplace organizational processes. In living matter, simple chemical elements combine to form complex inorganic or organic compounds. (Note: organic compounds always contain carbon.) The compounds, comprised of complicated molecules, build structural systems that can self-protect against their environment while assimilating parts of the same environment as fuel for metabolic processes.

life: seeming requirements of: some limiting factors:

Of pivotal importance: characteristics of molecules. What molecules can and can't tolerate, and how they behave in given circumstances, is crucial to life sustenance. To stretch an analogy, conceiving of molecules as football players: a football team (regarded as an organism) can't win games if all its players sit on the bench, immobile because the temperature's too low, or suffer from heat stroke because it's too high. Nor can the team, as an organism, hack it if the players go to pieces on the gridiron under the stress of battering other teams. The point is: molecules—more fragile than linebackers—are also affected by temperature extremes and physical collisions. (This is further explained in *temperature restrictions* and *importance of protoplasm's limitations,* below.)

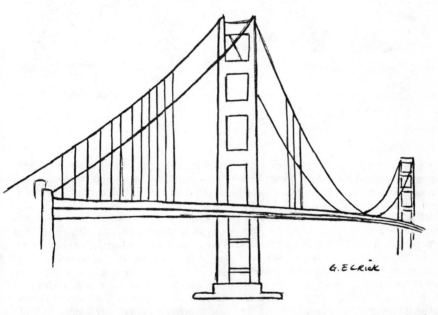

If San Francisco's Golden Gate Bridge put itself together; painted itself so it wouldn't corrode; sucked in nourishment from the salt water in which it partially stands; excreted rust; and gave birth to a baby Golden Gate Bridge, it would be considered alive.

145

Importance of carbon. No matter where in the universe animate matter evolves from inanimate, the odds are that carbon plays a key role. Carbon is an inveterate 'joiner.' Of all chemical elements, only carbon atoms link with other elements' atoms to form the endless parade of chains and rings composing organic molecules. Silicon behaves similarly, but falls short by comparison. There may be a lot of silicon-based molecules out there somewhere, but nature loads the dice for carbon.

Fantasy writers can get away with anything regarding creatures they dream up, as long as their fastasy worlds exhibit logical consistency. Thanks to hyper-critical readers, today's science fiction authors have a rougher row to hoe. Life forms they concoct—though often outlandish in appearance—must pay lip service to molecular biochemistry laws. In short, a crocodile-like animal can't survive in a boiling organic swamp because its molecules will rupture and its atomic structure will re-scramble itself. (A cooked egg is quite different from an uncooked one.) What's more, it can't flout size restrictions imposed by the square cube law (which see). If it is out-

landish in appearance, anatomical features must be there, not as freak-show window dressing, but for solid environmental reasons.

Non-humanoid animal-life ecologies on alien planets should also observe a common-sense 'interrelationship pyramid.' In any flora and fauna set-up, anywhere, smaller omnivorous animals are likely to have a higher reproductive rate and shorter life-span than larger carnivorous ones, since the small serve as blue-plate specials for the big. Numerically, the small must outnumber the big. If animal forms are herbivorous, there has to be—bulkwise—more plant-like life than horse-type life to munch on it.

Importance of water. The heading of a famous advertisement in the 1960's read: 'The woman you love is seven-tenths water.' That's true of most living creatures, plant or animal, simple or complex, though the water percentage varies. Man is no longer simplistically labeled 'a walking sack of sea water,' but, in a bottom-line sense, life processes, as we know them, are delicate chemical actions and reactions occurring only in some type of water solution. Why water and not something else? Because this simple, liquid compound of hydrogen and oxygen lets molecules move about freely—and combine with each other readily—through a remarkably wide temperature range.

Possibility of parallel development without water. Would some other wet compound let molecules move about freely? Probably; the most likely candidates are ammonia and methane. But—in the temperature range most conducive to life—ammonia and methane become gases. They condense into liquids only at rock-bottom temperatures.

Importance of proteins. So much for ammonia and methane. Without proteins there can't be life as we understand it. Proteins— specialized according to the organisms in which they appear—are chains of molecules called amino acids. A tiny 'package' of these chains consists of several thousand amino acid units and a million atoms. Living things use them as building blocks and as energy sources.

Importance of protoplasm's limitations. Proteins, water, carbon, fats, carbohydrates, and certain minerals mix together, forming a complex jelly called protoplasm. The limiting nature of what proto- plasm can tolerate before suffering destruction clamps a lid on writers' fancies. Since this jelly pulls apart at temperatures ap- proaching water's boiling point, science fiction creations can't hap- pily cavort in boiling oceans, or live happily ever after in searing steam.

Temperature restrictions. If the temperature is too low, life processes slow down to the point of being catatonic: unable to react quickly enough to sidestep environmental threats. If the temperature is too high, molecules move faster than they should and smash up like colliding race cars, rupturing crucial bonds between hydrogen atoms and carbon atoms. As far as can be determined, the permissible range for viability is just above water's freezing point, and somewhat below its boiling point.

Needed: a proper 'mix' of temperature, gravity, atmosphere, and liquid. This isn't a treatise in Biology 101, but it is obvious that, for a celestial body to support life, it must have a surface temperature spread similar to Earth's, and enough gravity to maintain an atmosphere and keep liquids from boiling off into space. Can these conditions be met elsewhere in our solar system and—if not in our solar system—elsewhere in the universe?

Possibilities of life on other celestial bodies in our solar system. We can erase Mercury, Pluto, the asteroids, and most planetary satellites, since they neither have an atmosphere nor the capacity to hold one. Besides, Mercury is too hot, as is Venus. Thanks to ultraviolet bombardment, Mars is antiseptic. Titan has an atmosphere, but its surface is too cold to support life. Regarding the warm, soup-like interiors of outwardly frigid Jupiter, Saturn, and Uranus, opinions are split. There *may* be a deep-down layer of water in each of these gas giants: water containing all needed chemical ingredients to sustain viable life-forms.

Life is probably common throughout the universe. Scientists estimate that in our Milky Way alone millions of stars have habitable planets.

See *habitable zone, square cube law,* and *intelligent life other than man.*

life support system. (Astronautics.) Because 'It's a cruel universe out there,' *life support system* refers to any of various fail-safe methodologies for sustaining human life, as well as mental and physical health, in a non-Earth environment. Complications grow by orders-of-magnitude in proportion to the duration of space missions or space colonization. Basically, whatever system is employed depends, to a great degree, on re-utilizing and recycling—either chemically or via photosynthesis—whatever usable material is available. Atmospheric condensate, exhaled carbon dioxide, urine, and other metabolic waste matter must be converted back into oxygen, drinking water, and edibles. Elaborate subsystems must control pressure, temperature, humidity, and other comfort requirements. Intellectual, recreational, psychological, and sociological needs must be provided for so neuroses and psychoses don't burgeon. Compare with *controlled leakage system.* See *algae and space travel, hydroponics, space suit, space colonies, breakaway phenomenon, atmospheric revitalization system, bioastronautics,* and *space hazards to the psyche.*

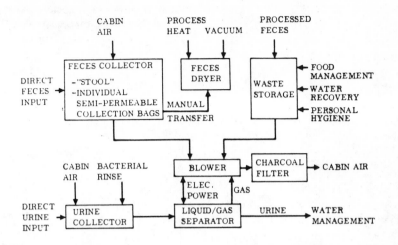

Most people secretly wonder how cosmonauts eliminate, or 'go to the bathroom,' during prolonged space flights. What happens to the inevitable waste products? The diagram above shows what takes place. (For relationship to water management and the habitability system, see page 113.)

The installed waste management subsystem is comprised of three basic modules. One contains components for both the collection and drying of feces and the collection and transport of urine. The other two are identical waste storage assemblies. Both collectors employ a ducted air stream to direct waste materials into collectors under zero-g, and to minimize cabin odors.

The fecal collection assembly resembles a conventional toilet stool with provisions for collection of solid waste in a semi-permeable bag through which the velocity air stream passes. Feces are vacuum-heat dried in either of two drying chambers located within the basic module. Following drying, feces still contained in the collection bag are placed in the storage assembly.

Urine is collected from crew members in a modified aircraft-type relief tube through which cabin air is drawn to facilitate transport of the urine to a liquid-gas separator. The separator, in turn, pumps the air-free urine to the water management subsystem. (Again, see page 113.)

lift-drift ratio. (Fiction.) The positional relationship of a stalled space ship to the gravitational pull of nearby asteroids.

liftoff. (Astronautics.) Same as blast-off or launch.

liftolite. (Fiction.) A putty-like substance that falls upward, made of magnetium fulminate and tetra-heliumite.

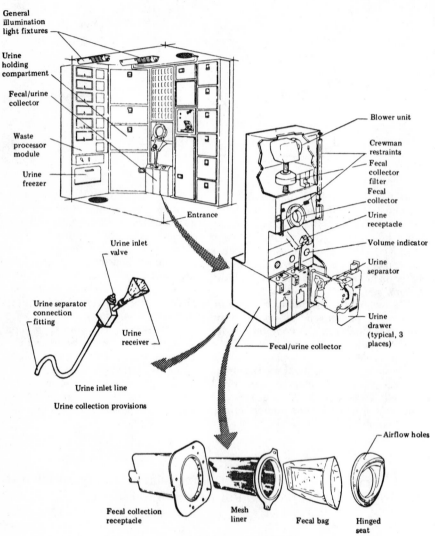

General illumination light fixtures

Urine holding compartment

Fecal/urine collector

Waste processor module

Urine freezer

Entrance

Blower unit

Crewman restraints

Fecal collector filter

Fecal collector

Urine receptacle

Volume indicator

Urine separator

Urine drawer (typical, 3 places)

Urine inlet valve

Urine separator connection fitting

Urine receiver

Urine inlet line

Urine collection provisions

Fecal/urine collector

Airflow holes

Fecal collection receptacle

Mesh liner

Fecal bag

Hinged seat

Fecal collector exploded view

light ray audio transmission. (Fiction.) A method of space-ship-to-space-ship or space-ship-to-planet communication. The result is a solidified light transcription disc run through a decoder so sophisticated it's said to be able to 'unscramble eggs.'

lightsaber. (Fiction.) A brilliant, blue-white beam, a trifle more than a meter in length, as thick as a man's thumb, activated when certain controls are depressed on a short, thick handgrip. Deadly as a face-to-face weapon, it slices anything in half with the ease of a knife sliding through whipped cream. Depicted by George Lucas in *Star Wars*.

light signature. (Fiction.) A known, unique, pre-recorded electro-magnetic configuration of a particular segment of any star field. Sought out, via automatic scanning, as a navigational coordinate so a space ship can maintain accurate bearings in interstellar travel.

lightspeed ship. (Fiction.) A space ship that travels at the speed of light: 186,284 miles-per-second.

light year. (Astronomy.) The distance light travels in one year: 5,878 trillion miles, roughly a third of a *parsec* (which see).

liquid air gun. (Fiction.) A cannon-like weapon used to shoot rocket shrapnel at enemy space ships.

liquid coal. (Fiction.) A viscous, greasy, combustible substance found on Mars.

liquid helium. (Fiction.) The liquid drunk by certain humanoids on Jupiter in place of ordinary water, because even ice water would burn their lips and tongues.

liquid luminate. (Fiction.) The type of fuel constituting the cargo of interplanetary oil tankers, which are sometimes referred to as space tramps.

liquid hydrogen. (Astronautics.) The lightest propellant used in space travel. One gallon weighs six-tenths of a pound. (An identical volume of kerosene weighs eight pounds.) Because liquid hydrogen is super cold, all space ship components contacting it must be heavily insulated. This entails double-walled piping for fuel lines, with a vaccum interface. Valves must be protected with fittings surrounded by a pump-maintained insulating vacuum.

liquid oxygen. (Astronautics.) A rocket fuel commercially called LOX. Must be kept at 300 degrees below zero Fahrenheit to prevent it from boiling away.

locator beam. (Fiction.) Also called a magna locator. A beam, activated by a parked space ship, that enables crew members to explore unknown terrain without fear of getting lost regarding the ship. It emits a periodic signal inaudible to those who don't wear special-frequency helmet earphones.

Lorentz-Fitzgerald contraction. (Physics.) Also called the Lorentz transformation. Along with most aspects of relativity, it is as difficult to comprehend as radiation simultaneously acting as a wave and as a particle, the characteristics of black holes and neutron stars, or any other esoteric 'reality' phenomena that make wildly imaginative flights of fancy as prosaic as automotive parts catalogues.

Moving bodies are shortened in the direction of motion. The Lorentz equations state that bodies are deformed by motion, with a

According to the Lorentz-Fitzgerald contraction, a moving body approaching lightspeed velocity shortens itself in the direction of motion. A person so shortened would be unaware that he was compressing in depth to micro-thin proportions and spreading out like a pancake in width and height. These startling effects would be detectable only to an observer in a stationary frame of reference removed from the affected individual.

concomitant slowing down of apparent time. The physical shrinkage and temporal slowdown, however, are obvious only to an observer in a frame of reference that is stationary and removed from the moving body. And only when bodies approach lightspeed are such relativistic effects discernible. At ordinary speeds, detectable telescoping of objects, and time dilation, are virtually nil, though these effects have been documented with elementary particles.

The greater the speed, the greater the contraction. If a yardstick moved at 90 percent lightspeed, it would shrink to roughly half its length. As its velocity continued to increase, its contraction would accelerate. Should the stick actually attain lightspeed, it would shrivel to zero, length-wise. (Compare this with the reference below that its mass would concurrently increase.) A clock traveling at light-speed would cease ticking and come to a dead stop.

The velocity of light is the universal constant. Despite fictional references to warp factors and supralight travel, nothing in the universe apparently moves faster than the speed of light, no matter what forces are applied. Lorentz transformation equations enshrine light-speed as the universal constant. (This doesn't mean poetic license shouldn't be employed for the sake of effect, or that speculation should cease.)

How an object can simultaneously get shorter and heavier. According to relativity, a moving body's mass—relative to an observer in a non-moving frame of reference—increases with velocity. This seems to contradict the fact that a yardstick traveling at light speed would shrivel to zero length, but it doesn't. Width and breadth wouldn't shrivel. Instead, infinite 'sideways' and 'up-and-down' mass would be attained. So limited is the conceptual capacity of the human mind that all one can conjure up mentally at this point is a type of enormous, micro-thin pancake.

Effects of these phenomena on a space traveler. Would a space traveler experience length shrinkage, mass increase, and time retardation? No. Everything would appear normal *to him.* Perception-wise, he wouldn't notice that his heart would be beating slower than a hibernating chipmunk's (if at all), that his physical proportions had altered, or that the hands of his watch were 'frozen.'

See *relativity, paradox of the twins, time dilation, time slippage,* and *mass.*

low shock power. (Fiction.) One of the settings on a paralysis ray pistol.

M

Mach number. (Astronautics.) Sometimes abbreviated to 'M.' A number representing the ratio of a spacecraft's speed to the speed of sound. Sonic speed—Mach 1—is 760-miles-per-hour at sea level (the speed of sound decreases with altitude). Progressively, a spacecraft moving at five times the speed of sound is traveling at Mach 5; at ten times the speed of sound at Mach 10; and so on.

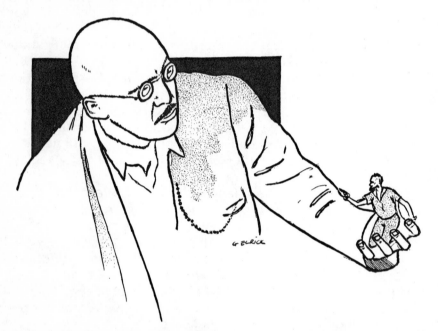

'Mad scientists'—usually with thick German accents, even thicker spectacles, and an unholy passion for tampering with human flesh—perpetrated foul deeds in early science fiction horror movies, Stone Age science fiction pulps, and repulsively lurid comic books. Their dark laboratories, situated in decaying mansions, featured crackling machines and bubbling test tubes. Even if, through some slip-up in their genes, they momentarily meant well, dull-witted assistants invariably slipped pickled criminal brains into the wrong skull cases. Most cinematic mad scientists were delightfully psychotic. To pursue their vivisection-like studies, they needed an endless supply of virgins' blood or spinal fluid from kidnapped brides. Pictured is Albert Dekker, as Doctor Cyclops, after using radium rays to reduce some unfortunate to doll size. The mad scientist represented plot conflict to yesterday's uneducated man. Today he's as extinct as the passenger pigeon.

Mackenwald distorter. See *time travel.*

macrobinoculars. (Fiction.) Wide-angle binoculars with intensely powerful lenses.

mad scientist. (Fiction.) A stock character in early 20th Century science fiction, particularly in movies, pulp magazines, and comic strips. He usually has a beautiful daughter chastely desired by the stalwart protagonist.

Magellanic clouds. (Astronomy.) A pair of small, irregular galaxies, roughly 60 kiloparsecs away, regarded as spatial companions of the Milky Way.

magic eye. (Fiction.) A self-protecting, hidden, beam-emitting device used by space pirates on certain planetoids. Any human or humanoid on foot, who accidentally passes through its emission and breaks the circuit, triggers a blast from a concealed death ray gun.

magna-detector. (Fiction.) A sensory gauge in a submersible rocket ship. Picks up the presence of sunken metallic craft.

magna-gamma proto-neutralizer. (Fiction.) A hand-held device that enables one to safely enter a radioactive room and avoid contamination. The person holding the device is temporarily covered with Saint Elmo's light, caused by electro-beta particles absorbing each other.

magna-soli-ray missile. (Fiction.) Also called a permalite bomb or magnetic death bomb. At an appropriate time, it is fired from a space ship as a beam of 'chemical light.' Starting as a ray, it solidifies—after ten miles—into a super-explosive magnetic bomb hurtling through space at 82,000 miles-per-hour, attracted to the nearest metal field of attraction: hopefully an enemy spacecraft.

magna-sonic fix. (Fiction.) A space ship viewplate gauge that 'cross-hairs' the position of another spacecraft.

magnetic drift. (Fiction.) The force of charged interstellar particles: an attraction—however so slight—for metallic bodies that's a factor in space ship navigation.

magnetic grapples. (Fiction.) Large-circumference magnetic plates, at the ends of long tubes shooting out from a space ship's underside, that immobilize another spacecraft on contact, providing the latter has a metallic surface.

magnetic neutralizer. (Fiction.) A device that—in conjunction with turned-off lights and power—makes a space ship difficult to detect if a hostile spacecraft is trying to find it.

magnetic projector. (Fiction.) Used by space gangsters. An enormous, searchlight-type projector mounted on a swivel base on an artificially cloud-shrouded small planet. Projects demon-like images into space, to confuse ships, then pulls them downward by magnetic force, so they can be looted.

magnetic ray. (Fiction.) Also called M-ray. Establishes a momentary, extremely powerful electromagnetic field. When properly broad-focused on hostile space ships, the ray makes them crash together.

magnetic shoes. (Fiction.) Shoes that prevent one from drifting off into space when exploring the exterior of an enemy space ship or a derelict space ship.

magnetic towline. (Fiction.) Also called a magnetic tow ray. A carefully focused magnetic force used by one space ship to tow another behind it.

magnetic vibration cycle. (Fiction.) Used, in conjunction with a known space zone, to pinpoint the presence of an oncoming distant space ship.

magneto gravity generator. (Fiction.) Also called a magneto gravitator. A power supply that makes 'down' a point inside a space ship's base, preventing the haphazard tumbling about of free fall in a weightless environment.

magnetohydrodynamics. (Physics.) The interaction between an ionized gas and a magnetic field.

magnetosphere. (Astronomy.) A planetary magnetic field that strongly affects charged particle movements and deflects solar wind. See *solar wind*.

magnetum ore. (Fiction.) A type of metal sometimes used to counterbalance the reverse-weight effect of inertron.

magni bomb. (Fiction.) An unsportsmanlike device used by rocket ship dog-fighters who lack a sense of honor or integrity. If, in an aerial or planetary atmospheric one-to-one battle, one is downed by the other, he can always project a magni bomb at the supposed victor. The magnetic apparatus will then trail, close in on the supposedly 'winning' ship, and blow it to bits.

magnitude. (Astronomy.) Also called apparent magnitude. A logarithmic measure of a celestial body's brightness. The smaller the number, the brighter the object.

magno-locater needle. (Fiction.) A gauge attached to a cannon-like disintegrator gun, revealing the presence and position of distant metallic targets, even when they're out of sight range.

magno ray. (Fiction.) A magnetic ray used to moor a space ship in a fixed position above the Earth, another planet, or an asteroid.

main propulsion unit. (Fiction.) An engine that uses matter and antimatter for propulsion. Contact between contrasting particles results in instant annihilation and a tremendous energy release. (Star Trek.) See *warp factor*.

One of Mars's mountains—a volcanic cone—is twelve miles high: two-thirds larger than the island of Hawaii.

main stabilizer fin. (Fiction.) A space ship protuberance resembling a shark's or killer whale's dorsal fin, gyro-stabilized to keep the vehicle from pitching and yawing.

mainstream literature. (Generic.) Non-science fiction literature.

mantle. (Generic.) The outer portion of a planet's interior, just beneath its crust and just above its core.

mare. (Astronomy.) A flat, dark region on the moon's surface, normally round in outline.

marriage by tele-radio. (Fiction.) A legal method of formalizing and sanctifying marital vows when lovers are in a space ship far from Earth.

Mars . . . as it really is. (Astronomy.) One of the so-called terrestrial planets: the fourth celestial body from the sun, orbiting in an oval path at an average distance of 141,640,000 miles. Due to its distinctive reddish color, and the fact that it is essentially cloud-free, it is the easiest planet to observe.

Size: Its diameter is 4,200 miles, slightly more than half the Earth's; its total surface two-sevenths the Earth's; its volume one-seventh the Earth's; and its mass one-ninth the Earth's. However, its 56-million-square mile surface equals Earth's over-all land area.

Density and composition: Mars's chemical composition is similar to that of the Earth and Venus, but its density is lower because there is less gravitational inward-squeezing. However, its density isn't as low as the moon's.

Temperature: Since Mars has a desert climate, it experiences wide temperature-scale shifts. Mid-day summer temperature at the equatorial surface is 70 degrees Fahrenheit. A few yards up it's below freezing, thanks to the thin atmosphere. At night, the temperature plummets to nearly 150 degrees below zero. In addition to the thin atmosphere, there are two reasons for this: no oceans modify the extremes, and the red planet, being farther from the sun than is the Earth, receives less sunlight.

Atmosphere: Extremely rarefied, comparable to Earth's at an altitude of 20 miles. Unlike Earth's, which is basically oxygen and nitrogen, it is almost pure carbon dioxide, with such minute traces of water vapor that, were the latter condensed, it would cover the planet with a film only a few thousandths of an inch thick. In short, the humidity of Mars resembles that of extremely dry central Arabia. Because of this, whispy white clouds are rare, and, except near the

158

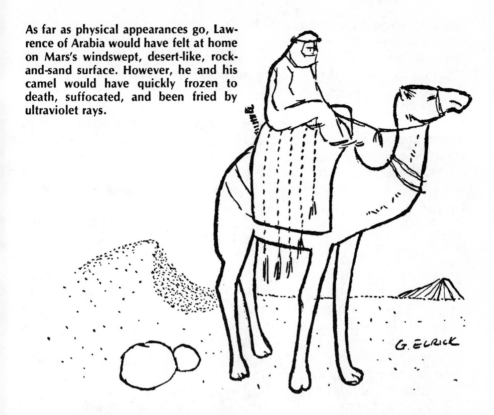

As far as physical appearances go, Lawrence of Arabia would have felt at home on Mars's windswept, desert-like, rock-and-sand surface. However, he and his camel would have quickly frozen to death, suffocated, and been fried by ultraviolet rays.

G. ELRICK

surface, the atmosphere is crystal clear. (See reference to dust storms and sand storms below.)

Since there is no protective layer of ozone overhead, deadly ultraviolet rays slam down unblocked. If the same situation existed on Earth, life as we know it would cease. (Hospitals use ultraviolet radiation as a germicide.)

Surface conditions and features. Mars is a bastardization of the Oklahoma 'Dust Bowl' of the 1930's crossed with a Sahara sand storm. Winds blast across its cratered face, depositing quantities of vari-colored dust and sand here, there, and everywhere. What formerly were considered areas of colorful vegetation are really areas of chromatic mineral matter. There are bright patches predominantly orange-ocher in hue; and darker areas predominantly orange-gray in hue. Some of these regions boast gigantic sand dunes.

As is the case with Mercury and the moon, the terrain is rough and heavily pocked by meteors on one side; relatively flat and smooth on the other. In some places, craters have been erased, eroded, and

159

replaced by jumbled ridges. High mountains—actually giant, extinct volcanoes—poke their cones skyward. One towers twelve miles: two-thirds larger than the island of Hawaii.

Brilliantly white polar caps dominate each end of the axis. More meteorological than geographical, they seasonally spread and shrink. The south cap vanishes completely at the southern summer's peak, but the north cap's hub never melts. Astronomers believe both caps are frozen carbon dioxide, probably mixed with ice, though the frozen water is conjectural.

Yet there may have been a considerable amount of liquid something-or-other on Mars at one time, because of winding canyons, apparently cut by rivers, and what seem to be tributary stream beds. The planet possibly experiences periodic warming trends when the polar caps melt and the atmosphere is dense and soggy rather than thin and dry.

Seasons: Mars has seasons similar to the Earth's, though each is roughly twice as long, since the Martian year is approximately double ours. Vegetation doesn't change quarterly, because there is no known plant life, but windblown dust and sand deposits do. Paralleling the Earth, each hemisphere alternately receives the lion's share of sunshine, but Mars's orbit is eccentric, so the planet receives 50 percent more sunlight at perihelion than at aphelion.

Possibilities of life: At present, practically none, due to the absence of water and the presence of ultraviolet radiation. (See *life: seeming requirements of.*) What happens when, and if, the planet periodically becomes wet rather than dry is anyone's guess.

Perils to spacemen: A human wearing a complex space suit could survive. Without a space suit, it would be the 'deep six' in a few thumb-snaps. According to Frederik Pohl, in *Man Plus*, an unprotected, air-breathing, water-based creature like man wouldn't last fifteen minutes. His blood would boil away because of extremely low atmospheric pressure . . . and while his blood boiled he'd concurrently strangle. If he wore an oxygen-supplying face mask and his blood didn't boil, ultraviolet radiation would fry him. If he were shielded against radiation, sub-arctic night-time cold would crystallize him. If he were protected against *that*, he'd soon perish from thirst and hunger, since there wouldn't be a drop of water to sip or a sliver of edible food to munch. As the saying goes, without a space suit and its accoutrements, 'better he should stay home.'

Rotation: The Martian day almost duplicates Earth's. Mars turns on its axis once every 24½ hours.

Orbital period. 687 days.

Satellites: Mars has two: Phobos and Deimos, meaning Fear and Terror. Both are tiny, irregularly shaped, cratered rocks. They orbit relatively close to the planet's surface near its equatorial plane. Oddly, Phobos revolves faster than Mars rotates.

Gravity: Earth = 1. Mars = 0.39.

Mars and/or Martians . . . as depicted in early pulp magazine-type science fiction. The red planet has an atmosphere like Earth's, pale, greenish-yellow sunshine, jagged mountain ranges of crystal clear quartz, vast deserts, large metropolitan areas, and jungle regions with bizarre plants and enormous flowers.

The surface of one of the deserts is so hot that flames crackle on the sand.

Enormous canals, ten to twenty miles wide, form intricate patterns. These waterways feature periodic pumping stations.

Mars and/or Martians . . . as depicted by semi-modern and modern science fiction novelists. *H. G. Wells,* in *The War of the Worlds,* depicts a Martian as follows:

A big grayish rounded bulk, the size, perhaps, of a bear, was rising slowly and painfully out of the cylinder. As it bulged up and caught the light, it glistened like wet leather.

Two large, dark-colored eyes were regarding me steadfastly. The mass that framed them, the head of the thing, was rounded, and had, one might say, a face. There was a mouth under the eyes, the lipless brim of which quivered and panted, and dropped saliva. The whole creature heaved and pulsated convulsively. A lank, tentacular appendage gripped the edge of the cylinder, another swayed in the air.

Those who have never seen a living Martian can scarcely imagine the strange horror of its appearance. The peculiar V-shaped mouth with its pointed upper lip, the absence of brow ridges, the absence of a chin beneath the wedgelike lower lip, the incessant quivering of this mouth, the Gorgon group of tentacles, the tumultuous breathing of the lungs in a strange atmosphere. There was something fungoid in the oily brown skin.

Wells also describes the 'sword of heat' used by Martians. The sword actually is 'a ghost of a beam of light' flickering from a ray gun. Focused by a curved mirror, it drops men and horses in their tracks, and ignites anything combustible.

Edgar Rice Burroughs calls Mars *Barsoom,* and depicts its peculiarities in eleven novels. To encapsulate Burroughs would require pages, so the following extreme telescoping is simply a sip from a barrel of head-twisting wine.

Physically, much of Barsoom is falling apart, like Rome before the Vandals sacked it. Many of its cities are deserted ruins; and most of its seas are evaporating, leaving dried-out, moss-covered basins. Yet certain glories remain. There's the River Iss, the Valley Dorr, the Lost Sea of Korus, the incredible mountains and valleys of Otz, and the mysterious Sea of Omean. Crowning it all, Thuria, one of Mars's moons, still has vast mountains of platinum and gold, plus huge

Crimson-skinned, egg-laying Deja Thoris.

G. ELRICK

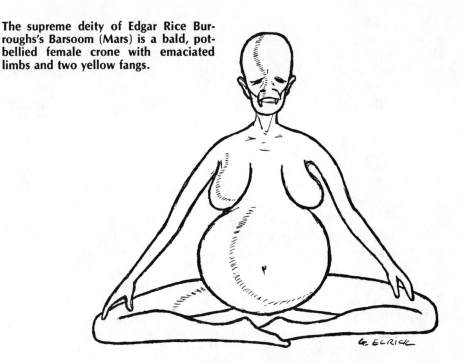

The supreme deity of Edgar Rice Burroughs's Barsoom (Mars) is a bald, pot-bellied female crone with emaciated limbs and two yellow fangs.

plains carpeted with precious stones. (Contrast this with the second-rate real thing: tiny Phobos and Deimos.)

Beautiful women who lay eggs. The populace of Barsoom rivals anything out of L. Frank Baum's *Oz* or *Grimm's Fairy Tales.* A variety of human or humanoid races, all with different-colored skins, hate each others' guts with a passion. Each racial nation has its own unique religion, gods, and science. No male or female Martian—unless a slave—ever voluntarily walks, hulks, or slinks around without a weapon of destruction. Whatever the skin or hair color, average life expectancy is 300 years. This could be stretched to the thousand-year mark, except that most meet violent, messy deaths. All Martian women lay eggs (thirteen a year), but this barnyard trait doesn't stop them from enthusiastically mating with Earthmen.

Black-skinned Martians are delusionally like Hitler's super race: the 'First Born of Barsoom.' Unlike World War II Germans, they're an aristocracy living luxuriously in an inner world under Mars's surface. Deliberately non-productive, they've decreed it a crime for anyone with ebony skin to labor or think. Reveling in prolonged idleness, they're waited upon by shapely female slaves: kidnapped princesses of other Martian races. Their supreme deity—and, by extrapolation, the supreme deity of all Barsoom—is an ancient, pot-bellied female black with emaciated limbs, a hairless head, and a mouth that's toothless except for two yellow fangs.

Brains the size of a Boston baked bean. Red-skinned Martians are notable for producing curvaceous, intellectual Deja Thoris, Princess of Helium, who marries Earthman John Carter. Green-skinned Martians are famed for being fifteen feet tall and having four arms. White-skinned Martians are 'dirty old men,' yet, strangely enough, keep naked, fifteen-year-old Thuvia as a virgin plaything. Yellow-skinned Martians dwell in the Carrion Caves up north, at the entranceway to which they pile dead bodies and garbage, so the stench will drive intruders away. Plant men are bisexual, like true vegetables, have brains the size of a Boston baked bean, and are frightful foes in battle because they lack a sense of self-preservation. Great white apes and Holy Therns are always there in the background if things get dull.

Burroughs's typically imaginative bestiary includes *soraks*, which are cat-size pet animals favored by Red-skinned Martian women; *calots*, which are Martian dogs; *thoats*, which are green Martian 'horses'; *zitidars*, which are draft animals resembling mastodons; *siths*, which are bald-faced hornets the size of a prize Hereford bull; and *apts*, which are enormous, white-furred creatures with six limbs, four of which are for locomotion and two of which, in the shape of arms with hairless hands, are used for grasping prey.

C. S. Lewis, in *Out of the Silent Planet,* refers to Mars as *Malacandra*. It's a world strikingly different from Burrough's Barsoom: philosophically and esthetically dignified.

In its highlands—where breathing is difficult—Malacandra displays tall, needle-like mountains, plus great patchworks of green and red rock. Its valleys harbor indigo-blue warm-water lakes; pink, resilient groundweed; and purple vegetables twice the height of trees, shaped like enormous umbrellas blown inside out. In both regions the air is cold, but not abrasive.

Three highly intelligent, but scarcely humanoid, species inhabit Malacandra: *sorns, hrosses,* and *pfiftriggi.*

Covered with creamy white feathers, *sorns* are eighteen feet high; have spindly, bird-like legs; top-heavy, pigeon-breasted chests; narrow conical heads; elongated, droopy-mouthed faces; fan-shaped, seven-fingered hands; and foghorn-deep voices.

Hrosses dwell in or near water; are six feet high when erect; resemble black-coated, skinny hybridizations of penguins, seals, beavers, and otters; and have basketball-round heads with tiny mouths.

Pfiftriggi live in caves; are the size of German shepherds; enjoy digging; soften what they dig with fire, so they can sculpture it, and also sculpture in stone. More freakish in appearance than the other two species, they're tapir-headed and frog-bodied, with long fore-limbs.

Ray Bradbury, in his sinister, allegorical *The Martian Chronicles,* gives Mars the outward appearance of McKinley-era America, replete with white wooden houses, red brick cottages, church steeples, green lawns, gingerbread architecture, and a plethora of stained glass windows.

Martian meridian. (Fiction.) A point of reference used in space travel.

Martian scourge squad. (Fiction.) Martians who torture captured Earthmen in unspeakable ways.

maser. (Physics.) Acronym for Microwave Amplification by Stimulated Emission of Radiation. An apparatus that converts incident electromagnetic radiation from a broad frequency range to one or more discrete frequencies of highly amplified, coherent, microwave radiation. Compare with *laser.*

mass. (Physics.) A fundamental quantity of physics: a measure of the total amount of material in a body, and a measure of that body's inertia, or resistance to change of motion or acceleration. Unlike weight, from which it is different but to which it is proportional, mass is not dependent on the force of gravity at the site of measurement. According to relativity, a body's mass increases with velocity. See *relativity* and *Lorentz-Fitzgerald contraction.*

mass-energy equation. (Physics.) Einstein's famous formula: $E = mc^2$, meaning a body's mass is a measure of its energy content. See *matter and energy: equivalence of.*

mass ratio. (Astronautics.) Weight-wise, the vast differential between a launch vehicle's massive poundage and the lesser poundage of its payload. See *payload.*

master slave driver. (Fiction.) A radio-controlled robot, fixed in one position, with the capability of swinging a mining pick locked in its metallic hands. Electroplated human or humanoid slaves, tuned in to its pick-swinging motions, helplessly duplicate them.

mate/demate. (Astronautics.) A device for engaging or disengaging a piggyback-riding orbiter. Used in the so-called 'mated taxi' phases of a mission.

matter and energy: equivalence of. (Physics.) Einstein said that matter is a kind of frozen energy; that the two are interchangeable; that the distinction is simply one of temporary state. When matter sheds mass and travels at the speed of light, it is referred to as radiation or energy. When energy thickens and assumes a different form, it is referred to as matter. See *mass, mass-energy equation,* and *relativity.*

matter: what causes properties of. (Physics.) Color, hardness or softness, plus chemical characteristics, are determined by the way electron wave patterns in atoms interact with electromagnetic radiation.

maximum entropy. (Generic.) The postulate that the universe and all its phenomena are gradually, but inexorably, winding down; that the sun will sputter out, as will all the stars; that electromagnetic radiation is fizzling away; and that, eventually, every natural process will shuffle to a halt in an ultimate 'heat death.' No energy will remain; all space will be the same temperature; there'll be no light, life, or warmth; and time itself will cease. See *entropy* and *time.*

Max Q. (Astronautics.) Short for Maximum Q: the period of greatest strain on a space vehicle immediately following launch . . . reached when the spacecraft's velocity equals the speed of sound, accompanied by a sonic boom and shock wave.

mech. (Fiction.) Also referred to as mek, or mekkano, it has two meanings: (1) a robot or automaton; (2) a robot or automaton technician.

mechanical claw. (Fiction.) A large, expanding and contracting claw-like device extendable from an opening at a space ship's bottom. Used to pick up objects and unwilling victims, such as shrieking nymphets.

mechanical hand. (Fiction.) An expanding, multi-clawed artificial hand directed, cantilever fashion, from the nozzle of a device closely resembling a disintegrator pistol. Used to physically detain someone at a considerable distance.

medical tricorder. (Fiction.) A hand-held apparatus that has two functions: (1) it selectively measures, compares, and diagnoses vital clues regarding alien life forms; (2) it senses, measures, and compares environmental health conditions. (*Star Trek.*)

mega-gravitational push-pull power. (Fiction.) Replacing ordinary rocket power, this force multiplies, or entirely screens out, gravity's pull, then alternately activates reverse gravity.

megaparsec. (Astronomy.) A million parsecs. See *parsec.*

memorator. (Fiction.) A pocket-size apparatus for recording on-the-spot memos. (*Star Trek.*)

mentaloscope. (Fiction.) A memory-probing device that tunes in on cerebral frequencies, then projects motion picture-like images on a screen. Normally used only after the administration of a sleep ray. See *sleep ray projector.*

Mercury . . . as it really is. (Astronomy.) Smallest of the so-called terrestrial planets, and the celestial body closest to the sun, with a mean distance of only 36.2 million miles.

Size: Its radius is roughly 1,500 miles, less than half the Earth's, and its mass is slightly over one-twentieth the Earth's.

Density and composition: Mercury, with its rocky mantle and iron core, has a density approaching Earth's though its internal pressure is much lower, due to its smaller dimensions. The reason for this seeming discrepancy is that it contains more iron than does the Earth, Venus, or Mars, the other three terrestrial planets. It has a small magnetic field.

Temperature: Because of proximity to the sun, its searing surface temperature hovers between 500 and 770 degrees Fahrenheit: hot enough to melt lead and tin. Venus also has a red-hot surface, but Mercury is the solar system's heat champion.

Surface conditions: Since it lacks atmospheric protection against downward-slamming meteors, and experiences no erosion, its bare, rocky surface is pocked like the moon's, complete with pits, scarps, and extensive plains. One side of the planet is more cratered than the other.

Mercury's searingly hot surface is pitted and pock-marked like the surface of Earth's moon, and for the same reason: there's no atmosphere to burn up downward-slamming meteors.

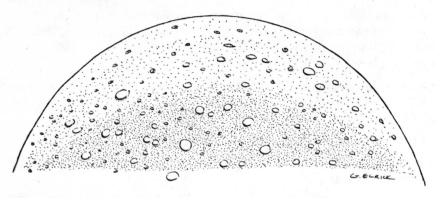

Atmosphere: Mercury has none, because of high surface temperature and low gravity.

Rotation: In every two revolutions around the sun, Mercury spins precisely three times on its axis.

Orbital period: 88 days.

Satellites: None.

Gravity: Earth = 1. Mercury = 0.38.

Mercury and/or Mercurians . . . as depicted in early pulp magazine-type science fiction. The tiny planet has mountain ranges, freshwater lakes, trees, shrubbery, and a torrential underground river. It also has a blue moon.

Because Mercurians love solitude, and emphatically dislike associating with people from other planets, they avoid building cities. There are less than a thousand families on the planet, and they live as far apart as possible.

Backwoods natives of the Caliban Hills will commit murder to get a chocolate bar capsule.

Mercury and/or Mercurians . . . as depicted by a modern science fiction novelist. Arthur C. Clarke, in *Rendezvous with Rama*, states that most solar system inhabitants consider Mercury a replica of Hell. However, Mercurians—known as Hermians—are proud of the planet's double sunrises and sunsets, and its molten metal rivers.

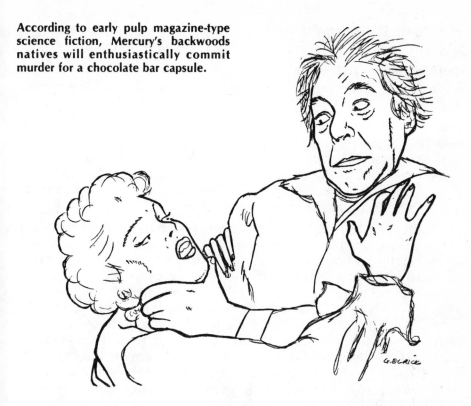

According to early pulp magazine-type science fiction, Mercury's backwoods natives will enthusiastically commit murder for a chocolate bar capsule.

Thanks to its closeness to the sun, plus its metallic and heavy-element composition, Mercury is a source of unlimited energy and metal. Via enormous magnetic launchers, Hermians catapult manufactured products to purchasers throughout the solar system. They also export energy in the form of synthetic transuranium isotopes of pure radiation.

metal cloth. (Fiction.) Protects its wearer against the debilitating effects of a *de-energizing rod* (which see) by short-circuiting the latter's force.

metalloglass. (Fiction.) Glass with the strength of stainless steel: a basic constituent of atmosphere domes. It is used to contain and confine atmospheric pressure and livable temperatures in antiseptically enclosed cities, as well as to keep out bacteria.

metallo-scope. (Fiction.) A space ship device that electronically sniffs out the whereabouts of any nearby spacecraft the identity of which is unknown.

metallo-sonic detector. (Fiction.) A super-sensitive sensor that can pick up the slightest sound through ten feet of solid metal.

metal softening paste. (Fiction.) A purple-colored colloid that, when rubbed on a metal such as steel, softens it to the pliability of wet macaroni.

meteor. (Astronomy.) Also called a meteoroid. Any of numerous solid celestial objects moving through interplanetary space, ranging in size from specks slightly bulkier than dust granules to asteroids. When a meteor's stony or metallic substance survives flaming passage through the atmosphere and smacks the Earth's surface, it is known as a meteorite. See *meteorite* and *carbonaceous chrondites.*

meteorite. (Astronomy.) A meteor large enough to survive downward passage through the Earth's ever-thickening atmosphere without being totally consumed, though it is likely to have a fusion crust caused by friction's searing heat. Meteorites are 4.6 billion years old; more ancient than the Earth or other planets in the solar system. Thousands have been found on the ground, ranging from lightweight pebble-size objects to misshapen clumps of stone, iron, or a mixture of both, weighing several tons. The genesis of some may be solid material from the nuclei of old, disintegrated comets, but most are small asteroids whose orbits have criss-crossed the Earth's due to perturbation. See *asteroids, perturbation,* and *fusion crust.*

meteor shower. (Astronomy.) Also called a meteor swarm: meteors that group together like buckshot. Frequently a stream of debris from an old comet, with all particle fragments having roughly parallel trajectories. The particles occasionally enter Earth's atmosphere with a spectacular fireworks display.

methusaleh enzyme. (Fiction.) A biochemical catalyst that prevents the typical cross-linking in genes that speeds up aging. Gene cross-linking causes molecules, and therefore the entire organism, to function below par. The methusaleh enzyme—so named because it enables an individual to prolong his life indefinitely—dissolves unwanted cross-links between molecules. A space ship crew periodically injected with this laboratory-produced substance could traverse space for thousands of years, facing only the peril of boredom, the threat of mind-squashing claustrophobia, or the danger of getting on each other's nerves unendurably. As a means of sustaining starship life, compare with *egg ship* and *sleeper ship.*

Every day 75 million sporadic meteoric bodies 'flame out' in the Earth's atmosphere, but these don't constitute meteor showers. The latter are swarms of meteors, orbiting the sun, that sometimes slice across the Earth's own orbit. A meteor swarm can pose a hazard to a spacecraft, puncturing its living quarters and causing personnel-damaging decompression. Fortunately, the parameters-of-motion of most swarms are known quantities. Spacecraft trajectories are carefully selected to avoid them.

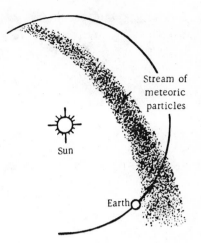

Stream of meteoric particles

Sun

Earth

micro-ultronic detector. (Fiction.) A sensing device that picks up the whereabouts—by pinpointing force vibrations—of a space ship that has just been destroyed.

microvac. (Generic.) A miniaturized analog computer. See *analog computer.*

microwave. (Physics.) The shortest-wavelength, highest-frequency portion of the radio segment of the electromagnetic spectrum: the boundary between short-wave radio wavelengths and infrared wavelengths. See *electromagnetic spectrum.*

midcourse guidance. (Astronautics.) Any type of selected guidance applied to a spacecraft between the end of its launching phase and the beginning of its terminal guidance phase.

midget disintegrator. (Fiction.) A tiny, hand-held de-atomizing instrument used by interplanetary secret agents.

milk run. (Astronautics.) Slang for an uneventful space flight.

Milky Way. (Astronomy.) Our galaxy, in which the solar system is an infinitesimal speck. Its diameter is almost 800 million billion miles in length; it's roughly ten times as long as it is thick; light takes 120,000 years to travel from one end to the other; and it rotates like a stupendously large wheel. The Milky Way is composed of billions upon billions of stars, dark dust clouds, and gas.

The sun

The Milky Way is lens-shaped: thick in the middle and thin at the edges. Among other entities (see entry) it contains star clouds, star clusters, and star associations. A star cloud is an enormous area filled with individual stars scattered at random. A star cluster, normally found in a constellation, is either 'open' or globular, and contains a dense stellar concentration. A star association is less crowded than a cluster, is unstable, and contains stars with a common origin.

mini ray. (Fiction.) A tiny, but effective, disintegrator beam released from a tube no larger than a thick pencil.

mobile disintegrator. (Fiction.) A tunnel-creating, tractor-size, totally enclosed conveyance that can burrow underground like a giant mole.

module. (Astronautics.) A self-contained portion of a launch vehicle or spacecraft, doubling as a building block for the entire structure. Usually designated by its primary function, such as *command module* or *lunar landing module*.

Moebius strip. (Generic.) (Topology.) In a rather eerie way, a real-life parallel to the time-warp or space-warp concept: a one-sided surface that can be formed from a rectangular strip by rotating one end 180 degrees and attaching it to the other end. Compare with *Klein bottle*.

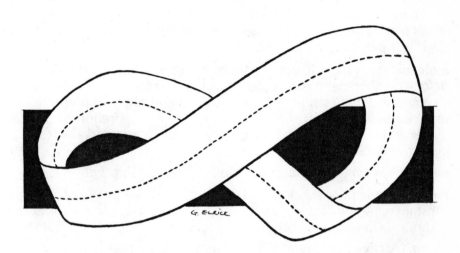

G. ELRICK

Science fiction authors sometimes rely on the mathematics of distortion (topology) to have a space ship zip from one part of the universe to another without wasting time. In doing so, they tend to use the Moebius strip principle, first exclaimed over by a German mathematician in the 17th Century. A Moebius strip absolutely defies common sense, but it's for real: an actual one-sided surface. A straight line traced along the center of this seemingly two-sided surface eventually arrives back at it starting point without crossing any 'edge' to get to the apparent other side. In fact, the quickest way to get from the starting point to the strip's half-way point is to push directly through. From a twisted paper strip to equally twisted spacetime is a short imaginative skip. To instantly blast to another part of the cosmos, a space ship simply plows straight though a warp or a 'gateway,' like a pencil point puncturing the Moebius strip's weird one-sided surface.

molecular disruptor. (Fiction.) A devastating ray used by space predators. When directed downward upon a 'sitting duck' spacecraft, it causes great cracks to occur in the latter, totally disabling it.

molecular permeator. (Fiction.) Also called a permeator ray or molecule separator. An apparatus that separates a solid wall's molecular structure—rearranging molecules so they offer no more resistance than gas—enabling a person to pass through unimpeded. When the device is clicked off, the wall re-solidifies. It can also be used to de-molecularize floors, dropping suspects into dungeons without the need to open trap doors.

molecule. (Physics.) Just as an atom is the smallest identifiable particle of an element, a molecule is the smallest identifiable particle of a compound that exhibits all the chemical and physical properties of that compound or substance. It is a stable configuration of atomic nuclei and electrons bound together by electrostatic and electromagnetic forces. See *atom*.

monitor screen. (Astronautics.) A type of space ship viewplate.

monopropellant. (Astronautics.) A rocket fuel comprised of a single substance, usually liquid, capable of producing a jet blast without the addition of a second substance.

moon. (Astronomy.) Generally, any natural satellite revolving around any planet. (For example, Saturn has either nine or ten moons.) Specifically, Earth's only natural satellite. Despite comedian Ernie Kovac's comment, 'Although the moon is smaller than the Earth, it is farther away,' our moon isn't as far away as most people believe: an average of 239,000 miles, or only thirty Earth-diameters.

Appearances to the contrary, the moon rotates on its axis. The moon doesn't hang in the sky like a silver coin with only one face turned toward the Earth: it spins on its axis. However, because its spin is precisely synchronized with its orbital revolution, we only *see* one face from the Earth.

Temperature extremes due to lack of atmosphere: In sunlit portions, the moon's surface temperature is higher than that of boiling water; in immediately adjacent portions, it is cold enough to crystallize an unprotected person's blood.

Other facts: The moon's gravity is one-sixth that of the Earth's; its diameter is 2,160 miles; and its mass is roughly one-eightieth that of the Earth's.

moon bug. (Fiction.) A small, plated, bird-like creature faintly re-sembling a duck. Its metabolism enables it to exist on the moon's airless surface; its shell-like plating holds it together in the absence of air pressure; and it hears via vibrations picked up through its feet. When captured and brought to Earth, it can only survive in a vacuum.

motion: first law of. (Physics.) A body at rest remains at rest unless acted on by an outside force; and a body in motion continues to move with the same velocity, in the same direction, unless acted on by an outside force.

motion: second law of. A moving body's velocity changes at a rate proportional to the forces acting on it. Also, the capacity of a force to accelerate a moving body is in inverse ratio to that body's mass.

Because the moon seems only a stone's throw away, early space travel stories centered on it as the target destination. Big-nosed Cyrano de Bergerac, 17th Century sword-fighter, poet, musician, and physicist, wrote wildly fanciful yarns about getting there and back. In one, he returned to Earth by clinging to the devil's ankle, as shown.

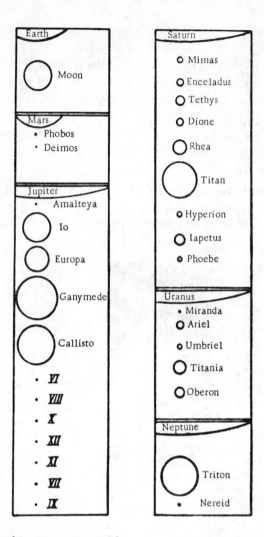

Earth	
○	Moon

Mars	
·	Phobos
·	Deimos

Jupiter	
·	Amalteya
○	Io
○	Europa
○	Ganymede
○	Callisto
·	*VI*
·	*VIII*
·	*X*
·	*XII*
·	*XI*
·	*VII*
·	*IX*

Saturn	
○	Mimas
○	Enceladus
○	Tethys
○	Dione
○	Rhea
○	Titan
○	Hyperion
○	Iapetus
◉	Phoebe

Uranus	
·	Miranda
○	Ariel
○	Umbriel
○	Titania
○	Oberon

Neptune	
○	Triton
·	Nereid

Relative size of Earth's moon compared to the satellites of other planets.

motion: third law of. When two bodies exert forces on each other, both forces have the same strength but are opposite in direction.

motion sickness. (Astronautics.) A messy combination of pallor, sweating, nausea, and vomiting caused by unusual spacecraft accelerations.

moto belt. (Fiction.) Evolutionary precursor of the full-fledged *flying belt* (which see), combining the principles of the *degravity belt* and the *moto tube* (which see). It is more convenient than a moto tube, though less convenient than a flying belt.

moto tube. (Fiction.) Hand-held predecessor of the *flying belt* (which see). Roughly the size of a 20th Century bicycle pump; shaped like a capital T; worn in conjunction with a degravity belt (for better balance); and attached to a clothing harness with a small chain. It operates via *non-recoil energy* (which see), which exerts itself in whatever direction the tube is pointed when its trigger is pressed. If

The author's awareness of this particular 1932 comic strip panel, when he was a ten-year-old in Evanston, Illinois, initiated him into the wondrous universe of Buck Rogers. Note the dramatic, no nonsense, clean-lined simplicity of the art-work depicting Buck, Wilma Deering, and their moto tubes. From the sequence known as 'Beneath the Greenland Ice Cap.' Artist: Dick Calkins. Writer: Phil Nowlan.

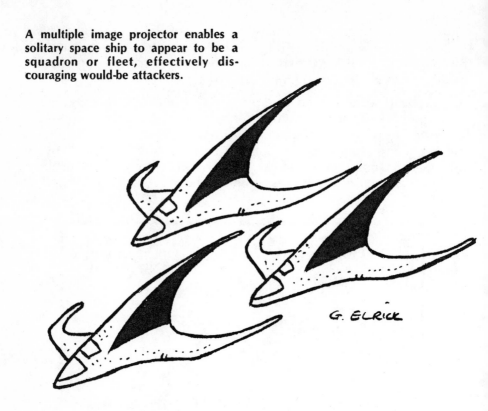

A multiple image projector enables a solitary space ship to appear to be a squadron or fleet, effectively discouraging would-be attackers.

G. ELRICK

the cap is unscrewed from its base, the moto tube can be used as a *force tube* (which see). Though a moto tube's power is controllable, if an unchained, activated one is released, it can flash across space as a dangerous projectile.

multiple image projector. (Fiction.) Also called a multiple mirage ray. A space ship electromagnetic frequency device that projects multiple optical-illusion images of the ship, to confuse spacecraft that might be pursuing and trying to draw a bead on it. Makes one ship appear to be a squadron or fleet.

multistage rocket. (Astronautics.) A space vehicle featuring two or more rocket units or modules, each unit firing after the one in back of it has exhausted its propellant. A unit is jettisoned after completing its firing operation.

178

multiverse. (Fiction.) A series of parallel universes.

'mummifying of time' theory. (Fiction.) The hypothesis that every event on Earth travels into space on rays of invisible light. For example, if you were ten light years from Earth, you could see ten years into the past.

N

nausea: danger of in space. (Fiction.) Graphically described by Arthur W. Ballou in *Marooned in Orbit*. In a weightless environment, the misery of active nausea is coupled with the horror of strangulation because gravity can't drain the nose and throat.

nebula. (Astronomy.) Generally a bright cloud of interstellar gas. A dust cloud is sometimes called a dark nebula. A nebula is visible as a luminous area or dark region depending on how its mass absorbs or reflects incident radiation. Specifically: an *emission nebula* is one that absorbs ultraviolet radiation from stars and re-emits it as visible light; an *absorption nebula* is one that absorbs incident radiation without re-emitting it; and a *reflection nebula* is one that reflects visible radiation. In previous practice, the word nebula also referred to a galaxy. This is no longer so. See *interplanetary dust* and *interplanetary gas*.

needle gun. (Fiction.) A machine gun-type apparatus that shoots tiny, chemically treated, needle-like darts that burn frightfully.

needle ray. (Fiction.) An emission blasted in a thin stream from a special hand gun's nozzle. The threat of its searing pain makes potential torture victims faint.

Neptune. (Astronomy.) One of the so-called Jovian planets, a 'gas giant,' and the eighth celestial body from the sun, with a mean distance of 2.8 billion miles. It can't be seen with the naked eye, but it resembles a small green globe when observed through a telescope. Because of its immense distance, astronomers know little about it.

Size: Its dimensions are impressive though, size-wise, it plays second fiddle to Jupiter, Saturn, or Uranus. Its volume is 27 times, and its mass 15 times, that of the Earth. Its diameter ranges between 27,000 and 31,000 miles, more than three times the Earth's.

Density: Similar to Jupiter's.

Composition: Less massive than Jupiter, and less compressed by strong gravity, its make-up features a higher ratio of medium-weight and heavy elements.

Temperature: Minus 300 degrees Fahrenheit. (The Earth receives 900 times as much light and heat per square mile.)

Atmosphere: As is the case with all Jovian planets, its atmosphere is 'thick.' Hydrogen is the basic constituent. There is a great deal of methane, but Neptune is too cold for ammonia to exist in gaseous form, as it does on Jupiter.

Rotation: Neptune makes a complete turn on its axis every 16 hours.

Orbital period: 164.8 yeas. (Contrast to Mercury's 88 days.)

Satellites: Neptune has two satellites, both unusual. The larger, Triton, the size of our moon, orbits in a reverse direction. It's big enough and cold enough to retain an atmosphere, but none is detectable. If there *is* an atmosphere, it may be frozen out as a solid layer on the surface. The second satellite is tiny and moves in a huge, eccentric orbit.

Gravity: Earth = 1. Neptune = 1.23.

Billions of neutrinos slam through our bodies every moment, yet we're totally unaware of the puncturing.

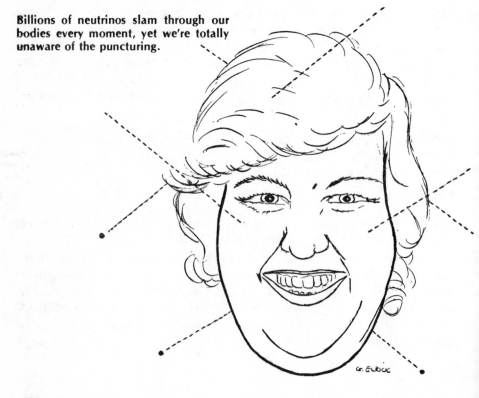

net formation: (Fiction.) A flying pattern occasionally assumed by a space ship fleet.

neutrino. (Physics.) A fundamental sub-atomic particle, basically an electron with no charge: massless, neutral, and stable. Neutrinos are produced during the radioactive breakdowns of nuclei. Though perfect for testing the weak nuclear force, they basically ignore other sub-atomic particles. Billions pass through our bodies every moment, like painless machine-gun fire. According to physicist Leon Lederman, they zip straight through the Earth as if the latter weren't there. See *weak nuclear force, radioactive decay,* and *radioactivity.*

neutro graph. (Fiction.) A spacecraft sensing device that warns of impending atomic explosions, no matter how distant. When its indicator displays condition red, it means an atomic explosion is about to take place locally.

neutro-metabolic tube. (Fiction.) A six-foot-high hermetically sealed tube that de-activates but does not destroy life. It is capable of holding a vertical human or humanoid in suspended animation indefinitely.

neutron. (Physics.) A neutral elementary particle slightly larger than a proton, with which it is normally coupled in an atom's nucleus (with the exception of hydrogen). Its mass is 1,830 times greater than an electron's. Though stable in a nucleus, a free neutron is unstable, decaying in a few minutes into an electron, proton, and neutrino. Neutrons sustain fission chain reactions in nuclear reactions. See *proton, neutrino, fission, atom,* and *nuclear reactor.*

neutron bomb. (Fiction.) Not to be confused with the actual neutron bomb developed in 1977. A small—but deadly explosive—bomb that can be set to fly in a tight circle for four minutes, behind an escaping spacecraft, while concealed with a smoke screen. Perfect for wiping out pursuing space ships.

neutronic-cycle anti-rocketcraft gun. (Fiction.) A howitzer-size weapon that spits deadly green flame at attacking rocket ships.

neutron lifter. (Fiction.) A smaller, pencil-size version of the standard *non-recoil-energy force tube* (which see). When pointed downward, it can be used to hoist oneself off the ground to any desired height. It is often employed, in conjunction with a molecular separator or permeator, to raise a person upward from floor level to floor level, by going *through* the floors.

neutron star. (Astronomy.) Other than a black hole the most compressed stellar configuration in the universe, just a few miles in diameter: a tightly squeezed clump of neutrons as compact as an atom's nucleus. In a sense, it *is* a freakish, oversize atomic nucleus. However, gravitation pushes it together, not nuclear forces. So great is the gravitational pressure that its electrons have been jammed into its protons; as a result, its protons have become neutrons; and only neutrinos and high-energy photons can break free. Formed in the final stages of a star's evolution, it features an intense magnetic field and is totally invisible. A universe composed of neutron stars would be near maximum entropy. Compare with *black hole*. See *neutron, photon, neutrino, entropy,* and *maximum entropy.*

neutron pistol. (Fiction.) Employs controlled atomic force to unlock doors that aren't meant to be opened by causing a fission in the barrier's atomic structure. By reducing its force, a small hole can be drilled silently. By increasing its force, large obstructions can be noisily blown to oblivion.

neutron projector. (Fiction.) Also called a bomb buster. A globular device fastened, via an anchor ray, in a fixed position above the Earth's surface, it can destroy any approaching atomic warheads by shooting atom-splitting neutrons 2,000 miles up and beyond the exosphere.

'new wave' science fiction. (Generic.) Science fiction that emphasizes raw sex, bone-crunching violence, and deep pessimism about 'the meaning of it all.' It tends to be self-consciously stylistic, and heavily underscores such present-day problems as pollution, racism, and overpopulation.

nitrocoric acid. (Fiction.) Destroys whatever it touches, except glass. One drop on his skin will kill a human being or a humanoid.

nitro vitriolite. (Fiction.) An explosive used in interplanetary warfare.

non-Euclidean geometry. (Generic.) If existentialism is science fiction's refreshing philosophy, non-Euclidean geometry is its head-snapping mathematics. In non-Euclidean geometry—also known as differential, elliptic, or hyperbolic geometry—parallel lines eventually *can* meet under certain circumstances; lines are finite though unbounded; the shortest paths between points are curved lines; and triangles change shape when shifted about. Garden-variety Euclidean geometry serves well enough for everyday three-dimensional Earth-time experience, but only non-Euclidean geometry—along with topology—paves the way for understanding spacetime and the overarching properties of the universe in its entirety. See *Euclidean three-space* and *topology*.

non-ex fluid. (Fiction.) Short for non-existence fluid. A chemical compound used by alien-planet foreign agents if cornered. When they have no recourse except to surrender, they inject themselves with it and vaporize after ten seconds. Compare with *disintegrating fluid* and *vaporizing pill*.

non-recoil energy. (Fiction.) Also called one-way energy. A type of energy beam with a powerful, controllable 'push,' but no recoil whatsoever, whether used in a small flashlight-size tube (called an energy tube), or a larger force tube. Based on carefully balanced electronic and sub-cosmic energy control, it is similar in effect to a repellor ray. Provides ideal motive power for innumerable spacecraft, technological, and industrial applications. See *force tube, neutron lifter,* and *repellor ray*.

Earlier traditional science fiction virtually ignored sex. To draw an exaggerated parallel to old-fashioned Western movies, it was permissible for the protagonist to lightly kiss the surface of his spacecraft [just as it was okay for a cowhand to platonically kiss his 'good old boy' horse), but the hero seldom kissed the girl, whatever her function might have been in the story. By contrast, in 'new wave' science fiction, the girl is likely to be subjected to 'anything goes' bedroom gymnastics.

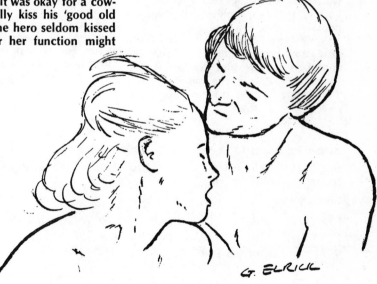

G. ELRICK

Whether a person becomes invisible by injecting non-ex fluid, swigging disintegrating fluid, by popping vaporizing pills, or just willing himself or herself into the state (super heroes, 'I Dream of Jeannie,' etc.), the concept has immense popular appeal. The vampire-type alien agent pictured here is cross-dissolving into temporary nothingness. This, of course, is fantasy, not science fiction (despite H. G. Well's 'The Invisible Man'). The trouble is, even in fantasy some unsolvable problems present themselves. In the first place, only the biological body would disappear, not clothing, which means a person would have to run around naked, no matter how cold it might be outside. In the second place, any food a person consumed would be visible until digested. But this is splitting hairs. Though scorned by savvy science fiction fans, the concept itself will stubbornly refuse to vanish.

non-viso camouflage ray. (Fiction.) An electromagnetic emission perfected by Martian space lane raiders. When activated, it renders their space ships invisible.

nose cone. (Astronautics.) The cone-shaped 'point' of a rocket, missile, or spacecraft. Constructed to withstand searingly high temperatures generated by air-particle friction, it is normally coated with *ablating materials* (which see).

nova. (Astronomy.) A variable star that suddenly flares to many times its normal brightness—sometimes 60,000 times as much—due to a surface explosion or explosions. The new brightness remains steady for a few weeks, then fades to its original intensity in several weeks, months, or years. See *supernova*.

nuclear force. (Physics.) Also known as *strong nuclear force* (which see): a powerful non-electromagnetic force between sub-atomic particles, responsible for the binding of a proton to a neutron in an atom's nucleus.

nuclear power as applied to spacecraft. (Astronautics.) There are three ways to use nuclear power in space flight, depending on how nuclear reaction is controlled and contained:

    1. heat-transfer. A propellant is heated while passing through a nuclear reactor's core.

    2. consumable nuclear rocket. Nuclear fissioning takes place in the fuel itself.

    3. 'firecracker-under-the-can.' Nuclear reaction is slowed down so energy is released in seconds rather than microseconds; in short, controlled-expansion nuclear bomb propulsion.

    See *nuclear reactor* and *fission*.

nuclear reactor. (Physics.) Also called an atomic furnace, atomic pile, atomic reactor, chain-reacting pile, or reactor. Any of several basic devices for creating nuclear energy, a nuclear reactor initiates, maintains, and controls a fission chain reaction. It produces heat, typically used for power generation, and also produces neutrons and fission products, used for a variety of medical and experimental purposes. Its primary components are a core with fissionable fuel, a moderator, a reflector, shielding, coolant, and various control mechanisms. See *fission*.

nucleonic oscillator. (Fiction.) A device invented by the humanoid inhabitants of certain large asteroids, capable of flooding the Earth, or any other planet, with impalpable sub-atomic deadly vibrations destructive to all living flesh.

nucleosynthesis. (Physics.) The nuclear reaction processes by means of which atomic nuclei are formed.

null-gee. (Astronautics.) Also called anti-grav. The condition of weightlessness. See *zero gravity: effects of*.

nutation. (Astronomy.) A very small, periodic motion of the Earth's celestial pole with respect to the ecliptic pole. See *celestial sphere* and *ecliptic*.

O

oblate. (Astronautics.) Regarding spacecraft, having a spheroid shape. Compare with *prolate*.

observo ray chart. (Fiction.) An interplanetary navigational aid consisting of an adjustable viewplate with grids.

occultation. (Astronomy.) The passage of a celestial body between an observer and another celestial object, as when the moon intervenes between the Earth and the sun during an eclipse. Also, the progressive blocking of radiation from a celestial source during occultation.

Official Earth Band. (Fiction.) The band—on the spread of interplanetary radio frequencies—used by space ships when contacting Earth.

offplanet. (Fiction.) A science fiction 'street talk' phrase. Typically used as follows: 'Let's see if we can arrange for passage offplanet.'

one-way transparo-dyne atomizer. (Fiction.) A spray that, when directed at a solid wall, enables one to see through to the other side without being seen in return.

optical illusions in space travel. (Fiction/Astronautics.) Navigating a starship at ever-increasing velocities isn't like driving a Porsche on an expressway, since light registers on the retinas of astronauts' eyes in weird ways, due to the Doppler effect. At medium-rate speeds, as the spacecraft approaches a star, the star's light reddens. As the spacecraft pulls away from a star, the star's light turns blue. At 36 percent lightspeed, the straight-ahead destination star erases itself from the visible spectrum and becomes a narrow cone of blackness. As the starship slams forward at stepped-up accelerations, other stars reappear as a multi-colored ring, gradually bunching together toward the bow and thinning out toward the stern. This visual effect stems from aberration: light appearing to shift, like slanting rain, in the direction of motion. All of this renders navigation by positional astronomy as impossible as climbing Mount Everest in open-toed sandals. A lightspeed ship *must* rely on sophisticated inertial navigation. See *Doppler effect* and *inertial guidance*.

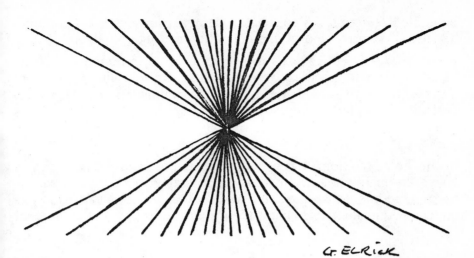

Because of visual tricks played by the Doppler effect, when a spacecraft attains 36 percent lightspeed, the straight-ahead destination star erases itself from the visible spectrum and becomes a narrow cone of darkness.

oralphone. (Fiction.) An electronic language decoder and interpreter that unscrambles various interplanetary tongues so they're understandable in at least a rudimentary fashion. In appearance, it resembles a mid-20th Century washing machine.

orbit. (Astronomy.) The regular path of a celestial body, or man-made satellite, as it travels around another body. Also, the movement of an electron with respect to an atom's nucleus. See *spacecraft orbits*.

orbital decay. (Astronautics.) The effect of atmospheric drag on an Earth-orbiting satellite's velocity, so that gravitational pull eventually forces re-entry. Compare with *deorbit*.

orbital maneuvering system. (Fiction/Astronautics.) OMS for short. A space ship maneuvering system engine that provides calculated thrusts to perform orbit insertion; orbit circularization; orbit transfer; rendezvous and docking, if planned; and deorbit.

orbit chart. (Fiction.) A graph used to calculate the square of a space ship's displacement.

organic. (Fiction.) A non-android being or a non-robot.

outer circle route. (Fiction.) A particular route used by Earth space ships when approaching the moon.

outer shell. (Fiction.) A space ship carapace in which atmospheric heating is counteracted by the activation of friction valves.

oxidizer. (Astronautics.) A rocket propellant component—such as liquid oxygen, liquid hydrogen, fluorine, or nitric acid—that combines with fuel to support rocket engine combustion in outer space. Basically, it replaces the oxygen of the Earth's atmosphere and is needed because there's so little oxygen above the *exosphere* (which see).

ozone hole. (Fiction/Physics.) A hole in the Earth's ozone layer, above an enemy country, caused by a nuclear bomb. The opening exposes people on the ground to deadly ultraviolet radiation. Its effect is equivalent to placing them, unshielded, on the surface of Mars.

P

pandemic disease. (Fiction.) A widespread infection brought to Earth by returning space travelers, or via some other interplanetary or interstellar source.

Pangaea. (Generic.) The ancient, enormous land mass that, through continental drift, gave rise to Earth's present continents and their jigsaw puzzle configurations.

panspermia. (Fiction.) The drifting or migration of life-producing spores, through space, from one planet to another.

paradox of the twins. (Generic.) Let's say there are identical twins named George and Gordon. If George departed on a ten-year space trip at a velocity approaching lightspeed, he'd be a year younger than Gordon when he returned, due to the effects of time dilation, relativity, and the Lorentz-Fitzgerald contraction. If Gordon were telemetering George's trip from a data-input station on Earth, time on the space ship would appear to drag its feet, though George, possibly manipulating controls in the distant ship, would experience time passage as normal. If George extended his space trip and spent 28 years traveling at a velocity approaching lightspeed, he'd be a middle-aged man when he returned, but would be unable to share his adventures with Gordon. The latter would have died of old age, or whatever, and would have been crumbling to dust in the family plot for 150 Earth years. See *spacer, telemetry, time dilation, relativity, time slippage,* and *Lorentz-Fitzgerald contraction.*

In the paradox of the twins, the cosmonaut twin becomes younger than his stay-at-home brother. How much younger? That depends on the duration of the trip and the velocity involved. Substitute sweethearts for twins, and you have one of the prime plot-twists of science fiction: a real heart-breaker.

parallel world. See *alternate reality.*

paralysis gas. (Fiction.) Paralyzing vapor emitted from a small, explosive capsule. It affects nerve centers, rendering those exposed to it alive but helpless.

paralysis gun. (Fiction.) Also called a par gun. A ubiquitous pistol used in virtually all science fiction: a futuristic 'Saturday Night Special' that flashes a faintly visible, crackling beam of high-frequency energy vibrations that paralyze certain brain centers. With adjustment, it is capable of blasting a triple-power ray. A person hit by the gun's emission instantly drops, remains rigid and comatose for minutes or hours, then recovers with a splitting headache. See *paralysis ray.*

paralysis ray. (Fiction.) Body-stiffening energy emitted by a paralysis gun or a non-hand-held device, temporarily making joints and muscles as rigid as steel. It is normally a crackling beam, pale and green in hue, that can be set for narrow focus or wide angle, full voltage or reduced voltage. When a unit is inconspicuously concealed in a wall, it is employed as an automatic guard against room entry, controllable via an invisible ultraviolet light 'barrier' and a selenium cell. See *paralysis gun.*

paralysis rod. (Fiction.) A four-foot-long rod with a paralyzing bulb at its tip. Used to 'teach a lesson' to those who act in an insubordinate manner.

paralyzing force ray. (Fiction.) A type of barrier device. Taut wires, strung close to the ground between unobtrusive electronic pylons, emit a paralyzing force that 'freezes' in mid-air anyone trying to pass over them with a flying belt.

paramagnetic. (Physics.) Pertains to an induced magnetic field that is stronger than a normal magnetizing field.

parity. (Physics.) A 30-year-old 'law' that was kicked to pieces in 1956 by two Chinese-born American physicists: Tsung Dao Lee and Chen Ning Yang. In disproving the conservation of parity assumption, the young men drilled yet another peep-hole into the staggeringly complex nature of ultimate reality. The previous viewpoint regarding parity had been that elementary particles emitted in an atomic nucleus's decay would, like the flip of a coin, be just as likely to spin in one direction as another. Lee and Yang validated that each particle has its own characteristic spin: in short, it tends to be 'left-handed' or 'right-handed.' They shared the Nobel Prize in 1957.

parking orbit. (Astronautics.) The self-sustaining orbit of a satellite, roughly 200 miles above the Earth's surface, traveling at 18,000 miles-per-hour. This is the speed at which it maintains its endless revolution, with no boosts from fuel-induced power, counterbalanced by its centrifugal thrust into space and the tug of gravity trying to pull it downward. A parking orbit is used as a 'waiting' position for the add-on assembly of additional components, or as a 'marking time' period prior to conditions favorable for departure from orbit. Compare with *synchronous satellite.*

parsec. (Astronomy.) The basic unit of interplanetary and intergalactic measurement used by astronomers: equivalent to 206,000 times the distance from the Earth to the sun, or 3.26 light years.

parsec computer. (Fiction.) A bank of computerized instruments used to determine the interstellar positions of objects being tracked.

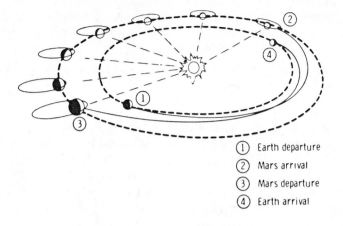

① Earth departure
② Mars arrival
③ Mars departure
④ Earth arrival

Diagram of a spacecraft in a parking orbit around Mars.

particle reference. (Astronautics.) A spacecraft frame of reference used in interplanetary and interstellar navigation and guidance. Consists of a microscopic glass ball floating in a balanced electric field. When the apparatus with the floating ball is moved, forces acting on the ball itself can be calculated with extreme accuracy.

passive homing. (Astronautics.) Space ship homing in which the craft directs itself toward its target via natural energy waves transmitted or radiated from the target, in place of 'bounce back' waves transmitted by the craft itself. Compare with *active homing.*

passive thermal control system. (Fiction/Astronautics.) A non-active heat control system that helps maintain other space ship systems and components within specified temperature tolerances. It employs available space ship heat sources and heat sinks supplemented by insulation blankets, thermal coatings, and thermal isolation techniques. Note: active heating elements are used on components and systems where passive thermal control methods are inadequate to maintain required functioning temperatures. See *thermal protection system.*

payload. (Astronautics.) On a space mission, the personnel, life-support systems, and equipment needed to accomplish the mission. Expressed in poundage, it's over and above the weight of propellants, frame, fuel tanks, or nose cone.

pellet of high explosive. (Fiction.) An aspirin-size weapon easy to conceal that detonates if someone steps on it.

penetratelescope. (Fiction.) Utilizing a sending beam, and manipulated by dials, it has a lens that easily penetrates solid objects, revealing what's behind them. (It must be focused in such a way that it doesn't see through *those* objects too.) It is ideal for long-distance surveillance. When the desired focal range has been reached, a faint purple glow appears on the viewplate. When the focus is pinpointed, the viewplate emits a greenish hue.

penetrato gerryscope. (Fiction.) A device that filters light rays in such a manner that camouflage rays are counteracted, rendering that which was invisible visible.

A penetratelescope enables its user to see through solid objects, focusing the lens—and his attention—on what lies beyond them.

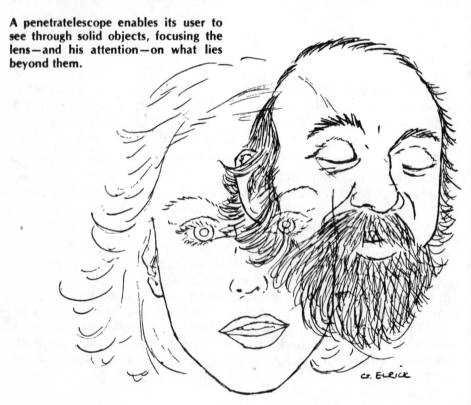

penumbra. (Astronomy.) With reference to a celestial body, such as the moon or another planet, a semi-shadow region, sometimes referred to as a fringe, between areas of complete shadow and total illumination, caused by another celestial body coming between *that* celestial body and the sun. Compare with *umbra*.

perigee. (Astronautics.) The point nearest the Earth in a satellite's orbit. In terms of astronomy, the point nearest the Earth in the moon's orbit. The opposite of *apogee* (which see).

perihelion. (Astronomy.) The point closest to the sun in the orbit of a planet or other body. Opposite of *aphelion* (which see).

permutation symmetry. (Physics.) A situation in which one object in a system can be replaced by another object without changing the system's behavior or characteristics. For instance, any electron in an atom can be replaced by another electron without altering the atom's properties.

personal sub-cosmic emanations. (Fiction.) Electromagnetic radiations from a person's body that enable him to open secret passageways simply by pressing his hand on the right spot on a wall, or on a space ship's bulkhead.

perturbation. (Astronautics.) A force that causes variations in a designated orbit, whether of a planet, a satellite, or an electron, stemming from the disturbing influence of one or more external bodies.

petri-ray. (Fiction.) A type of hardening and debilitating energy used by space pirates on certain planetoids. When petri-rays are turned on captured women, the latter are transformed into rock-hard 'living statues,' positioned on pedestals, and worshipped. Compare with *plastic paralysis ray*.

phoneme. (Generic.) The smallest sound unit in any language which makes a difference in meaning to the speaker or listener. If mispronounced, omitted, or slurred, confusion results.

photoelectron. (Physics.) An electron that has been ejected from a substance by incident electromagnetic radiation, particularly by a photon of visible light. See *photon*.

photoionization. (Physics.) Removal of an electron from an atom through absorption of a photon that has more than enough energy to ionize the atom. See *ionization, phoeoelectron,* and *photon*.

photometry. (Physics.) The accurate measurement of the properties of light, especially its brightness.

photon. (Physics.) A photon is almost impossible to describe, let alone comprehend; it exists in a way that 'passeth all understanding.' Just as matter consists of incomprehensibly small elementary particles, radiation consists of particles called photons.

An individual photon is variously described as a discrete wave-particle entity; a tiny packet of radiation; a quantum of electromagnetic energy; a virtual seed of pure energy; and the mediator of electromagnetic interactions.

A photon has no mass at rest, and doesn't exist unless traveling at the speed of light, when it has an indefinitely long lifetime. Each photon is absorbed or emitted by a single atom, and has no electric charge.

Educated humans are dimly aware that visible light beams—and *all* forms of radiation—are comprised of machine-gun streams of photons. They're also dimly aware that photons are invisible in and of themselves. The same educated humans also intellectually pay lip-service to the fact that energy is simultaneously wave-like and particle-like, but no one has ever really succeeded in 'picturing' this most puzzling of all paradoxes of modern physics. It's akin to believing something can be round and square at the same time.

A photon's energy is inversely proportional to electromagnetic wavelength. The impact of an individual photon's energy is in direct proportion to the radiation frequency producing it, and in inverse ratio to the wavelength it travels. Therefore, in long-wavelength radio-wave radiation, the impact of an individual photon's energy is relatively slight; in short-wavelength X-ray radiation, the impact of an individual photon's energy is relatively momentous.

Why short-wavelength radiation is physiologically damaging. Because photons are bunched closer together in short-wavelength radiation, their cumulative effect is comparable to that of a small hand grenade exploding. They wreak invisible havoc and 'let loose the dogs of war' in human flesh they impinge upon. For example, absorbing gamma rays rather than sunlight is like being punctured with bullets rather than pelted with rose petals.

The intensity of light depends on the number of photons present. In a beam of light, every photon has the same energy as every other photon. It follows that, the more intense the beam, the greater the number of photons zapping forward each second. 'Brighter' simply means 'more.'

All in all, it's almost as difficult to grasp the concept of photons as it is to comprehend the concept of infinity. For a particle that's equally weird, see *quark*.

photon engine. (Astronautics.) A projected type of reaction engine in which thrust would be obtained from a stream of electromagnetic radiation in the form of light rays. Though the engine would eject a minimum of mass and its push would be negligible, in space— where no resistance is offered by air particles—it could build up indefinitely to a velocity approaching lightspeed. Through the use of a solar cell, a specific impulse from 30 million seconds up is conceivable. See *reaction engine, solar cell, specific impulse,* and *photon*.

physics: four basic forces of. (Physics.) The four primary forces of nature traditionally are: gravity; electromagnetism; the weak nuclear force, which controls radioactive decay; and the strong nuclear force, which binds the nuclei of atoms together. See separately, as well as *color,* a newly discovered force which may be the most powerful of them all.

piggyback satellite. (Astronautics.) A secondary satellite riding on the back of a primary satellite. When the latter's in orbit, the secondary satellite is released to fulfill its own independent mission.

pinhead H-bomb. (Fiction.) A hydrogen bomb so minute it can be concealed in one's hand. Can be timed to blow up in 21 minutes.

piracy in high space. (Fiction.) A punishable breach of interplanetary law.

pistol phaser. (Fiction.) A pistol-shaped device consisting of a beam shield, beam emitter, photon accelerator, dilithium crystal cell, forward lockplate, deflector shield, rear lockplate handle with magnatomic adhesion areas, and a force-setting dial. Depending on the dial twist, it can de-materialize, heat, or stun. It is useful as an emergency metal-cutting torch. (*Star Trek.*)

pitch. (Astronautics.) A spacecraft's rotation about an axis that is perpendicular with respect to the vehicle's length and horizontal regarding the Earth's surface, or any other celestial body's surface.

Planck's constant. (Physics.) A constant of proportionality linking the quantum of energy possessable by radiation to the radiation's frequency. See *quantum theory.*

planet. (Astronomy.) A word meaning wanderer in Greek, referring to one of nine relatively large celestial bodies revolving around the sun. Beyond our solar system, a planet is any nonluminous body orbiting around a star. In order, from nearest to the sun to farthest, the planets are Mercury, Venus, Earth, Mars, Jupiter, Saturn, Uranus, Neptune, and Pluto (which see separately). In general, the farther away planets are from the sun, the more distant they are from each other. Each planet has two motions: it revolves around the sun and rotates on its own axis. The distinction between planets and asteroids or planetoids is arbitrary, based on size. See *asteroids, Jovian planets,* and *terrestrial planets.*

planetoid. See *asteroids.*

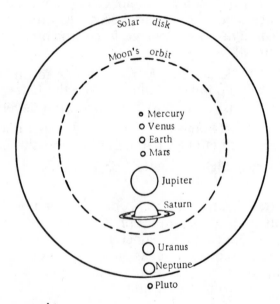

Relative sizes of the planets compared to the solar disk and the orbit of Earth's moon.

Planetoids were treated lightly by German writers of the 1920's. One wrote a story about a man named Buffke who decided to spend the summer with his wife and daughter on planetoid 2017, located between Mars and Jupiter. The illustration shows the family perched on the chunk of rock, which they've found to be artificial, manufactured by the Ford Motor Company. Note the flapper costumes and hair-do's.

plasma. (Astronomy.) An extremely thin gas—thinner than any vacuum man has been able to create on Earth—pervading the universe in varying degrees of concentration. It's an extension of the flung-off atmosphere of stars, referred to as solar wind. Plasma is electrically neutral, comprised of ions, electrons, and non-charged particles. See *interplanetary gas, solar wind,* and *ions.*

plasma jet. (Astronautics.) A high-temperature jet, heated and ionized by the magnetohydrodynamics effects of strong electrical discharge. Though the expansion of hot plasma creates rocket thrust, energy is supplied electrically rather than via combustion, fusion, or fission. Plasma jets are ideal for space ship travel where short-duration bursts of speed at high specific impulse are needed. See *magnetohydrodynamics* and *specific impulse.*

plasma sheath. (Astronautics.) A compressed blanket of electrically neutral, highly ionized gas that sometimes surrounds a spacecraft during re-entry into the Earth's atmosphere. Caused by atmospheric friction, it, in turn, causes temporary communications blackouts. See *plasma, interplanetary gas,* and *gas cap.*

plastic air cylinder. (Fiction.) A cylinder in which captives can be solidified—without suffocating—like insects in hardened amber. Those so entrapped can be stored indefinitely, or until they die of hunger and thirst. Victims sealed in this manner have enough facial latitude to continue to see, hear, and talk.

plastic paralysis ray. (Fiction.) A de-energizing emission used to transform captives into living statues. Victims, properly posed and positioned on pedestals, are normally stripped, then given a powdered or glazed coating to render them marble-like in appearance. They're

Results of plastic paralysis ray exposure and treatment. The victim may be twisted into other postures.

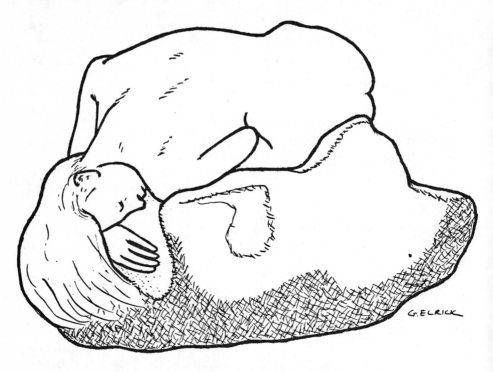

G.ELRICK

kept alive by periodically pouring life-sustaining nutrients down their throats. They continue to breathe, but in such a restricted manner that chest movements are almost non-existent. Limbs are flexible enough to be rearranged to suit the whims of caretakers. Regardless, living statues remain comatose indefinitely until an antidote is administered. The ray itself is pink, as opposed to the pale green hue of an ordinary paralysis ray. Compare with *petri-ray*.

Pluto. (Astronomy.) The ninth and farthest planet from the sun: at its maximum distance, 4.6 billion miles, almost 40 times as far from the sun as is the Earth, and difficult to accurately observe. Though it roams the solar system's outer fringes, normally the domain of the 'gas giant' Jovian planets; it differs from them radically and is sometimes classified as a terrestrial planet due to its size.

Thanks to its maverick traits and properties, some astronomers refuse to classify it as a simon-pure planet, suggesting it began as a satellite of Neptune that subsequently escaped.

Size: Roughly as small as Mars or Mercury. As far as can be determined, it has a diameter approximately half, and a mass one-tenth, that of the Earth.

Density and composition: Little is known about either, but it is theorized that its density approximates the Earth's.

Temperature: Incomprehensibly cold.

Atmosphere: None. Though its gravitation could retain one, the temperature is so frigid that gases would crystallize. As is the case with Neptune's satellite, Triton, any potential atmosphere would be deep-frozen as a solid surface layer.

Rotation: Unknown.

Orbital period: 248.4 years. (Contrast to Mercury's 88 days.) Pluto has the most eccentric of all planetary orbits, meandering all over the place.

Satellites: One, discovered in July, 1978.

Gravity: Earth = 1. Pluto = 0.16.

pocket altimeter. (Fiction.) A device carried in the pocket of someone airborne with a flying belt, used to determine exact elevation when darkness, fog, or smoke prevent gauging vertical distance with ordinary eyesight. See *flying belt.*

pod. (Fiction.) In astronautics, a streamlined housing enclosing engines or fuel carried externally on an aerospace craft. In science fiction, an encapsulated, rocket-powered escape vehicle just large enough to hold three or four people. Compare with *escape bullet* and *space boat.*

point of no time. (Fiction.) As conceived by Gordon R. Dickson in *Three to Dorsai!,* it is a point of high-level energy shuttled back and forth in a three-step tubular accelerator until it virtually reaches light-speed, at which moment it 'breaks' (disappears) and becomes a point of no time zapping back and forth on the same path. If perfectly synchronized with another point of no time in a similar laboratory on another celestial body, it creates a causeway for instantaneous, timeless transmission between both locations. Since a point of no time has universal dimension, it can be used to transport objects of any size from one planet to another with the speed of a cheek-twitch.

positron. (Physics.) The positively charged antiparticle of an electron, which is always negatively charged. Positrons are short lived; when one encounters an electron, both disappear. Positrons are emitted in certain radioactive disintegrations, and are also formed in pair production by the interaction of high-energy gamma rays with matter. See *antiparticle* and *electron*.

precession. (Astronomy.) The slow wobbling of a rotating body's axis. The Earth's axis wobbles slightly because of the attractions of the sun and moon. This causes the apparent positions of stars to change.

pressure suit. (Astronautics.) A space suit providing carefully calculated pressure on its wearer's body so his respiratory and circulatory functions continue normally under low-pressure conditions found at high altitudes, or in the near-vacuum of outer space exterior to a pressurized space ship, cabin, or pod. Compare with G-suit. See *explosive decompression* and *space suit*.

printout. (Generic.) Same as *readout* (which see).

prisma-toric fog piercing eye. (Fiction.) An optional component of space helmets, enabling the helmet's wearer to see clearly, no matter how dense or opaque the fog, cloud, or alien-emitted smoke through which he's progressing.

probe. (Fiction/Astronautics.) Also called a space probe or lander/probe. An unmanned, automated, exploratory spacecraft used to locate planets suitable for habitation by humanity's expanding population, or simply to prepare the way for a manned landing. Probes are programmed to transmit requisite data to Earthbase, or to physically return with soil, atmospheric, and other environmental samples.

prolate. (Astronautics.) With respect to a spacecraft, rod-shaped or cigar-shaped. Compare with *oblate*.

propellant. (Astronautics.) A mixture of fuel and oxidizer in liquid or solid form which, when ignited in a combustion chamber, produces gases and a tremendous pressure increase. The gases, emitted through a nozzle in a jet stream, force a reaction in the opposite direction, rapidly shoving the vehicle in that direction. In a liquid-propellant rocket engine, propellants obviously are in liquid form prior to engine injection, and the oxidizer is conjoined as a separate entity. In a solid-propellant rocket engine, chemicals used as fuel are in a solid state before combustion, and are pre-mixed with an oxidizer.

See *auxiliary fluid ignition, blast chamber, boil-off, burn-out, chamber pressure, chemical fuel, cluster engine, composite propellant, double-base propellant, electric propulsion system, flame-out, force field propulsion system, hypergolic, ionic pro-*

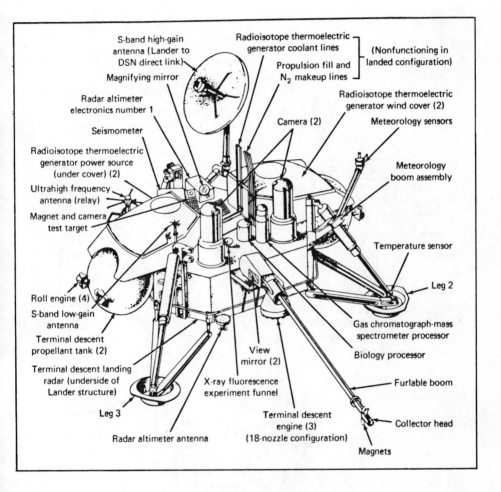

Detailed view of typical probe in position on planetary surface.

pulsion, liquid hydrogen, liquid oxygen, magnetohydrodynamics, monopropellant, multistage rocket, nuclear power as applied to spacecraft, oxidizer, photon engine, plasma jet, reaction engine, rocket cluster, rocket thrust, solid rocket booster, spacecraft orbits, spacecraft propulsion, specific impulse, and *thermal propulsion system.*

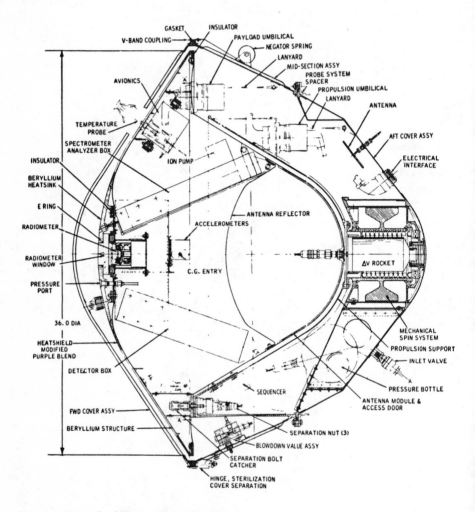

Cross section of a different type of probe.

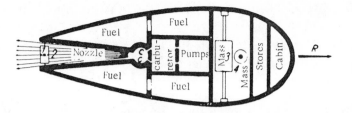

Simplified diagram of reactive space-craft indicating how a propellant is used and forward thrust is attained. Fuel is pumped into the mixing chamber (carburetor), then into the combustion chamber (cc), where it burns explosively. Gaseous combustion products discharge rearward through the gradually widening nozzle. Necessary thrust is created by reaction (R) to this hot gaseous jet. For flight navigation and control, vanes inserted in the jet are used as an elevator (1) and a rudder (2). Masses (3 and 4), adjustable in position along two mutually perpendicular axes, serve a companion purpose.

prothesiologist. (Fiction.) One who creates a *cyborg* (which see).

prosthesis. (Generic.) A functional, artificial replacement for any part of the human body. See *android*.

protective deflector. (Fiction.) An instantly activated, 'pop up' defensive force field that serves as an invisible shield for space ships that encounter dangerous interplanetary or interstellar objects and radiation belts. See *force field*.

proton. (Physics.) A stable, positively charged elementary particle slightly smaller than a neutron, with which it is normally coupled in an atom's nucleus. In and of itself, it is the nucleus of a hydrogen atom. It interacts with the strong nuclear force. If an atom has a given number of electrons, its nucleus must have the same number of protons in order to hold them in orbit. See *atom, neutron,* and *strong nuclear force*.

proton-proton chain. (Physics.) A nuclear reaction series starting with the fusion of two protons and terminating in the fusion of four hydrogen nuclei, forming a helium nucleus. See *fusion*.

protostar. (Astronomy.) A configuration of interstellar material, collapsing inward toward its own center because of gravitational pull, increasing in temperature as it does so, and on its way to becoming a star.

Proxima Centauri. (Astronomy.) Along with its companion star, Alpha Centauri, the nearest star to Earth: 4.3 light years or 25 trillion miles away.

pseudogravity. (Fiction.) Not identical to an artificial gravity field in a space ship, but equally efficient. The creation of pseudogravity requires that a spacecraft spin endlessly on its main axis, in conjunction with a contrary spin generated by a centerline flywheel, producing an angular acceleration, or centrifugal force, that keeps crewmen and passengers firmly on their feet. The calculated rotation commences when the vehicle's rockets cease firing after blast-off, and stops when the vehicle maneuvers to a landing.

psionics. (Fiction.) A general term for telepathy, telekinesis, and similar phenomena.

psychic shock. (Fiction.) The state of internal psychological shattering experienced by a human instantaneously transported from one location to another via a *point of no time* (which see). A person so transmitted experiences a moment of consciousness during which he's spread out to infinite proportions before being recondensed at the receiving end. This 'smearing' sometimes results in insanity or death.

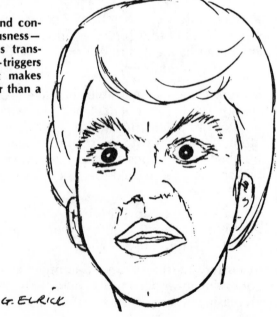

The spreading out, 'smearing,' and condensing of a person's consciousness— brought about by instantaneous transportation via a point of no time—triggers a state of psychic shock that makes ordinary shell shock seem milder than a slight headache.

G. ELRICK

psycho attracto ray. (Fiction.) A ray, emitted from a searchlight-type projector, that draws people toward it in a zombie-like, sleepwalking fashion. Those exposed to the beam feel they must reach the projector at any cost. Perfect for making one's enemies walk helplessly into one's arms.

psychomechanics. (Fiction.) See *time travel.*

psychomyth. (Fiction.) A term coined by Ursula LeGuin to describe her tales dealing basically with psychological reactions to concepts suggested by science and technology.

pulsar. (Astronomy.) A neutron star whose rapid rotations, variations in light radiation, and strong magnetic field cause its extremely short-period radio emissions to register as a sequence of brief pulses. See *neutron star.*

pulsating star. (Astronomy.) Not to be confused with a pulsar. A pulsating star is one whose interior balance is unstable. The layer just below its surface oscillates, storing up energy, then releasing it. As the surface periodically shrinks and swells, the star alternately becomes fainter and brighter.

Q

quantum jump. (Physics.) The leap of an electron between levels of an atom due to absorption of a quantum of energy. See *quantum theory.*

quantum theory. (Physics.) Propounded by physicist Max Planck in 1900. Energy is emitted and absorbed in tiny units, or discrete 'packets,' not as a steady stream. Every substance that radiates energy contains a certain amount of quanta. This theory applies only to energy transmitted by waves.

quark. (Physics.) Also called 'ace.' Though quark is a word coined by James Joyce, the Irish novelist, and is meant to be an imitation of a sea gull's cry, it is actually the ultimate of ultimates: the microworld's truly fundamental unit of matter. Quarks, discovered in 1964, are souped-up, overweight particles from which all other elementary

Quarks—the most elusive of all elementary particles—are named after a sea gull's cry. In one of his novels, James Joyce used the phrase: 'Three quarks for Mrs. Marks.' High-energy physicists, forever seeking new names for subatomic phenomena, eagerly made use of the reference.

G. ELRICK

particles are composed. They exist inside protons in groups of three and combine, in different ways, to make all heavy particles known. Quarks have electric charges equal to one-third or two-thirds that of an electron. Though no one has ever seen one, in essence, the universe is comprised of them.

Up, down, and strange. The three definitely known types of quarks have been baptised up, down, and strange. There may be a fourth type of quark tentatively dubbed *charm*. Because of the charge they carry, quarks cling together in threesomes. Since physicists are running out of names, the charge is called *color*.

See *proton, elementary particles, electron, charm,* and *color.*

quasar. (Astronomy.) Short for quasi-stellar radio sources. Per present-day observations, the brightest, most energetic objects in the entire universe. They're explosive, star-like entities more luminous than an entire galaxy, yet smaller than a galaxy's center. Red shifts indicate apparent fantastic speeds and enormous distances from Earth. It's not yet known what they really are, how far away they actually are, or what makes them 'tick.' See *red shift.*

R

radar altimeter. (Astronautics.) An airborne, low-altitude, terrain-tracking, altitude-sensing apparatus used for precise touchdown guidance. Its usage is based on a precise measurement of turn-around time needed for an electromagnetic energy pulse to travel from a spacecraft to the nearest object on the ground and then return.

radar anti-collidescope. (Fiction.) A space ship sensing device that enables it to dodge through crowded asteriod fields.

radia-luminous flux. (Fiction.) A blinding green light powered by a sub-spectro cathode. When accurately aimed, neutralizes the 'seeing' power of infra-lavender goggles.

radial velocity. (Astronautics.) That part of a body's velocity that lies along the line of sight, measurable by means of the *Doppler effect* (which see).

radiation. (Physics.) Energy particles, in the form of photons, moving in waves at such speed that a single particle could encircle the Earth more than seven times in one second. Radiation refers to any stream of photons, whether in the guise of light rays, heat radiation, radio waves, X-rays, or gamma rays produced by splitting atoms. See *photon* and *electromagnetic radiation*.

radiation belt. (Astronomy.) Also called the Van Allen radiation belt: a layer of charged electrons and protons, emitted primarily by the sun, trapped in the Earth's magnetic field. The belt begins 500 miles above the Earth's surface and extends upward 40,000 miles.

radiation: genetic effects of. (Generic.) Absorption of ionizing radiations by living organisms can lead to effects straight out of a horror story: chiefly bizarre mutations. Effects are additive, and there is no recovery.

radiation illness. (Generic.) As in the preceding reference to genetic effects, the results are straight out of a horror story: nausea, vomiting, diarrhea, blood cell alterations, internal hemorrhaging, and loss of hair.

radioactive boranium. (Fiction.) A uranium concentrate, regularly shipped by space freighters from Venus to Earth.

radioactive decay. (Physics.) Also called radioactive disintegration: a spontaneous transformation of an atomic nucleus into another type of nucleus, or a different nuclear state, usually by ejecting elementary particles, catalyzed by the weak nuclear force. See *elementary particles* and *weak nuclear force.*

radioactivity. (Physics.) The spontaneous—or nuclear reaction induced—breakdown of atomic nuclei, with the emission of alpha particles, nucleons, electrons, and gamma rays. Not to be confused with *radiation* per se (which see).

radio astronomy. (Astronomy.) The observation and analysis of celestial objects by aiming radio-frequency waves at them, and measuring and timing the reflections; or the study of radio waves naturally radiated by celestial bodies. See *radio waves.*

radio guidance. (Astronautics.) Also called command guidance. A system in which the input for a spacecraft's here-to-there path stems from a source, or sources, exterior to itself. The space ship contains a receiver that accepts directions from one or more Earth-based—or other planet-based—ground stations, and executes these commands through its control system.

radionum. (Fiction.) A metallic element from Venus, regarded, in its radioactive state, as a source of virtually infinite power. It is much sought after by space predators.

radiotel. (Fiction.) A space ship sensing device that detects the presence or approach of another spacecraft.

radio waves. (Physics.) The most stretched-out, lowest-frequency waves in the electromagnetic spectrum, including all wavelengths longer than infrared. Radio waves fall into several categories: shortest in length are microwaves, used in radar . . . next in length are waves used in television and FM radio . . . then come 'short waves,' erroneously named because—at one time—they were the shortest used . . still longer waves are used in the narrow band delineating AM broadcasting. The longest waves of all are used in esoteric long-distance communication systems. Regardless of individual radio wavelengths, all travel at the speed of light. See *infrared rays, electromagnetic spectrum, electromagnetic radiation,* and *wavelength.*

Ram augmented interstellar rocket. (Fiction/Astronautics.) A ramjet/rocket hybrid proposed in 1974 by Alan Bond, British propulsion engineer. Its thrust is produced by a fusion rocket that uses hydrogen isotopes—deuterium and tritium—as fuel, augmented by magnetically-scooped interstellar matter electrically accelerated to boost rocket performance. Compare with *Bussard interstellar ramjet.* See *isotope.*

range finder. (Astronautics.) Any optical, electronic, or acoustical apparatus used to determine an object's distance.

ray bat. (Fiction.) An airborne, sporadically remote-controlled electronic surveillance device, roughly a foot long, fat for its length, powered by weightless neutron batteries. Controlled by someone who carries a negative beta-tron disc, it zeroes in on a tiny positive beta-tron disc, known as the target point, slipped in the pocket of an unsuspecting person from whom information is secretly extracted via electronic 'watching' and 'listening.' The ray bat leaves no trace and stops at nothing till it reaches its target point. It can penetrate solid

The floating surveillance device known as a ray bat easily penetrates solid walls by de-molecularizing a hole sufficient for its silent passage. The hole immediately re-solidifies behind it.

Buck Rogers changed drastically in appearance over the years. Compare this 1948 representation with the way he's depicted on pages 177 and 224. The illustrative style has evolved from 'primitive simplistic' to 'comic-book slick.' Here Buck and Flame D'Amour dodge a ray rifle blast in the city of Zoogar on Saturn. Flame is a Venusian secret agent whose code name is 'Thermal.' The twosome's mission is to capture the insidious, cat-eyed Doctor Modar, Saturn's ghoulish dictator. By this time, after 19 faithful years, Wilma Deering has been phased out of the strip. Artist: Murphy Anderson. Writer: Bob Barton.

walls by de-molecularizing a hole sufficient for passage. The hole immediately closes behind it. Adjusted to approach no closer than 15 feet from he or she carrying a positive beta-tron disc, it is constructed to unobtrusively seek shadows and the high point of any room it silently enters. Every word overheard and action observed is automatically recorded and relayed to a distant viewplate. If the viewplate reveals that the bat is in danger of discovery, because of the physical postures of those near it, the hovering device can be extracted from a particular site via remote control.

ray knife. (Fiction.) A commando-type personal combat weapon featuring a crackling, knife-edged electromagnetic emission instead of a blade.

ray repellor screen. (Fiction.) When the requisite device is activated, a protective electromagnetic shield emitted by a space ship. It deflects, or at least tones down, the effect of disintegrator rays and other 'attack' emissions.

ray rifle. (Fiction.) A weapon whose emission force is almost as strong as that of a full-fledged disintegrator.

reaction engine. (Astronautics.) A rocket engine operating in accordance with Newton's third law of motion: 'For every action or force there is an equal and opposite reaction or force.' It develops thrust by a focused expulsion of ignited fuel gases in the form of a jet stream. See *rocket* and *spacecraft propulsion.*

readout. (Generic.) Also called printout. Computer data presentation, generally in digital form, either from storage or from 'right now' calculations.

recon pod. (Fiction.) Short for reconnaissance pod or reconnoitering pod.

red shift. (Astronomy.) Caused by the continuing expansion of the universe: a displacement—or Doppler shift—of a star's or galaxy's spectral lines toward the red end of the electromagnetic spectrum. See *Doppler effect, Big Bang Theory,* and *electromagnetic spectrum.*

reducto gun. (Fiction.) A hand weapon, with an adjustable nozzle, that emits a reducing ray. By means of graduated scale adjustments, it shrinks objects to one-fifth normal size or less. Unless zero dimensions are reached, the process reverses itself in an hour.

re-entry. (Astronautics.) The successful, non-self-destructive return plunge of a spacecraft into the Earth's atmosphere. Intense heat caused by atmospheric friction poses great peril unless special protective materials are used on the craft's outer surface. Without such protection, the spacecraft would burn up and dissipate like the typical meteor. See *ablating materials, plasma sheath, atmospheric entry, entry corridor, window, air friction,* and *air drag.*

reflectocosmic spectrometer. (Fiction.) Called spectro for short: a device used for measuring cosmic rays absorbed by various substances. Useful for detecting—from space—the presence or absence of specific metals on other planets.

reflecto-scope. (Fiction.) Comes in two versions: (1) A small, hand-held apparatus used to detect the presence or absence of cosmo-magnetic emanations. By holding it against a wall—no matter how thick—it is possible to determine if there is any type of living creature on the other side. (2) Broader-focus, more powerful beams are used on space ships to pinpoint the whereabouts of people trying to hide on a planet's surface.

refractory metals. (Astronautics.) Metals which are highly heat-resistant and can withstand extreme temperatures experienced during blast-off and atmospheric re-entry.

refractoscope. (Fiction.) An intricate device, several times larger than a human being, that bends light rays so a person can see around corners. When focused on the moon from Earth, it enables an observer to see the moon's other side.

relativistic travel. (Astronautics.) A synonym for lightspeed travel.

relativity. (Physics.) A complicated, mind-jarring 'double' theory—proven out in many respects—advanced by Albert Einstein. Some of its dicta are: all motion is relative to the frame of reference from which it is measured . . . the speed of light never varies . . . no object having mass can travel faster than lightspeed . . . and there is no such thing as *absolute* space, time, distance, or mass, since everything is relative to everything else. In a nutshell, relativity deals with the behavior of objects moving at extremely high velocities, and the activity of objects exposed to extremely strong gravitational fields. It doesn't contradict classic Newtonian physics, but merely regards previous concepts as limiting cases applying uniquely to man's everyday experiences.

Relativity is split into a special theory and a general theory. Both deal with applications of natural laws to moving things. The distinction lies in the types of moving things the laws are concerned with.

Overview of the special theory of relativity. The special theory, formulated before the general theory, states that natural laws are the same for all non-accelerated frames of reference moving at a steady pace regarding each other . . . that light is propagated at a fixed, unvarying speed, in straight lines, in all directions . . . that matter and energy are equivalent: simply different aspects of the same basic matrix . . . and that rapidly moving objects experience mass increase, time dilation, and the Lorentz-Fitzgerald contraction.

Essentially, the special theory applies to inertial motions in inertial systems; that is, to objects and observers moving at uniform speed, in straight lines, but comparatively 'fixed' with respect to each other. In short, a person traveling in an inertial set-up of uniformly moving objects perceives and reacts to all phenomena from a 'frozen' frame. He's oblivious to the system's motion, since he's moving right along with it, at the same velocity. Other aspects and implications of the special theory directly follow.

Why lightspeed must be invariant. Newton demonstrated that mechanical laws apply equally to all of an inertial system's components. Springboarding from that, Einstein demonstrated that— if electromagnetic laws are to be identical in all inertial systems— light velocity must forever be the same. Put another way, if a group of scientists measures the velocity of light in a particular inertial system, other scientists, in tandem motion regarding the first group, will obtain the same lightspeed measurement.

Discordant perceptions of a weight, a yardstick, and a clock. This example has become shopworn with over-use, but it is still valid:

A person traveling in an inertial set-up of uniformly moving objects perceives and reacts to all phenomena from a 'frozen' frame. He's oblivious to the system's motion, since he's moving right along with it, at the same velocity.

G. ELRICK

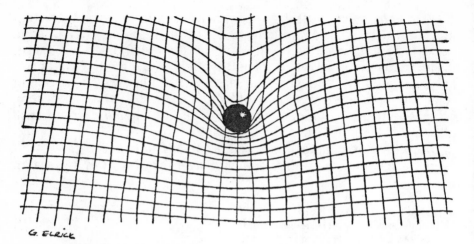

G. ELRICK

According to Einstein's general theory of relativity, the presence of large, compacted masses of matter accounts for local curvatures of space. Our sun, the stars, and all planets and planetary satellites create dimpled 'pockets.' (The dimpling is the same from whatever direction the body is approached.) Light rays bend slightly as they near these pockets. Space ships wobble around and through the depressions like golf balls rolling across uneven putting greens.

there are two keen-eyed observers, one with his feet firmly planted on the Earth's surface, the other flashing past at great speed in a spacecraft or some other vehicle. Each has in his possession a ten-pound weight, a yardstick, and a clock. Oddly enough, if each attempts to measure the weight, speed, and length of his possessions by the *other's* perceptions, he'll find that the weight seems heavier, the clock slower, and the yardstick shorter.

When objects approach lightspeed, mass increases and time slows down. Let's continue the example of the two keen-eyed observers. If the one who zoomed by actually approached the limiting speed of light, and each was somehow able to keep an eye on the other, the possessions of the other would appear to change remarkably. The increasingly heavy weight would seem to approach infinity, proportion-wise (though only in two directions: see *Lorentz-Fitzgerald contraction*), the clock would seem to stop, and the yardstick would seem to vanish. The word 'seem' is used purposely, because neither would note any apparent change in his *own* possessions . . . only in the *other* party's.

Proven out in laboratories. None of this is 'blue sky,' or applicable only to vast galactic scenes. Time dilation has been recorded in cyclotron experiments, as has the linkage of growing mass with increased velocity. Lightweight elementary particles become disproportionately heavy, and short-lived particles reach wrinkled 'old age' as they slam through detection apparatus at relativistic speeds.

$E = mc^2$. This, the mass-energy equation is, without doubt, the most famous formula man has developed. E stands for energy, m for mass, and c for the velocity of light in a vacuum.

Overview of the general theory of relativity. The general theory—an outgrowth and refinement of the special theory—has had less impact on popular imagination than has the latter. Propounding a fresh outlook on gravity and its effects on motion, it states that a light ray will bend as it passes a massive object . . . extends the special theory to accelerated reference frames: to non-inertial as well as inertial set-ups . . . and emphasizes that gravitational and inertial forces are equivalent. A brief rundown of the general theory directly follows.

The principle of equivalence. A non-inertial observer—one who's undergoing acceleration, such as spinning—cannot distinguish between the effects of acceleration and gravity. Ergo, inertial forces derive from gravitation.

The sun bends the space in which it is embedded. (Aspects of this tenet are still hotly debated by physicists.) Rather than being a force, gravity is conceived as space curvature. Instead of the sun—or any other star—controlling its orbiting planets through traditional gravitational pull, it deeply dimples space, and encircling planets merely follow the resultant curve. The sun's dimpling also bends light rays and radio waves aimed so they achieve near proximity to the dimpling. This posits a non-Euclidean spatial geometry.

See *mass, mass-energy equation, matter and energy: equivalence of, gravity, gravitation, time, time dilation, Lorentz-Fitzgerald contraction, cyclotron, elementary particles,* and *inertial reference frame.*

the relativity of simultaneity. (Generic.) The hypothesis that man cannot assume that his strictly subjective sense of 'now' applies to all parts of the universe. Elsewhere, 'now' might be 'then,' or not yet experienced. See *time.*

relief ship. (Astronautics.) A rescue space ship.

remote sensing. (Astronautics.) An orbiting or manned spacecraft method that measures and analyzes—via panoramic, automatic scanning devices—electromagnetic energy emanating from the Earth's surface, or from the surface of any other celestial body. It is based on the phenomenon that any object whose temperature is above absolute zero reflects, emits, absorbs, transmits, or scatters photons, whether the object is organic or inorganic. Because each object, or class of objects, has a unique atomic and molecular structure, it yields a distinctive, easily identifiable spectral signature or 'fingerprint.' A remote sensing apparatus can 'see' and record through darkness, clouds, haze, vegetation, snow, and layers of rock. Perfect for taking surveys of usable resources, the whereabout of some of which may previously have been unknown. See *photon*.

repellor ray. (Fiction.) A form of non-recoil energy used by certain space ships when cruising through Earth's atmosphere, or when close to another planet's surface. Repellor rays take the form of columns of scintillating light that push downward with terrific force against the

The use of repellor rays is beautifully depicted in this 1929 Buck Rogers panel from the sequence labeled 'Capturing the Mongol Emperor.' The strip was only 164 days old when this drawing—now a collectors' item—appeared. The initial sequences weren't concerned with other planets or galaxies, but with an Earth that had been taken over by airborne Orientals from the Gobi Desert. Artist: Dick Calkins. Writer: Phil Nowlan.

ground, and upward with equal force against the keel of the ship generating them. The ship is maneuvered by altering the slant of the rays. See *non-recoil energy*.

resonance. (Physics.) Two coordinated phenomena reacting again and again regarding each other, always in the same relationship.

retarding rocket blast. (Fiction.) A blast from the stern of a space ship that has been spun around so its nose points upward, away from a landing site. It slows the ship's descent so it can land gently.

retro rockets. (Astronautics.) Also called retrograde or braking rockets. A spacecraft's rear rockets, providing counterthrust to the vehicle's forward movement; used to slow a space ship down before re-entry into the Earth's friction-producing atmosphere, or to maneuver it for a landing.

retrothrust. (Astronautics.) Reverse rocket thrust employed in a braking maneuver.

revolution. (Physics.) The orbital motion of one body around another, central body. For instance, the Earth revolves around the sun; the moon revolves around the Earth; and an electron revolves around an atom's nucleus. Compare with *rotation*.

ring of electric death. (Fiction.) Created by a small electro tube, employed to guard oneself against hand-to-hand combat. A deadly circumference of vibrating shock waves is formed around the person holding the tube. If an attacker passes through the waves, he is electrocuted.

ring ray. (Fiction.) A finger ring emission that prevents atomic fission in someone else's atomic pistol: useful when the latter is pointed at one and its trigger is squeezed. To activate the ray, all the ring's wearer has to do is clench his or her fist.

robot. (Fiction.) The word derives from a Czechoslovakian term for 'worker,' and was first used by Karel Capek in his play, *R.U.R.*, produced in 1921. R.U.R. means 'Rossum's Universal Robots.' These initial robots were essentially man-like androids mass-produced chemically. (In a pure sense, *android* is a science fiction term for a human-appearing robot, as opposed to a metal one, though the distinction is frequently ignored.) Capek wasn't the first writer whose theme was the creation of artificial life. He'd been preceded by Mary Shelley, with *Frankenstein*; and by Ambrose Bierce, with *Moxon's Master*.

All-metal robots came on stage in 1929. All-metal robots, known as homunculi, first appeared in Franz Harper's novel, *Plus and Minus*, published the year of Chicago's St. Valentine's Day Massacre. They soon became stock science fiction props that, lacking emotion, normally destroyed the protagonist in a bloody manner. Over the years, thanks largely to Isaac Asimov in such works as *I, Robot*, and *The Last of the Robots,* metal-and-electronic creations became virtually human. A key example of this is George Lucas's treatment of See Threepio and Artoo Detoo in *Star Wars*. Despite the Laurel and Hardy-type appeal of metallic See Threepio and Artoo Detoo, the current tendency in science fiction is to utilize robots and androids that are superficially indistinguishable from humans, as Asimov himself has also done.

Robots and androids indistinguishable from humans:

What they look like: You can sit beside one on a plane trip to Miami and never suspect he or she isn't born of woman. (We're not discussing Frankenstein-type monsters patched together from a grab-bag of human parts, but electronic-and-plastic creations, or electronic-and-human flesh creations.) It has muted eyes with irises that work . . . carefully veined hands, with smooth bands of con-

Traditional 'metal' robots, typified by the now-famous C3PO and R2D2, can perform tasks in environments inimical to humans, or undertake work disliked by flesh-and-blood beings. Metal robots have had a variegated science fiction history. Some have been hostile to man; others subservient; and still others have longed to be 'people.' A few have felt sorry for humans because the latter have soft, perishable bodies.

tractile plastic that articulate the fingers . . . hairy eyebrows that raise, lower, and bunch together realistically . . . and a positronic brain or its equivalent (see *What makes them 'tick,'* below) that can reason as well as yours, if not better. Its skeleton is fashioned from porous silicone plastics. Its 'flesh' and 'skin' may or may not be soft plastic that defies detection: it may be *real* human flesh and skin, grown over a skeletal structure via an adroit usage of hormone-controlled human ova.

Humanoid robots, such as this one whose head has been temporarily detached, are so similar to real people that the distinction smudges. In Gene Wolfe's 'Going to the Beach,' one of them becomes a hip-swinging streetwalker. Humanoid robots have emotions; they're not unfeeling, plastic-skinned store-window mannequins. They've even marched for their rights.

What makes them 'tick:' The various parts of its body are pains-takingly assembled along outwardly invisible dividing lines of self-resealing micromagnetic fields. For repair work, an arm, leg, the head, or the torso, comes apart at a proper touch, then snaps together again at a contrary touch. Under the plastic skin and flesh, or real skin and flesh if the latter are used, are silent servomotors . . . omni-directional auditory sensors . . . photoreceptors and ocular circuitry . . . epidermal sensors . . . locomotors for fluid movement purposes . . and a host of logic circuits and integrated logic terminals. The posi-tronic brain, or its equivalent, is a spongy globe about the size of a real brain, programmed to respond realistically and reflexively to given stimuli.

What they can and can't do: The 'he' or 'she' sitting beside you on the flight to Miami can discuss anything in a learned, witty, natural manner. It can also go through the motions of eating, drinking, and smoking, and even excuse itself to go to the bathroom. Once inside the water closet, however, it won't eliminate normally. Instead, it will open its chest, remove a plastic bag filled with solid food and liquid—ingested via suction and apparent chewing—and flush the bag away. It may seem as 'real' as you, but doesn't feel actual hunger or thirst, and lacks a sense of taste. It doesn't require true sleep, but may deactivate itself when there's nothing purposeful to accomplish. It may even experience electronic hallucinations if deprived of sensory inputs too long. Chances are, its over-all behavior is governed by what has become almost sacred in modern science fiction writing: Asimov's Three Laws of Robotics.

Asimov's Three Laws of Robotics: (1) A robot may not injure a human being, or through inaction allow a human being to come to harm. (2) A robot must obey the orders given it by human beings except where such orders would conflict with the First Law. (3) A robot must protect its own existence as long as such protection doesn't conflict with the First or Second Law.

See *android, cyborg,* and *anti-robot gun.*

roboticist. (Fiction.) A robot expert or robopsychologist.

rocket. (Astronautics.) A self-contained reaction engine that pushes forward at great speed by ejecting a stream of hot gases to the rear through an exhaust nozzle. It requires no air intake for combustion, since it carries its own oxidizer as well as a propellant. A rocket's force is measured in pounds of thrust. See *reaction engine, oxidizer, propellant,* and *spacecraft propulsion.*

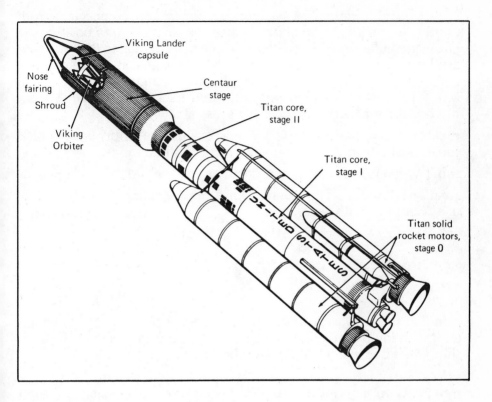

Viking Lander
capsule

Nose
fairing

Shroud

Viking
Orbiter

Centaur
stage

Titan core,
stage II

Titan core,
stage I

Titan solid
rocket motors,
stage 0

In this Titan III space vehicle configuration, two solid rockets, each 10 feet in diameter and 85 feet long, burn powdered aluminum in a rubber matrix, along with ammonium perchlorate, generating 1,200,000 pounds of thrust each at liftoff. After two minutes they burn out and are jettisoned. The Titan core—consisting of a two-stage liquid rocket, also 10 feet in diameter—ignites just before the solid rockets burn out. The core's liquid stages burn a blend of hydrazine and unsymmetrical dimethyllhydrazine fuel with a nitrogen tetroxide oxidizer.

rocket cluster. (Astronautics.) Two or more adjacent rockets functioning as a single propulsion unit.

rocket pistol. (Fiction.) A weapon similar in appearance to a 20th Century automatic. Ammunition rounds are snapped into position via clips, and bullets are fired with explosive power equal to 20th Century artillery shells. If aimed—at too close range—at something as resistant as a four-foot-thick-metal door, concussive effects can knock the pistol's user unconscious, and back-blowing fumes from the bullet's explosion can sear his eyes.

rocket thrust. (Astronautics.) A rocket engine's forward-directed force, push, or impetus, normally expressed in pounds.

roll. (Astronautics.) A spacecraft's rotation about a longitudinal axis.

rotation. (Physics.) The spinning of a body around its own internal axis. Compare with *revolution*.

S

safe flight. (Fiction.) A flight launched between solar storms which emit so many charged particles that they are hazardous to both space ship crews and space ship instrumentation.

safety mat. (Fiction.) An electronically-activated door mat at the entranceway to a germ-free building, enclosure, or spacecraft. When stepped on, a high-frequency current courses through the entrance-seeker's clothing, body organs, circulatory, gastro-intestinal, and respiratory systems, instantly killing any spores, seeds, or bacteria inadvertently picked up on the outside.

safety net. (Astronautics.) A restraining device used by space ship crew members when in a free fall condition, often attached to a bucket seat or contour couch. See *free fall*.

sailship. (Fiction.) a 1,000-ton starship that gradually approaches lightspeed under the pressure of laser-produced photons alone: a technique known as beamed power propulsion. The ship features a plastic fabric sail 155 miles across and adjustable shroud lines 20 miles in length. After it breaks away from the Earth's atmosphere,

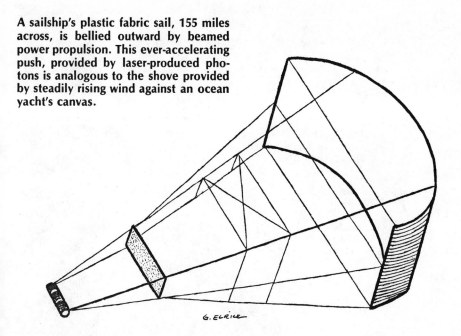

A sailship's plastic fabric sail, 155 miles across, is bellied outward by beamed power propulsion. This ever-accelerating push, provided by laser-produced photons is analogous to the shove provided by steadily rising wind against an ocean yacht's canvas.

G. ELRICK

it's pushed faster and faster into outer space via laser-focused photons stemming from asteroid-base set-ups. A galaxy's magnetic fields—tapped into by means of two long wires with a charge of several million volts—enable the craft to maneuver at will. See *photon* and *laser*.

sandwich skin. (Astronautics.) Two layers of material with a different material between them. A spacecraft's housing normally is fashioned from graphite epoxy honeycomb sandwich skins.

Sargasso. (Fiction.) A planet held together by a magnetic force instead of gravity, covered with the wrecks of crashed space ships.

Saturn . . . as it really is. (Astronomy.) One of the so-called Jovian planets, Saturn is an enormous 'gas giant' without a solid surface; the sixth planet from the sun.

Size: Nearly as large as Jupiter, but with less mass than the latter. However, its mass is 95 times that of the Earth, and its diameter is 74,000 miles.

Density: Saturn is seven-tenths as dense as water and one-eighth as dense as the Earth. It is so light that, if it were possible to position the planet on water, it would float.

With a sublime disregard for the hazards of explosive decompression—or the need for a pressure suit—Buck Rogers, as depicted in 1932, sallies forth on the rings of Saturn, protected only by a space helmet. What's he doing? He's looking for a man named Gadarxtl, who has gone spinning off into God knows where on one of those colliding boulders. From the safety of a nearby spacecraft, a woman named Kaxla has pleaded: 'Oh, no! Don't jump out with only a helmet on! You'll freeze instantly!' Using abominable English, Buck has self-confidently snapped back: 'Nix, sister, nix! Nothing like as fast as if we were going out into cold air. That's vacuum out there, so I won't lose much heat!' In actuality, he'd soon resemble a messy inflated balloon. Artist: Dick Calkins. Writer: Phil Nowlan.

Composition: Basically a hydrogen/helium 'soup,' with a warm, liquid metal interior. Oddly, it radiates more heat than it receives from the sun, though its outer layer is cold beyond belief. It has a slight magnetic field.

Temperature: Minus 250 degrees Fahrenheit.

Atmosphere: There is a great deal of methane, but not enough oxygen to support life as we know it (at least near the gaseous surface). Cloud belts made of ammonia hover overhead.

Rotation: Saturn spins rapidly, so much so that it's more flattened than Jupiter, and its day is a fraction over ten hours.

Orbital period: 29.5 years.

Satellites: Some astronomers say there are nine; others claim there are ten. It is possible that smaller satellites remain undetected. The largest satellite, *Titan* (which see), has an atmosphere containing methane and hydrogen. Whatever their size, the satellites are icy material.

Rings: Only a mile thick, but with a diameter of 170,000 miles. Each ring is composed of small bodies, each lies in Saturn's equatorial plane, and each goes around in its own circular orbit. Components of the rings jostle each other gently, and are far enough apart for stars to be seen through them. Their composition is probably ice-covered rock, ranging from snowball to iceberg size. Total mass is roughly that of a medium-size satellite.

Gravity: Earth = 1. Saturn = 1.17.

Saturn and/or Saturnians . . . as depicted in early pulp magazine-type science fiction. The rings of Saturn consist of billions of grinding, clashing rocks, all vibrating with sub-electronic pulsations; all rich in radioactive thorium, which can be used in space ship power generators.

The planet has a lushly variegated solid surface. Its principal metropolis is surrounded by upwardly thrusting deadly gamma rays, the purpose of which is to exclude interlopers.

Four of Saturn's moons shine all night, so it never gets dark. The planet has an unpopulated jungle region. Wild mountain tribesmen lurk in the hinterlands.

S-band link. (Astronautics.) Used with a lander/probe. (See *probe.*) A steerable dish, 30-inch parabolic reflector high-gain antenna that tracks the Earth from its site on a distant celestial body, transmitting high-volume scientific, photographic, and telemetric data directly to

Earth at selectable rates of 250, 500, or 1,000 bits-per-second. It receives command data from Earth at four bits-per-second.

SCC. (Fiction.) Short for Standard Communications Channel. Usage of its radio frequency band is mandatory for every spacecraft approaching any of a solar system's planets, so clearance and landing instructions can be obtained via some variety of mutually understood galactic language or code.

schematic. (Generic.) A procedural or structural diagram, sometimes depicting a 'critical path.'

science tricorder. (Fiction.) A device for selectively sensing, measuring, analyzing, comparing, and identifying surrounding environmental conditions. It features multiple channel recording and readout capability. (*Star Trek.*)

scientific method. (Generic.) Not an elaborately outlined formal procedure, nor a detailed road map into the unknown, but a generally

G. ELRICK

The so-called scientific method of inquiry and hypothesis validation is as much a chess game as a mentally computerized approach to ultimate answers, since Aristotle's 'Aha!' experience is frequently a factor in the discovery of final solutions.

adhered to approach-pattern to conceptualization, data collection, and hypothesis validation. In its totality, it's an 'overturn-every-stone' style of inquiry; a 'Show me, I'm from Missouri' attitude; and a respectful watch-and-wait philosophy regarding nature's reluctance to reveal secrets. In essence, scientists pose questions; collect pertinent evidence; form a postulate; deduce the postulate's implications; test the implications experimentally; then accept, reject, or modify accordingly. Many scientific discoveries, of course, derive from flashes of inspiration or sudden perceptions akin to Aristotle's 'shock of recognition.' (The 'Aha!' experience.)

scrub. (Astronautics.) To cancel—for any of a variety of reasons—a scheduled spacecraft launching before or during countdown. See *countdown.*

secondary neonic force-ray battery. (Fiction.) An apparatus capable of clearing interplanetary radio channels, so the approach of an attacking space ship is undetectable.

semi-inertial guidance. (Astronautics.) A spacecraft navigation system employing the same equipment and techniques as those used in inertial guidance, augmented by equipment capable of receiving instructions or commands from Earth, another planet, or another spacecraft. See *inertial guidance.*

sensor. (Generic.) An extremely sensitive apparatus that perceives and responds to stimuli. The latter may be nuclear, electromagnetic (including visible and invisible portions of the spectrum), chemical, biological, thermal, mechanical, auditory, olfactory, or vibrational. The simplest example of a sensor is the common photoelectric cell.

separation velocity. (Astronautics.) Not to be confused with *escape velocity* (which see). Separation velocity has two meanings: (1) the speed at which a space vehicle is thrusting ahead when some part or section is deliberately dropped away from it, as in a multistage rocket; (2) the velocity of a satellite or space probe at separation-time from its launch vehicle.

servomechanism. (Generic.) Also called a servo. A closed-loop feedback system that automatically controls a mechanical or electronic operation by measuring the difference between a standard and a process being monitored, constantly regulating the procedure to nullify errors. The controlled variable is often a mechanical position or rate. The servomechanism generally consists of a sensing element, an amplifier, and a servometer. See *cybernetics*.

shaving ray. (Fiction.) The futuristic equivalent of a razor blade or electric shaver. Disintegrates facial hair without harming the skin.

ship's complement. (Astronautics.) The number of crew members on a space ship.

shock absorbo chamber. (Fiction.) Also known as a recoil chamber. A space ship compartment that dampens or nullifies the effects of a high-speed collision.

sidereal. (Astronomy.) A synonym for *stellar*; anything concerning stars or constellations.

simulacrum. (Generic.) A realistic image, 'double,' or representation of something or someone.

skycycle. (Fiction.) A small, single seat, double-rocket 'open' version of a 20th Century motorcycle, used for airborne recreational pleasure jaunts.

skyhopper. (Fiction.) A powerful little suborbital manned spacecraft.

sleeper ship. (Fiction.) A space ship carrying occupants in suspended animation.

sleeping gas. (Fiction.) Has two meanings: (1) Anesthesia sprayed on a subject before his mind pictures are examined via an *infra-quantum hypnotiscope* (which see). (2) A gas emitted by a time-release capsule a quarter-of-an-inch wide. When dropped behind if one is being pursued on foot, it temporarily incapacitates those who are trying to catch up.

sleep ray projector. (Fiction.) A hand-held, flashlight-like object that, when clicked on, emits a ray that causes those it's pointed at to fall into a deep, though temporary, sleep. As a side effect, it instigates a brief fever that burns up superficial diseases.

S.L.S. (Fiction.) Also known as super life span or super life serum. A miracle compound that extends longevity indefinitely. When used in liquid form, one injection must be administered daily. When used in capsule form, one tablet must be swallowed every 24 hours.

social science fiction. (Generic.) Along with adventure SF and gadget SF, one of the genre's three primary divisions. Concerned with the moral, psychological, metaphysical, sociological, and philosophical

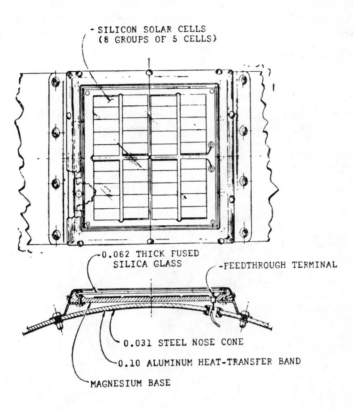

SILICON SOLAR CELLS
(8 GROUPS OF 5 CELLS)

0.062 THICK FUSED
SILICA GLASS

FEEDTHROUGH TERMINAL

0.031 STEEL NOSE CONE

0.10 ALUMINUM HEAT-TRANSFER BAND

MAGNESIUM BASE

Solar cells on space vehicles convert the sun's energy photovoltaically. In a typical spacecraft installation, fused quartz windows 1/16 inch thick protect against damage from ionized particles and micrometeorites. Molded rubber gaskets temper stresses caused by launch vibrations and extreme temperature changes.

ramifications of technically advanced milieus, interrelationships, and lifestyles, this is the subtlest and most difficult type of science fiction to write. See *adventure science fiction* and *gadget science fiction*.

soft landing. (Astronautics.) Also called touchdown. The landing of a spacecraft on a solid celestial body 'softly' enough to avoid self-destruction or self-damage, accomplished by carefully slowing the spacecraft's descent via retro rockets. See *hard landing* and *retro rockets*.

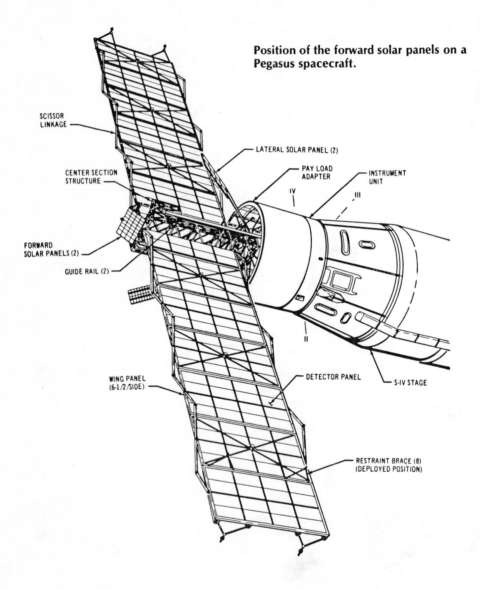

Position of the forward solar panels on a Pegasus spacecraft.

SCISSOR LINKAGE

LATERAL SOLAR PANEL (2)

PAY LOAD ADAPTER

INSTRUMENT UNIT

CENTER SECTION STRUCTURE

IV

III

FORWARD SOLAR PANELS (2)

GUIDE RAIL (2)

II

WING PANEL (6-1/2/SIDE)

DETECTOR PANEL

S-IV STAGE

RESTRAINT BRACE (8) (DEPLOYED POSITION)

solagonic line projection. (Fiction.) A space travel navigational reference term.

solaradio. (Fiction.) A radio transmitter and receiver utilizing specific space-ship-to-space-ship frequency waves.

solar cell. (astronautics.) A semiconductor device used to convert the energy of sunlight into electric energy.

solar cyclone. (Fiction.) A type of solar system disturbance occasionally encountered by space ships.

solar fin. (Fiction.) Either a two-sided or a pyramid-shaped space ship protuberance functioning as a solar panel, covered with thousands of solar cells that convert stellar radiation into electric power.

solar panel. (Astronautics.) A portion of a satellite, or any other spacecraft, covered with thousands of solar cells that convert sunshine into electric power. A battery pack may be used to store electricity for use when the craft is in the Earth's shadow. See *solar cell.*

solar silhouette book. (Fiction.) A reference volume, carried by Earth-based space ships, depicting recognition silhouettes of all other known space ships.

solar solidifier. (Fiction.) Also known as metallic air. A ray, zapped from a space cannon, that instantly solidifies an attacking space fleet in transparent armor plate.

solar system: chemistry of. (Astronomy.) The solar system is basically hydrogen—as is the universe in its entirety—with a mixture of other chemical elements. In our planetary set-up, the heavier elements that comprise rocks and metals tend to be relatively close to the sun. Moving outward, the more volatile, or easily evaporated elements, compounds, and mixtures prevail.

solar system space lanes. (Fiction.) Celestial 'beaten paths'; the most frequently traveled routes between Earth and the solar system's eight other planets. Used by interplanetary liners, freighters, even space tramps. Occasionally ducked in or out of by space pirates. To deviate from the routes is to risk being smashed by cosmic storms.

solar timeless belt. (Fiction.) An area—in the interplanetary space of another galaxy—where time is frozen. When in that region, one's body maintains its particular status quo indefinitely. If one leaves the region, inevitable entropy sets in, sometimes followed by total decomposition.

solar wind. (Astronomy.) A flow of *plasma* (which see), or gas, spreading outward in all directions from the sun at 250-miles-per-second. A million tons of gas are ejected each second. Solar wind has a temperature of a million degrees, and is a mixture of chaotic magnetic fields carried by currents of electrons in the plasma, which is almost totally ionized. See *ionization*.

solid rocket booster. (Astronautics.) SRB for short. A booster rocket containing a solid propellant.

soma. (Fiction.) In Aldous Huxley's *Brave New World*, a drug that eases all tensions, concurrently inducing a state of euphoric contentment.

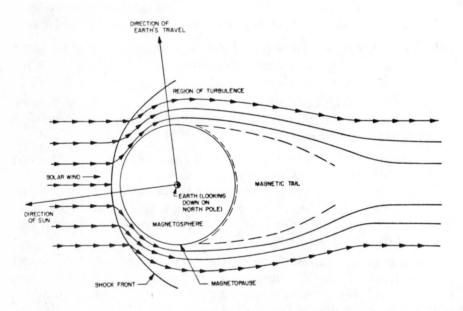

When solar wind arrives in the vicinity of the Earth, it encounters the latter's magnetic field. The airfoil-shaped region created by the solar wind's interaction with the magnetic field, compressing and confining it, is the magnetosphere. The boundary is the magnetopause. Since the Earth's magnetic field deflects all particles, a disturbance is created in the solar wind's smooth flow, just as a rock protruding from a stream disturbs the smooth flow of water.

sonic detonator. (Fiction.) A small pendant worn by female interplanetary agents. Actually a self-protection device rigged to a concealed on-the-body disintegrator pistol. One loud shout or scream fires the pistol, destroys whoever's trying to capture, manhandle, or molest the agent, but leaves the latter unscathed.

sonic disintegrator. (Fiction.) An ultimate defensive weapon, capable of reducing the Himalayas to heaps of loose dust. Creates supersonic frequencies of such force that even its echoes de-atomize large objects.

sonic-gyroscopic neutro-stabilizer. (Fiction.) A space ship control device that prevents dangerous midship vibrations when a craft blasts off at a 4,000 miles-per-hour velocity. Without its balancing influence, sub-dynamic leverage stress can produce dangerous turbo-torque. Once a ship is in flight, the stabilizer is switched off.

sonic speed. (Physics.) The velocity of a body traveling at Mach 1. See *Mach number.*

sonic vox projector. (Fiction.) A loudspeaker in controlled orbit, usually not far above the surface of the Earth or some other planet, used to give commands, issue warnings, or utter threats, depending on who controls it.

sound: absence of in space. (Generic.) With the exception of a few areas closely surrounding certain planets, interstellar and intergalactic space is as silent as the interior of a closed and buried casket, because there is no atmosphere to propagate sound waves. Space ships don't make exterior hissing or whooshing noises, and rocket battles between spacecraft would be as quiet as a picture on a printed page, or, to quote Samuel Taylor Coleridge's *The Rhyme of the Ancient Mariner*: 'As silent as a painted ship upon a painted ocean.' All communications in space must be via radio—the signals of which travel on magnetic waves—or via some form of light beam technology. See *anacoustic zone.*

soundless siren. (Fiction.) An assembly or warning signal, emitted at wavelengths beyond the perceptive powers of the unaided human ear, but perfectly audible to those whose helmet radios or tiny ear plugs are adjusted to its frequency.

space. (Generic.) Space is as difficult to define as *time* (which see) or *photon* (which see). Though linked with time as a form of intuitive perception, like time it has no objective reality as an entity in and of itself. It's nothing but the order—or spatial relationships—of things regarding each other; nothing but the distance between objects. The concept of interstellar space or intergalactic space is meaningless minus the presence of stars and galaxies. Without objects occupying it, space is a zero.

But there *are* billions of objects 'out there,' and when we conceptualize space with respect to the universe, in some ways it's less of an abstraction, and in some ways more so. In any case, it's a different ball game, and a puzzling one.

Space has no direction or boundaries. The universe is as restless as a school of fish exploding away from a pursuing shark. That's a colorful simile, and true, but the analogy peters out. There's an 'up' and a 'down' in the ocean, but no up, down, or sideways in space. There's no north, south, east, or west in space. All movements of all

There's no up, down, sideways, north, south, east, or west in the universe's 'space.' The movements of celestial bodies can be described only with respect to each other. Nothing ever 'gets' anywhere, for there's no fixed place at which anything can possibly 'arrive.'

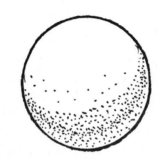

G. ELRICK

bodies in space can be described only with respect to each other. Taken as a whole, the movements don't result in anything 'getting' anywhere, because, composite-wise, there's no 'place' at which anything can possibly arrive.

Space is warped near matter. According to Einstein, space is curved near matter: the heavier the matter, the greater the adjacent curvature. Space curvature around a celestial body is referred to as its gravitational field. A star's gravitational field can be conceived as a

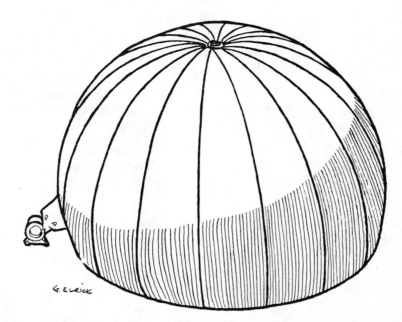

G. ELRICK

Though many space colonies will simply orbit in 'living bicycle wheels' shaped like giant doughnuts (known as Stanford Toruses), others will stake out claims on the surfaces of celestial bodies. Before these off-Earth cultures build domed or underground cities, 'advance men' will erect temporary structures such as the inflatable, igloo-type affair pictured. These will be made of fabric, rubber, or Fiberglas, covered with heavy metallic fabric to deflect micrometeorites. Interior artificially produced atmospheric pressure will be 14.7 pounds per-square-inch, as on Earth. Some colonies may thrive in the form of synthetic worlds in hollowed-out asteroids.

'hill,' with the star at the summit. Planets and other bodies moving in the star's gravitational field slide around the star rather than over it, for a curved path is easier to follow that a hill or a flight of stairs. And, despite lip service to the pull of gravity, bodies don't really attract each other at a distance: they simply follow lines of least resistance through space curvature's crests and troughs.

See *spacetime* and *relativity*.

space apple. (Fiction.) A type of fruit, some varieties of which are poisonous, found on certain planetoids.

spacebane. (Fiction.) A Venusian 'old-wives'-tale' interplanetary monster that supposedly causes death and destruction.

space bell. (Fiction.) A metal, globe-shaped, self-contained 'life raft,' for use when a space ship must be abandoned. It has the same internal atmospheric pressure as the space ship of which it was a part, and is capable of sustaining several people.

space boat. (Fiction.) Not to be confused with a space bell. The equivalent of a 20th Century life boat, though enclosed and rocket-powered. Compare with *escape bullet* and *pod*.

space burial. (Fiction.) Futuristic counterpart of the sea burial of earlier centuries. A body, properly shrouded and bound, is ceremoniously cast adrift in outer space, where it presumably orbits indefinitely.

space cane. (Fiction.) A type of jointed grass found on certain asteroids.

space colonies. (Fiction/Astronautics.) The first bona fide space colony undoubtedly will be on the moon's surface, or below the moon's surface. Why the moon? Because of its size, proximity, and abundant raw materials. Even when other, perpetually orbiting space colonies are built, they'll use the moon's raw materials for construction purposes, though such volatile elements as hydrogen, carbon, and nitrogen will be Earth-supplied. Oxygen is plentiful on the moon —compounded with other materials—and recyclable water could easily be 'manufactured' in conjunction with hydrogen transported via space shuttle.

Eventual use of asteroids for raw materials: When the moon's colonies, and its mines, are in full operation, asteriods can be engaged and broken down for *their* minerals, hydrogen, carbon, and nitrogen, avoiding depletion of the Earth's resources.

Creation of artificial gravity at two spins a minute: In time, huge structures—cylindrical, sphere-shaped, or doughnut-shaped—will be erected in space, capable of housing tens of thousands of people from birth to death. These moon-material and asteroid-material structures, each with its own solar energy station, will spin twice a minute, creating a 'feet on the ground' effect similar to that of gravity.

See *life support system, algae and space travel, hydroponics, space suit, space platform, space shuttle, space processing, asteroids,* and *expandable space structure.*

spacecraft orbits. (Astronautics.) Space ships follow orbits, just as do planets, comets, asteroids, and satellites. They're subject to identical laws of motion and gravitation. The difference resides in the fact that a ship is provided with initial motive power to place it in a desired orbit, and can later be shifted to another orbit, if desired. Because orbital motion persists with no force other than gravitation, propulsion power can be cut off for most of a spacecraft's journey.

spacecraft propulsion. (Astronautics.) If a space ship needs some thrust in order to change its orbit, it must thrust against its own exhaust gas, for there's nothing else in space to push against. This is the source of all interplanetary or intergalactic acceleration, when the latter is needed.

space drowning. (Fiction.) Suffocation in the virtual vacuum of space, due to space suit malfunctioning.

spacefaring men. (Fiction.) Also known as spacefarers. The futuristic equivalent of seafaring men. See *spacer.*

space hazards to the psyche. (Astronautics.) Crew members of space ships—particularly on prolonged flights—struggle with a variety of psychological problems, including physical isolation from all but fellow crew members, who may be getting on each other's nerves; boredom; kinetic activity restrictions; curtailed sensory inputs, which can give rise to hallucinations; prolonged weightlessness; and time-and-place disorientation. See *breakaway phenomenon.*

space inertial navigation system. (Fiction.) The fundamental guidance base for a starship's onboard navigational complex, perpetually realigned with galactic coordinates. (*Star Trek.*)

space mine. (Fiction.) An explosive device orbiting around a planet as a defense against enemy space ship encroachment.

space opera. (Generic.) A derisive term applied to science fiction that relies on cardboard characters, cliche situations, and 'hardware.'

space pirates. (Fiction.) Also known as space bandits, space gangsters, or space predators: criminals who prey on interplanetary shipping. They usually single out space freighters as targets.

space platform. (Astronautics.) Also called a space station: a large orbiting satellite serving as a habitable space base, with scientific observation, military, or exploratory applications. Facilities include adequate nourishment for those who man the station, plus adequate space for supply storage. It is frequently used as a launching pad for other space vehicles, or as a warehouse and personnel pool for other spacecraft. See *space shuttle.*

spaceport. (Astronautics.) Futuristic equivalent of an airport, where spacecraft are loaded and unloaded, fueled, and serviced.

space prober. (Fiction.) Also known as a salvage prober or sonic eye. An electronic sensing device at the end of a long, flexible cable, used by cosmic current space-combers who seek out and search derelict spacecraft for whatever valuables they contain. By means of remote control, the prober is directed toward, or enters, any derelict ship spotted. What it sees with its eye-sensors is depicted on the controlling ship's tele-plate. The front of the prober is equipped with a disintegrator, so it can blast apart closed doors and hatches, or eat its way through bulkheads.

space processing. (Generic.) The creation, manufacture, and processing of physical and biological materials in encapsulated, orbiting, gravity-free environments. Space processing permits the growth or development of larger, purer crystals for use in semiconductors, new metallurgical alloys, metal foams, new forms of optical glass, and new strains of biological molecules.

spacequake. (Fiction.) A disturbance in space equivalent, in its effects, to an earthquake.

spacer. (Fiction.) A futuristic Ishmael: an inveterate professional space ship crew member, in whatever capacity. Accustomed to taking voyages which seemingly last several years, but actually

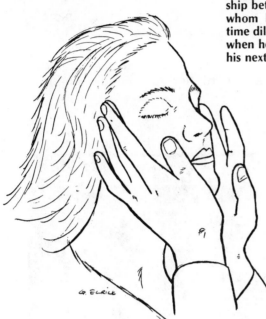

There's nothing sadder than the relationship between a 'spacer' and a woman to whom he makes love, for—thanks to time dilation—she'll be dead and buried when he swings back to Earth-base after his next prolonged mission.

extend many decades, Earth-time-wise, a spacer usually spends each Earth layover drinking heavily and enthusiastically—but heartlessly—womanizing, totally aware that each female he beds will be dead, and will have long since mouldered away, when he next returns. See *paradox of the twins.*

space rat. (Fiction.) A mutant-type of rodent that occasionally infests space ships.

space ship avionics. (Fiction/Astronautics.) The over-all electronic, cybernetic interrelationships that pertain in a space ship. Normally, there are roughly 200 major 'black boxes' employed for guidance, navigation, and control; for transmission of data to and from various subsystems; and for monitoring. In essence, computers process information from the guidance, navigation, and control systems; then perform computations and transmit requisite commands to flight-control black boxes, which immediately position applicable control surfaces. This parallels what happens with human body sensors: eyes and ears sense what's taking place, then signal the brain to react. The latter instantly forwards proper instructions to appropriate body parts. Usage of multiple computers with redundancy management guarantees fail-operational/fail-safe performance. Not only do computers act and react automatically, they display 'real time' readout information to the flight crew. See *black box, fail operational/fail-safe performance, cybernetics,* and *servomechanism.*

AND A MILLION MILES AWAY NOW—ARDALA SAT AT THE CONTROLS OF OUR SPACE SHIP.

I'LL BE RID OF ROGERS AND WILMA — WHEN THAT PLANETOID SMASHES THEM UP ON EARTH — I'LL DROP BARNEY OFF ON PLUTO AND —

No redundant computers or 'black boxes' here: flight control is simpler than grinding corn between two stones. Ardala Valmar—the most black-hearted wench ever spawned by mass audience fiction—steers her space ship as though pushing levers on a Caterpillar D9 Tractor. The speech balloon denotes her casual attitude toward interplanetary distances. From a 1934 Buck Rogers sequence known as 'The Planetoid Plot.' Artist: Dick Calkins. Writer: Phil Nowlan.

space ship cradle. (Fiction.) The half tubular 'nest' in which a space ship is positioned after returning to an Earth—or other planetary—spaceport and all controls have been cut off.

space ship flight control. (Fiction/Astronautics.) Generally speaking, a space ship's guidance, navigation, and control system is comprised of four redundant computers tied into appropriate software and numerous 'black boxes,' plus a fifth computer employed for backup flight control. The space ship's commander or pilot selects flight control system operational modes via pushbuttons on the display-and-control panel. There are three modes to choose from: automatic, control stick steering, and direct. In the automatic mode, the ship basically acts like a missile, with the flight crew occasionally monitoring instruments to verify that the vehicle is following the correct orbit or trajectory. This provides human workload release, since computers execute flight control equations 25 times per second, governing movements of aerodynamic control surfaces. If the vehicle at any time diverges from trajectory or orbit, the flight crew takes over by switching to control stick steering or the direct mode. In the control stick steering mode, the flight crew flies the ship by deflecting a small pistol-grip stick called the rotation hand control. The flight control system interprets rotation hand control motions as rate commands in pitch, roll, or yaw: the larger the deflection, the larger the command. The system compares commands with inputs from rate gyros and accelerometers, then generates control signals to produce desired rates. In the direct mode, space ship control surfaces respond only to flight crew inputs, but the inputs continue to be routed through computers. See *backup flight control system, space ship avionics, caution/warning system, displays and controls, instrumentation system, electrical power system, orbital maneuvering system, flight deck, fail-operational/fail-safe performance,* and *black box.*

space ship yards. (Fiction.) Areas where space ships are designed and assembled.

space shuttle. (Astronautics.) A space transportation system that carries passengers, equipment, and supplies to and from an orbiting space platform on a routine, aircraft-like basis. See *space platform.*

space shuttle main engine. (Fiction/Astronautics.) SSME for short. Features an engine controller based on a digital computer that monitors such performance parameters as pressure and temperature, automatically adjusting for required thrust and constant mixture ratio.

space suit. (Astronautics.) A pressurized suit worn by a space venturer that provides him or her with a normal, Earth-type human environment when away from a space ship, or when the command module or

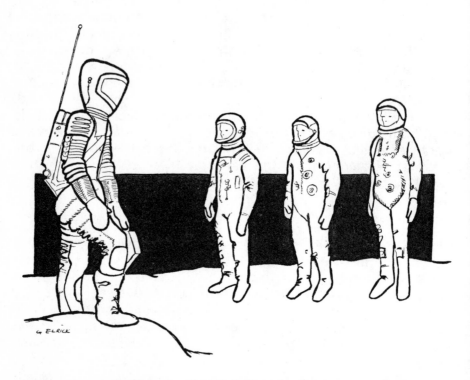

Real-life space suits and science fiction space suits are virtually identical, both having developed from old-fashioned underwater diving suits. Portrayed are a variety of outfits, all kissing cousins in appearance except for the 'lobster shell' suit at left. Each cosmonaut wears a polycarbonate plastic helmet with two additional external visors that filter out deadly ultraviolet rays. Under the thick-skinned outer garment, each wears complicated underwear consisting of a comfort layer, a pressure bladder, a restraint layer, a bumper layer, an aluminized thermal layer, a felt layer, and an outer layer of non-flammable Fiberglas cloth. Each also wears a snug-fitting skullcap featuring a built-in headset and microphone.

crew cabin is depressurized. Generally, it must have its own oxygen supply set-up, humidity control system, communication system, and ingenious arrangements for eliminating or recycling metabolic and bodily wastes. The suit must be of a material that protects its wearer against micrometeorites, cosmic rays, X-rays, gamma rays, and unexpected 'things that go bump in the night.' Specifically, it must: (1) Protect its wearer from the vacuum of space. (2) Keep the ambient temperature in the suit comfortable, whether in blazing sunlight or dark shadow, and during unpowered space flight when the spacecraft's heating system may be turned off. (3) Feature a backpack whose oxygen supply is renewable—for periods lasting several weeks—via periodic pluggings into the mother ship's oxygen supply. (4) Allow its wearer to ingest food and liquid, under zero gravity conditions, without breaking the suit's sealed atmosphere. (5) Enable its wearer to regain footing unaided, should he or she stumble and clumsily sprawl like an overturned turtle. (6) Permit its wearer to do work requiring a considerable degree of manual dexterity. See *pressure suit, cosmic rays, X-rays, gamma rays, explosive decompression,* and *FORB.*

space tender. (Fiction.) A small rocket ship that is stowed in a compartment in a larger space ship. Used to explore planets and asteroids while the mother ship hovers nearby. Compare with *pod.*

space tide. (Fiction.) A dangerous, sucking turbulence of interstellar gas and dust.

spacetime. (Generic.) Also called the spacetime continuum or fourth dimension: a four-dimensional indivisible 'whole' of three spatial coordinates (height, width, and depth) and one temporal coordinate (time) in which all events and physical objects are positioned. As such, though difficult to conceptualize, it is the ultimate matrix of reality. Any separation of space from time is totally subjective, for all measurements of time actually are measurements in space, and measurements in space depend on measurements of time. Yet space and time are intuitive perceptions, each dependent on the other; relative quantities varying with individual observers.

Impossible to construct a four-dimensional model of spacetime. Since time can't be held in one's hands or dropped on the floor, it is impossible to erect a meaningful mock-up depicting height, width, depth, and a fourth dimension that is forever in one's head. But it

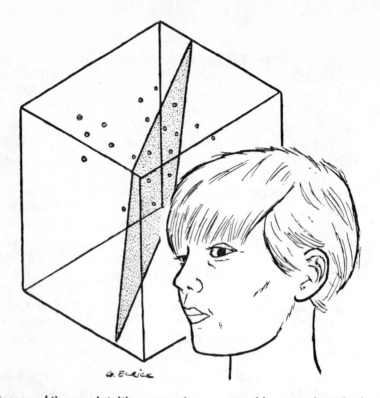

G. ELRICK

Space and time are intuitive perceptions, each leaning against the other for existence. It follows that the difficult-to-grasp twin entities are strictly relative quantities, varying radically from observer to observer, and from period to period with each observer. The perceptual field of a two-year-old bears little resemblance to that of a harassed forty-year-old. What's more, the perceptual field of a male may differ from that of a female. As King Canute muttered when sitting on the beach, 'Time and tide wait for no man' . . . but time, tide (and space) are perceived and reacted to differently by each individual.

definitely can be conceived in the abstract, and it emphatically can be represented via complicated equations that 'work.'

Spacetime manifests local irregularities. The geometrical structure of the universe, in toto, is shaped by the sum of its material content; and the universe's material content distorts the continuum here, there, and everywhere. As mentioned under *space* (which see), the heavier the concentration of matter, the greater the adjacent space-time curvature. Each galaxy, and every celestial body, can be thought of as an archipelago or island protruding from a sea, with eddies swirling around it.

244

No straight lines; only great circles. Though light is emitted isotropically—theoretically in flat trajectories in all directions—it actually doesn't follow arrow-straight lines. Light radiation bends slightly when traversing gravitational fields, for the geometry of the fields permits no straightness. Because of gravitational buckling and dimpling, the shortest path light can follow is faintly circular on a relatively local level; vastly circular on the macrocosmic level.

A great closed cosmic curve. The end result of the adding up of all local spacetime curvature is an incomprehensibly massive *Moebius strip* (which see) or *Klein bottle* (which see), in which the continuum bends back on itself in an unbroken curve.

Looking outward in space means looking backward in time. Light radiation from a distant star, registering 'just now' on an astronomer's photographic plate, may have left that stellar body eons before the first long-extinct dinosaur flopped out of its leathery egg.

See *invariance of interval, relativity, time, universe,* and *isotropic.*

space trade routes. (Fiction.) Interplanetary routes used for space shipments.

space warp. See *alternate framework.*

space warp engine. See *main propulsion unit.*

space whirlpool. (Fiction.) An eddy or vortex of interstellar gas.

spaceworthy. (Fiction.) As applied to space ships, comparable to the 20th Century term seaworthy.

spacewreck. (Fiction.) The equivalent of a 20th Century shipwreck, sometimes used as a decoy by space predators.

spatiography. (Generic.) The study of interplanetary, interstellar, and intergalactic space and its characteristics.

specific impulse. (Astronautics.) The amount of thrust developed by burning one pound of fuel for one second in a spacecraft rocket. Specifically: the ratio of thrust to fuel-mass flow.

spectrograph. (Physics.) An instrument producing a spectrum of the light radiating through it.

spectrum. (Physics.) The array of an object's radiation—in colors or wavelengths—when its emissions are dispersed through a prism or grating.

spectrum analyzer. (Astronautics.) An instrument that separates and measures individual frequencies comprising a complex electrical signal, obtaining a full-resolution scan and providing a signature analysis or 'fingerprint.'

speedtalk. (Fiction.) A form of verbal communication devised by Robert Heinlein in his story 'Gulf.' Speedtalk compresses a language so that, meaning-wise, a word equals a sentence, and two or more words equal a paragraph.

splinter cultures. (Fiction.) Alien cultures that have broken off from, or developed differently than, mainstream galactic cultures.

split S turn. (Fiction.) A rapid maneuver made by a space ship to avoid colliding with a suddenly looming object, such as a large meteor.

spring soles and heels. (Fiction.) Foot gear worn with any type of anti-gravity back pack to ease the shock of landing and taking off when bounding from point to point.

spy eliminator. (Fiction.) A polarized ray, activated between two harmless looking pillars flanking a door, which temporarily knocks out anyone who walks through it.

square cube law. (Physics.) Makes many of early science fiction's conventions concerning giant ants and other enormous creatures laughable in light of today's knowledge. Here's why: doubling the linear dimensions of a beast quadruples the cross-sectional area of its legs; quadruples the absorptive area of its lungs and intestinal tract or gut; and multiplies its total mass by eight. If a writer triples the linear dimensions of a monstrous creation, the results are even more downward-crushing and self-defeating. Anything that large (unless it stayed in water, like a whale) would need legs like an underpass's concrete pillars to support it; lungs the dimensions of a grade school gymnasium to suck in enough oxygen or whatever gaseous compound it breathed; and a daily food intake capable of supplying the Chinese army on full field rations.

stage. (Astronautics.) In a space vehicle powered by successive units, each component is referred to as a stage. Generally, rocket vehicles are referred to as one-stage, two-stage, or three-stage.

star. (Astronomy.) A massive, self-luminous sphere of hot gas—primarily hydrogen—held together by its own inward-pulling gravi-

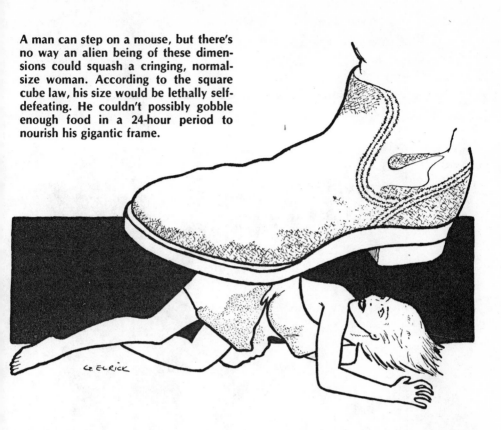

A man can step on a mouse, but there's no way an alien being of these dimensions could squash a cringing, normal-size woman. According to the square cube law, his size would be lethally self-defeating. He couldn't possibly gobble enough food in a 24-hour period to nourish his gigantic frame.

tation. It sustains itself by a self-perpetuating creation of nuclear energy at its center, basically through a slow conversion of hydrogen to helium, and emits radiation throughout the electromagnetic spectrum, from the longest waves to the shortest, all of which travel at lightspeed.

star cluster. (Astronomy.) A group of stars held in relatively close proximity by mutual gravitational attraction.

Star Fleet. (Fiction.) The armed, peace-maintaining forces of the United Federation of Planets, consisting of the following classes of starships: dreadnoughts, heavy cruisers, destroyer/scouts, cruisers, and transport/tugs. (*Star Trek.*)

starship. (Fiction.) A space ship capable of interstellar or intergalactic travel.

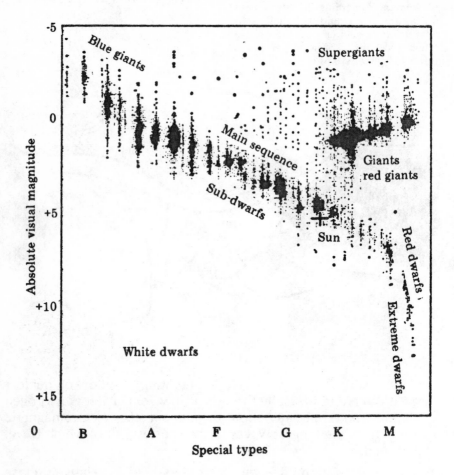

Absolute visual magnitude

-5

0

+5

+10

+15

Blue giants

Supergiants

Main sequence

Giants
red giants

Sub-dwarfs

Sun

Red dwarfs

Extreme dwarfs

White dwarfs

O   B   A   F   G   K   M

Special types

Early astronomers classified stars in two categories: brightness and color. They called the brightest stars, such as Alpha Centauri, magnitude 0. The magnitude of less bright stars increased to magnitude 6. This basic scale is still in use. Since magnitude 0 is defined by the brightness of a particular star, the magnitudes of other bodies such as the sun, moon, and some planets have negative values. A star's color is a measure of its temperature. Ten different major classifications of stars now exist according to color or temperature. In this Hertzsprung-Russell diagram, there's a distinct sequence (right to left) from red M stars of absolute magnitude 15 to blue stars of magnitude 5.

248

star formation. (Fiction.) One of the many flight patterns available to a space ship fleet.

star tracker. (Astronautics.) A space ship navigational device designed to fix on a star. See *celestial guidance.*

stasis. (Fiction.) In certain science fiction stories, a condition of timelessness in which the entropy arrow is motionless. Everything stays 'as is.' Derived from a physiological reference to the stagnation of body fluids, particularly blood.

static generator. (Fiction.) A device that emits powerful blasts of static that can disrupt enemy-used wavelengths, particularly when the wavelengths are employed for remote control of mechanical men.

statico detector. (Fiction.) An electronic sensor used by space predators to register the cosmic oscillation frequencies of strangers.

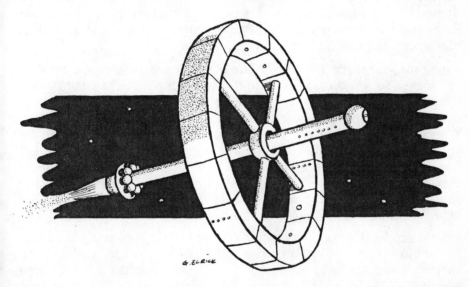

Interstellar travel beyond our solar system is so prohibitive that generations of nomadic colonists—in rotating starships such as this—could be born, grow up, and die without setting foot on an ultimate destination other-planet. These computer controlled 'generation ships,' or 'traveling arks,' using plasma drive or ionic propulsion, might take advantage of supralight jumps via hyperspace. Even so, particularly ambitious trips would take centuries. To stave off claustrophobia, boredom, or worse, crew members could conceivably opt for periodic, 'deep-freeze' suspended animation made possible through cryogenics.

steadyscope. (Generic.) A lightweight, hand-held, gyro-stabilized surveillance instrument that provides a clear view of distant objects, even when its user is in a violently maneuvering aerospace vehicle.

steam rifle. (Fiction.) A rifle, the staccato-like bullet-firing of which is activated by steam rather than explosive powder.

Stefan's law. (Physics.) The total radiation rate from a black body is proportional to its surface area and the fourth power of its temperature. See *black body.*

stratosphere. (Astronautics.) A layer of the Earth's atmosphere, beginning about six miles above sea level and lying just above the troposphere. Its temperature is steady; motions are horizontal, without vertical mixing; and there is virtually no weather activity.

streamlining: lack of need for. (Astronautics.) Since there is no atmosphere in space to impede motion, space ships needn't be shaped like elongated bullets. A spacecraft shaped like an elaborate Christmas tree ornament, or an Easter basket, will go just as fast as one structured like a pointed pencil.

strong nuclear force. (Physics.) One of the four fundamental entities in nature. (See *physics: four basic forces of,* and *weak nuclear force.*) Roughly a hundred times more powerful than electromagnetism, its overwhelming short-range attraction 'glues' atomic nuclei together. Whereas the force ranges of electromagnetism and gravity can be considered theoretically infinite, the range of the strong nuclear force's influence extends no farther than the outer boundary of an atomic nucleus, where it abruptly terminates. The fire-maker of the sun and other stars, it is employed, on Earth, in bombs, and in nuclear power stations. See *nuclear reactor.*

structo scope. (Fiction.) Operating on the principle of refracted light, it combines rays to form a deliberately created mirage: an 'air shell' shaped like a building. Used to mislead and confuse an attacking enemy.

stun pistol. (Fiction.) A device for temporarily incapacitating without killing.

sub-atomic cell reversion of solid chemi-tissue. (Fiction.) A means of vaporizing—and then re-solidifying—groups of men at will.

sub-atomic particles. See *elementary particles.*

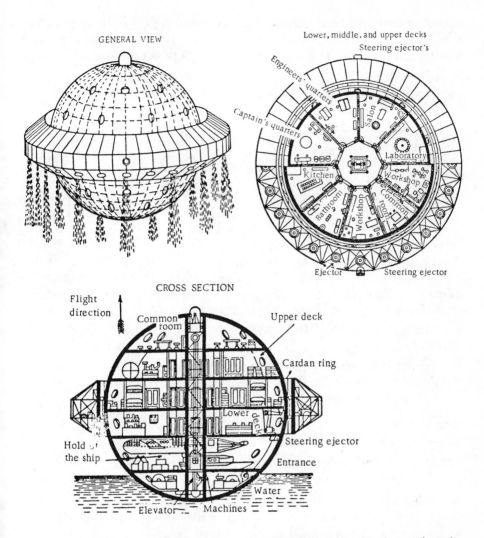

GENERAL VIEW

Lower, middle, and upper decks

Steering ejector's

Engineers' quarters

Captain's quarters

Salon

Laboratory

Kitchen

Workshop

Common room

Bathroom

Workshop

Ejector   Steering ejector

CROSS SECTION

Flight direction

Common room

Upper deck

Cardan ring

Lower deck

Steering ejector

Hold of the ship

Entrance

Water

Elevator   Machines

There's no need for streamlining in a spacecraft, but most pictorial representations assume there is. The shape of Austrian scientist F. A. Ulinsky's 'cosmic ship,' proposed in the 1920's, is that of a globe. In this case it makes sense, for a sphere is convenient for an integral universal joint necessary to change the direction of the vehicle's propellant reaction. When taking off on an interplanetary flight, the ship leaves from its starting point on water, or some other liquid, returning to a similar surface upon mission completion. The craft is propelled via the reaction force of electrons ejected from a row of nozzles arranged around its 'equator.' Electrons are obtained from solar energy captured by thermo-elements, or as atomic-matter decay products.

sub-cosmic directional radiofinder. (Fiction.) A device used to follow the 'now you see it, now you don't' course of a gyro-cosmically relativated space ship, by tracing its receding oscillations. See *gyro-cosmic relativator.*

sub-cosmic radio. (Fiction.) An extremely sophisticated type of radio, linked to a detector sensitive enough to pick out thought vibrations of selected individuals. Used for location and tracking purposes, it can be foiled only by the use of a ray-repelling metal shield. Thought emanations cannot be transmitted, perceived, or received through such a shield.

sub-ionic dematerializer. (Fiction.) Also known as a dematerializing ray tube. A hand-held device, slightly larger than a rocket pistol, shaped like an oversize kidney bean. Emits a ray that doesn't destroy substance, but temporarily robs it of material quality. It can even cause an impervium wall to briefly lose solidity, and makes barriers intangible, so a person can walk through them. If a human or humanoid is dematerialized, he temporarily turns wraith-like, quickly recovers his corporeal attributes, then faints from the after-effects. The dematerializer's batteries must be recharged periodically. See *impervium.*

sub-ionic oscillograph tape. (Fiction.) Picks up and registers such disturbances as distant paralysis ray vibrations. Directional lines on the tape locate the source.

sublight travel. (Fiction.) Space ship velocity slower than lightspeed. Compare with *supralight travel.*

submersible rocket ship. (Fiction.) Variation of a flying submarine, with a dorsal gun mount and flared fins.

subterrain. (Fiction.) Also called a flying corkscrew or flying mole. A space ship shaped like a giant auger, capable of going underground and spinning through rock strata.

success probability. (Generic.) A computer evaluation.

suction chute. (Fiction.) A means of floating helpless, unconscious subjects into a laboratory for experimentation purposes.

suit up. (Astronautics.) To put on a space suit.

super cardioid inductor. (Fiction.) Used to produce a 'ghost' image of oneself when one is supposedly dead. The device, worn like a belt, is activated by a remote converter ray which, via a refractor, can shift the seeming position of the 'ghost.'

superconductivity. (Physics.) The flow of electric current through metal, without resistance, at temperatures approaching absolute zero. Compare with *superfluid*.

super electro magnet. (Fiction.) A large, hemisphere-shaped magnet that can be lowered from the bottom of a space ship to engage and capture another space ship.

superfluid. (Physics.) A fluid, or an electric current, exhibiting frictionless flow at temperatures approaching absolute zero. Compare with *superconductivity*.

supernova. (Astronomy.) A star that suddenly explodes with a brilliance as much as 200 million times that of its previous state, possibly outshining an entire parent galaxy. Energy released is comparable to that radiated by an ordinary star in its whole lifetime. Only a small remnant of the supernova remains following the spectacular flare-up. The Milky Way seems to have no more than one supernova explosion per century. Compare with *nova*.

supertel. (Fiction.) A super-powered two-way television transmitting and receiving apparatus capable of communicating with Venus and other planets. A message is preceded by audio activation of a microwave sounder, after which a directional finder zeroes in.

supralight jump. (Fiction.) An incredible surge of velocity: a space ship equivalent of an electron's quantum jump from one atomic shell to another. See *quantum jump, electron,* and *supralight travel.*

supralight travel. (Fiction.) Space ship velocity faster than lightspeed. To attain supralight speed, a ship must have a dual-drive system: both antigrav and supralight. Antigrav is needed to pull away from a celestial body's gravitational tug, after which faster-than-light speed is achieved via a supralight jump. Compare with *sublight travel.* See *supralight jump.*

surface sampler. (Astronautics.) Used with a lander/probe, (see *probe*) a surface sampler consists of a ten-foot retractable boom; a powered, shovel-like head that can dig, backhoe, lift, and deposit;

and a protective shroud. Its purpose is to pick up samples of another planet's soil and position them—for analysis—in biology, gas chromatograph spectrometer, and X-ray fluorescent spectrometer inlets.

sustainer engine. (Astronautics.) An engine that sustains a spacecraft's velocity once a booster engine has given it its programmed speed. See *booster.*

symbiont. (Fiction.) In real-life zoology, a symbiont is one of two or more different organisms existing in a close relationship of benefit to each. Examples: a hermit crab lugging a sea anemone around on its back; an ant tending an aphid, protecting the helpless creature so it can imbibe its nectar; or a flagellite bacterium dwelling in a termite's intestine, so its blind white host can digest the wood it relentlessly gnaws through. Similar relationships are depicted in science fiction, but normally they're more bizarre. In some science fiction, a symbiont is a head piece that imparts human or humanoid intelligence

In science fiction, not all head pieces are worn to prevent explosive decompression. Some—known as symbionts— impart human or humanoid intelligence when fitted on the heads of animals.

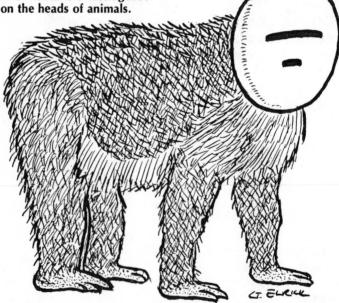

when worn by an animal. In fact, it can be any input device worn by a creature to 'flesh out' what it lacks physically, emotionally, or intellectually.

synchronous satellite. (Astronautics.) An artificial satellite, orbiting the Earth from west to east, precisely matching the Earth's rotational speed so as to remain at the same fixed point above the equator. Compare with *parking orbit*.

synchroton radiation. (Physics.) Radiation emitted by high-energy electrons as they gyrate in a magnetic field.

synthetic air. (Fiction.) The type of air generated, sustained, and refreshened in space ships. It matches the atmospheric composition of a space ship's home planet.

synthetic atmosphere producer. (Fiction.) Used to create an atmosphere on the moon, or other celestial body, similar to that of Earth. As long as the machine continues to spew forth an Earthlike gaseous mixture, one can freely move about on the treated body's surface minus a space suit or oxygen helmet. Compare with *terraform*.

synthetic foods. (Fiction.) In general, compressed, organic food tablets produced from pure energy—by a process of disintegration and electronic recombination—using sand or some other mineral compound as raw material. They are frequently used instead of ordinary foodstuffs grown on mechanized farms. In the field, or in space, a tablet slightly larger than an aspirin suffices as a normal day's ration, easily assimilated by a human or humanoid digestive system. Synthetic delicacies include, but aren't restricted to, fried chicken capsules, sirloin steak tablets, lamp chop capsules, and T-bone steak pills. Jailers sometimes contemptuously toss food pills to prisoners, as though the latter were bears in zoos.

When—for the sake of intestinal health, variety, and psychological satisfaction—bulkier synthetic foods are ingested during space flight, kitchen utensils are equipped with magnetic strips or clamps so they won't drift away from metallic tables or trays.

In *Lucky Starr and the Pirates of the Asteroids*, Paul French features self-heating cans that automatically unfold into dishes with enclosed cutlery. In this novel, a broad spectrum of imitation food is made from yeast-based material grown on Venus. As nourishing as the real thing, it's shaped like—and tastes like—almost anything you can dream up, including steaks, nuts, butter, and candy.

The ultimate solution to space travel nutritional needs is to zap along at velocities approaching lightspeed. At such speeds (See Lorentz-Fitzgerald contraction), an astronaut's digestive system slows down, along with his wristwatch, by a factor of 70,000. He needs only one meal for each 6,750 eaten by comrades left on Earth. Until such velocities are attained, he must ingest 2,500 calories daily, roughly split as follows: 17 percent protein, 32 percent fats, and 51 percent carbohydrates. Since an astronaut is weightless, in a weightless environment, his food also is weightless. Prepared basically by freeze-dehydration, it needs no refrigeration. It can be consumed in baby-food form, from balloon-like squeeze tubes; in whole or sliced form, in plastic bags; as solid bite-size chunks, in edible wrappers; and in powdered form, in plastic bags. Food containers are opened with clippers; water is added via a pistol-like squirt gun. There's no need to carry extra water for this purpose, as plenty is available from fuel cells.

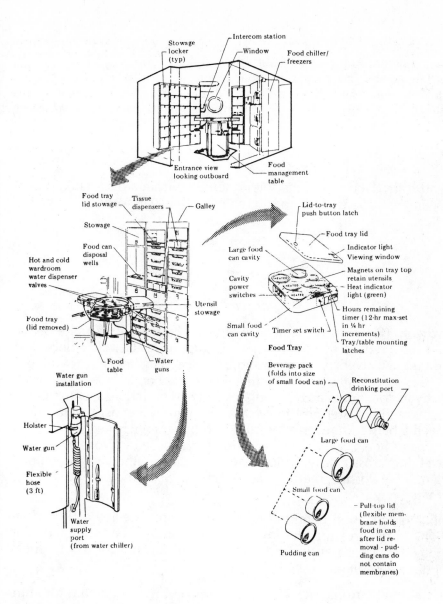

Typical proposed eating facilities in a large spacecraft.

Regarding real-life present-day space travel, several companies have developed feeding systems in which an entire day's nourishment requirement is contained in what is virtually an ordinary toothpaste tube. When the tube's contents have been squeezed into the ingester's mouth, the tube itself is munched as a dessert, because it is vitamin-packed and edible.

synthetic water machine. (Fiction.) A device that creates fresh drinking water in a space ship.

syntho air. (Fiction.) Space suit air supplied from a back tank, used in an emergency when a spacecraft's artificial atmosphere is out of kilter.

T

tachyon. (Fiction.) A theoretical 'ghost' elementary particle—as yet undiscovered in actuality—that, according to Gerald Feinberg of Columbia University, might be able to exceed lightspeed providing its mass is representable with an imaginary number. Feinberg claims the tachyon concept in no way violates Einstein's relativistic equations. A tachyon zips faster and faster the less energy it has, making lightspeed a barrier in reverse, because infinite energy is needed to make it drag its heels. Some science fiction writers use tachyons to activate eye-blink cross-galaxy radio communication. Other writers employ them to transmit matter via beaming. See *beaming* and *atom projector*.

talk-o-ray. (Fiction.) Emitted by a gourd-shaped device activated via slight thumb pressure, this ray works on brain cells controlling hidden thoughts, in case an individual being interrogated refuses to speak without prodding.

telemetry. (Astronautics.) A system, employing a telemeter, for automatically taking speed, temperature, pressure, radiation, and other

technophobia. (Generic.) A fear and hatred of technological advancement. The opposite of technophilia, which is deep admiration for technological advancement.

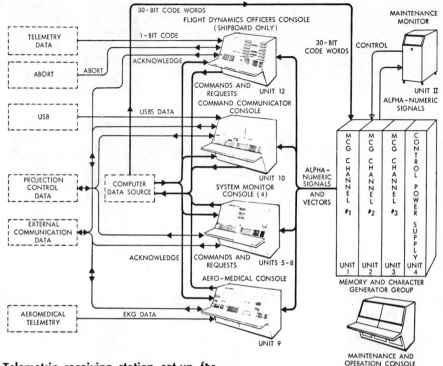

Telemetric receiving station set-up for the Apollo moon-landing program.

measurements, within a space vehicle during flight, and radio-transmitting them to a receiving station for recording and analysis.

telemetry and command antenna. (Astronautics.) A normally small apparatus by means of which an orbiting satellite transmits performance data and receives commands from ground stations.

teleportation. (Fiction.) Also called astral projection, or OOBE (short for 'out of body experience'): self-transportation across space by means of mind power alone.

televox control. (Fiction.) An audio/photo electric cell that activates the opening and closing of sliding panels via voice command, fine-tuned to obey specific voice patterns only.

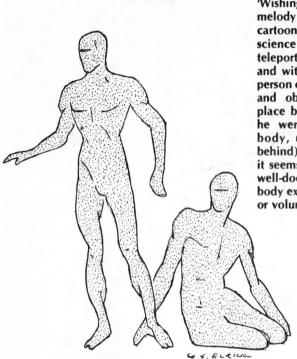

'Wishing Will Make It So,' a haunting melody from a 1940 full-length animated cartoon, has been utilized by some science fiction authors in the guise of teleportation. Under the right conditions, and with the correct frame of mind, a person can mentally 'go' somewhere else, and observe it on a real-time, real-place basis, simply by urgently wishing he were there (though his corporeal body, usually unconscious, remains behind). The concept isn't as 'far out' as it seems at first blush. There have been well-documented cases of actual out-of-body experiences, not all of the pleasant or voluntary.

G. S. ELRICK

terminal guidance. (Astronautics.) A spacecraft's final guidance, directing it to a target or into a last-stage orbital configuration, following *midcourse guidance* (which see).

terminator. (Astronomy.) The dividing line between the illuminated and dark portions of a celestial body that is non-self luminous. Compare with *gibbous, umbra,* and *penumbra*.

terraform. (Fiction.) To make another planet habitable for Earth-based humans.

terrestrial. (Fiction.) An inhabitant of the Earth.

terrestrial planet. (Astronomy.) A planet that features certain Earth-like properties. Included are Mercury, Venus, and Mars. Pluto is sometimes added to the list. Compare with *Jovian planet*.

tesseract. (Fiction.) Variously described as a wrinkle in time, a momentary fragment of nothingness, and a fifth dimension obtained by squaring the fourth. One can edge in and out of tesseracts. As useful as the Moebius strip and Klein bottle concepts for depicting instantaneous time-and-space warp travel, or the portrayal of alternate realities. See *Moebius strip, Klein bottle, alternate framework,* and *alternate reality.*

tetra-dyn. (Fiction.) A powerful explosive used in remote-controlled rocket warheads.

thermal propulsion system. (Astronautics.) Uses a heat-produced gas or plasma forced out of a nozzle at up to 4,000 seconds of *specific impulse* (which see).

thermal protection system. (Fiction/Astronautics.) TPS for short. A space ship's external skins, constructed primarily of aluminum and/or graphite epoxy, designed to withstand temperatures up to 2,300 degrees Fahrenheit, and reusable for at least 100 missions. A space ship's internal insulation, heaters, and purging facilities—all used to control interior compartment temperatures—are not part of the TPS. See *sandwich skin* and *passive thermal control system.*

thermodynamics: first law of. (Physics.) Energy can neither be created nor destroyed: it merely changes place or form. See *conservation law.*

thermodynamics: second law of. (Physics.) Everything, including energy and—supposedly—the universe itself, eventually 'runs down' because entropy increases with the passage of time. See *entropy* and *maximum entropy.*

thermonuclear reaction. (Physics.) The fusion of atomic nuclei, at high velocities, through high-temperature exposure. See *fusion.*

thermo-quantic generator. (Fiction.) A type of gigantic generator used as a defensive device by space gangsters. Emits a destructive blast of force-energy-heat in the shape of a vast, expanding fireball.

thermo skin. (Fiction.) A skin-tight, specially treated space suit that keeps its wearer warm.

thermo space gear. (Fiction.) A type of emergency space suit immediately slipped into when a spacecraft's internal heating system malfunctions and exterior interplanetary temperatures drop as low as 278 degrees below zero. It prevents its wearer's body fluids from crystallizing.

thrust. (Astronautics.) Forward or upward force exerted on a space ship by its power plant and rocket engine or engines. The force must be powerful enough to lift the vehicle off its launching pad and break away from Earth's downward-tugging gravitational pull.

time. (Generic.) Though toyed with and treated in various ways in science fiction, time is a mysterious entity that defies pigeonholing. Saint Augustine commented: 'When no one asks me what time is, I know . . . but when I would give an explanation of it in answer to a man's question, I do not know.' Most moderns, including physicists, are in the same boat.

Regardless of the definition dilemma, the following are pretty much taken as 'givens': time is a nonspatial continuum in which events occur in a seemingly irreversible succession from the past through the present to the future; as a quantity, it is the 'measure of change,' forever changing in one direction; it is a system of relationships that involve before, after, and contemporary; it is particularized and idiosyncratic; and events become, but there is no corresponding unbecoming of events. The following also are more or less accepted as 'givens':

Time has no independent existence. Time doesn't exist apart from the order of events by which we measure it. In other words, there isn't a steady, unvarying, inexorable time-flow per se, streaming from an infinite past through the present and on into an infinite future.

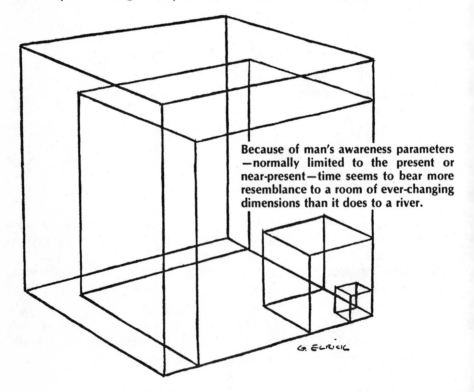

Because of man's awareness parameters —normally limited to the present or near-present—time seems to bear more resemblance to a room of ever-changing dimensions than it does to a river.

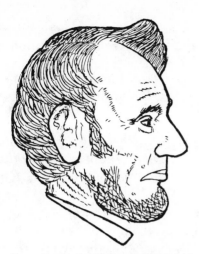

G. ELRICK

Though we're presently cognizant of long-dead Lincoln, and he knew nothing about us in the 1860's, we're more like vaporous 'non-persons' with respect to him than he is to us, despite the fact that he's dust. The rail-splitter can be compared to a deceased movie star who continues to flicker on a mental screen whenever he enters our consciousness. There's no way, as individuals, that we could have flickered on a screen in Lincoln's mind.

Time is essentially subjective and psychological. The sense of time is a form of perception, as is the sense of color. There's no such thing as color without an eye to behold it. There's no such thing as an instant, an hour, or a day without an event to mark it or a consciousness to perceive it. The dead are beyond time.

Time may be more like a room than a river. Despite the human mind's tendency to compare time to a road or a stream, beside which —if one were high enough—the beginning, middle, and end could be perceived simultaneously, it may be more boxed-in. John Fowles, in *The French Lieutenant's Woman,* compares it to a room . . . a *now* so close that we typically fail to see it. That may be true, but:

There's no such thing as 'now' independent of a frame of reference. Relativity states that a fixed time interval can't exist separate from a referral system. Simultaneity doesn't manifest itself in and of itself. Another truism:

We're related to the past, but the past isn't related to us. This may seem like a belaboring of the obvious, but it bears examination. We're keenly aware of Abraham Lincoln as an individual, but Lincoln was in no way aware of us, except as the nebulous concept: 'people in the 20th Century.' Lincoln is past to us, not because we haven't studied his photographs, but because he couldn't possibly pore over ours. Despite science fiction fancies, there's a non-relationship here that can't be rectified.

Which leads to one final axiom: past events needn't be classified as non-entities. Time being a measure of change needn't involve the destruction of previous realities. That which has been continues to exist in our one-sided awareness.

See *invariance of interval, spacetime, time travel, time reversal, time slippage, maximum entropy, relativity, Lorentz-Fitzgerald contraction, time corridor, alternate framework, alternate reality, alternity, aperture,* and *the relativity of simultaneity.*

time corridor. (Fiction.) As delineated by Poul Anderson in *The Corridors of Time,* a tube of force whose length has been rotated on the time axis. Entropy and temporal flow exist inside the corridor but, from the standpoint of one experiencing the force tube's reality, cosmic or outside time is completely 'frozen.' By selecting an appropriate gate, one can enter any past era and experience it as 'here and now,' with a conversion factor of approximately thirty-five days per linear foot. Every few centuries a twenty-five-years-wide portal opens. If the portal manifested itself at less than two-hundred-year intervals, weakened force fields would fold inward and collapse. Compare with the *alternate framework, alternate reality, alternity,* and *aperture.*

time dilation. (Physics.) The slowing down of time in space. See *Lorentz-Fitzgerald contraction, time slippage,* and *paradox of the twins.*

time retarder. (Fiction.) A projection apparatus capable of showing events that took place at any point in time preceding the present. It operates by retracting light waves.

time reversal. (Physics.) Not to be confused with theoretically sliding back in time, entering the so-called time-stream at a preselected point, and moving forward again. (See *time travel.*) Even though events seem to unfold unidirectionally along the time axis:

Natural events are time-reversible in principle. Many reversals are conceivable but unlikely. It's possible that a star's radiation could be reversed; that its energy could converge again to its source via backward-running nuclear reactions. However:

Boundary conditions militate for one-way events. In a one-way universe, enormous improbabilities are involved in reversing even a

G. ELRICK

simple event, such as beta decay. Beta decay reversal requires that an electron, a proton, and an anti-neutrino be fired from the 'rim' of things with such unerring aim that all three particles strike an identical nucleus and create a neutron. That's statistically far-fetched: more difficult than removing shampoo from someone's hair and squeezing it back in a bottle. In addition, there is:

A communication problem inherent in reversing the entropy arrow. Once more we're not discussing sliding back in time, then moving forward again. We're discussing a time-reversed universe with the entropy arrow flying the other way. If you succeeded in communicating a fact to someone experiencing time-reversal, he'd immediately forget the fact, since the information would instantly become part of his future instead of part of his past.

See *time, time travel, entropy,* and *time-reversal invariance.*

time-reversal invariance. (Physics.) The empirical observation that some simple, relatively gross processes work equally well in either direction. In short, a physical system experiencing a given chronological sequence of states or events can experience an exact reversal of the same states or events in an inverse chronological order. For statistical improbabilities at both the microcosmic and macrocosmic levels, see *time reversal.*

time slippage. (Generic.) The quantitative time differential experienced by someone on a prolonged space flight compared to the supposedly identical length of time experienced by someone on Earth. See *paradox of the twins, Lorentz-Fitzgerald contraction,* and *time dilation.*

time travel. (Fiction.) Shuttling back and forth in time is as integral to science fiction as space ships, androids, alien beings, electromagnetic emissions, and force fields. The concept, offering psychedelic plot possibilities, has been enthusiastically explored by writers as diverse as H.G. Wells in *The Time Machine,* Poul Anderson in *The Corridors of Time,* and Piers Anthony in *Ox.* Problems inherent in time travel—chiefly how to *arrive* somewhere in the future or past, and then return—are handled differently by each author. Here's how Gordon R. Dickson develops temporal back-and-forth transit in *Ancient, My Enemy:*

Disciplined mind propulsion. By means of a Mackenwald distorter, the physics sub-discipline of psychomechanics can pinpoint —and capitalize on—the seemingly tenuous connection between a human body's perception of, and experience of, time. A trained body reacts to what it perceives as quickened time-flow by accelerating its own functions as much as three times, concurrently affecting nearby inanimate objects, sweeping them along with it in its awareness. Not only can a body, as a gestalt, be distorted relative to time; time can simultaneously be distorted, vis a vis a body, so the latter is in a suspended 'timeless' state. Once in limbo, it employs the propulsive force of its finely-honed mind to slip *into* the time-stream at any point it desires, and slip *out* of the time-stream at any point it desires.

Here's how L. Sprague De Camp develops temporal back-and-forth transit in *A Gun For Dinosaur:*

Positively curved spacetime warp. Utilizing a fusion process in conjunction with sea water, so much power can be concentrated in a tiny area that the entity known as spacetime is distortable, permitting objects and people to travel in time the way machines traverse space. Instead of being permanent, the time-translation has an impermanence similar to that of a billiard ball given a 'reverse English,' remaining in a desired era for a period proportionate to the power used to propel it there, then returning spontaneously to the time and place from which it started.

Experiencing time-translation involves pain and a sense of being slammed outward by an enormous catapult. The machine used per-

Imagined time travel in early science fiction tales involved the use of special machines, such as Nikolskii's chronomobile, shown here. The chronomobile moves forward or backward in time via ultra-high frequency electrical oscillations. Inside the spherical craft are engines, electric generators, lamps, two armchairs, and a switchboard. When a meter needle hovers at zero, time stops for the passengers. When it dips to the right, they're carried into the future; when to the left, into the past.

267

mits forward or backward projection, within a working tolerance of two months temporally and one-and-three-quarter miles spatially. Built-in safety devices and controls position the time traveler anywhere on Earth, above its surface; most emphatically not in a place occupied by a solid object. The eventual snap-back to the present entails another pain and sense of outward-slamming.

What if the time traveler, dipping into the past, should literally change history by, let's say, preventing Julius Caesar's murder? As is the case with all science fiction writers, L. Sprague De Camp has a ready answer: spacetime curvature is positive, so any disturbance in the past will iron itself out in subsequent history, and everything will eventually be the same as it would have been regardless. (If spacetime curvature were negative, however, subsequent events would diverge more and more from their original pattern with the passage of time.)

See *time corridor, alternate framework, alternate reality, alternity,* and *aperture.*

time warp. See *alternate framework* and *time corridor.*

Titan . . .as it really is. (Astronomy.) The largest of Saturn's nine satellites, easily visible with a small telescope, Titan—twice as heavy as the moon—orbits its gaseous mother planet at a distance of 760,000 miles. Though similar to Jupiter's frozen-mud-and-ice satellites, Titan differs in having an atmosphere. Its spectrum reveals methane and a considerable amount of hydrogen. Why Titan should have an atmosphere, while Jupiter's similar-size satellites do not, remains a mystery.

Titan . . . as depicted in early pulp magazine-type science fiction. The satellite features fresh air, an elaborate palace, and flowering forests of stunning beauty.

Titan . . . as depicted by modern science fiction novelists. In Ben Bova's *As On a Darkling Plain*, Titan has enormous, mysterious towers —not made by man but being investigated by man—with smooth metal walls and interiors featuring throbbing machinery erected by an alien type of intelligence centuries before.

The satellite's surface is primarily frozen wastes. There's also an impressively large gray ammonia sea, colder than any of Earth's deep-freeze polar oceans.

In Arthur C. Clarke's *Imperial Earth*, Titan is blanketed by low, thick, reddish clouds composed of the same organic compounds as

Jupiter's Great Red Spot. Under this covering, the satellite is the solar system's most hospitable spheroid, with the exception of Earth. Its temperature is periodically so mild that a spaceman can move about in a simple oxygen mask and an even simpler thermofoil suit. Some of this warmth is due to a greenhouse effect akin to that manifested on Venus, but much stems from radioactive internal sources spewing forth megatons of hydrogen compounds.

Regardless, a methane monsoon rages throughout the long winter, condensing methane into shallow lakes dotted with ammonia ice flows. Whenever clouds pull apart, the lakes vaporize.

topology. (Generic.) Also called 'rubber-sheet geometry': the study of the unchanging properties of three-dimensional figures that can be twisted, deformed, molded, pulled inside out, and stretched in a variety of ways called transformations. To a topologist, a sphere and a cube are one and the same, since each can be squeezed into the shape of the other. However, a sphere and a doughnut-shaped torus cannot be molded into each other's configuration. A comprehension

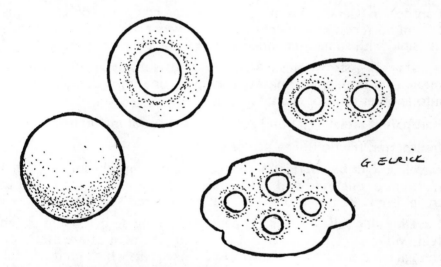

Various topological objects whose physical properties blow the minds of mathematicians. A sphere is referred to as genus 0; a doughnut or torus as genus 1; an object with two holes as genus 2; and an object with more holes as genus any number of holes there are.

of topology is crucial to an understanding of the 'shape' of the four-dimensional universe, because it concerns itself with how an area is 'glued together' in terms of its parts, and how many intersections are formed by a curve with itself. See *Klein bottle, Moebius strip,* and *spacetime.*

total contact. (Fiction.) As exemplified by Gordon R. Dickson in *Three to Dorsai!*, a non-physical but oceanic 'touching' of the fundamental pattern underlying the objective universe. He who establishes such mystic contact can perfectly pivot his identity into the most appropriate, satisfying position within the over-all structure.

touchdown. (Astronautics.) Another word for *soft landing,* which see.

tracking. (Astronautics.) The process of following a spacecraft's movement via radar, radio, and photographic observations. See *telemetry.*

tractor beam. (Fiction.) Short for *attractor beam* or *attraction beam.*

transceiver. (Generic.) A hand-held module comprised of a combination radio receiver and transmitter 'joined at the hip' in a single housing, with some components utilized by both units.

transducer. (Astronautics.) Any of various substances or devices—often used in telemetering—that convert one form of energy input into another form of energy output.

transparent metal. (Fiction.) A type of structural material.

transporter. (Fiction.) See *beaming.*

traveling light beam. (Fiction.) A controllable light beam with a flat platform or enclosed pod at the forward-thrust end. Can be used to travel from one point to another, at any desired speed.

traveling sidewalk. (Fiction.) A perpetually moving belt, eight to ten feet wide, similar to a 20th Century department store escalator, though horizontal. Carries rows of pew-like seats which metropolitan dwellers use when tired of walking.

tricynoline. (Fiction.) A deadly poison. One drop in a city's water mains would wipe out the entire population.

tridimensional. (Generic.) Synonym for holographic or three-dimensional.

triffid. (Fiction.) A huge, perambulating vegetable with poisonous tendrils. First described in John Wyndham's *The Day of the Triffids.*

G. ELRICK

The more exotic plants in 'far out' science fiction and fantasy bear no resemblance to a head of lettuce. They're able to sing; slither about in a strange shuffling manner; react violently to thought waves; drop deadly snares with the skill of a trained terrorist; cunningly pretend to be friendly when they aren't; develop a craving for human muscle tissue; look down on people as parasites; or, as this triffid is doing, behave like lust-crazed sailors on shore leave.

Possibly inspired by imaginative portrayals in horror films and on the printed page, scores of serious experiments were conducted, in the late 1960's and early 1970's, zeroing in on the possibility that plants can feel pleasure and pain, or react—in a not-yet-understood fashion—to extensive spreads of electromagnetic emanations, including well-wishing or hateful attitudes.

triple redundancy. (Astronautics.) As applied to space ship digital and analog computers, a triple-checking of ongoing data for greater reliability. Each circuit produces identical data, instantaneously voted upon by the other two for accuracy. Data errors and inconsistencies are rejected.

tripodal. (Fiction.) Three-footed: used with reference to a specialized robot or android.

tropopause. (Astronautics.) The region between the upper *troposphere* (which see) and the lower *stratosphere* (which see). It varies in altitude from five miles at the poles to eleven miles at the equator.

troposphere. (Astronautics.) The lowest layer of the Earth's atmosphere, roughly six miles deep, through which the temperature decreases upwardly. In a steady turmoil due to rising and falling air currents, it is responsible for clouds, storms, rain, and snow.

turnover. (Astronautics.) The maneuver made by a spacecraft when backing into a landing. See *retro rockets* and *retrothrust*.

type 24 converter ray. (Fiction.) A space ship electromagnetic camouflage emission that, when activated, diffuses reflective light rays in such a manner that the craft resembles a comet.

U

ultraviolet. (Physics.) Solar radiation that causes sunburn: that portion of the electromagnetic spectrum at the short-wavelength, high-frequency side of the visible region, packed with more photons than visible light, bounded by an even shorter wavelength area comprised of X-rays. Fortunately, most ultraviolet rays are blocked out by the Earth's atmosphere, since unprotected full-intensity exposure—as it occurs in space—would be lethal, frying living things like eggs on a grill. See *electromagnetic radiation, electromagnetic spectrum, X-rays, wavelength,* and *photon.*

ultraviolet bath. (Fiction.) A diluted electromagnetic cleansing shower that dispenses with the need for water.

ultrawave communicator. (Fiction.) Called 'ultra' for short. As portrayed in *World Well Lost,* by John Aiken, a device that pulses beats on an electromagnetic carrier frequency, sending messages at 200,000 times the speed of light.

ultrono radio. (Fiction.) A space ship radio used for tuning in on Earth Central (which see) on ultrono channels. Occasionally capable of receiving messages from, and transmitting messages to, other planets. If the wrong type of impulse is transmitted or received, the device may explode.

umbilical cord. (Astronautics.) Any fuel or electrical line connecting a spacecraft with ground units during a pre-flight servicing period. Propellant transfer devices are sometimes called mechanical nurse-maids. Also a line that supplies a spaceman with oxygen while he's outside a space ship.

umbra. (Astronomy.) On a non-self-luminous celestial body, such as a planet or moon, the darkest part of a shadow from which all light is cut off. See *penumbra*.

uncertainty principle. (Physics.) Also called the Heisenberg uncertainty principle. A basic cornerstone of quantum physics, which states that it is impossible to measure both the position and velocity of a particle with infinite precision, or to determine accuracy values for energy and time intervals. Similar to the cynical so-called Harvard law of animal behavior: 'When stimulation is repeatedly applied under conditions in which environmental factors are precisely controlled, the animal will react as it damn well pleases.' See *quantum theory*.

under jets. (Astronautics.) Position-controlling rockets on a space ship's underside.

Unified Field Theory. (Physics.) Einstein spent much of the latter part of his life postulating that all the forces of physics—though seemingly separate—are but different facets of a single, all-embracing, basic phenomenon. Physicists, still on the theory's trail, know that matter is affected by and interacts with many kinds of fields. They're burning midnight oil deducing that nuclear, electro-magnetic, and gravitational forces are somehow interrelated in a tightly-knit, previously unrecognized manner. See *physics: four basic forces of, mass-energy equation, matter and energy: equivalence of, relativity, gauge theories,* and *basic laws: seeming simplicity of.*

universal focus. (Fiction.) Wide-angle setting for a paralysis ray.

universal translator. (Fiction.) A hand-held device employed to unscramble unknown alien languages. Components include speech characteristic sensors, a decoding/encoding section, and an operator's speaker/microphone. (*Star Trek.*)

'Picturing' the universe as it really is, or actually may be, is beyond the capacity of the human mind, which is why most attempts end up like the two fanciful but simplistic drawings shown here. Einstein's basic conception of spacetime is almost 100 percent accepted today. That great mover-and-shaker of modern thought used the non-Euclidean thinking of German mathematician George Friedrich Bernhard Riemann as his point of departure. Riemann's concept of the macrocosm was a hypersphere: a four-dimensional analog of a Euclidean sphere. A ray of light in a Riemannian universe eventually curves back on itself, like the Earth's equator. The universe doesn't have infinite volume, because it's constantly expanding, but it also lacks an 'edge.' In 1917, the Dutch astronomer William de Sitter, pondering Einstein's field equations, worked out another non-Euclidean model of the cosmos. In de Sitter's model—a modification of Riemann's and Einstein's—space curvature becomes steadily less pronounced with the passage of time, and a light ray travels in a perpetually expanding spiral rather than a circle. Regardless of which projection is 'right,' the universe is a place with its center simultaneously everywhere and nowhere; despite the brain-bending number of galaxies, the average density of matter is equivalent to one hydrogen atom every 60 cubic feet; and everything isn't expanding into space because space is expanding along with it.

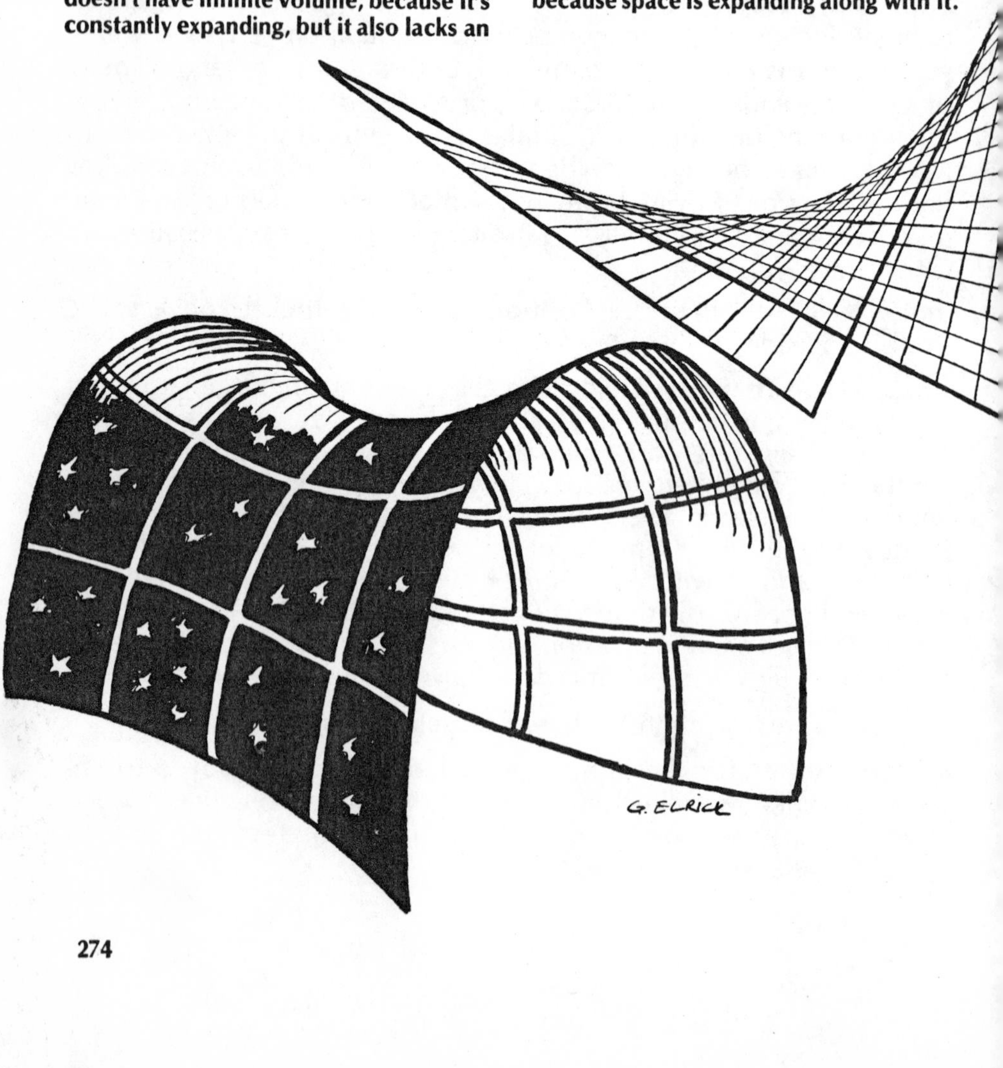

G. ELRICK

universe. (Generic.) The macrocosm, or entire cosmos, regarded as a unit: an all-inclusive system of all conceivable types of astronomical bodies, forces, and energies. There are as many galaxies in the universe as there are stars in the Milky Way; it's 15 billion years old, according to the *big bang theory* (which see); and no one knows its full dimensions, since it curves back on itself. The word 'dimensions' may not even be applicable.

Finite but unbounded. According to Einstein, there's no 'edge' to the universe, and any point in it may be considered as central. Field equations of the general theory of relativity utilize non-Euclidean geometrical values that postulate a three-dimensional analog of a sphere's two-dimensional surface.

The distribution of galaxies seems uniform. According to continuing astronomical inputs, and data analyses, the distribution of galaxies throughout the universe appears homogeneous and isotropic: identical in all directions.

Evolutionary, yo-yo, and steady state theories. Though most astronomers feel the universe began with the so-called big bang, some do not. Some believe it was once a rarefied gas that collapsed, exploded, and will forever expand. Others, proponents of the 'yo-yo theory,' think it periodically inflates and contracts in an endlessly repetitious cycle. Still others, advocates of the 'steady state theory,' which casts aside the conservation of energy principle, feel the universe has always been—and always will be—essentially unchanged, and that new hydrogen atoms are being created continuously.

See *cosmic egg, spacetime, galaxy, relativity, conservation law,* and *isotropic.*

Uranus . . . as it really is. (Astronomy.) One of the so-called Jovian planets, a 'gas giant,' and the seventh celestial body from the sun, orbiting at a distance of approximately 1,790,000,000 miles.

Size: Not nearly as large as Jupiter or Saturn, it is still huge compared to the Earth, with a diameter between 28,500 and 32,000 miles, fifteen times Earth's mass, and 64 times Earth's volume.

Density: Similar to Jupiter's.

Composition: Since it's less massive than Jupiter, and therefore not as squeezed together by strong gravity, it probably has more medium-weight and heavy elements in its make-up than the solar system's colossus.

Temperature: Minus 300 degrees Fahrenheit.

Climate: Strange beyond belief. Because the planet's equatorial plane remains fixed as it moves around the sun, each polar region spends roughly 42 years in sunlight and 42 years in darkness.

Atmosphere: 'Thick,' with a great deal of hydrogen, much methane, but no ammonia, since Uranus is too frigid for ammonia to exist in gaseous form.

Rotation: Uranus spins moderately fast, making a complete turn on its axis every eleven hours.

Orbital period: 84.02 years.

Satellites: Five in number, with orbits virtually perpendicular to the planet's. However, they revolve from east to west, in an opposite direction from most solar bodies. In order outward from the planet, their names are Miranda, Ariel, Umbriel, Titania, and Oberon.

Rings: Five rings, previously undetected, but discovered in 1977, are similar to those that encircle Saturn, yet much thinner. They're named after the Greek Alphabet's first five letters: alpha, beta, gamma, delta, and epsilon.

Gravity: Earth = 1. Uranus = 1.05.

Uranus and/or Uranians . . . as depicted in early pulp magazine-type science fiction. There's a great green desert, a bleak polar region where ice is five miles thick, and mountains towering twenty miles.

Human-type inhabitants dwell in houses one story high, with matted rubbery vines stretching between the roofs. So elastic are the vines' interwoven upper surfaces, they serve as trampolines.

The capital city, surrounded by purple-flashing death rays, is called 'The Traveller's Last Rest,' since no visitor ever leaves it alive.

urban monads. (Fiction.) Completely self-contained skyscrapers one mile high, with different floors representing the habitations of different social strata. They are described in detail in Robert Silverberg's *The World Inside.*

V

vaporizing pill. (Fiction.) A suicide pellet swallowed by anyone who wants to avoid capture, especially if torture is implicit in the situation. The pill causes the ingester's body to disintegrate. Compare with *non-ex fluid* and *disintegrating fluid.*

vector. (Physics.) Any force or influence—such as velocity or acceleration—which can be totally specified regarding magnitude and direction at each point in space.

Venus . . . as it really is. (Astronomy.) One of the so-called terrestrial planets, with a rough surface, like the Earth's; and the second celestial body from the sun, after Mercury, at a mean distance of 67.2 million miles. It's the solar system's most brilliant planet, reflecting more than half the light that hits it, rendering it eight times as luminous as the moon.

Size: With a 3,800-mile radius, and a mass 0.816 that of the Earth, Venus, though slightly smaller, is virtually the Earth's twin, dimension-wise.

Density and composition: Its mean density parallels the Earth's, indicating the internal structure is similar: rocky mantle and iron core.

Temperature: Totally unlike the Earth, Venus has a 700 degrees Fahrenheit surface temperature, hot enough to melt lead. If the Earth were as blistering, its oceans would evaporate. Due to intense heat

A spaceman poking around on the surface of Venus would immediately wish he weren't there. He'd experience a steaming sauna bath to end all sauna baths; the thick, soupy atmosphere would distort light rays, creating bewildering optical illusions; and hurricane-force winds would knock him about like a ping pong ball.

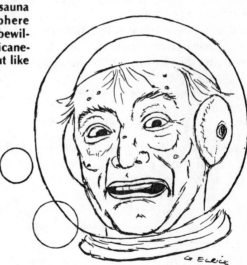

energy, the planet emits a continuous radio signal.

However, the temperature of the perpetually overhanging clouds is much lower than that of the surface, which is searingly hot because of the *greenhouse effect* (which see below).

Greenhouse effect. Carbon dioxide in Venus's atmosphere blocks most wavelengths by means of which it could throw back heat absorbed by the sun. In brief, energy easily reaches the planet's surface, but has a tough time escaping. The result is a sauna bath to end all sauna baths.

Atmosphere: As noted above, Venus's atmosphere—a hundred times more massive than Earth's—is basically carbon dioxide. Water vapor, nitrogen, and hydrochloric acid also are present. So 'thick' is the air, anyone staggering through it—properly protected by a pressure suit—would swear he was thrashing through thin gruel a tenth the density of water. The same intolerably hot broth would bend light rays and create fun-house optical illusions.

A spaceman would also battle hurricane-calibre winds caused by hot air rising and cool air sinking. These winds whip Venus's unbroken cloud layer around the planet in four days, whereas the planet itself seemingly rotates lethargically. The clouds, whose composition is unknown, are 40 miles above the surface, which means the troposphere—or 'weather mixing' area—is 40 miles deep. Earth's is only six.

All in all, Venus is a nightmare.

Rotation: Many astronomers think Venus turns only once on its axis in its 224.7-day revolution around the sun. Other observations indicate a faster rotation.

Orbital period: 224.7 days.

Satellites: None.

Gravity: Earth = 1. Venus = 0.88.

Venus and/or Venusians . . . as depicted by semi-modern and modern science fiction novelists. *Edgar Rice Burroughs,* in several novels about Venus, pictures a world that no way resembles the real thing.

Venus, called *Amtor,* is divided into three concentric-circle areas: Trabol, a temperate zone; Strabol, a tropical country; and Karbol, a frigid region. Amtor rotates once a year, forever turning the same face to the sun.

There are mile-high plants, Earth-like Venusians, some of whom dwell in tree houses, and the usual Burroughs pantheon of monsters and weird beasties.

The living dead are humanoids into whom synthetic life has been instilled. Their thoughts—mostly inimical—are transmitted to them via telepathy. They do dirty work for their masters.

C. S. Lewis, in *Perelandra*, depicts an endless green sea; floating, orange-colored islands; a golden sky; and a lovely naked green lady totally unaware of evil.

The lovely green lady from Perelandra.

John Ball, Jr., in *Operation Springboard,* postulates a musty jungle with giant ferns, pungently sweet odors, and spongy soil.

vibro-destructor ray. (Fiction.) A ray so powerful that, when used in conjunction with a disintegrator ray, it has the capacity to wipe out an entire civilization.

vibro-revivor. (Fiction.) An electrode-studded device used to counter-act the debilitating effects of exhaustion ray exposure. One jolt of cosmo-electric juice snaps an afflicted person back to normal. See *exhaustion ray.*

visible radio. (Fiction.) A form of skywriting used by space ships when other types of communication fail.

visio-perception refractoscope projector. (Fiction.) Projects mental images into space—entoptic phenomena based on the theory of Purkinje's figures* —meant to confuse space predator pursuers. Causes a spacecraft to appear in double or triple image. If luck persists, the predators fire at the phantom ships. (* Science fiction lingo for the delectation of readers—not to be taken over-seriously.)

visio phone. (Fiction.) A two-way, audio-visual console with a three-foot-square viewplate, used for one-to-one, face-to-face consulta-tions between the captain of a space ship and any selected individual on Earth. One needn't stand near the console to have one's voice picked up and transmitted.

visio-scope. (Fiction.) A large electronic sensory cabinet in a space ship, with a gridded video screen viewplate. It picks up images, at any distance, at whatever focal range desired. When switched to infrared, it can see through dense smoke or fog.

vita-comp tablets. (Fiction.) Special nutritional tablets, a handful of which will sustain a person for a month in an emergency situation.

vita-lex 7. (Fiction.) A spray that—when directed at a spot where a seed has been planted—causes a full-grown, tree-size plant to sprout and flourish in seconds.

vito-vibral ray. (Fiction.) An emission that heals most injuries by means of unique vibrational frequencies.

vitrolium noxide. (Fiction.) A deadly gas produced by space ship rocket malfunctioning.

voice-altering sound wave transmitter. (Fiction.) An apparatus used to disguise vocal tones.

Volapuk. (Generic.) An international mathematical language invented in 1879.

Vulcan. (Fiction.) A planet diametrically opposite Earth, orbiting in precise synchronization with the latter, though on the other side of the sun. Because of its position, it's visible only to roving space ships. Since it doesn't spin on its axis, Vulcan enjoys perpetual sunshine in its habitable zone, suitable for colonizing. Flanking the habitable zone are the torrid zone, where the temperature reaches a blistering 386 degrees Fahrenheit; and the ice zone, more frigid than the coldest spot on Earth.

The mythical planet Vulcan revolves around the sun diametrically opposite the Earth, which is why it supposedly remains forever invisible to Earth-based telescopes.

W

warnometer. (Fiction.) A space ship gauge that registers intra-hull air pressure.

warp factor. (Fiction.) A propulsion system enabling a space ship to travel faster than the speed of light, based on a controlled contact of matter with antimatter and the overwhelming energy release that results. Velocity is measured in 'warp factors.' Warp factor one is the speed of light; warp factors two, three, four, and so on are based on a geometric progression of light velocity. For example: warp factor two is eight times the speed of light, and warp factor four is 64 times the speed of light. (*Star Trek*.) In reality, a warp factor is an impossibility according to the Lorentz-Fitzgerald contraction. See *main propulsion unit, antimatter,* and *Lorentz-Fitzgerald contraction.*

wavelength. (Physics.) A quantity measurement used to differentiate different portions of the electromagnetic spectrum: the distance between successive oscillations of electromagnetic fields comprising the radiation. Wavelengths determine how radiation interacts with matter. See *electromagnetic spectrum* and *electromagnetic radiation.*

weak nuclear force. (Physics.) One of the four fundamental dynamic entities in nature. (See *physics: four basic forces of,* and *strong nuclear force.*) All elementary particles except photons seem capable of exerting it. Despite its name, it's more than a trillion trillion times stronger than gravity. Like the strong nuclear force, it operates only at short range. Controlling radioactive decay, it seems to catalyze some elementary particles—particularly beta particles—to break down into simpler ones, thereby changing the quality of matter. It helped form the heavy atoms needed for life. Neutrinos are ideal for testing the weak nuclear force. See *photon, elementary particles, beta particle,* and *radioactive decay.*

white hot cosmic dust. (Fiction.) The super-heated ejecta from a comet.

wide formation. (Fiction.) A space ship flotilla flight pattern, with control ships flying at thousand-mile intervals.

window. (Astronautics.) A computer-selected and guided path to any celestial object.

X

xenobiologist. (Generic.) A biologist who studies alien forms of life. See *probe* and *exobiology*.

X-rays. (Physics.) Also called Roentgen rays: high-frequency, short-wavelength electromagnetic radiation between ultraviolet and gamma rays on the electromagnetic spectrum. X-rays are streams of relatively high-energy photons. They are produced whenever fast electrons are quickly brought to rest, or when electrons in atoms make transitions to inner shells. When occurring extraterrestrially, they are blocked out by the Earth's atmosphere. When created and controlled terrestrially, their penetrating power is used in radiography, radiology, radiotherapy, and research. See *electromagnetic spectrum, electromagnetic radiation, wavelength,* and *photon.*

Y

yaw. (Astronautics.) Rotational or oscillatory movements of a space-craft about a vertical axis, always a deviation from the craft's intended course.

Z

zero gravity: effects of. (Astronautics.) Per Isaac Asimov, astronauts who've been subjected to gravity for three months have experienced no permanent ill effects and have been capable of doing hard, mentally demanding work. However, their bodies evince a slow, steady loss of bone calcium, their blood tends to pool; and they suffer a slight impairment of the circulatory system, correctable by having them work out on trampolines.

Z-ray chair. (Fiction.) A strap-down chair interrogation device designed to overcome a captive's will power and force him to divulge information. Actually a mind-reading set-up. The prisoner is forced to face a Z-ray emitting apparatus in such a manner that the emission penetrates his cerebrum.

zodiacal light. (Astronomy.) A faint cone of light briefly visible after sunset in the west and before sunrise in the east, caused by inter-planetary dust scattered near the ecliptic plane, and by meteoric particles surrounding the sun. See *ecliptic* and *interplanetary dust.*

A Line-Up of Genuine
Space Ship 'Originals'

Earth-based Battle Cruiser BC77Y.
Speed: 15,500 miles-per-second.
Crew: 2,000 fighting men.

Martian Flash Blast Attack Ship
TS310Z. Speed: 16,700 miles-per-
second. Crew: 1,500 Space
Marines.

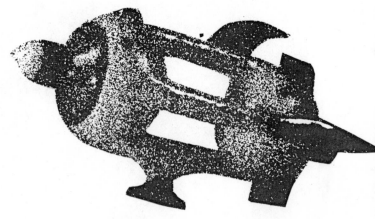

Martian Police Ship MP83Z.
Speed: 12,500 miles-per-second.
Crew: 250 men with deadly gas ray
guns.

Earth-based Pursuit Ship PS91ZX.
Travels virtually at lightspeed.
Crew: 1,000 men who have volun-
teered for death.

Venusian Fighting Destroyer
FD69Z. Speed: 14,900 miles-per-
second. Armament: 9 aerial tor-
pedo tubes.

287

Jovian Super Dreadnought SDF1X.
Speed: 9,500 miles-per-second.
Crew: 5,000 men. Armament: 269
force ray guns.

James Stark, of Wheeling, Illinois, doubtless was a germinal influence in shaping the man-in-the-street's conception of space ships in the 30's and 40's. His models, six of which are pictured here, had a tremendous impact on pulp magazine illustrators and comic strip artists, most of whom used his creations as prototypes. Jim's bizarre flights of fancy, prosaically referred to as 'sky wagons,' made their maiden appearance in a stop-action motion picture at the Chicago World's Fair in 1933 and 1934. When musing about the balsa wood rocketship kits he produced in the years that followed, he admits his greatest competition was kits featuring World War I biplanes. 'We were thirty years ahead of time,' he chuckles wryly. Regardless, modern science fiction authors, artists, and film-makers are still heavily indebted to his 'sky wagons.'

288

Science Fiction Titles

Writing outstandingly different science fiction novels, novelettes, or short stories is hard enough. So is dreaming up titles that stop readers in their tracks (aided by eye-grabbing cover illustrations in the case of novels). Where do science fiction authors get their titles? Some rely on whimsy and blatant word-play. Others adroitly adapt phrases found in Shakespeare, the Bible, poetry, and songs: a fact much appreciated by those 'in the know.' Still others give pretzel twists to titles of mainstream novels and plays. Most, of course, cut titles from whole cloth, deriving them totally from narrative subject matter. Whatever their title source, science fiction authors are a cultured lot, deeply versed in many fields, as is clear from the following examples of derivations and adaptations.

Derivations and Adaptations

Brian Aldiss's *Barefoot in the Head* is derived from Neil Simon's play 'Barefoot in the Park.' Poul Anderson's *Planet of No Return* is derived from John P. Marquand's 'Point of No Return.' James Blish's *And All the Stars a Stage* is adapted from Shakespeare's 'All the world's a stage' (*As You Like It.*) Ben Bova's *As On a Darkling Plain* is a phrase from Matthew Arnold's 'Dover Beach' (And we are here as on a darkling plain/Swept with confused alarms of struggle and flight/Where ignorant armies clash by night.) Ray Bradbury's *When Elephants Last in the Dooryard Bloomed* is adapted from Walt Whitman's 'When lilacs last in the dooryard bloomed.' The same author's *The Golden Apples of the Sun* is a phrase from William Butler Yeats ('The silver apples of the moon/The golden apples of the sun.') L.P. Davies's *Psychogeist* is a play on the word poltergeist. Philip K. Dick's *Eye in the Sky* is a take-off on 'pie in the sky by and by.' Robert Heinlein's *The Green Hills of Earth* is derived from Ernest Hemingway's book 'The Green Hills of Africa.' The same author's *I Will Fear No Evil* is a phrase from the Twenty-Third Psalm. Michael Moorcock's *Behold the Man* was one of Pilate's comments before Christ was crucified. Lewis Padgett's *A Gnome There Was* is derived from 'The Vampire' by Robert Louis Stevenson ('A fool there was and he made his prayer/Even as you and I!/To a rag and a bone and a hank of hair.') H. Beam Piper's *Fuzzy Sapiens* is a take-off on Homo sapiens. Eric Frank Russell's *Somewhere a Voice* is derived from the song 'Somewhere a Voice Is Calling.' Kate Wilhelm's *Where Late the Sweet Birds Sang* is a phrase from one of Shakespeare's sonnets (Upon these boughs which shake against the cold,/bare ruined choirs, where late the sweet birds sang.)

Word Frequency

An analysis of 1,020 titles reveals that certain words appear more frequently than others, with 'star' leading the list.

Word	Number of times used	Word	Number of times used
Star	57	Island	6
World	45	Beyond	6
Space	42	Robot	5
Time	36	Voyage	5
Earth	26	War	5
Moon	25	Universe	4
Man (or Men)	24	Tower	4
Mars (or Martians)	22	Alien	4
Planet	19	Atom	4
Sky	14	Infinity	3
Sun	13	Saturn	3
Galaxy (or Galactic)	9	Destination	2
Venus	9	Jupiter	2
God (or Gods)	7	Titan	2
Sword	7		

The following title list is representative but by no means complete. New titles appear regularly, like mushrooms popping from the ground. Regardless, a perusal of these eye-catchers reveals an imaginative spectrum as broad as the electromagnetic spectrum.

1,020 Representative Titles

Edwin A. Abbot
Flatland

Robert Aickman
Cold Hand in Mine

Joan Aiken
The Green Flash
Not What You Expected

John Aiken
The World Well Lost

Brian Aldiss
Barefoot in the Head
Cryptozoic
Frankenstein Unbound
The Long Afternoon of Earth
Starswarm
Galaxies Like Grains of Sand
The Male Response
Report on Probability A

The Saliva Tree
Earthworks
The Eighty-Minute Hour
Greybeard
The Moment of Eclipse
Neanderthal Planet
Who Can Replace a Man?
Hothouse
The Shape of Further Things
The Hand-Reared Boy
Soldier Erect

Kingsley Amis
  The Alteration

Poul Anderson
  The Corridors of Time
  Enemy Stars
  The High Crusade
  The Star Fox
  Tau Zero
  Three Hearts and Three Lions
  The People of the Wind
  The Broken Sword
  Ensign Flandry
  Mirkheim
  Seven Conquests
  We Claim These Stars
  Beyond the Beyond
  The Dancer from Atlantis
  The Day of Their Return
  Fire Time
  Homeward and Beyond
  Let the Spacemen Beware!
  There Will Be Time
  Time and Stars
  Twilight World
  The War of Two Worlds
  World Without Stars

Piers Anthony
  Chtom
  Macroscope

  Omnivore
  Orn
  Ox Prostho Plus
  Rings of Ice
  Var the Stick

Christopher Anvil
  Pandora's Planet

Robert Ardrey
  The Brotherhood of Fear

Edwin Lester Arnold
  Gulliver of Mars

Isaac Asimov
  The Caves of Steel
  The Currents of Space
  Fantastic Voyage
  The Gods Themselves
  I, Robot
  The Naked Sun
  Pebble in the Sky
  The Rest of the Robots
  Is Anyone There?
  Jupiter
  Of Matters Great and Small
  Only a Trillion
  The Stars in Their Courses
  The Stars, Like Dust
  Buy Jupiter
  The Currents of Space,
  Earth Is Room Enough
  The End of Eternity
  The Heavenly Host

Brian Ball
  Probability Man
  The Space Guardians

J. G. Ballard
  Chronopolis
  Terminal Beach
  Vermillion Sands

The Crystal World
The Disaster Area
The Drowned World
The Wind from Nowhere
Concrete Island
Crash
The Atrocity Exhibition

Arthur K. Barnes
  Interplanetary Hunter

William Barton
  A Plague of All Cowards

Peter Beagle
  A Fine and Private Place
  The Last Unicorn

Alfred Bester
  The Demolished Man
  The Stars My Destination
  The Computer Connection

H. U. Bevis
  Space Stadium
  The Time Winder

Lloyd Biggle
  All the Colors of Darkness
  The Fury Out of Time
  The Metallic Muse
  Monument
  Watchers of the Dark

James Blish
  Black Easter
  A Case of Conscience
  Cities in Flight
  Jack of Eagles
  The Seedling Stars
  Vor
  And All the Stars a Stage
  Anywhen
  A Clash of Cymbals
  Earthman, Come Home
  Midsummer Century
  A Torrent of Faces

Ralph Blum
  The Simultaneous Man

Pierre Boulle
  Planet of the Apes

Ben Bova
  As On a Darkling Plain
  Forward in Time
  Millenium
  The Star Conquerers
  Star Watchman
  The Weathermakers
  Out of the Sun
  The Dueling Machine
  Escape
  Exiled from Earth
  Flight of Exiles
  The Winds of Altair

Chris Boyce
  Catchworld

John Boyd
  The Rakehells of Heaven
  Andromeda Gun
  The Doomsday Gene
  The Last Starship from Earth

Leigh Brackett
  The Big Jump
  The Long Tomorrow
  The Starmen

Ray Bradbury
  Fahrenheit 451
  The Illustrated Man
  The Martian Chronicles
  S Is for Space
  When Elephants Last in the
    Dooryard Bloomed
  R Is for Rocket
  Switch On the Night
  The Golden Apples of the Sun
  A Medicine for Melancholy

Marion Zimmer Bradley
The Bloody Sun
Star of Danger
Endless Voyage
The Heritage of Hastur
The Sword of Aldones

Kurt Brand
Blockade: Lepso

Franklyn M. Branley
Lodestar: Rocket Ship to Mars

Frederick Brown
The Lights in the Sky Are Stars
What Mad Universe
Angels and Spaceships
The Bloody Moonlight
The Dead Ringer
The Far Cry
Here Comes a Candle
Knock Three-One-Two
Martians, Go Home
Space On My Hands

John Brunner
Jagged Orbit
The Sheep Look Up
Stand on Zanzibar
Age of Miracles
Bedlam Planet
Times Without Number
The World Swappers
A Plague on Both Your Causes
Quicksand
*The Stone That Never Came
  Down*
Total Eclipse
From This Day Forward
The Shockwave Rider
The Wrong End of Time

Peter Bryant
Two Hours to Doom

Algis Budrys
Rogue Moon
Who?

Kenneth Bulmer
City Under the Sea
The Doomsday Man

Anthony Burgess
A Clockwork Orange
Honey for the Bears
The Wanting Seed

Edgar Rice Burroughs
At the Earth's Core
Carson of Venus
The Chessmen of Mars
Escape on Venus
A Fighting Man of Mars
The Gods of Mars
Llana of Gathol
Lost on Venus
The Mad King
The Master Mind of Mars
The Monster Men
The Moon Maid
The Moon Men
Pellucidar
Pirates of Venus
A Princess of Mars
Swords of Mars
Synthetic Men of Mars
Tanar of Pellucidar
Thuvia, Maid of Mars
The Warlord of Mars
John Carter of Mars
The Wizard of Venus
Savage Pellucidar

John W. Campbell, Jr.
The Black Star Passes
The Incredible Planet
Islands of Space

The Mightiest Machine
The Moon Is Hell

Karel Capek
R.U.R.
War with the Newts
The Absolute at Large
An Atomic Phantasy

Paul Capon
The Other Side of the Sun

Robert Spencer Carr
Beyond Infinity
Creatures from Beyond
An Exaltation of Stars

Jeffrey L. Castle
Vanguard to Venus

Robert W. Chambers
The Dark Star
The Gold Chase
The Green Mouse
In Search of the Unknown
The Maker of Moons
The Slayer of Souls
Some Ladies in Haste

A. Bertram Chandler
The Way Back

C. J. Cherryh
Hunter of Worlds
Brothers of Earth

Michael Chrichton
The Andromeda Strain
The Terminal Man

John Christopher
No Blade of Grass
Pendulum

James Churchward
The Children of Mu
Cosmic Forces of Mu

Arthur C. Clarke
Childhood's End
The City and the Stars
Earthlight
A Fall of Moondust
Rendezvous with Rama
Across the Sea of Stars
The Deep Range
Expedition to Earth
Islands in the Sky
The Other Side of the Sky
Sands of Mars
2001: a Space Odyssey
The Wind from the Sun

Hal Clement
Ice World
Mission of Gravity
Needle

Mark Clifton
When They Come from Space

Stanton A. Coblentz
The Blue Barbarians
After 12,000 Years
In Caverns Below
The Sunken World
Under the Triple Suns

Padraic Colum
The Voyagers

D. G. Compton
The Steel Crocodile
Synthajoy
The Missionaries

Michael Coney
*The Girl With a Symphony in
Her Fingers*

Edmund Cooper
Kronk
Seed of Light
The Slaves of Heaven

Five to Twelve
A Far Sunset
The Overman Culture
Seahorse in the Sky
The Tenth Planet
Transit
Who Needs Men?

Lee Correy
Starship through Space

Richard Cowper
Breakthrough
Clone
Kuldesak
Phoenix
The Twilight of Briareus
Worlds Apart

Ray Cummings
The Girl in the Golden Atom
The Shadow Girl

Leonard Daventry
Degree XII
A Man of Doubled Deed
Twenty-one Billionth Paradox

Avram Davidson
Or All at Sea with Oysters
Masters of the Maze
Mutiny in Space
Peregrine: Primus
The Phoenix and the Mirror

L. P. Davies
The Alien
The Artificial Man
Dimension A
Psychogeist
Twilight Journey

Samuel Delany
Babel-17
The Einstein Intersection

The Fall of the Towers
The Jewels of Aptor
Nova
The Ballad of Beta 2/Empire Star
Captives of the Flame
The Towers of Toron
City of a Thousand Suns
Triton
Driftglass

Lester Del Rey
Nerves
And Some Were Human
Attack from Atlantis
The Mysterious Earth
The Mysterious Sea
Rocket Jockey
Rockets to nowhere
Helen O'Loy

Philip K. Dick
Do Androids Dream of Electric Sheep?
Clans of the Alphane Moon
Eye in the Sky
The Man in the High Castle
The Simulacra
Game Players of Titan
The World Jones Made
A Scanner Darkly
Ubik
Galactic Pot-healer
A Maze of Death
Our Friends from Frolix 8
The Preserving Machine

Gordon R. Dickson
The Alien Way
The Genetic General
Naked to the Stars
The Pritcher Mass
Soldiers, Ask Not

Spacepaw
Sleepwalker's World
None But Man
The Star Road
Ancient, My Enemy
Danger: Human
The R Master
Tactics of Mistake

Arthur Conan Doyle
The Lost World
The Poison Belt
The Land of Mist
The Disintegration Machine
When the World Screamed
The Marcot Deep

David Duncan
Beyond Eden
Occam's Razor

Lord Dunsany
The Gods of Pegana
Time and the Gods

Eric R. Eddison
The Worm Ouroboros

Max Ehrlich
The Edict

Harlan Ellison
*The Beast That Shouted Love at
   the Heart of the World*
Alone Against Tomorrow
Approaching Oblivion
Partners in Wonder

Sylvia Louise Engdahl
Enchantress from the Stars
Journey Between Worlds
This Star Shall Abide

George Allan England
The Afterglow
Darkness and Dawn

The Flying Legion
The Golden Blight

Mark Epernay
The McLandress Dimension

J. Jefferson Farjeon
Death of a World

Ralph Milne Farley
The Radio Beasts
The Radio Planet

Philip Jose Farmer
The Fabulous Riverboat
Lord Tiger
Tarzan Alive
The Lovers
To Your Scattered Bodies Go
Behind the Walls of Terra
The Stone God Awakens
The Wind Whales of Ishmael

Howard Fast
A Touch of Infinity

Kenneth Fearing
Loneliest Girl in the World

John Russel Fearn
Liners of Time
The Trembling World

Arnold Federbush
*The Man Who Lived in Inner
   Space*

E. M. Forster
The Machine Stops

Alan Dean Foster
Icerigger

Nancy Freedman
Joshua, Son of None

David Gerrold
When Harlie Was One
The Man Who Folded Himself

Diana and Meir Gillon
  The Unsleep

Reginald Glossop
  The Orphans of Space

Ron Goulart
  The Hellhound Project
  Odd Job
  After Things Fell Apart

Robert Grant
  The King's Men

Joseph Green
  Conscience Interplanetary

Percy Greg
  Across the Zodiac

Mary Griffith
  Three Hundred Years Hence

James Gunn
  The Listeners
  Breaking Point
  The End of Dreams
  The Joy Makers
  This Fortress World
  Star Bridge
  Station in Space
  Future Imperfect

H. Rider Haggard
  Allan Quatermain
  Ayesha: the Return of She
  Child of Storm
  The People of the Mist
  Treasure of the Lake

Edward Everett Hale (Author of
  'The Man Without a Country')
  The Brick Moon (1869) (the earli-
    est known concept of an
    artificial Earth satellite)

Edmond Hamilton
  Battle for the Stars

  City at World's End
  The Haunted Stars
  The Horror on the Asteroid
  The Star Kings
  The Star of Life

Thea Von Harbou
  Metropolis
  The Rocket to the Moon

Harry Harrison
  Deathworld
  The Stainless Steel Rat
  Skyfall
  The California Iceberg
  One Step from Earth
  A Sense of Obligation
  *Star Smashers of the Galaxy
    Rangers*
  War with the Robots

M. John Harrison
  The Centauri Device
  The Committed Men

Milo Hastings
  City of Endless Night

Julian Hawthorne (son of
    Nathaniel Hawthorne)
  The Cosmic Courtship

Gerald Heard
  Doppelgangers

Lafcadio Hearn
  The Romance of the Milky Way

Robert Heinlein
  The Door Into Summer
  Doublestar
  Farnham's Freehold
  The Green Hills of Earth
  Have Space Suit—Will Travel
  Methuselah's Children
  The Moon Is a Harsh Mistress
  Orphans of Tomorrow

Podkayne of Mars
The Puppet Masters
Starship Troopers
Stranger in a Strange Land
The Star Beast
Between Planets
Citizen of the Galaxy.
Red Planet
Rocket Ship Galileo
The Rolling Stones
Space Cadet
Time for the Stars
Tunnel in the Sky
I Will Fear No Evil
Time Enough for Love
Assignment in Eternity
Beyond This Horizon
The Man Who Sold the Moon
The Menace from Earth
Orphans of the Sky
Starman Jones
Frank Herbert
Dune
Children of Dune
The Dragon in the Sea
The Eyes of Heisenberg
The God Makers
Hellstrom's Hive
Soul Catcher
The Green Brain
Destination Void
Whipping Star
Herman Hesse
Steppenwolf
Daemion
J. Hunter Holly
Encounter
The Green Planet
The Mind Traders

Robert E. Howard
The Incredible Adventures of
Dennis Dorgan
The Lost Valley of Iskander
The Moon of Skulls
Fred Hoyle
The Black Cloud
October the First Is Too Late
L. Ron Hubbard
Typewriter in the Sky
W. H. Hudson
A Crystal Age
Aldous Huxley
Brave New World
Brave New World Revisited
Cutcliffe Hyne
The Lost Continent

Dennis F. Jones
Colossus
The Fall of Colossus
Implosion
Raymond Jones
Renaissance
The Secret People
This Island Earth
The Toymaker

Stephen King-Hall
Post-war Pirate
Otis A. Kline
Maza of the Moon
The Outlaws of Mars
Damon Knight
Beyond the Barrier
Hell's Pavement
A for Anything
C. M. Kornbluth

Gladiator-at-Law
The Space Merchants
Wolfbane
Henry Kuttner
Fury
The Mask of Circe
Mutant
Ahead of Time
Destination Infinity

R. A. Lafferty
Fourth Mansions
Past Master
The Reefs of Earth
Philip Latham
Missing Men of Saturn
Keith Laumer
Dinosaur Beach
Galactic Diplomat
Graylon
A Plague of Demons
Retief: Ambassador to Space
The Big Show
The Long Twilight
Assignment in Nowhere
The Day Before Forever
Thunderhead
Deadfall
Galactic Odyssey
The Glory Game
The House in November
The Infinite Cage
The Monitors
Night of Delusions
Once There Was a Giant
The Other Side of Time
The Other Sky
Retief's Ransom
The Shape Changer

The Star Treasure
The Time Bender
The World Shuffler
Ursula K. LeGuin
The Lathe of Heaven
The Left Hand of Darkness
The Wizard of Earthsea
City of Illusion
Planet of Exile
Rocannon's World
Very Long Way from Anywhere
    Else
The Wind's Twelve Quarters
The Farthest Shore
The Tombs of Atuan
Wild Angels
Fritz Leiber
Conjure Wife
A Spectre Is Haunting Texas
The Wanderers
The Big Time
Green Millenium
The Mind Spider
Swords Against Death
Swords and Deviltry
Swords Against Wizardry
Swords in the Mist
The Swords of Lankhmar
You're All Alone
Our Lady of Darkness
Gather, Darkness!
Night's Black Agents
Murray Leinster
The Pirates of Zen
The Brain Stealers
Sidewise in Time
Colonial Survey
The Forgotten Planet
The Last Space Ship

The Listeners
The Monster from Earth's End
Operation: Outer Space
Space Platform
Stanislaw Lem
  The Invincible
  Solaris
  The Cyberiad
  The Investigation
  Memories Found in a Bathtub
Gaston Leroux
  The Bride of the Sun
C. S. Lewis
  Out of the Silent Planet
  Perelandra
  That Hideous Strength
David Lindsay
  A Voyage to Arcturus
John Uri Lloyd
  Etidorpha or the End of Earth
Richard A. Locke
  The Moon Hoax
Frank Belknap Long
  It Was the Day of the Robot
  John Carstairs, Space Detective
  The Rim of the Unknown
  Three Steps Spaceward
H. P. Lovecraft
  The Color Out of Space
John Lymington
  The Hole in the World
  Froomb!
  Night of the Big Heat
  The Nowhere Place
  Ten Million Years to Friday

Charles Eric Maine
  Alph

He Owned the World
The Isotope Man
The Man Who Couldn't Sleep
Spaceways Satellite
Timeliner
Edward Maitland
  By and By
Barry N. Malzberg
  Down Here in the Dream Quarter
  In the Enclosure
Douglas R. Mason
  Omega Worm
  Pitman's Progress
  Matrix
  The Phaeton Condition
  The Tower of Rizwan
Anne McCaffrey
  Dragonflight
  The Ship Who Sang
  Dragonsinger
  Dragonsong
  To Ride Pegasus
J. T. McIntosh
  Born Leader
  A Coat of Blackmail
  The Fittest
  Flight from Rebirth
  One in Three Hundred
  Six Gates from Limbo
  The Space Sorcerers
  Time for a Change
  World Out of Mind
Shepherd Mead
  The Big Ball of Wax
Louis B. Mercier
  Memories of the Year Two
    Thousand Five Hundred
Judith Merril
  The Tomorrow People

A. Merritt
  The Moon Pool
  Through the Dragon Glass
  The People of the Pit
  The Conquest of the Moon Pool
  The Metal Monster
  The Face in the Abyss
  The Ship of Ishtar

Walter Miller, Jr.
  A Canticle for Leibowitz

Edward Page Mitchell
  The Crystal Man

Michael Moorcock
  The Black Corridor
  Stormbringer
  Behold the Man
  The Condition of Muzak
  The End of All Songs
  Legends from the End of Time
  The Sailor on the Sea of Fate
  An Alien Heat
  The Hollow Lands
  The Land Leviathan

Catherine L. Moore
  Doomsday Morning
  Judgment Night

Ward Moore
  Bring the Jubilee

John Morressey
  Nail Down the Stars
  Starbrat
  Under a Calculating Star

William Morris
  News from Nowhere

Larry Niven
  Ringworld
  Protector

John Norman
  Tarnsman of Gor

Andre Norton
  Star Rangers
  The X-Factor
  Android at Arms
  Beast Master
  Breed to Come
  Catseye
  The Crossroads of Time
  Dark Piper
  Daybreak 2250 A.D.
  Defiant Agents
  Dragon Magic
  Dread Companion
  Exiles of the Stars
  Eye of the Monster
  Forerunner Foray
  Galactic Derelict
  High Sorcery
  Huon of the Horn
  Ice Crown
  Iron Cage
  Judgment on Janus
  Key Out of Time
  The Plast Planet
  Lord of Thunder
  Moon of Three Rings
  Night of Masks
  Plague Ship
  Postmarked the Stars
  Quest Crosstime
  Sargasso of Space
  Sea Siege
  Secret of the Lost Race
  Shadow Hawk
  The Sioux Spaceman
  The Time Traders
  Year of the Unicorn
  The Zero Stone

The Jargoon Pard
Merlin's Mirror
No Night Without Stars
Small Shadows Creep
Alan Nourse
Raiders from the Rings

Lewis Padgett
A Gnome There Was
Mutant
Robots Have No Tails
Edgar Pangborn
Davy
West of the Sun
The Judgment of Eve
A Mirror for Observers
Alexei Panshin
Masque World
Rite of Passage
Star Well
Chapman Pincher
Not with a Bang
H. Beam Piper
Fuzzy Sapiens
Little Fuzzy
Charles Platt
Planet of the Voles
Frederik Pohl
Drunkards Walk
Slave Ship
Man Plus
The Gold at the Starbow's End
Gustavus W. Pope
Journey to Mars
Christopher Priest
The Inverted World
Real-time World

John Rankine
Astral Quest
The Fingalnan Conspiracy
Interstellar Two-Five
Lunar Attack
Moon Odyssey
Moons of Triopus
One Is One
The Plantos Affair
The Weisman Experiment
Mack Reynolds
Rolltown
Ability Quotient
Satellite City
Section G: United Planets
Looking Backward from the Year 2000
Keith Roberts
The Grain Kings
Frank Robinson
The Power
George Rochester
The Black Mole
Roy Rockwood
By Air Express to Venus
By Space Ship to Saturn
Five Thousand Miles Underground
On a Torn-away World
Under the Ocean to the South Pole
Victor Rousseau
The Sea Demons
The Messiah of the Cylinder
Joanna Russ
And Chaos Died
The Female Man
Picnic on Paradise

Eric Frank Russell
Deep Space
Dreadful Sanctuary
The Great Explosion
Like Nothing on Earth
Sentinels from Space
Sinister Barrier
Somewhere a Voice
Wasp
With a Strange Device

Nathan Schachner
Space Lawyer

Robert Scheckley
Journey Beyond Tomorrow

James H. Schmitz
Agent of Vega
The Demon Breed
The Eternal Frontiers
The Witches of Karres

Arthur Sellings
The Long Eureka
The Quy Effect
Time Transfer
The Uncensored Man

Garrett P. Serviss
A Columbus of Space
The Moon Metal

Bob Shaw
Other Days, Other Eyes
The Two Timers
Cosmic Kaleidoscope
A Wreath of Stars
Orbitsville
The Palace of Eternity
Tomorrow Lies in Ambush

M. P. Shiel
The Purple Cloud
The Yellow Danger

The Lord of the Sea
The Yellow Wave

Robert Silverberg
Dying Inside
Hawksbille Station
The Masks of Time
Thorns
Tower of Glass
The World Inside
Downward to the Earth
The Feast of St. Dionysus
To Open the Sky
Parsecs and Parables
Recalled to Life
The Second Trip
Starman's Quest
The Stochastic Man
The Time Hoppers
A Time of Changes
Time of the Great Freeze
To Live Again

Clifford Simak
City
Goblin Reservation
Time and Again
Way Station
Enchanted Pilgrimage
Our Children's Children
Aliens for Neighbors
All the Traps of Earth
Cemetery World
A Choice of Gods
Cosmic Engineers
Destiny Doll
Out of Their Minds
Ring Around the Sun
Shakespeare's Planet
Strangers in the Universe
Time Is the Simplest Thing
Way Station

Curt Siodmak
  City in the Sky
  Donnovan's Brain
  Hauser's Memory
  The Third Ear
William Sloane
  The Edge of Running Water
  To Walk the Night
  Space Space Space
Cordwainer Smith
  The Planet Buyer
  The Game of Rat and Dragon
  Space Lords
Edward Elmer Smith
  Children of the Lens
  First Lensman
  Galactic Patrol
  Grey Lensman
  Second Stage Lensman
  The Skylark of Space
  Skylark of Valeron
  Skylark Three
  Spacehounds of IPC
  Subspace Explorers
  The Vortex Blaster
George O. Smith
  Hellflower
  Lost in Space
  Nomad
  The Path of Unreason
  Pattern for Conquest
  Venus Equilateral
Jerry Sohl
  The Altered Ego
  Costigan's Needle
  The Haploids
  The Odious Ones
  Point Ultimate
  Prelude to Peril
  The Transcendant Man

Norman Spinrad
  Bug Jack Barron
  The Last Hurrah of the Golden
    Horde
  The Iron Dream
  Passing through the Flame
Brian Stableford
  The Face of Heaven
  The Paradise Game
  Promised Land
Olaf Stapledon
  Last and First Men
  Odd John
  Starmaker
  Old Man in New World
  Darkness and the Light
  Last Men in London
  Nebula Maker
  To the End of Time
George R. Stewart
  Earth Abides
Theodore Sturgeon
  The Cosmic Rape
  The Dreaming Jewels
  More than Human
  Venus Plus X
  Case and the Dreamer
  A Touch of Strange
  Without Sorcery
Walter Sullivan
  We Are Not Alone
Thomas Burnett Swann
  The Tournament of Thorns

John Taine
  The Cosmic Geoids
  The Crystal Horde
  The Forbidden Garden
  G.O.G. 666
  The Gold Tooth

The Greatest Adventure
Green Fire
The Purple Sapphire
Quayle's Invention
Seeds of Life
The Time Stream

William Tenn
A Lamp for Medusa
The Wooden Star

E. C. Tubb
Alien Dust
Breakaway
City of No Return
Century of the Manikin
Collision Course
Escape Into Space

Wilson Tucker
The Year of the Quiet Sun
The City in the Sea
Ice and Iron
The Lincoln Hunters
The Long Loud Silence
The Time Masters

Jack Vance
The Dragon Masters
The Languages of Pao
The Brains of Earth
The Gray Prince
The Eyes of the Overworld
The Palace of Love
Star King

Jules Verne
20,000 Leagues Under the Sea
The Mysterious Island
Journey to the Center of the Earth
An Antarctic Mystery
Around the World in Eighty Days
The Adventures of Captain
  Hatteras

The Begum's Fortune
Black Diamonds
The City of the Sahara
The Clipper of the Clouds
Dropped from the Clouds
Five Weeks in a Balloon
A Floating City
Flood and Flame
From the Earth to the Moon
Master of the World
The Masterless Man
The Sphinx of the Icefields
Propellor Island
Round the Moon
The Wilderness of Ice

A. E. Van Vogt
Slan
The Weapon Shops of Isher
The World of Null A
Children of Tomorrow
Quest for the Future
The Silkie
The Universe Maker
The Secret Galactics
The Players of Null A
Away and Beyond
The Beast
The Book of Ptath
Destination: Universe!
Empire of the Atom
The House that Stood Still
The Mind Cage
The Mixed Men
Rogue Ship
The Violent Man

Kurt Vonnegut, Jr.
Cat's Cradle
The Sirens of Titan
God Bless You, Mr. Rosewater

Edgar Wallace
  The Day of Uniting
  Planetoid 127
  King Kong
F. L. Wallace
  Address: Centauri
  Deathstar Voyage
  Dr. Orpheus
  Pan Sagittarius
Ian Watson
  The Martian Inca
  The Embedding
  The Jonah Kit
Stanley Weinbaum
  A Martian Odyssey
  The Black Flame
  The Red Peril
Manly Wade Wellman
  The Dark Destroyers
  Giants from Eternity
  Islands in the Sky
  Worse Things Waiting
H. G. Wells
  The First Men in the Moon
  The Time Machine
  The War of the Worlds
  In the Days of the Comet
  Men like Gods
  Things to Come
  The War in the Air
  The World Set Free
Kate Wilhelm
  The Killer Thing
  The Infinity Box
  Let the Fire Fall
  Where Late the Sweet Birds Sang
Jack Williamson
  The Humanoids
  The Cometeers

  Darker Than You Think
  Dragon's Island
  The Legion of Space
  The Legion of Time
Bernard Wolfe
  Limbo
Gene Wolfe
  The Fifth Head of Cerberus
Donald A. Wolheim
  Destiny's Orbit
  The Martian Missile
  One Against the Moon
  The Secret of the Martian Moons
Sydney Fowler Wright
  Spiders' War
  The Throne of Saturn
  The World Below
Philip Wylie
  The Disappearance
  When Worlds Collide
  After Worlds Collide
John Wyndham
  The Day of the Triffids
  The Midwich Cuckoos
  Re-Birth
  The Chrysalids
  Out of the Deep
  Trouble with Lichen

Roger Zelazny
  Creatures of Light and Darkness
  Damnation Alley
  Lord of Light
  Jack of Shadows
  Isle of the Dead
  The Dream Master
  Four for Tomorrow
  This Immortal
  To Die in Italbar
  Today We Choose Faces

Science Fiction Publishers

A & W Pubs., Inc. / *Hard cover and paperback*
Academy Press, Ltd. / *Hard cover*
Ace Books / *Paperback*
Aeonian Press, Inc. / *Hard cover*
Algol Press / *Hard cover and paperback*
Arbor House Pub. Co., Inc. / *Hard cover and paperback*
Arkham House Publishers, Inc. / *Hard cover*
Arno Press, Inc. / *Hard cover*
Atheneum Pubs. / *Hard cover and paperback*
Aurora Pubs., Inc. / *Hard cover and paperback*
Avon Books / *Paperback*
Award Books / *Paperback*
Ball-Stick-Bird Pubs., Inc. / *Hard cover*
Ballantine Books / *Hard cover and paperback*
Bantam Books, Inc. / *Hard cover and paperback*
Barlenmir House, Pubs. / *Hard cover and paperback*
Baronet Pub. Co. / *Hard cover and paperback*
Barron's Educ. Series, Inc. / *Paperback*
Berkley Pub. Corp. / *Hard cover and paperback*
Beta Book Co. / *Hard cover and paperback*
The Borgo Press / *Paperback*
Brasch & Mulliners, Pubs. / *Hard cover*
CPI Publg., Inc. / *Hard cover*
Chatham Square Press, Inc. / *Hard cover*
College Notes & Texts / *Hard cover*
Condor Pub. Co., Inc. / *Paperback*
Coral Reefs Pubns., Inc. / *Hard cover and paperback*
Coward, McCann & Geoghegan, Inc. / *Hard cover and paperback*
Creative Arts Books Co. / *Hard cover and paperback*
Crown Pubs., Inc. / *Hard cover and paperback*
DAW Books, Inc. / *Paperback*
Dell Pub. Co., Inc. / *Hard cover and paperback*
Donning Co. Pubs. / *Hard cover*
Doubleday & Co., Inc. / *Hard cover and paperback*
Dover Pubns., Inc. / *Paperback*
Drake Pubs., Inc. / *Hard cover and paperback*

Educational Insights, Inc. / *Hard cover*
Fawcett Books / *Paperback*
Filter Press / *Hard cover and paperback*
Eleanor Friedle, Inc. / *Hard cover*
Garland Publg., Inc. / *Hard cover*
Globe Book Co., Inc. / *Hard cover and paperback*
Gregg Press / *Hard cover*
G. K. Hall & co. / *Hard cover*
Harper & Row, Pubs., Inc. / *Hard cover*
Houghton Mifflin Co. / *Hard cover*
Hyperion Press, Inc. / *Hard cover and paperback*
National Textbook Co. / *Hard cover*
The New American Library, Inc. / *Paperback*
Newcastle Pub. Co., Inc. / *Paperback*
Penguin Books / *Paperback*
S. G. Phillips, Inc. / *Hard cover*
Pinnacle Books, Inc. / *Paperback*
Piper Publg., Inc. / *Hard cover*
Popular Press / *Hard cover*
Prentice-Hall, Inc. / *Hard cover and paperback*
G. P. Putnam's Sons / *Hard cover and paperback*
Rand McNally & Co. / *Hard cover*
Random House, Inc. (See Ballantine)
The Ward Ritchie Press / *Hard cover and paperback*
Scott, Foresman & Co. / *Hard cover*
The Seabury Press, Inc. / *Hard cover and paperback*
Peter Smith / *Hard cover*
Southern Illinois Univ. Press / *Hard cover*
Stein & Day Pubs. / *Hard cover and paperback*
Strawberry Hill Press / *Hard cover and paperback*
Sun Pub. Co. / *Hard cover and paperback*
Taplinger Pub. Co., Inc. / *Hard cover*
Tower Pubns., Inc. / *Paperback*
Transatlantic Arts, Inc. / *Paperback*
Troubador Press, Inc. / *Paperback*
The Two Continents Pub. Group, Ltd. / *Hard cover and paperback*
Vanguard Press, Inc. / *Hard cover and paperback*
Wade Publg. Co., Inc. / *Hard cover*
Walker & Co. / *Hard cover and paperback*

Science Fiction and/or Fantasy Organizations

Science Fiction Research
  Association
Marshall Tymn
English Department
Eastern Michigan University
Ypsilanti, Michigan 48197

The Science Fiction Writers'
  Association of America
Theodore R. Cogswell
108 Robinson Street
Chincilla, Pennsylvania 18410

The National Fantasy Fan
  Federation
Route 1, Box 364
Heiskell, Tennessee 36645

The British Science Fiction
  Association Limited
David Wingrove
4 Holmside Court
Nightingale Lane
London SW128JW, England

The British Fantasy Society
Jon M. Harvey
37 Hawkins Lane
Burton-on-Trent
Staffordshire, England

The Fantasy Foundation
Forrest J. Ackerman
2495 Glendower Avenue
Hollywood, California 90027

The New England Science Fiction
  Association
Box G, MIT Branch PO
Cambridge, Massachusetts 02139

The Science Fiction Foundation
North-East London Polytechnic
Longbridge Road
Dagenham
Essex RM82AS, England

Bibliography and Information Sources

Non-Fictional Sources

Aldiss, Brian W. *Billion Year Spree*. Doubleday & Company, Inc.; Garden City, New York, 1973.

Allen, L. David. *The Ballantine Teachers' Guide to Science Fiction*. Ballantine Books, New York, 1975.

Amelio, Ralph J. *The Filmic Moment: Teaching American Genre Film Through Extracts.* Paper delivered at 1977 Science Fiction Research Association Conference.

Ansfield, Esther K. *Utopian Fantasy.* Paper delivered at 1977 Science Fiction Research Association Conference.

Asimov, Isaac, et al. *Physical Science Today.* CRM Books; Del Mar, California, 1973.

Barnett, Lincoln. *The Universe and Dr. Einstein.* Harper Brothers, 1948.

Bergamini, David. *Mathematics.* Life Science Library, 1963.

Bergaust, Erik,. *The Next Fifty Years in Space.* The Macmillan Company, 1964.

Bracewell, Ronald N. *The Galactic Club.* W.H. Freeman and Company, San Francisco, 1975.

Bretnor, Reginald. *Science Fiction Today and Tomorrow.* Harper & Row, Evanston, 1974.

Clareson, Thomas D. *Extrapolation—A Journal of Science Fiction and Fantasy.* The Collier Printing Company, Wooster, Ohio. (Scores of issues.)

Clarke, Arthur C. *The Exploration of Space.* Harper & Brothers, 1959.

DeCamp, L. Sprague. *Literary Swordsmen and Sorcerers: The Makers of Heroic Fantasy.* Arkham House, 1976.

Finder, Jan Howard. *Heroic Fantasy.* Paper delivered at 1977 Science Fiction Research Association Conference.

Firsoff, V.A. *Exploring the Planets.* A. S. Barnes and Company, 1964.

Flammarion, Gabrielle Camille. *The Flammarion Book of Astronomy.* Simon and Schuster, New York, 1964.

Friend, Beverly. *Science Fiction: The Classroom in Orbit.* Educational Impact, Inc.; Glassboro, New Jersey, 1974.
The Science Fiction Fan Cult. Doctoral dissertation, Northwestern University, 1975.

Frisch, Karl Von. *Man and the Living World.* Time Incorporated, New York, 1965.

Gentle, Ernest J., and Reithmaier, Lawrence W. *Aviation and Space Dictionary.* Aero Publishers, Inc., 1974.

Honig, Edwin. *Dark Conceit: The Making of Allegory.* Oxford University Press, 1966.

Huxley, Aldous. *Literature and Science.* Harper & Row; New York, Evanston, and London, 1963.

Irwin, W. R. *The Game of the Impossible: A Rhetoric of Fantasy.* University of Illinois Press, 1976.

Johnson, Eric R. *Servomechanisms.* Prentice-Hall, Inc., 1963.

Jung, Carl G. *Man and His Symbols.* Doubleday & Company, Inc., Garden City, New York, 1964.
Key to the Universe. Two-hour television special report, aired on Chicago's Channel 11 from 7:30 to 9:30 PM on Tuesday, May 24th, 1977.

King, Ivan R. *The Universe Unfolding.* W. H. Freeman and Company, San Francisco, 1976.

Kyle, David. *A Pictorial History of Science Fiction.* The Hamlyn Publishing Group Limited, 1975.

Lapp, Ralph E. *Matter.* Time/Life Science Library, 1963.

Lee, Stan. *Unknown Worlds of Science Fiction.* Magazine Management Co., Inc., 1976.

Manlove, C. N. *Modern Fantasy: Five Studies.* Cambridge University Press, 1975.

Molson, Francis J. *Juvenile Fantasy.* Paper delivered at 1977 Science Fiction Research Association Conference.

Moskowitz, Sam. *Seekers of Tomorrow.* The World Publishing Company, New York, 1966.
Explorers of the Infinite. Hyperion Press, Inc., 1963.

Newton, Clarke. *1001 Questions Answered About Space.* Dodd, Mead & Company, 1964.

Porges, Irwin. *Edgar Rice Burroughs: The Man Who Created Tarzan.* Brigham Young University Press, 1975.

Rabkin, Eric S. *The Fantastic in Literature.* Princeton University Press, 1976.

Rudaux, Lucien, and De Vaucouleurs, G. De. *Larousse Encyclopedia of Astronomy.* Prometheus Press, New York, 1959.

Schlobin, Roger C. *On the Nature of Fantasy.* Paper delivered at 1977 Science Fiction Research Association Conference.

Scientific American Magazine. (Scores of articles.)

Shelton, William R. *Man's Conquest of Space.* National Geographic Society, 1968.

Sitchin, Zecharia. *The 12th Planet.* Stein and Day Publishers, New York, 1976.

Taylor, Edwin F., and Wheeler, John Archibald. *Spacetime Physics.* W. H. Freeman and Company, San Francisco, 1966.

Todorou, Tzvetan. *The Fantastic: A Structural Approach to a Literary Genre.* Cornell University Press, 1975.

Vickery, John B. *Myth and Literature.* University of Nebraska Press, Lincoln, Nebraska, 1966.

Wertham, Fredric. *The World of Fanzines.* Southern Illinois University Press, 1973.

Wilson, Michael. *Energy.* Life Science Library, 1963.

Fictional Sources (Novels and Anthologies)

Aiken, John.
World Well Lost.

Aldiss, Brian.
Space Opera
The Shape of Further Things
The Eighty Minute Hour
Moment of Eclipse

Amis, Kingsley, and Conquest, Robert.
Spectrum
Spectrum 5

Anderson, Poul.
The Enemy Stars
The Corridors of Time
Trader to the Stars
Firetime
Homeward and Beyond
Midsummer Tempest
Operation Chaos

Anthony, Piers.
Ox
Omnivore

Anvil, Christopher.
Pandora's Planet

Asimov, Isaac.
I, Robot
Nightfall and Other Stories
Nine Tomorrows
The Rest of the Robots
The Hugo Winners, Volume Two
Fantastic Voyage
Second Foundation

Ball, John Jr.
Operation Springboard

Ballard, J.G.
The Crystal World

Bellow, Arthur W.
Space Relations

Biggle, Lloyd Jr.
Monument
The Light That Never Was
This Darkening Universe
The Rule of the Door
All the Colors of Darkness
Watchers of the Dark

Bodelson, Anders.
Freezing Down

Boulle, Pierre.
Planet of the Apes

Bova, Ben.
Analog 9
Starcrossed
As On a Darkling Plain

Blish, James.
Midsummer Century
And All the Stars a Stage
Earthman, Come Home

Bradbury, Ray.
R Is for Robot
Something Wicked This Way
  Comes
The Illustrated Man
The Martian Chronicles

Brown, Fredric.
Angels and Spaceships
Rogue in Space

Brunner, John.
The Shockwave Rider
The Sheep Look Up
From This Day Forward
Total Eclipse
The Wrong End of Time
Quicksand
The Jagged Orbit

Bryant, Edward.
Among the Dead

Campbell, John W.
Analog 7

Clarke, Arthur C.
The Wind from the Sun
Across the Sea of Stars
The Nine Billion Names of God
Rendezvous with Rama
A Fall of Moondust
Tales of Ten Worlds
The City and the Stars
Imperial Earth
Time Probe

Cooper, Edmund.
Five to Twelve
The Slaves of Heaven
Sea Horse in the Sky

Cordell, Alexander.
If You Believe the Soldiers

Cowper, Richard.
Clone

Crowley, John.
The Deep

Daventry, Leonard.
A Man of Double Deed
Twenty-One Billionth Paradox

Davidson, Avram.
Strange Seas and Shores

Lucas, George.
Star Wars

Davies, L. P.
The Alien
Twilight Journey
Dimension A
The Artificial Man
Psychogeist

De Camp, L. Sprague.
The Compleat Enchanter
A Gun for Dinosaur

De Ford, Miriam Allen.
Elsewhere, Elsewhen, Elsehow

Del Rey, Lester.
Pstalemate
The Year After Tomorrow
The Book of C.L. Moore
Early Del Rey

Dick, Philip K.
The Preserving Machine
Flow My Tears, the Policeman
  Said
The Three Stigmata of Palmer
  Eldritch

Dickinson, Peter.
The Green Gene.

Dickson, Gordon R.
Tactics of Mistake
The R Master
The Pritcher Mass
The Star Road
Three to Dorsai!
Hour of the Horde
Sleepwalker's World
Ancient, My Enemy
Mutants

Disch, Thomas M.
Fun With Your Head
The New Improved Sun

Edmondson, G. C.
T.H.E.M.
Chapayeca

Effinger, George Alec.
What Entropy Means to Me

Ehrlich, Max.
The Edict.

Ellison, Harlan.
Approaching Oblivion.

Elwood, Roger.
Continuum 1
*Androids, Time Machines and
   Blue Giraffes*
Saving Worlds

Farca, Marie C.
Complex Man

Farmer, Philip Jose'.
To Your Scattered Bodies Go
Tarzan Alive

Fast, Howard.
A Touch of Infinity

Freedman, Nancy.
Joshua, Son of None

French, Paul.
*Lucky Starr and the Pirates of
   the Asteroids*

Gerrold, David.
The Man Who Folded Himself

Greg, Percy.
Across the Zodiac

LeGuin, Ursula K.
The Wind's Twelve Quarters
The Dispossessed

Heinlein, Robert A.
The Past Through Tomorrow
Tunnel in the Sky
Time for the Stars
The Moon Is a Harsh Mistress

Herbert, Frank.
The God Makers
Whipping Star

Hipolito, Jane.
Mars, We Love You

Hoskins, Robert.
The Shattered People

Hoyle, Fred.
Fifth Planet

Laumer, Keith.
The Shape Changer
Time Trap
The Great Time Machine Hoax

Lem, Stanislaw.
The Invincible

Norton, Andre.
Star Man's Son

Pohl, Frederik.
Man Plus
The Early Pohl

Siodmak, Curt.
Skyport
City in the Sky

Individual Inputs and Suggestions

Cornish, Edward S.
President
World Future Society
4916 St. Elmo Avenue
Washington, D.C. 20014

Erlich, Richard D.
Department of English
Miami University
Oxford, Ohio 45056

Krulik, Theodore.
High school English instructor
69020 Kissena Boulevard
Flushing, New York 11367

Milstead, John.
Professor of English and
Chairman, English Honors
Oklahoma State University
Stillwater, Oklahoma 74074

Nedelkovitch, Alexander.
Professor of English
Zahumska 39, 11050
Belgrade, Yugoslavia

Presley, Horton.
Ottawa University
10th and Cedar Street
Ottawa, Kansas 66067

Swanson, Roy Arthur.
Department of Comparative
 Literature
The University of Wisconsin
P.O. Box 413
Milwaukee, Wisconsin 53201

Williamson, Jack.
Science Fiction author
Box 761
Portales, New Mexico 88130

Organizational Inputs and Suggestions

British Aircraft Corporation
Publicity Department
Electronic and Space Systems
 Group
Filton, Bristol, England.

Martin Marietta Corporation
Public Relations Department
Denver, Colorado 80201

Rockwell International Space
 Division
12214 Lakewood Boulevard
Downey, California 90241